THE
FIGHTING SPIRIT

Charles Gidley

FONTANA/Collins

First published in Great Britain by Collins 1989
First issued in Fontana Paperbacks 1990

Copyright © Charles Gidley Wheeler 1989

Printed and bound in Great Britain by
William Collins Sons & Co. Ltd, Glasgow

THE FIGHTING SPIRIT

CHARLES GIDLEY joined the Royal Navy when he was sixteen, and in the course of a twenty-five-year career qualified as a Fleet Air Arm pilot and flying instructor, flew Airborne Early Warning Gannets from the deck of HMS *Eagle*, captained the minesweeper HMS *Ashton* and was First Lieutenant of the anti-submarine frigate HMS *Yarmouth*. During this time he wrote constantly, contributing articles to *Blackwood's Magazine* and numerous television scripts to the BBC (*Warship* and *Wings*) and Yorkshire Television (*The Sandbaggers*).

Since leaving the Navy in 1980 to take up writing, Charles Gidley has written a number of successful novels: *The River Running By*, *The Raging of the Sea*, *The Believer*, and *Armada*. *The Fighting Spirit* is his fifth novel. Charles Gidley is married and lives in Hampshire

'A brilliant piece of "faction" covering the fall of France and the retreat to Dunkirk . . . a totally riveting account, leaving the reader feeling that he has been personally present throughout the campaign. In short a gripping story, not easily put down.'   *The Naval Review*

By the same author

The River Running By
The Raging of the Sea
The Believer
Armada

In memory of
James Gidley Wheeler
who fought at Boulogne

PART ONE

ONE

That was a marvellous summer, the summer of '39, and Kent was a lovely part of England in which to enjoy it. Most days Simone was awake by five, and one night they heard the nightingale sing. She stood listening with Griff at the open window, spellbound by the range and purity of that magical solo, which seemed to be performed for their benefit alone. 'I don't suppose we shall hear the like of that again,' Griff had whispered when they were back in bed; and it was then, lying in his arms with the dawn creeping in at the window and the sparrows cheeping under the eaves, that she first became positively aware that the clouds which had been gathering for so long would not go away, that a storm was surely coming, and that this waking dream of peace and security which England and France shared, like sleeping lovers, must soon be shattered.

It was as if they were all in a boat – that was the comparison that came most often to mind – as if they were in a boat, rowing lazily downstream over smooth water, the oars dipping in unison, the willows slipping by on either side, the steersman reassuring them with soothing words; and as she pulled at her oar she could hear – behind her, in the direction the boat was moving – a dull roar, a sound she recognized but could not immediately identify. Was she awake or asleep? Both and neither. The boat, that fleeting moment between the future and the past, slipped on through the summer, and the roar became louder – until suddenly, that night when she was in Griff's arms after hearing the nightingale, she knew that the roaring was the sound of the smooth stream turning into a fury of white water as it went over the cliff.

That was the comparison, the simile, but the premonition was simpler and more terrifying: it was an inward certainty that she dare not speak aloud, one she recognized, for she had experienced a similar second sight when she was in her teens. It was the sure knowledge that this man, Griff, who was making love to her as if his life and reputation depended on it, was 'on the list' as they used to say in 1917, and must soon be taken from her.

But of course, she told herself, picking strawberries in the fruit cage, bottling plums with the housemaid, working at her tapestry in the evenings while Griff marked history essays or listened to violin concertos on the wireless, every other woman in England must be having similar forebodings.

Or were they? It was difficult for her to be sure. Though she had lived in England since marrying Griff in 1919, she had never been able to regard herself as English, to feel that she belonged to this green and pleasant land – or, for that matter, to the community of staff and friends of Prowse School for Boys. She had never ceased to be conscious of herself as a foreigner among these comfortable county people. She knew that she could never be entirely accepted as 'Simone' or even 'Mrs Wilmot' but must remain the history master's wife, or, to be more precise, the history master's *French* wife. Nor was there one single person in the world – not even Griff – to whom she could pour out all her heart, for there were things which she had kept from him: secrets and memories of another life, another storm whose constant fury had been all about her during her teens and which had faded only gradually after coming to England.

Had it ever gone completely? Not really. The new turmoil ahead was, after all, nothing more than a continuation of the first, the same water going over a different weir. Nevertheless she found this new torrent more frightening because it lay ahead, out of sight, behind her as she rowed downstream, the only way one could row, into the future.

The summer term ended; speech day came and went. Usually they took a fortnight's holiday in Wales and stayed with Griff's sister and her family in Pembrokeshire, but earlier that year Griff had bought a new Standard coupé, and had decided they must economize. They would have a quiet summer: Griff would potter in the greenhouse, weed the herbaceous border, roll velvet stripes diagonally across the lawn.

Griff was very good at pottering. Simone had found it amusing in the early years of their marriage. But that was a long time ago. Griff was still in the army and they were presumptuously 'waiting a year or so before starting a family'. Those were the years before they discovered that Griff's mother had frittered away a fortune on doctors' fees and trips to London. They were the years of flat chests and cloche hats, short skirts and silly dances.

They were also the years before it dawned on them both that Griff could not, however energetically and persistently he tried, give her a baby.

Griff's mother had died in '22, and when the medical and legal fees had been paid she had left a far smaller estate than Griff had expected, and he had been forced to accept that he could not keep a wife as well as pay his way in the regiment. So he had resigned his commission as a cavalry officer and had taken a job as a history master here at his old school, Prowse, and Simone had been required to metamorphose almost overnight into the wife of a humble schoolmaster.

The arrival of young Captain Wilmot and his twenty-one-year-old French wife acted like a shot of adrenalin injected straight into the school's arteries. With the petite figure of Simone on the touch line, the Prowse first fifteen became unbeatable. Head boys and prefects became infatuated with her. On hot summer evenings, fourth-formers took it in turns to crane out of their bathroom window for a glimpse of Wilmot's wife through the French windows at the back of Prowse Lodge. A standing invitation to late-night cocoa at Captain Wilmot's became as highly prized as a first eleven cricket cap.

For a year or so Simone basked in a glow of adolescent adoration. But then one of the school's classics scholars fell in love with her and began sending her secret – and highly sentimental – love poems, one of which was intercepted.

Griff was taken to one side by the headmaster and Simone was taken to one side by Griff. The school had an impeccable reputation. In an attempt to protect the boy, Simone said nothing of previous *billets doux*, unaware that her inamorato had already been tricked into an admission that he had sent some. As a result, Simone was judged, as Griff put it, to have discouraged his advances with insufficient energy. She had placed a brilliant career in jeopardy. It must never happen again.

It never did: from that day onward, Simone took little part in the life of the school. Her interest in it was stone dead. She no longer felt any obligation to stand on a touch line or mother the new boys or bring cocoa in on a tray when Griff invited his sixth-formers in for a late-night chat. She had no wish to help out in the art classes, teach French conversation, or volunteer to design the school production of *The Rivals*. She did not wish to volunteer for anything. She was not English, and she did not enjoy volunteering. She liked breakfast in bed, hot sunshine, new clothes, good shoes, white wine and plenty of loving – all the things that every French woman took for granted as her birthright, all the things which seemed to be in such short supply this side of Dover.

Her marriage to Griff, which had started so romantically, turned suddenly humdrum. The fire of their early love died down. And of course everything would have been quite different between them if they had been able to have children.

Griff rolled heavily out of bed and went to the window, peering between the curtains in his striped pyjamas. 'Looks like it's going to be another scorcher,' he announced, and made a rasping noise as he stroked the stubble on his chin.

He took his paisley silk dressing gown from the hook behind the door and headed for the bathroom. A few moments later, Simone heard him stropping his Rolls razor. It was the morning ritual.

She threw back the coverlet and put her feet on the rug. It was indeed going to be a scorcher. The sun was already brilliant upon the verdigris spire of the school chapel. Wood pigeons were cooing in the copse behind the house.

From the bathroom came the sound of Griff singing as he shaved. Another of his rituals. Sometimes it was Gilbert and Sullivan, sometimes *The Messiah*, occasionally what he was singing this morning for some reason known only to himself:

> I vow to thee, my country — all earthly things
> above —
> Entire and whole and perfect, the service of my
> love.

She sat down at her dressing table, and was putting her hair up when he returned. The lingering odour of tobacco which never left him was now partially masked by the smells of soap, toothpaste and shaving cream.

'What's this?' he said. 'Getting up for breakfast?'

She smiled and nodded to his reflection, and while he dressed she caught fleeting glimpses of him in the mirror as he pulled on a shirt in his bungling way, putting his head in first and then struggling like a stranded turtle to get his arms into the sleeves.

'Nothing the matter is there, Simone?'

She inserted a tortoiseshell comb in her hair. 'No. Nothing the matter.'

'It's a boring old summer,' he said. 'I'm sorry.'

But it was not the boring old summer that was upsetting her. It was the roaring of troubled waters. She could hear it much louder this morning. It was as if they were already beginning to accelerate towards an unseen gorge.

He came to her and put his hands on her shoulders. She reached up and took one in her own. She never quite gave up hope that Griff might one day understand that it was not enough simply to love her – which he undoubtedly did – but that what she needed above all was to *feel* loved. Perhaps even now he might cast aside his English reserve, plant a hundred kisses on her neck and breasts and tell her that he worshipped the very ground she trod. Oh, but if only he would!

'Would you like Peggy to poach you an egg for breakfast?' he asked, and then: 'What's funny about that, Simone?'

She shook her head. 'It's nothing. Tell Peggy just coffee and toast.'

She heard him go downstairs and say his good mornings to the housemaid. Suddenly she had an overwhelming feeling of terror: she wanted somehow to stop time, to put her shoulder up against the door to the future and slam it shut.

They breakfasted in the dining room as usual, and Peggy waited on them. Griff immersed himself in *The Times* and while Simone was sitting over her second cup of coffee, the postmistress rode up on a bicycle and delivered three letters.

'Ha!' Griff said, opening the first. 'Archie! He's back from the far flung. Well, that should cheer you up, sweetheart. I mean you've got a bit of a soft spot for old T-H, isn't that right?'

She felt herself colour, and was annoyed about it. Archie Trendle-Home was a naval officer and Griff's oldest and closest friend. He had been married to a lovely Irish comedy actress called Olivia Fitzgerald. The Trendle-Homes had been regular visitors here at Prowse, and Archie had become the only friend of Griff's in whose company Simone felt genuinely at ease. But Olivia had died in a motor smash when their only daughter Christine was twelve years old, and Archie had reverted to his bachelor existence, disappearing in lean grey ships to the outposts of the British Empire and returning bronzed and debonair for fleeting calls upon his old friends.

Simone had last seen him four years before at the Spithead Review. Lieutenant Commander Trendle-Home had requested the pleasure of the company of Captain and Mrs Griffith Wilmot at a jubilee cocktail party on board HMS *Calcutta* to be held after the review of the fleet by His Majesty King George V. Under a striped awning and the influence of too many gimlets she had allowed Archie to persuade her to accompany him to the bridge. There, looking out over the lines of battleships, cruisers and destroyers that were anchored in neat lines off Gilkicker Point, he had interrupted his explanations about how orders were passed down a voicepipe to the man on the wheel to tell her that she was the most fascinating woman he had ever encountered. There had followed a few snatched moments in each other's arms behind something Archie had called the Fire Control Position. It had been for Simone an isolated experience of infidelity, a little island of deceit, a treasured oasis of romance in a dry desert of tweeds and sensible shoes.

'Oh, that's very decent of him,' Griff was saying. 'Listen to this, sweetheart. He's on leave until September and he'd like us to join his house party at Eggardon for the last week in August.' He looked up. 'That's really quite an honour. Archie only invites his closest friends to Eggardon. What do you say? I think we must accept, don't you?'

He had opened another letter, and his cheerful manner was suddenly gone. He sagged visibly. 'Ah,' he said softly. 'Damn. Still, I can't say it comes as a surprise . . . The governors have said no.' He tried to smile. 'You're not going to be a headmaster's wife after all.'

'Oh Griff – I'm sorry –'

He looked away. 'I shouldn't have raised your hopes, should I?'

'It's all right, Griff. I don't mind –'

'Well I do.' He breathed out suddenly. 'It would have been so – nice – to make a success of something. Just this once. Just for a change.'

She thought desperately for the right thing to say. 'You should have been given the post, Griff.'

'No I shouldn't. Reffel will get it, and a damn fine head-master he'll make, too. I'm a has-been, Simone. Do you know what a has-been is?'

'Yes, of course I do. But I don't agree –'

He got up from the table. 'Here, there's one for you. I shall be in the garden. Eating worms, probably.'

Her letter had that smart, semi-official look: the address on the cream envelope was typed, and the stamp bore a West End postmark. While Griff went out through the conservatory to the garden (she really did not mind at all that he was not going to be headmaster of Prowse), Simone slit it open and found inside two letters, one typed, the other handwritten on expensive, headed notepaper. She read the typewritten letter first. It was from the Marie Gould Adoption Agency in Wigmore Street.

Dear Mrs Wilmot,

We have recently received the enclosed letter from Mr David Odell which we have decided, after careful consideration, to forward to you at your last known address. Mr Odell has not been informed as to the disposal of his letter.

As it is our experience that reunions such as Mr Odell proposes seldom fulfil the expectations of the parties concerned, it is our custom to advise natural parents against making contact with children who have been adopted. However, if you wish to reply to Mr Odell's letter, may we suggest that you do so through this agency, without revealing your address?

If there is any other way in which we may advise

you or be of assistance, please do not hesitate to let us know.

Yours faithfully,
T. E. Winkup (Miss),
Families Advisor

The other letter was written in a large, untidy copperplate, with generous loops and flourishes. The signature was underlined twice.

Park House
Nassau Lane
Island Park
New York.

18 June 1939

Dear Mother,

I do not know if this will ever reach you, but I certainly hope it does. My name is David Odell and my adoption papers – which I saw for the first time only a week back – say that I was born on 31 December 1918 at the Westow Croft nursing home, Westow, North Riding, Yorkshire. I never figured out why I had to be adopted, all I know is that since I found out I have been set on meeting you, my real mother. Trouble is, I do not even know your name, just the adoption agency, so I am sending this letter to them and asking them to send it on to you. As you see, I live in New York, but my father (adoptive father) died three months back and now I'm planning on taking a trip to England this fall.

What I'd really appreciate, is for you to write me and give me your address – and your permission to come visit you. That way, maybe we can exchange letters before I take the steamer for Britain, and get acquainted. Even if you don't care to meet with me (and I guess you may not feel so inclined after all these years) could you write me a letter? You don't have to put your address on it – nor even your name if you don't want. But it would be really something to hear from you, my real mother. A man needs to know who he is, if you understand my meaning.

    With the sincere respect of your son,
    David Odell.

Simone read the letter through twice. Then she put her head down among the plates on the breakfast table and wept.

iv

Griff was in the greenhouse, pottering.

'Sweetheart,' he said when he saw her face. 'It's not the end of the world!'

It took her a moment to realize what he was talking about. 'It's something else,' she said, and held out the two letters.

She watched him while he read. Though he had been a schoolmaster for seventeen years now, Griff had never quite lost his military bearing. His hair was neatly parted and trimmed, and his moustache was nothing more than a carefully clipped square of bristles on his upper lip. And in a way, he had never entirely stopped being a cavalry officer: he still bore in his general bearing the indelible stamp of an élite regiment of lancers, still carried on a love affair with leather, and the tautness of his jaw line still gave witness to the rigours of a Sandhurst training.

'Poor old girl,' he said eventually, and put a protective arm round her shoulders. 'My poor sweetheart!'

'It's not for me you should be sorry, Griff. It's for that poor child.'

He released her, and bent to remove leaves from the tomato stems. And immediately she sensed his hostility. She could almost see his hackles go up. 'He's not a child any longer, Simone. He's a grown man. He must be – what – twenty-one?'

20

'Twenty,' she whispered. 'He's still twenty.' She looked down at the back of his head. 'I always knew that one day, one day –' She wept a little, then controlled herself and said in a low voice, 'I used to pray every night that we would be reunited. Did you know that?'

He turned to face her. He had deepset eyes beneath dark and very bushy eyebrows. They were sad eyes, has-been eyes.

She said: 'I want to write to him, Griff. You don't mind, do you?' But as soon as she had asked the question she knew that he *would* object. How could he do otherwise, he who had stipulated adoption of her baby as a condition of marriage, who had threatened to break off their engagement and land her back on the streets if she did not cooperate, who had insisted on her crossing to England and going up to Yorkshire to have her baby out of sight of his regiment, his old school and his mother; who had never visited her once during her confinement, who had never even set eyes on her child, the wonderful baby she had suckled daily for five weeks, weeping over him in loneliness and bewilderment and fear? Griff was a gentleman, yes, but even at the age of twenty-two he had been no sapling, but a war-hardened, resolute young officer with an unbending will and, at times, a breathtaking lack of compassion.

'I think –' he started, and even now she knew that he was genuinely concerned and anxious not to hurt her, 'I think the best thing to do with this is to ignore it, Simone. It may sound heartless, I know, but –'

'No,' she said quickly, and took the letters back from him. 'I can't do that. I must write to him.'

'But sweetheart – haven't you read the other letter? These people aren't fools, you know. To ignore their advice –'

'Damn their advice,' she said.

He tried again. 'Then let me write back for you. Via the agency. Wouldn't that make a great deal more sense?'

'And what would you say?'

'I would say, very tactfully, that you have decided in the interests of all parties that it would be better not to attempt such a reunion.'

'In other words, that his mother has no interest in him.'

'Not at all,' he said. 'That is not at all what I meant, and you know it, Simone.'

They had left the greenhouse and now stood together – yet significantly apart – on the lawn by his beloved rose beds. But Simone was no longer listening to him. She was remembering a long, wintry train journey she had made up to Yorkshire. She remembered the spartan nursing home, the long and difficult labour and the final delivery of a red-faced, yelling boy. She remembered the very first time she put him to her breast and suckled him. She remembered weeping for hours every day by his cot. But most clearly of all she remembered a morning when the baby was five weeks old and she had watched from the window of an upper room in the Westow Croft nursing home.

For a moment, instead of seeing this lawn, these roses and that swing seat with the green and white awning where they had tea on summer afternoons, she looked down in her mind's eye upon a wintry drive where a large chauffeur-driven black limousine was parked. She saw a man in an expensive overcoat and a brown bowler hat, with a glamorous woman on his arm. She saw the nanny in a starched apron and cap, carrying the baby – her baby. She watched them shake hands with the matron before getting into the car, the baby crying all the while, and felt again that physical sensation of loss, of having part of herself ripped out, carried away.

'Don't you understand, Griff? He's my *son*!'

He glanced at her and somehow – she never knew how he did it – managed to make her feel in the wrong. 'Of course . . . he may not be. Had you considered that? He may be an impostor. America, and New York in particular, is the breeding ground of confidence tricksters and shysters. Anyone with access to the adoption papers could have written that letter. So our Mr Odell could quite easily be an adventurer out to make what I believe the Yanks call a "fast buck".'

She said nothing.

'Also, before you put pen to paper, Simone, I think you should give thought to some of the very possible consequences. Because if you write to him the chances are that it won't stop there. It'll be the thin end of the wedge. He'll have his foot in the door, so to speak. You'll end up agreeing to meet him.'

'Would that be such a disaster?'

'No, but it might be very embarrassing for you.' He hesitated a moment. 'I don't think you would find it easy to admit, after all these years, that you had an illegitimate baby when you were a child of seventeen. People would look at you with new eyes, and that's putting it mildly.'

'At least they might look at me. At least they might start acknowledging my presence.'

Griff summoned reserves of patience. Simone had done very little to help herself in the past twenty years. She took little part in village life, held herself aloof from the school and even refused to return to France for holidays. But it was no good telling her that she was cutting off her nose to spite her face. It was no good telling Simone anything.

'Listen. He's twenty. He's a grown man. You can't be a mother to him, you can't even guarantee that you'll like him. He's been brought up on the other side of the Atlantic. He'll have quite different values, tastes. He's not the baby you gave up, sweetheart –'

Her temper blazed. Suddenly they were back in the quarrel that had grown up like a blight on their marriage, an issue that had lingered unresolved between them since their wedding day. 'And why did I have to give him up, Griff? Because you insisted on it, that's why. Because you were afraid of what might be said in your – your precious regiment!'

He appealed to her: 'Sweetheart – I didn't force you to do anything! We took the decision together. Didn't we? It was the only way we could have got married! We both had to make sacrifices. That's what love involves –'

'*We* made sacrifices? What sacrifice did you ever make, Griff?'

He shook his head. 'I'm not going to rake all that up again, Simone. I've told you what I think. If you decide to act against my advice, that's up to you. But if things go wrong, please don't come to me for sympathy.' He smiled sadly. 'Yes, of course you made the bigger sacrifice. But there was a time when the sacrifices we made bound us closer together and proved how much we were in love, wasn't there? Isn't it better to look on them in that way than – than to use them as ammunition to hurl back and forth at each other?'

'You don't understand, Griff. You never did, and you never will.'

She saw a muscle tighten in his jaw. 'I think I understand very well, Simone. I proposed in good faith, but you accepted knowing damn well you were pregnant.'

'I did *not* know! I was seventeen, Griff! Seventeen!'

His voice had become cold and clipped. He was no longer the gentle schoolmaster but the officer again, war-hardened, embittered by seeing too many good men die. 'Of course you damn well knew. You saw me coming, didn't you? You were pregnant by some common *poilu* –'

'He was an officer! He was a pilot! He died for France!'

'It matters not a jot who he was, Simone. The fact remains that you were carrying his child when you agreed to be my wife and you said nothing whatsoever about it.'

'I did not know, Griff! How many times must I tell you that? How many times?'

'You saw me coming, that was my trouble.' He gave a short, bitter laugh. 'Well then, go ahead. You write to your long lost son. And while you're about it, I suggest you tell him what his mother got up to before he was born. I suggest you tell him about your time as one of the Paris "godmothers", one of the "little angels" we saw so much of on the boulevards, each with her spotty-faced "hero of the republic". I suggest —'

She swung round and hit his face as hard as she could with the palm of her hand. Suddenly she was the fighter again, the Parisienne teenager who had rebelled against her bourgeois upbringing, one of the easy girls who gave soldiers a reason to fight.

'You shall be sorry you ever said that,' she whispered, and went quickly across the lawn and into the house.

v

He went back into the greenhouse and stared at his tomatoes. He was already sorry. He had not meant to say what he had said. He was afraid that he had broken something fragile, something he had been at pains to preserve for many years. He had never before hinted at what he knew about Simone. He had always given her the impression that when he first approached her that sparkling May afternoon in the Bois de Boulogne, he had never set eyes on her before.

But he had seen her — many times — during the spring of 1918. The previous autumn, he had been sent back from the front after taking a shell splinter in the thigh, and as soon as he could walk again had volunteered to return to duty. But instead of going back to the trenches he had been given a light duties post as assistant liaison officer on the French General Staff at Vincennes. He took lodgings in Paris and came to know the city well. He sat outside the cafés and saw the teenage girls — some of them only thirteen or fourteen — picking up the young French soldiers and taking them off for half an hour's love before they went to the front to be killed or maimed.

Simone had been one of those girls, and one of the most popular. He had seen her once with a soldier on each arm and three or four following behind. There had been — still was — something about her that drew men to her like moths to a bright light, a sex appeal so strong you sensed it even when she was round a street corner and out of sight.

Having noticed her once, Griff noticed her again and again. To him she appeared young, innocent, carefree – and far too good for the company of ordinary *poilus*. For Griff, every girl with a soldier on her arm was a tart, but Simone was different. Simone had confidence, flair. He watched her from a distance. Petite, with wonderful chestnut hair drawn into a topknot on her head, she captivated him without even knowing it.

War has strange effects on men: in the shadow of death no man, however disciplined, educated or religious, is proof against the instinct to reproduce, especially when confronted with the ideal mate. Griff was no exception. He had been too close to death and had seen too many soldiers die in the waterlogged trenches of Ypres. Coming back to Paris, walking about in the sunshine with the daffodils bursting forth in white and yellow hosannas, he felt a great burden of guilt at having survived when others had fallen. He needed desperately to love and be loved, to forgive and to be forgiven, and when he found Simone weeping alone on a bench in the Bois de Boulogne, it was unthinkable that he should do anything other than limp to her rescue.

She told him her story. Her name was Simone Billotte. She came from a good family. Her uncle was a colonel in the army. Her mother and all her brothers were dead, and her father, an entrepreneur, had taken up with a woman who had thrown her out of the house in a fit of jealousy. She was destitute and alone.

Griff took pity on her. He found rooms for her and paid the rent. He met her every day, fell quickly in love with her and proposed marriage. She accepted without delay, and without delay he put a ring on her finger and announced the engagement in *The Times*. His mother, his regiment, his old headmaster – even his friend Archie – were appalled.

But Griff was unmoved: marrying Simone against such a weight of advice somehow eased the burden of guilt. He was paying back something to somebody in a complicated way. And he was also desperately in love.

And then one June day when they were taking coffee by the Seine, Simone vomited unexpectedly.

Griff was a regular customer, and the proprietor's wife knew him and liked him. 'If the young lady is not in the family way, M'sieur,' she told him, 'I am the Queen of Sheba.'

Griff asked Simone, and she broke down and admitted it. He was shattered by the discovery, but they were already too far along the road to marriage to turn back, and the story Simone gave him, and which he accepted, was to become the precarious raft upon which they were to build their marriage.

She said she had been engaged to be married to a French officer, a pilot who had since been killed in action. Knowing nothing of life, she had given herself to him. And, she insisted, she had had no idea that she was pregnant when she accepted Griff's proposal of marriage.

He had already almost convinced himself that her activities with French soldiers had been innocent, and he now fell over himself to believe her story and forgive her. To call off the wedding would not only cause him a huge loss of face but would condemn Simone to a life on the streets. He knew that he would never be able to live with his conscience if he did that.

He told her then and there that there was no question of breaking off their engagement. But different arrangements would, of necessity, have to be made. The wedding would have to be delayed until after she had had the baby, and the child would have to be adopted. That was the way things were done.

Simone agreed with hardly a murmur. They kept everything quiet, and towards the end of the year he brought her over to England. But at the last minute, he was unable to get leave to take her up to the private nursing home, and was obliged to enlist the help of his closest friend. So towards the end of December '18, it was Archie Trendle-Home who escorted Simone on the journey north, and it was Archie who was the only other person, apart from the staff of the nursing home and the Marie Gould Agency, who knew of the birth and the adoption.

vi

Simone avoided Griff all day, and lay awake most of the night thinking about their argument, the·letter, Archie, Griff's lost headmastership, the likelihood of war — everything.

Eventually, in the early hours, she abandoned hope of getting any sleep, tiptoed down to the sitting room and sat at her desk to write a letter to her son.

She wept over it a great deal. Although she longed to write a warm, loving letter inviting David to come and stay for as long as he liked, she knew that she could not do that because not only would Griff never agree to it but even the suggestion would put their future happiness at risk.

She saw what she was being forced to do: she was having to choose all over again, just as she had chosen in 1918, between her son and Griff. And in spite of the hurtful things he had said the previous morning, she still loved Griff. She knew how tender he was about never giving her a baby. She knew that he had indeed made sacrifices for her and had been a good husband to her. And even now she still carried with her the terror of finding herself alone and destitute.

So in the end she decided to write to David without giving her name or address and to say, very regretfully, that she thought that it was perhaps better, after all these years, that they did not meet.

It was not at all easy. She tried to explain why she was apprehensive of a meeting: that she was French, that she had married, that her husband's position was such that she could not afford to risk scandal. She sat and wondered what conclusion he might draw from that. Perhaps that she was titled or married to a public figure. Well, let him think so, poor boy! At least he would have something to hold on to . . .

She wept a little more, wrote a little more. She crossed out, tore up, started again. By the time she had completed the letter and had put it in an airmail envelope and left it out for Peggy to take to the post office first thing, it was getting light.

She crept back upstairs and into the double bed. The next thing she knew it was broad daylight and Griff was standing over her in his old brown corduroys and houndstooth hacking jacket, brandishing the letter in his hand.

He gave her no time to explain, that was what hurt her most of all. He presumed that because she had written direct to David in New York she had revealed her own address and welcomed the idea of a meeting. 'You've gone behind my back, Simone,' he said. 'You've betrayed my trust.'

Their argument – like so many they had had before – descended to the level of six-year-olds. He claimed that he had as good as forbidden her to write to David and that she had deliberately disobeyed him, her husband, whom she had promised to love, honour and obey. She said that at no time, at no time, had he forbidden her to write, and far from forbidding her had actually suggested – in a most insulting way – what she should write. He summoned all the condescension he could muster and explained, as if to a child, the rhetorical nature of that suggestion, saying that if she really inferred any other meaning from it she had a far lower level of intelligence than he had once supposed. She insisted, again, that he had not at any time forbidden her to write.

'Yes I did –'

'No, excuse me, you did not –'

'I did, Simone, I made it abundantly clear –'

She challenged him to open the letter and see for himself what she had written, but he got on his big white charger and said it had never been his practice to read other people's correspondence and that he didn't intend to start now.

She was no good at fighting with him, and had no wish to do so. She dissolved into tears and told him to tear the bloody letter up if he felt that strongly about it. He said that he didn't want to fight either and that all he wanted was to avoid raking over the past and having scenes like this, and that was why he had opposed her writing to David in the first place. She said she was sorry. He accepted her apology but did not apologize because Griff never apologized, it was something he had learnt not to do when he was in the army.

'What shall we do with this?' he asked.

'You can tear it up, Griff. I told you.'

He gave it to her. 'You do it. It's your letter.'

She tore it in four and gave him a watery smile.

'Peace in our time?' he asked, and when he held out his arms to her, she nodded, and leant against him in her nightdress; and he spread out her long shining hair over her shoulders, and gently kissed her; and she took his hand in hers and put it where she said it always belonged and held it there to make sure he would not take it away.

'I hope so,' she whispered. 'Oh, Griff! I do hope so . . .'

TWO

Eggardon House was one of those typical Victorian home-steads of flint and slate to be found dotted about Dorset. Nestling in the fold of the hill upon which stood the old Roman fortress Thomas Hardy had made famous, it faced southward over rolling pastures to the sea. The central porch was flanked on either side by a long, narrow verandah, and two small wings, one at either end of the main building, housed the wood store and the dairy. On the ground floor – which was flagged throughout – there was a large kitchen, medium-sized dining room and a poky sitting room. Up-stairs, giving off a narrow, creaking corridor, there were six sparsely furnished bedrooms with low ceilings, worm-eaten bare boards and arched lattice windows.

Attended only by a housekeeper and his personal servant, Rear Admiral Barty Trendle-Home (a battlecruiser man) had lived at Eggardon in solitary splendour for thirteen years after the Great War and, since inheriting the property from his uncle, Archie had made virtually no changes to the house apart from putting a ping-pong table in the old cheeseroom over the woodstore and installing a rather temperamental refrigerator in the dairy. Otherwise very little had been altered. The drains still stank, the walls still wept, the ceilings still sagged and the floorboards upstairs still creaked diabol-ically – wherever you went and however carefully you tip-toed; while in the kitchen, covering almost an entire wall, Archie had preserved his uncle's extraordinary montage of postcards, photographs, drawings and doggerel, as well as a copy of every letter, published and unpublished, that the admiral had sent to *The Times*.

The Wilmots arrived in their little blue coupé soon after

four o'clock, when Archie and his guests were sitting in front of the house having tea; and when Griff had parked on the grass (there was no drive) between Archie's Lagonda and a very sporty looking little MG, Simone braced herself for the usual hellos and hoorays she had come to expect at English house parties.

It was a smaller gathering than they had expected. Archie's daughter, Christine, was pouring the tea and her admirer, a large, ginger-haired RAF pilot called Nick Massingbohm, was in the middle of explaining to her how to shake the enemy off your tail at three hundred miles an hour. A jolly lady called Beeby Perowne (was she Archie's latest? Simone wondered) was sunk deep in a deck chair eating a scone loaded with strawberry preserve and clotted cream, and Christine's friend Celia and her fiancé, Leslie, a bearded intellectual in green corduroys and Fair Isle pullover, completed the collection.

Archie was as bronzed and brown-eyed and beaky-nosed as ever, and the very sight of him made Simone feel weak with excitement. Dressed in cricket flannels, blazer and a battered old Prowse boater whose crown was missing, he advanced to the Standard and as soon as Griff got out shook him by the hand, hit him between the shoulder blades, struck him a glancing blow on the back of the head and then punched him in the stomach when he wasn't expecting it. Having completed this display of public school camaraderie, he turned to Simone, hugged her, kissed her on the cheek and in doing so informed her – accidentally, of course, but in a way that was intimate in the extreme – that his ardour for her was every bit as strong now as it had been four years before on the bridge of HMS *Calcutta*.

He made all the introductions, organized two extra deck chairs, ribbed Griff for going thin on top and then proceeded to outline to the new arrivals what he called the 'routine'. This included matters such as the use of the bathroom, how to manage the 'heads' (you had to count to ten – slowly – before letting go the chain), and the ghost.

'What do you mean, the ghost, Arch?' Beeby roared. (Beeby was an officer in the recently resurrected Women's Royal Naval Service.) 'I simply refuse to believe in this ghost of yours!'

'My dear Beeby, I do assure you there *is* a ghost. He stomps up and down the corridor at two in the morning. I think it must be Uncle Barty. He probably thinks he's still on his bridge. But he's quite harmless. Last time I heard him I simply bellowed "Get turned in, you old fool!" and it worked like magic.'

Christine turned to Simone. The last time they had met, Christine had been all puppy fat and pigtails. Now she was a demure rose of nineteen in a white blouse and pleated skirt. 'I've never heard anything. It's just one of Pater's inventions.'

'Not at all,' her father insisted, 'Blashford won't go into the west wing. I can't even drag him.'

'Who the Dickens is Blashford?' Griff asked.

'My new Labrador,' Archie said. 'I thought as I'm going to have a spell ashore I might get an animal trained up again.'

'You won't have much time for shooting the way things are looking,' Beeby observed darkly.

Celia giggled. 'Here we go again.'

'Simone,' Christine said. 'How do you like it? Milk or lemon? It's only Lyons, I'm afraid.'

Griff had turned to Beeby. 'You mean Poland?'

There was a general shout of protest.

'What have I said?'

'We were having a very boring argument about the crisis just before you arrived,' Beeby explained. 'And Leslie suggested we drop the whole subject while we're here.' She looked back at Archie, who was reclining in a deck chair with his crownless boater tipped over his eyes. 'Actually, there's very little we can do about it, isn't there, Arch? And if we're going to have a holiday, I suppose we may as well have a holiday from all that as well.'

They all looked to him for a decision and he played up to

the situation in true Archie fashion, peering out at them from under the straw brim of his boater.

'All those in favour say "aye".'

'Aye,' said the majority, which did not include his daughter.

He smacked the arm of his deck chair. 'Carried. It is the will of this house that the world crisis be declared taboo, that no newspapers be purchased or otherwise acquired, and that the wireless shall remain silent for the duration.'

'The duration?' Simone said, smiling. 'You make it sound as if we are in a prison!'

'Ah, *ma belle* Simone! With you here, I wouldn't mind a life sentence!'

She saw Griff glance quickly in her direction, but deliberately failed to meet his eye. On the way down from Kent, they had argued again about David.

ii

After tea, Griff and Archie took Blashford for a walk over Eggardon Hill in order to catch up on each other's news. They went up a steep path between fields where sheep grazed, and climbed over a stile onto springy turf.

'So what's in store for you now, old boy?' Griff asked. 'Isn't it about time your name came out of the hat for promotion?'

Archie cupped his hands round a vesta as he relit his pipe. 'No hope of that now. I'm passed over. Your obedient servant will be a two-and-a-half-striper to his dying day. Haven't found sufficient favour with Their Lordships, you see. Bit of a bore, but there it is. Of course, if this war we've promised not to talk about materializes, that might change matters somewhat. So . . . you know the old wardroom toast, don't you?'

'Which one's that? "Sweethearts and wives"?'

'No! "A bloody war or a sickly season." That's the only way I'll get myself promoted now.'

Griff chuckled. It was good to be in Archie's company again. Archie always managed to put you in good heart and make you take life less seriously.

'So what's this new job of yours?' he asked.

'Chatham.' Archie pulled a face. 'Admiral's staff. The usual thing. Looks as though yours truly's going to be stuck behind a cheap tin desk for the next two years. That is not a prospect that fills a chap with glee, if you know what I mean.'

They reached the top of the ancient fort and stood facing into the southerly breeze.

'I expect you already know about Reffel getting the head-mastership?' Griff said.

'Yes. Damn shame, that. Never've happened if Uncle Barty had been alive. I voted against it, of course, but I don't suppose that's much consolation.'

'Well . . . thank you.'

'Will you stay on?'

'I don't see what else I can do. If I owned the house it might be a different story. But you governors have got me in your pocket, haven't you? You say jump, I jump.'

'But what about this idiotic idea of moving the school to Somerset? If that happens you'll be moving anyway.'

Griff prodded the turf with his stick. 'As a matter of fact, I supported that idea. It'll only happen in the event of hostilities, you know. But I think it makes sense. After all, we are within howitzer range of Calais.'

Archie stooped to relight his pipe again and flung the spent match away downwind. 'Yes, but Jerry has to get to Calais first, old boy, doesn't he? And I don't see him doing that overnight.' He glanced at Griff. 'What would you do? If the balloon did go up?'

'Join up, I suppose. If they'll have me.'

Archie sucked at his pipe and gazed seaward.

'Wouldn't it make a lot more sense to join up *before* it goes up? I mean, there'll be a mad scramble for the plum jobs, won't there, and if you were crafty and got in with your bid before the rush —'

'You mean throw up teaching altogether?'

'Not necessarily. I know I could talk the board of governors into keeping your post open for the duration if you volunteered to join up again. Might be a very welcome move. Set a fine example to the boys. Besides, since this idea of moving the school has been going around, there's been muttering in some quarters about shell dodging. So if the head of the history department were seen to be one of the first reserve officers in the country to volunteer, well . . .'

'It would be a feather in the school's cap.'

'Exactly that, old boy. You've taken the blessed words out of my mouth.'

They walked on over the hill and after rejoining the road decided on a quick pint at the village local.

'Christine's grown up to be very lovely,' Griff remarked when they had settled themselves on the bench outside the pub.

Archie looked as if he had been paid a personal compliment. 'She'll do,' he said gruffly.

'And this RAF type she's got in tow. Is that what you might call "serious"?'

'Don't ask me, old boy. That's on the secret list. But what about your good self? Your literary ambitions? Wasn't there some slim volume of poetry on the stocks last time we talked?'

Griff gazed into his beer tankard. 'That? I put it aside some time ago. It's all too easy to convince oneself that one has more talent than is the case.' He laughed, a little sadly. 'So I continue to muddle along, you know. The village schoolmaster, that's me. Chalky Wilmot.'

'I think you underestimate yourself,' Archie said.

'You do? I doubt if Simone would agree with you there, old man.'

Griff took a gulp of bitter and looked out over the mellow

evening landscape. From a hillside half a mile away came a series of short, shrill whistles, and a sheepdog went racing off in a wide arc round the flock. Nearer at hand, the village church clock struck the half hour, and the bell notes hung in the summer evening air.

How did those lines go from Gray's Elegy? That verse which went, *Some mute inglorious Milton, here may rest, Some Cromwell guiltless of his country's blood* . . .

'You may as well know,' he said. 'Things aren't too grand between us at the minute. She – had a letter not long ago.' He glanced at Archie, who was fondling Blashford's silky black ears. 'Does the name Odell ring a bell?'

'Odell . . . Not –?'

'Yes. That Odell.'

'Good God!'

'David Odell. Lives in New York. Wanted her to write back. I put the tin hat on that very quickly, as you can imagine. So . . . if relations seem a little strained, you'll understand the reason why.' He forced a smile. 'Just thought I'd mention it.'

Archie said, 'I am so sorry, old boy.'

Griff watched the flock of sheep come slowly down the hill, the sheepdog crouching and moving at each whistled command. 'I – er – was wondering if you might be able to help,' he said.

'My dear chap, if there's anything at all I can do –'

'Simone's very fond of you, we both know that.' Blashford had transferred his affections and was now looking soulfully up at him, his saliva-flecked jaw resting on his knee. 'And if the subject were to crop up, well, I'd be grateful to you if you could help her see it from my point of view.'

'Which is?'

'Which is that I don't want this Odell chap to be instrumental in opening up old wounds.'

'It sounds to me as if he's already done that, Griff.'

'He's begun to, certainly. But if Simone could be persuaded that my decision was made for her own good . . .'

He shook his head and turned to Archie. 'I just thought she might take it from you better, that's all.'

'The trouble is, old boy, *is* it for her own good? I mean, would it be so very harmful to allow her to contact her own son?'

Griff looked away, his jaw clamped firmly shut, a muscle working in his cheek.

'You never forgave her, did you?' Archie said quietly. 'That's the root of the trouble. You never forgave her, and Simone never forgave you. You're both still fighting the same battle you were fighting in 1918.'

Griff drained his tankard and stood up. 'Hadn't we better be making a move? Won't do to leave your guests unattended too long, will it?'

When they arrived back, Nick, Christine, Leslie and Celia were playing quoits on the grass in front of the house.

'Gin time!' Archie announced. 'Nick, you can make yourself useful. There's Pimm's and lemonade for the ladies, and ice and lemon in the fridge. Jump to it, lad!'

Massingbohm sprang to attention and saluted. 'Aye aye, sir!' he roared, and hastened to obey.

iii

Outwardly, the house party was a great success, because everyone mucked in very well and there was no shortage of food, drink, conversation or humour. Archie organized, chivvied and teased his guests with unfailing bonhomie; Nick Massingbohm talked to anyone who would listen about his beloved Hurricanes; Beeby ate a great deal and did quite a lot of laughing, and Celia's arty boyfriend produced a sketch of the house which Archie tactfully decided was worthy of the kitchen wall.

They played ping-pong in the cheeseroom and backgammon on the lawn. They drove down to Bridport and walked along the sands and up over the cliffs to Golden Cap. They dined late, and sat over their coffee. They set each other puzzles and anagrams, recited poetry they had learned in the fourth form and played 'Chopsticks' on an old, honky-tonk piano. It was like stepping back fifty years: there were no outside entertainments so, as Beeby put it, they jolly well had to buckle to and entertain themselves.

But something was missing. By forbidding conversation about the crisis and banning the wireless and newspapers, Archie inadvertently caused a strange atmosphere of false security, a sense of unease, which Griff felt particularly keenly.

His difficulty with Simone was partly to blame: it was one thing having to avoid mentioning Poland, but quite another to have to bottle up the threat of this other conflict, which was much closer to home. And there was no question of discussing it further with either Archie or Simone. She was careful to place herself in another group when they went for walks, sat at the far end of the table from him at meals and refused to speak to him when they were getting ready for bed. As for Archie, well, he had made it painfully clear whose side he was on.

It was their last afternoon. Griff drowsed outside in a deck chair, enjoying the sun. For once, everyone else seemed to have found themselves something to do, and it was not necessary to play games or make conversation. He had brought Maugham's latest book, *The Summing Up*, to read during the holiday, and was feeling depressed by the author's resigned scepticism. The awful part about it was that such a jaundiced view of life and morals seemed to be gaining ground wherever one looked.

He felt suddenly pessimistic. He was over forty, and here he was, still on the teaching treadmill and passed over for headmaster in favour of a younger man. He remembered his ambitions when his mother had still been alive. Once, when he had jokingly suggested that he might one day leave the army and go into business, she had been horrified. 'What on earth has put such a ridiculous idea into your head?' she had asked. 'You are in a job that you love, you have comradeship, good pay and security. If you were to go into business now, you would lose all those things, and a lot more besides.' He had remarked that his army service would provide him with excellent contacts in the city. She had replied that if he was at all like his father, he would become quickly disenchanted with the business world. Only a few months after that conversation, Mrs Wilmot had died, and the state of her own finances convinced Griff that however much he would like to take her advice, he was unable to do so.

The reason was Simone. She was spending his captain's pay faster than he earned it and leaving him so overdrawn at the bank that he couldn't keep his uniforms up to scratch or look his tailor in the eye. She didn't get on at all well with other officers' wives and was desperately lonely as a result. Worst of all, he was beginning to lose her respect because in spite of all their lovemaking, he had still failed to give her the baby she longed for.

That, along with the fact that her illegitimate child had been adopted, was the central issue. If he had been able to give Simone children – lots of them – the memory of the child she had been obliged to give up would have quickly faded and they might have been happy.

How desperately he had longed for her to come to him one day and tell him shyly that she was expecting! Even now, twenty years on, there were times when he still hoped for a miracle. But it had never happened and never would happen. She had not even had so much as a false alarm.

A month or two before leaving the army he had received a private letter from Archie's uncle, Rear Admiral Trendle-Home, who was one of the governors of Prowse, offering him a position as a teacher of history. Until that moment, teaching had never even occurred to Griff, but one visit to his old school and he was completely sold on the idea. A house went with the job; Simone would have an opportunity to help out with French conversation and art, and he would be able to surround himself with books and good company. He had fought for his country; he could retire with honour.

Given time, he might be able to publish a few poems, for like many of his contemporaries who had served in the Great War he had sought a release in the composition of verse. His mother had been right: he was not cut out for business and never had been. And wasn't the academic world infinitely preferable to that of high finance and the stock market?

So the decision had been taken. He had said farewell to the regiment and had hung up his cavalry sword for the last time; and here he was hardly any further on than he had been that first day when he entered 4b classroom and cracked that old Spoonerism about hissing a mystery lesson. How many times had he told that joke now? How many times had he warned of leaving by the town drain? Seventeen times, and in just a few weeks when term started again he'd be telling it to the junior year all over again.

The sound of a car approaching made him open his eyes. Archie and Simone had gone into Bridport in the Lagonda to buy provisions and were returning. He watched the car come slowly down the track towards the house, and for a moment tried to see Simone as the world saw her.

She was undoubtedly attractive. Petite, graceful, with wonderfully clear skin and an almost mediaeval quality about her high cheekbones and Gallic features, she possessed that flair some French women have for choosing clothes that emphasized her femininity – unlike the jumper, skirt and clodhopper outfits worn by so many English women. She looked young for her age, too: more like twenty-eight than thirty-eight. And sitting beside Archie in his pale grey Lagonda . . .

He wondered about them. That Simone was fond of Archie he had no doubt. But did it go any further? In an odd way, he almost hoped it did. It was as if he felt he owed Simone a little happiness, a little success. Nevertheless he could not entirely quell a nagging sense of jealousy and suspicion.

Really he would have felt much easier if they flirted openly and outrageously instead of sharing this indefinable empathy, this aura of happiness when they were together, which probably went unnoticed among the others but was quite obvious to Griff. Now, watching them as the open Lagonda bumped in through the gate and drew up alongside the house, he couldn't fail to see that in Archie's company Simone looked happier, prettier and more relaxed than he had seen her in years. She was radiant.

He strolled over to help unload the car.

'Chicken for dinner!' Archie announced, lifting a large hamper from the boot. 'Simone's going to cook us a *coq au vin à la Française*.'

Simone laughed. 'And for breakfast, Archie is going to make – *comment s'appelle*?' She put on a thick French accent. '"Sheet on ze raft".'

Archie turned to Griff and winked. 'Your wife is a very naughty lady, old boy. She means devilled kidneys on toast.'

Simone went into the house. During their shopping outing, she had opened up to Archie and told him all her feelings about the coming war and Griff and her son. He was a wonderful listener: really he was the only man she had ever known with whom she felt completely free to say what was in her mind. And on the way back – only ten minutes before – she had persuaded him to park in a lane off the road and they had trespassed further upon forbidden territory. She had lain in his arms, and his kisses had raised her to an impossible peak: she was still up there, riding a wave of sensual excitement that was almost unbearable.

She ran upstairs and locked herself in the bathroom. She buried her nose in the silk folds of her blouse to savour for as long as possible the lovely smell that was so uniquely Archie.

She was actually throbbing with excitement, even now. 'Oh God!' she whispered, sitting doubled up on the lavatory seat and hugging herself very tight. 'Oh God! Oh God! Oh God!'

As it was their last evening, Archie opened a bottle of Warre's '27 after dinner, and they sat at the table for a long time, talking and nibbling cheese and circulating the decanter.

Griff – who was on good form that evening – had a little brain-teaser for them which he had been saving up as a party piece. 'Here we are, ladies and gentlemen. Three tumblers and three table knives. Now the problem is to make a platform with the knives resting on the tumblers which will hold the weight of Simone's glass of port there. Anyone care to try?'

Beeby was a little flushed with Margaux. 'Oh I'm sure that's *very* easy,' she said, and proceeded to pile the knives haphazardly together on the upended glasses.

'My dear Beeby,' Archie said, 'if Griff sets you a problem you can be quite sure that it is *not* easy.'

'I think it's impossible,' Christine said after watching Nick's unsuccessful attempts.

Leslie declined to try. 'I have a suspicion it has something to do with cantilevers and mathematics, and neither is my métier.'

Archie turned to Griff. 'Go on, sir! Show the duffers how it's done!'

Griff arranged the tumblers in an equilateral triangle and fitted the blades of the knives together so that each rested on one of its neighbours and supported the other.

'*Violà!*' he said finally. 'Now if I may have your glass, *chérie –*' and he placed Simone's glass of port on the little triangular platform formed by the three knife blades.

'That is very, very clever!' Beeby exclaimed rather solemnly. 'It's like magic!'

Griff looked modestly pleased with himself, pushing his mouth forward as he smiled in the way he did in class when one of his jokes went down well.

'I've seen it before,' Simone said.

'I said it had something to do with cantilevers,' Leslie

remarked to Celia, who smiled adoringly and managed to touch his knee under the table.

'What about that poem of yours, Celia?' Christine asked when Griff's structure had been dismantled and Simone had her glass of port back. 'I do wish you'd read it to us.'

Celia had discovered, hidden under a loose floorboard in the cheeseroom, a poem she had written while on holiday at Eggardon seven years before. Now, after a little cajoling by the others, she was prevailed upon to read it aloud. She stood up at her place, a little flushed from the day's sun and the wine.

'It isn't all that good,' she apologized. 'But I think it's worth –'

'Oh – do get *on* with it, Celia!' Christine urged.

So she started.

> That year when we went
> It was early summer and
> We lay in the grass and watched the clouds
> And forgot the sea in the cold
> Of an English sun
> We played round the cars
> And dodged
> Between pillars, crumbling with age
> We ran laughing and shouting, flinging
> Ourselves among nettles, hiding
> Not caring
> While the grown-ups sat in deck chairs
> Torn and still tearing
> Soothed by the creaking trees
>
> At night we gathered reddened and hungry
> Warm in the damp of the walls and the stone floor
> The room was happy
>
> We trooped to the parlour
> Too scared of the night for games of murder

And things that move in the dark
And when we left and looked back from the road
The next day
It was bleak, stone, small against the hill
And we were sad in our goodbyes
But the house just stood
And listened to the sheep
And awaited the winds
Of another year.

'Gosh!' Beeby said. '"The winds of another year" – doesn't it sound ominous?'

'That's only because of the mood of our times,' Leslie said. 'You see – we all feel, well, insecure really.' He looked round. 'Don't we? I mean, it's only because of – of everything – that those lines sound ominous to Beeby.'

Christine exchanged glances with Nick and said: 'You mean if we'd never heard of Anschluss, or Czechoslovakia had never been occupied –'

'And Britain wasn't off the gold standard and there'd been no depression, no disarmament, no attack on Abyssinia and no bombing of Guernica we'd all be happy as sandboys, eh?' Nick finished for her.

'No!' Celia protested. 'Leslie didn't mean that at all, did you, Leslie? It was just a poem by a little girl. It wasn't supposed to sound ominous at all.'

'Out of the mouths of babes and sucklings,' Beeby said, and there was an unusually long silence.

It was broken by Simone, who turned to Archie and asked quietly, 'Do you think there really will be another war?'

Massingbohm gave a short, humourless laugh. 'I'd say it was inevitable.'

'That's because you *want* to fight,' Leslie said.

'Not at all. It's because when I see a socking great cloud of smoke on the horizon I know that there's a big fire somewhere, and sooner or later someone is going to have to put it out. And in aviation terms, it's also a very reliable indication of which way the wind's blowing.'

'I thought,' Archie said, 'that we weren't going to talk about the crisis.'

'Oh – Pa!' Christine said. 'Can't we have *one* serious conversation?'

'What do you think, Captain Griff?' Beeby asked. 'You're the veteran.'

'Thank you very much,' Archie said. 'I was at Gallipoli as a midshipman.'

'Here we go,' Christine said. 'What have I started?'

'You haven't answered my question, Griff,' Beeby said.

Griff shook his head. 'I'm just a frowsty old schoolmaster. I don't think my opinion is worth very much these days.'

'Ah, but you are an historian, Captain Wilmot,' Christine said.

'Come on, old boy,' Archie said. 'We're hanging on your every word.'

He smiled wryly. 'Well, I used to take the view that mankind could affect its own destiny, but now I'm not so sure. I have a feeling that whatever the politicians may tell us to the contrary, we humans are swept along by events rather than vice versa. And certainly the tide does seem to be taking us towards war at the minute.' He sighed. 'So I suppose it'll be the same old story. We'll send another expeditionary force. We'll fight each other to another standstill, lose the cream of another generation, sow another crop of bitterness and despair. No doubt the younger generation will rise to the occasion and do their bit –' He broke off and looked round. 'Sorry. I'm being rather depressing, aren't I?'

'You *are* rather, Captain Griff,' Celia said. 'I mean – surely things are quite different now, aren't they? Isn't the French army far bigger than last time? And what about the Maginot Line?'

'Oh didn't you know?' Simone put in. 'They don't count at *all*. All France is useful for is to provide a nice, big flat field for you British to fight your wars on. Isn't that right, Griff?'

Griff said gently: 'I think you've got the wrong end of the stick, darling heart. All I ever said was that it was dangerous to place too much faith in a line of fortresses, and that it was very shortsighted of Belgium – not France – to insist on neutrality, because Flanders, inevitably, will be where the main battle will be fought.'

Nick leaned forward, his elbows on the table. 'I'd take that a great deal further. You only have to read Liddell Hart to realize that the next war is bound to be one of mobility. And that means that the side with the strongest air force is bound, ultimately, to come out on top.'

Celia sighed impatiently. 'It all seems so unnecessary! So – petty! You'd have thought it would be the simplest thing in the world to sit down at a table with Herr Hitler and sort the whole thing out.'

'Oh – certainly,' Nick boomed. 'All we'd have to do is hand over Poland, and he'd be happy. For a week or so. Until he decided he wanted to annex Denmark or Holland or the Balkans.'

'I'm not sure if I agree with Captain Wilmot about events controlling mankind rather than vice versa,' Leslie said. 'After all, we only have ourselves to blame, really, don't we? If we'd treated Germany with a bit of compassion in the twenties instead of trying to extract the most absurdly punitive compensation –'

'Compassion!' Simone burst out. 'Compassion! You say we should have treated them with compassion! Don't you know anything at all about the Boches, Leslie? Shall I tell you something? Those people – they're like animals – worse than animals.' She looked round at their surprised faces. 'It's no exaggeration, you know. None of you knows what it was like for us French when those Prussian beasts were raping girls and killing babies. I might allow a hyena into my house – yes, I might – if it was on a strong chain and had plenty of guards. But I wouldn't do the same for a Boche. They are . . . they are *merde*.'

There was a shocked silence.

'I never realized,' Celia said quietly, 'that people really do hate the Germans as much as that. I'd heard about it, but I had always thought it was exaggerated.'

'Quite frankly, I'm sorry for you, Mrs Wilmot,' Leslie said. 'I think it's awfully, awfully sad that you should feel the way you do.'

'It's the children *I'm* sorry for,' Christine said, trying to steer the conversation onto a safer course. 'All this business over evacuation. War breaks so many homes, doesn't it? And losing a parent – well, it's the most terrible thing.' She glanced up the table to her father. 'I was just thinking – Mummy was alive when Celia wrote that piece. I can remember the holiday quite clearly. Even hiding in the nettles when we were playing hide and seek.'

'Well, at least you knew your mother,' Simone said. 'And that is more than can be said for many thousands of war orphans.' She drained her glass and allowed Archie to refill it for her before passing the decanter on to the left. 'At least you knew her,' she said again, and looked round the table. 'I mean, to be orphaned in early childhood as so many were in fourteen–eighteen. To have to live in a home. Or be adopted. That must be much worse.'

She looked down the table at Griff, who was being very careful not to look in her direction.

'My mother was adopted,' Beeby said. 'She only told us when we were grown up. She hates to talk about it. I think it left a sort of emptiness in her life that she can never fill.'

'Yes, well –' Archie began awkwardly.

'With me it was the other way round,' Simone said.

Leslie frowned and glanced at Celia. Celia said: 'How do you mean?'

'Simone,' Griff said gently. 'This really isn't the sort of subject –'

'Isn't it? Why not? Who says so? Why is it that you men are allowed to talk about war and fortresses and – and who has the most bombers, but when it comes to what women care about – the fate of orphans and adopted children – then that's taboo?' She turned back to Celia. 'I had a baby when I was seventeen.'

'Right,' Griff said. 'Right, you've told us. So now can we please change the subject?'

But there was no stopping Simone now. She needed to tell them. She needed to ram their over-weening complacency back down their throats.

'Illegitimate, of course. Don't look so shocked, Christine! These things happen! The father was probably a hero of the republic, though a rather spotty-faced one because of a nervous rash – but I think that's excusable, don't you, Leslie? When one has a life expectancy of three weeks?'

She picked up her glass by the stem and twirled it nervously back and forth.

'Well anyway, in spite of what Griff may tell you to the contrary, I didn't discover I was expecting until after we had agreed to marry. So the baby had to be adopted first. Well . . . it didn't *have* to be adopted I suppose, but we didn't want a scandal in the regiment, did we, Griff? No, of course we didn't, of course we didn't. So you fixed it all up and – and –'

'It's in the past, Simone,' Griff said. 'It's all in the past.'

'It's in your past, yes. But it's my present and it's my future. It's the opposite of the void Beeby's mother has in her life. For me, it's a great – great lump inside me, a lump like a cancer that grows bigger and bigger every day.'

Christine folded her table napkin and looked at Nick. 'Er – if you'll excuse me I think I'll –'

Simone brought the palm of her hand down on the table so that the glasses jumped. 'No! Why should you leave just because it makes you uncomfortable? I want you to hear this, Christine – I want you all to hear this. Do you think I don't know that you talk about me behind my back? Do you think I haven't guessed at what you think of me? Am I not allowed to say one single word in my own defence?'

Archie was looking at his plate. The muscle in Griff's jaw was twitching. Christine was sitting bolt upright on the edge of her chair, as if ready at a moment's notice to get up and leave. Celia was blushing furiously. Nick was looking angry. Beeby was making a play of sipping her port.

Only Leslie – who had aspirations in the field of psychology – appeared to be at ease and genuinely interested. 'I think it might help you,' he said earnestly, 'now that you've told us what you have, to tell us the rest.'

'Thank you very much, I shall,' Simone said much more calmly. 'Where were we? Up in Yorkshire, I think, in the nursing home where my baby was born. Griff had made all the arrangements most efficiently. But the baby was early, so I – I had him for five weeks before he was adopted.' She gave a little laugh. 'It's just occurred to me. None of you has actually had a baby, have you? So you don't know, really, what it's like. You don't know that even in the first five weeks a baby has a character, a personality. And he was a fighter, my baby. He was big, and he was healthy and – and he knew who his mother was too. Every day for five weeks . . . he knew who his mother was –'

'Surely that's enough,' Archie whispered. 'Surely you've tortured yourself enough, Simone –'

'Griff made all the arrangements, and the adoptive parents came up north to collect the baby and sign the papers. They were nice, well-to-do people, too. I was very lucky there. Everyone at the nursing home told me how lucky I was to have found such nice parents for my baby. The husband was an up-and-coming young American and his wife – his wife –'

She broke off, and suddenly her mouth had gone out of shape and her hand was fluttering nervously on the table, as if searching of its own accord for the wine glass.

She swallowed, and in a very strained voice said, 'His wife was a Boche. I expect she was one of Leslie's very charming and civilized Boches, and I'm sure I should feel much more compassion for her. But she was still a Boche and she was taking away my baby, and – and I – I – I –'

They stared at her, horrified. She was screaming silently, her eyes red, her mouth wide open, her knuckles white where she gripped the wine glass. Then suddenly she gave a terrible indrawn sob, and the stem of the glass snapped in her hand.

She ran from the room. Griff folded up his table napkin, rolled it and put it into its silver ring. 'I do apologize to you all for this,' he said stiffly. 'Now if you will excuse me –'

When he was out of the room, Archie looked at his daughter. 'Well, Christine. So much for serious conversation.'

'What I don't understand,' Celia said quietly to Leslie, 'is why she suddenly needed to tell us about it. I mean, I would have thought –'

Archie had overheard. 'I think,' he said, 'that if no one objects we should now drop this subject once and for all.'

'Hear blooming hear!' said Beeby rather loudly.

But the sound of Simone weeping in the room above still continued, and soon afterwards all except Archie decided on an early night.

v

She wept, off and on, into the small hours. In the twin bed beside hers, Griff lay on his back and dozed fitfully, never quite dropping off to sleep, jerked awake each time a fresh tide of sobbing swept over her. There was nothing he could say or do now, he knew that.

He dozed, and awoke again to realize that she was getting out of bed. He saw her dark shape slip out of the room and heard a board creak as she went downstairs. The silence she left behind was a blessed release.

Sometime later, he awoke again with a powerful feeling that something was wrong. The house was unnaturally quiet. He lay listening, then reached out a hand to the other bed to find out if Simone had returned; but she had not.

Well, no matter, he told himself. Better to let her get over this upset in her own way, even if that did mean pacing the lawn in her nightdress. He listened again. It was indeed a very quiet night. He turned his pillow over and tried to get comfortable. He had a long drive in the morning, so he wanted a decent bit of sleep.

But now he was thoroughly awake, and unable to stop wondering what Simone was up to. It was no good. It was as difficult to sleep with her out of the room as it had been while she had been weeping in the other bed. What had he once said to her before they were married? 'I'd rather be miserable together than apart.' He smiled sadly in the darkness. They had been happy, and he still loved her, and always would.

He got out of bed. The same board creaked as he went downstairs, but otherwise he made no noise. He stood in the hallway, the flagstones cold under his bare feet. It was just beginning to get light. The face of the grandfather clock which had stopped, according to Archie's uncle, at eleven o'clock on November the eleventh 1918, looked down on him from the corner by the front door. He tiptoed into the dining room and looked at the uncleared table. He stood and held his breath, listening.

And then he heard the gentle sound of breathing, of someone asleep nearby. He went back into the hall, and through to the sitting room.

He stood in the doorway for no more than two seconds, but those two seconds were enough. For just visible on the sofa in the grey darkness was Simone, fast asleep, her hair loose, her breasts spilling out of her nightdress and her lovely body cradled in Archie's arms.

vi

Why was it that he took no action? Why did he back away so quickly, his heart thundering in his chest, his fists tightly clenched? Why did he tiptoe silently back up the stairs – even managing to avoid the creaking floorboard this time – to return to his bed?

He couldn't explain why, he didn't understand. It was as if he had been running over a heath and a chasm had opened up suddenly, right in front of him. The only possible course had been to back away from the edge. Archie was his closest friend, his oldest, his only friend, the friend he needed, the friend he had always depended on for advice and moral support. And Simone: she was his wife, the lovely, infuriating, fascinating, wayward girl who had always demanded so much of him but whose very dependence he needed for his own self-respect.

And was it so surprising, really, that Simone and Archie should share a like relationship, a similar need for support and dependence? Hadn't he virtually guessed it only the previous afternoon, watching them return together from their shopping? What if he had behaved in the old-fashioned way, woken them, demanded explanations? Everything – the lives of each one of them – would have been reduced to ruins. His friendship with Archie would be over. And his marriage. Even his career as a schoolmaster, for there would be no question of staying on at Prowse if this got out.

So he lay on his bed as the light came up and thought on these things, and when he heard Simone tiptoeing up the stairs he pretended – for all their sakes – to be asleep, so that the love and friendship between the three of them should be preserved intact.

THREE

The Wilmots drove back to Kent in silence. At breakfast everyone had been very subdued. When the time for farewells had come no one had been able to say with any certainty when or where they might meet again. Now, bowling along at fifty miles an hour, it seemed to Griff that if he so much as spoke to Simone she would immediately know of the suspicion and worry she had aroused in him.

From time to time, as he drove, he saw evidence of the mobilization: neat rows of army tents in the New Forest, a barrage balloon floating like an inflated elephant over Portsmouth, a long convoy of army trucks full of conscripts that held them up outside Chichester. But the face England presented on that last day of August, as the Wilmots motored back to the real world of news bulletins and headlines, was much more that of a nation on holiday. Bognor Regis, Hove, Worthing, Brighton – it was the same all along the coast. The beaches crowded with bucket-and-spade holiday-makers; the family groups, the sun-flushed grannies, the ice-cream vendors, Punch and Judy shows, beach huts, deck chairs; the herds of nearly naked humanity lolling like sea-cows on the shore.

Eastbourne, Bexhill, Hastings, Rye. New Romney, Dymchurch, Hythe, Sandgate.

Folkestone.

Dover.

They climbed the hill out of the town and took the Deal road, turning right at the crossroads into the village of St Margaret's-at-Cliffe and right again along Reach Road, past Reach Court before turning left between the laurel bushes and along the gravelled drive to Prowse School.

Griff switched off the ignition and remained seated behind the wheel.

'Well. Home again.'

'Yes.'

'Not a bad holiday, was it?'

'No, not bad,' she said faintly. Then he turned to her and their eyes met for the first time that day, and he nearly said something, nearly told her what he knew; and at the same time he sensed that she was as close to some other brink herself and wondered if she was going to apologize for her outburst or confess to whatever it was she had done with Archie. But the moment passed. He got out of the car and took the luggage from the boot while Simone went ahead of him into the house.

He paused to examine the tea roses before going inside. They were looking exceptionally promising that year.

They had deliberately not cancelled the newspapers, and Peggy had stacked them on the hall stand, along with the mail. He put the suitcases down and began looking at the photographs and headlines, feeling suddenly hungry for news of the crisis.

EMERGENCY POWERS PASSED
STILL HOPE OF REASON AND SANITY
MOMENTOUS DAY IN LONDON:
PARLIAMENT REASSEMBLES

He scanned the columns, and his eye fell on a report of Dr Goebbels's latest speech, which referred to the British Prime Minister as 'a blind old idiot bound to an impossible policy and led by the nose by Jewish financiers'.

He felt a sudden hot fury of indignation. For Griff, that remark alone would have been sufficient excuse to go to war.

While he stood there, Simone came downstairs and collected her case. 'Let me carry that for you –' he offered instinctively, but she ignored him and lugged it upstairs herself.

He stood in the hall and scanned another newspaper, the

latest. There was a picture of an anti-aircraft unit setting up somewhere in Kent, with half a dozen Tommies in shirtsleeve order lining up to collect beef, boiled potatoes and butter beans at a field kitchen. The headlines seemed to have a strangely familiar quality, as if he had read them before in a previous existence:

CABINET REPLY TO LAST GERMAN NOTE
BRITISH GUARANTEE STANDS
FRANCE AND POLAND IN CONSTANT TOUCH
WARSAW CALLS UP MORE MEN AS
PRECAUTION

All the way back, during their silent drive from Dorset, he had been thinking about Simone and Archie and himself. Now these headlines suddenly put his personal problems into a new perspective. There was going to be a war, and war would change everything.

He threw the newspapers down and went to the foot of the stairs. 'I'm going out, Simone,' he called. 'For a walk.'

ii

He took the path that ran between the school grounds and Reach Court, descending into a narrow valley of scrubland before climbing a steep path to the cliff edge. There, he paused to gaze over the shimmering Channel to the low, blue coastline that was France.

Was there any smallest doubt now that Britain would be at war within the week? Not as far as he was concerned. He tried to imagine the nature of this coming war. Everyone had made much of the new threat from bombers, but bombers could not occupy and hold a position any more than could a submarine or a destroyer. There would have to be a major land battle, of that he was sure. And this time the allies were far better prepared. Hitler was a madman, there was no doubt of that. Nor were the Germans so convinced of the rightness of their cause as they had been twenty-five years before. So if (or when) conflict came, the allies wouldn't be fighting a united and determined nation so much as a mass of people stirred up into hysteria by a flawed ideology.

Also, given the sheer strength of numbers of the French army (how many men did they have under arms now? Was it really three *million*?) not to mention their air defences and Maginot Line, the Nazis would have little hope of success if they tried an attack through Belgium into Flanders and Picardy, on the lines of the old Schlieffen Plan.

But what if they did try? He cast his mind back to the old techniques of war, to digging in, putting up wire, running telephone lines, establishing artillery positions in the rear. Then the barrage, the attack at dawn, the confusion, the valiant rearguard action, the gaining – or losing – of a few more yards of blood-soaked mud and mire . . .

All that again.

Really the war had never finished, that was the truth of it. The German army had been able to blame defeat on their politicians, and to go home and tell their sons and nephews that they were unbeaten in the field. And France, poor France, had insisted on reparations so stringent and strangling that a generation of Germans had been brought up to hate the French every bit as intensely as the French hated them, and to be grimly determined to rub France's nose in the armistice of Compiègne.

He walked on, the white cliffs dropping sheer away beside him. What part had he to play in all this? His marriage was at breaking point, his teaching career was in a backwater and his oldest and most trusted friend was no longer able to look him in the eye. And now Britain was going to war and he would be out of that, too.

Or would he? He remembered what Archie had said on Eggardon Hill. He wasn't forty-three yet, and he had plenty of energy. He also spoke fluent French, and they'd be needing French speakers in the army again.

He stopped and watched as a formation of fighters – Hurricanes or Spitfires, he didn't know which – flew low over the sea beneath him. Would they take him if he volunteered? He was still on the reserve list, after all. And they'd be shouting out for experienced men soon.

He'd be in uniform again. The very thought of it cheered him. Discipline. Orders. Camaraderie. Hadn't he always been cut out to be a career officer? Hadn't leaving the army in '22 been the biggest mistake of his life?

He turned and began walking back. Rejoin the army! Archie was right, of course he was right! It would solve so many things. He would be an embarrassment at Prowse now that Reffel was taking over as headmaster, and the thought of presenting the school governors with a *fait accompli* and informing them that he had elected to serve his country and set an example to the boys was irresistibly attractive. A history master who did his bit in the making of history! Wouldn't that put meaning and purpose back into his life? Of course it would. He would be able to throw all his weight and enthusiasm into the task. There would be nothing at all to hold him back, not even Simone, for Griff was beginning to take the view that the only sure way to capture Simone's heart was to put on a uniform with brass buttons.

Going back into uniform might give him a second chance – a chance to recapture his self-respect. It was even possible, if the war lasted more than a few months, that he might climb back onto the promotion ladder and achieve a respectable rank. One of the things that had hurt most about leaving the army in '22 had been that he had never attained field rank, had never been able to style himself as 'The Major'.

'And if it comes to a real fight, I'll volunteer for the front, dammit,' he muttered to himself. 'And I won't go back into the cavalry, either.' He cast his mind back to 1918. Which regiment had he always admired? Which, out of them all, had he been happiest to fight alongside? Which had the reputation for brains and resourcefulness, for being the first into battle and the last out? The Royal Engineers, there was no question about it. So . . . he'd ask to be a sapper. Follow in the tradition of the greatest sapper of them all – Gordon of Khartoum, whose courage he had extolled so often in the classroom.

What was their motto? *Ubique*. Everywhere. 'The sappers,' he said softly, and punched the palm of his hand with a clenched fist. 'Yes, by George, the sappers . . .'

He actually ran some of the way back, still churning the idea furiously in his mind, already beginning to worry that war might not be declared and that his services might not be required. But all that was nonsense. Of course there was going to be a war. Everybody knew it.

iii

When he arrived back Simone was having a bath, an operation that usually took a long time. He hesitated on the landing, unwilling to have a conversation with her through the locked door, but at the same time impatient to tell her about his decision. There was so much to be done – so many letters to write and telephone calls to make. He must tender his resignation to the governors right away, that was the first thing. Or perhaps better not do that until he had contacted the War Office.

And what about uniform? He went up to the boxroom and lugged out his old army trunk. It still bore his rank, name and number in white paint on the lid: Captain G. Wilmot, P/3172. He summoned the housemaid and together they carried it down to the landing and into the spare room, Griff barking his knuckles on the door post in the process.

'You joinin' up are you, Mr Wilmot sir?' Peggy asked.

'Well, I think we ought to be ready, don't you, Peggy?'

'I don't know, I'm sure, sir. Whole world's gorn off it's blinking rocker, if you ask me.'

He chuckled. He was already certain in his mind that he was doing the right thing. 'Just put it down here, good girl. I'll manage the rest.'

He lifted the lid and looked down at the neatly folded uniforms, which gave off a strong smell of mothballs. He held up the tunic of his best service dress. The buttons needed a good polish, but there was nothing else wrong with it that a good batman couldn't put right in an hour or so. He took out his Sam Browne, his holster, his mess kit and his campaign medals. It was amazing: he felt as if he had put them all away only a few weeks before.

His cap was a bit squashed. He put it on and went to the mirror. 'I'll have to get a new one,' he told his reflection, and at the same moment he caught sight of Simone in her bathrobe at the door behind him.

He spun round to face her. 'Ah,' he said, feeling a little foolish. 'You're out.' He took off his cap and threw it carelessly on the bed. 'I've – been doing some thinking, Simone. I've decided to join up again.'

She made a little snorting noise and shook her head.

'Well, it isn't as ridiculous as all that, my dear. You do realize that we're virtually at war?'

'Yes, I know that, Griff.'

How wonderful she looked when she was fresh from her bath! Seeing her like this always reminded him of the days when she was his teenage bride. He felt younger already.

He appealed to her: 'Simone . . . let's try to put the past behind us, shall we?'

He had often said that she would make an excellent secret agent, and she had always been able to beat him at poker. When she looked at him now, there was not the smallest hint of guilt or deceit in her expression.

'Well?' he said. 'What do you think?'

The precipice was not far away now. Her boat was accelerating and there were little whirlpools all around in the otherwise smooth water.

'What do I think?' she said, and sighed deeply. 'I think – if you want to go off and join the army again, then – yes, I think it's a good idea.'

He thought about that for a second or two.

'You . . . wouldn't rather I stayed at home?'

She turned away. Archie was going to be in a shore job, only an hour away in Chatham. With Griff back in the army, everything would be easier.

'Does it matter what I want, Griff? I think you must do what you believe is your duty. I – I would hate to feel I was keeping you here against your will.'

He braced his shoulders back. 'Very well. That's settled then. I'll contact the War Office tomorrow.'

Simone went on along the passage to the bedroom. She was still quite flushed from her bath.

FOUR

Half an hour after the Wilmots left, Nick and Christine drove off with Leslie and Celia jammed together in the back of Nick's MG. After that, only Archie's Lagonda remained on the grass by the woodstore.

Beeby said she wanted to have a clear-up before they left. She said it was only fair to leave the place tidy, even though Mrs Peabody, the char from the village, was coming in that afternoon. Archie wasn't much of a hand at domestic duties, so he mooched about in the sitting room while she swept out the hall. He stared out of the window and reflected upon the events of the morning.

He tried to remember exactly how dark it had been, how much Griff might have been able to see, and whether he would have been able to make out that Simone was asleep in his arms on the sofa. Surely he must have seen! But why had he said nothing? Why had he slipped so quickly away, almost apologetically, as if he had intruded upon their privacy?

Why? because Griff was Griff, that was why. Most men would have stormed in, seized Simone by the arm and dragged her off. There would have been an unholy row. There would have been acrimony, hatred, an end to their friendship and probably a divorce. But Griff was too circumspect to precipitate such uncivilized behaviour. He would have either presumed that they were asleep or deliberately given them the chance of pretending to be; he might even have given them the benefit of the doubt and presumed that all that had happened was that Simone had sought a little comfort, that there had been no prearranged assignation, no 'conduct unbecoming' of any sort.

Poor old Griff! What a loser he was, but what a likeable loser and what a good friend and staunch ally for all that!

They had shaken hands only twenty minutes before. Archie had had to force himself to look Griff in the eye, and had been met with a gaze so steady that it seemed to penetrate his mind and see all that lay hidden there.

'Now you've been posted to Chatham, let's hope we'll see a lot more of you,' Griff had said, and Simone had added: 'You must come over for Sunday lunch whenever you're free, Archie.'

Archie had bowed, mock formal. 'Thankee kindly, sir, ma'am!' he had said in his Wessex accent. 'Always assuming,' he had added in his normal voice, 'that we don't have this blessed war, old boy.'

Then with a toot on the horn Captain Griff, with his gorgeous wife at his side, had driven the Standard 8 out through the gate and up the cart track, and when Archie and his guests had stopped waving goodbye it was as if there were only one thought in anyone's mind: When shall we ever be able to meet like this again?

'Penny for them?' said Beeby behind him, and he turned quickly. She had finished her sweeping and was standing in the doorway leaning on the broom. 'You look as if you're in a trance, Arch.'

He smiled. Beeby was trying very hard with him, and before this holiday he had even begun to think that she might make him a good wife. But Simone had changed all that. The trouble with Beeby was that she was too much of a good companion. She was too much of a *nice chap*, that was her drawback. Too big, too jolly, altogether too damned English. While on the other hand Simone . . .

But he really must try to stop thinking about Simone. What had happened must not on any account happen again. He owed it to Griff; he owed it to Simone; he owed it to himself.

'End of holiday blues,' he said aloud. 'Come on. Let's make a move.'

Things fell quickly apart. When Archie arrived at Chatham barracks, he found the whole place seething like a beehive before a thunderstorm. Lorries with emergency stores were being unloaded on the parade ground. Blackout materials and instructions were being issued to all accommodation blocks. Anti-aircraft gun and searchlight positions were being built out of sandbags and that evening in the wardroom, the anteroom was packed out with officers who had gathered for the nine o'clock news.

The news was bad: the invasion of Poland and the Anglo-French denunciation of it; the evacuation of children from London and other major cities; the passing of emergency measures and the futile newspaper headlines that shouted what everyone knew was at best a piece of wishful thinking and at worst a barefaced lie: BRITAIN STANDS READY.

Britain was not ready. Though the Royal Navy had been put on a war footing, its ships were too few and too lightly armed; though the air force had been considerably enlarged, it was barely a match for Hitler's new Luftwaffe; and though the army had the makings of a well-trained and professional fighting force, its mechanized equipment, its tanks, its artillery and its munitions were sadly – some said criminally – inadequate and out of date.

In Chatham itself there were queues at the recruiting offices and boy scouts had been put to work filling sandbags. In the dockyard, refits were being accelerated, pneumatic hammers were banging endlessly and the sheds were alight with the blue sparkle of oxyacetylene welders.

The last few days of peace passed so rapidly that it was difficult to remember, later, exactly what happened on which day, but one day and one moment stuck in everyone's memory that weekend at the beginning of September, for although everyone had known very well that the coming conflict was unavoidable, when the people heard Neville Chamberlain's solemn voice announcing 'this country is at war with Germany', his words caused a bleak sense of loss and failure, for there was hardly a family in the land that had not lost a father, an uncle, a cousin or a son in the great war to end wars, and their sacrifice now seemed to have been for nothing.

Half an hour after the announcement, the air raid sirens, recently purchased and tested by town councils up and down the land, wailed out their first devilish diapason.

iv

Archie received a letter from Griff a few weeks later, in which he told him that he had taken his advice and had got himself a job as a retired officer in the Military Secretary's branch at the War Office.

Griff was obviously in his element: although he was only 'pushing bumph' as he put it, he was involved with the order of battle and appointment of officers for the expeditionary force being sent to France, and had hopes of getting himself back into uniform before long. Archie read between the lines and saw that he was also pleased to be having a break from his wife.

Really it was a very curious letter: it was almost as if Griff were deliberately leaving the door open for him to have an affair with Simone.

Had that affair already begun? Archie was not sure: although he had gained something of a reputation as a ladies' man since the death of his wife, his experience in such matters did not match his reputation, and he now had difficulty in regarding the heart-tugging effect Simone had on him as an affair. He mentally listed the few snatched moments they had enjoyed together: the stolen kiss behind the bridge on board HMS *Calcutta*; a few minutes in the car on the way back from shopping in Bridport, and that last magical hour or so they had spent in each other's arms on the sofa at

Eggardon. Was that an affair? Hardly. Far worse things (or were they better things?) went on at other people's house parties.

Meanwhile, Christine had joined the Wrens, and after a month's training at a headquarters near Reading had emerged at the end of October in a navy-black suit, brass buttons and a tight, white shirt. Nick had by this time been given his own flight of Hurricanes and had been posted to Manston, so Archie pulled a few strings and organized matters so that his daughter should not be stationed too far away, with the result that she was appointed to the staff of the Vice Admiral, Dover.

There was little time to spare in those first weeks of war, and although Archie thought a lot about Simone, he saw nothing of her. As one of the governors of Prowse, he knew that the school had been moved to Somerset and that the army intended to take over the premises for the duration, and Griff had said in his letter that Simone was hoping to stay on at the Lodge. He wondered whether he might ring her, but something always held him back and he began to see that what had happened between them had not been the beginning of anything at all, but simply a little island of tenderness in the harsh discipline of his naval existence.

Then one November morning when he was preparing a briefing for the First Sea Lord who was to visit Chatham the next day, Archie's office telephone rang, and the unmistakable voice of Simone came over the line.

'Archie? Is that you? I say – did you know Griff's gone to France?'

'No –'

She sounded distraught. 'Well, he got his rank back and joined a battalion two weeks ago. They only gave him forty-eight hours' leave before they pushed him off.'

'But wasn't that what he wanted, Simone?'

'Yes of course it was, but –' She broke off and started again. 'Look, you know the army's taken over Prowse, don't you?'

66

'I had heard that, yes.'

'Well they have. And just ten minutes ago a snooty major knocked on my door and said that if I want to go on staying here I must have four officers billeted on me. Four officers! And on top of that my housemaid is going off to work in an aircraft factory. I'll be a landlady, Archie! I'm going to have to clean and cook and wash for them. It really is too much.'

He couldn't help smiling. He had been working long hours for two months since the outbreak of war, and this little inconvenience of Simone's seemed footling by comparison with the problems of anti-submarine warfare in the eastern approaches or minesweeping operations off the Nore.

But the very sound of her voice was having its effect on him, and with Griff out of reach, he felt it his duty to come to her rescue.

'Is there anything I can do?'

'Well, can't you pull strings or something? Apart from anything else, what's Griff going to think when he hears that I've got four men living with me?'

He laughed. 'Oh, I don't expect he'd object too much, in the circumstances.'

'I'm not so sure, Archie. You don't know Griff the way I know him.'

'Would it be more acceptable if your lodgers were women?'

'Well, I suppose it might be better than nothing. At least women can make their own beds. But with four army officers all demanding their – their bloody bacon and eggs in the morning and having to be fed and cleared up after and – and – you know what I mean, piddling on the lavatory seat, that sort of thing. Why are you laughing, for heaven's sake? It's no laughing matter, Archie, I can assure you.'

Leading Wren Carstairs had entered the office and stood waiting by his desk with an armful of classified charts. He pressed the telephone receiver tight against his ear so that she should not overhear the other half of his conversation.

'I'll see what I can do for you,' he said.

'Will you, Archie? I'd be so grateful. When am I going to see you?'

'It's a bit difficult –'

'Is there someone in the office with you?'

'Yes, there is.'

'Well, see what you can do, will you? I know you can fix something if you try. And Archie –'

'Yes?'

There was a pause, and her voice changed. 'I miss you. If you miss me, just cough or something, will you?'

He coughed. 'Yes,' he said. 'Yes, very well. I – I'll see what can be done.'

As soon as he had the office to himself again, he rang Christine, who was billeted at Dover in the Lord Warden Hotel. She confirmed that there was an acute accommodation problem in the town, and when he suggested that she and three other Wren officers might care to move out and stay with Simone at St Margaret's-at-Cliffe, she jumped at the idea. A telephone call to the first officer at the Vice Admiral, Dover's headquarters finalized the arrangement.

Three days later he found a picture postcard in his letter rack outside the anteroom bar:

> A: This is just to say a big thank you. Now that C.
> is staying here, you have no excuse for not visiting.
> So please come for lunch this and every Sunday
> you are free. That is an order.
> S.

While other members of the officers' mess went into the wardroom for breakfast, he stood in the corridor by the portraits of past commodores and re-read those few lines, aware that Simone was offering far more than just an invitation for lunch and that his loyalties were being cruelly divided. He owed it to Griff to give Simone a bit of support, but at the same time shrank from allowing an affair to develop behind his back. And it would be more than just an affair, too: Archie knew that he needed Simone's love just as much as she needed his. His career had gone wrong, his wife was dead and his daughter was grown up and no longer dependent on him. If he started seeing Simone now, he knew that he would be starting something which would be unstoppable, something which might destroy his friendship with Griff, break the bond of friendship between the three of them and leave none of them happier.

In the end he took the decision as if unconsciously. When Sunday came round he attended Divisions and went to church as usual. And then, almost watching himself to see what he would do next, he changed into a Gieves tweed suit and spotted silk tie, put a brown trilby on his head, got into the Lagonda and drove out of the barracks main gate with a roar.

v

When she saw the car draw up and he stepped out looking up at the house, she wanted to run out to him and wrap herself round him, hug him, tell him how much she had missed him, how she had been thinking of him constantly, longing for him, planning ways of meeting him, daydreaming about unrepeatable intimacies with him. She wanted to be completely alone with him just as they had been alone that last morning at Eggardon. She wanted his kisses and his caresses, the whole of him; she wanted to hear him say that he had thought only of her, and that she was all and everything to him, just as he was to her.

But Christine was there, and Christine was his daughter. Christine had to be allowed to go out to the car first, smart in her third officer's uniform and her newly permed hair, to give him a daughterly cheek-to-cheek kiss and to take his arm and come with him into the house.

And here he was, and her insides were turning over for him: she wanted to kiss him but with Christine present they had to content themselves with a handshake. 'Simone, my dear,' he said. 'You're looking splendid!' And the slightly shy way he said it, his look, his whole manner told her that although this war might have changed everything and everybody else, at least Archie was the same.

'I expect you'd like a drink,' she said, aware that Christine was watching her every move. 'Let me take your hat and coat. Christine – look after your father, won't you? I must see to the gravy. Oh – and this is Third Officer Marjory Lane. The other two are on watch. I've lit the fire in the sitting room, and there's some gin in the cabinet – do help yourself, Archie, won't you?'

She was in such a state she put the last of the icing sugar in the gravy to thicken it instead of cornflour, and had to scoop what she could of it out with a spoon, which made the gravy taste revolting, but Archie said it was delicious and managed to make the meagre little joint of roast pork seem like a side of prime beef because he had brought a bottle of wine from his private store in the wardroom cellars.

After lunch, they sat by the fire in the sitting room and talked about the war and what everyone was doing. Christine and Marjory were due on watch at four o'clock, and the other two, Betty and Elspeth, wouldn't arrive back until half-past, so she would have Archie to herself for about an hour. But then Archie offered to run the two girls down to the castle in his car, and her heart plummeted. 'Wait a minute,' she said, 'won't your bicycles be in the wrong place if you do that?' And Marjory came to her rescue and said yes, perhaps it was better if they went down by bike as usual, so a little after three they left, and as soon as they had disappeared round the laurel bushes at the end of the drive Archie turned back from the porch and she practically fell into his arms.

vi

They stood in the hall by the umbrella stand, the barometer and the little board upon which Griff used to keep his school

70

keys. They kissed, and in between kisses, they talked. She said: 'It's no use pretending that I don't want you, because I do.'

'I feel so guilty,' he said. 'I can't bear to think that I might come between you and Griff.'

She held his face in her hands and gazed into his eyes. 'I don't want to break with Griff, Archie. But there's no need for it to happen, don't you see? He doesn't suspect anything, and so long as he doesn't find out, so long as we're careful –'

He stared at her, wondering if he should tell her about Griff's silent appearance at Eggardon.

Then he was kissing her neck.

'Undo me,' she whispered. 'Explore me.'

'If we're going to meet, we shouldn't meet here,' he said.

'No, we shouldn't. I agree about that.'

'Where, then?'

'Down the coast somewhere? Deal?'

'Whereabouts in Deal?'

'I don't mind. Anywhere. The pier if you like.'

He thought: *I'm old enough to know better*. Aloud, he said: 'I may be able to get away on Tuesday afternoons.'

She looked at his tie. 'I'll say I've joined the WVS.' She giggled. 'Oh Archie, can't you just see me in one of those awful green hats?'

'You're very naughty, darling.'

'I know I am. But I *need* to be naughty. Archie – I want you so much! I want you *now*.' She pressed herself against him. 'We've got time, you know. We could.'

He felt himself shaking. He was astonished at his own weakness. 'What about . . . babies?' he asked huskily.

She looked straight up at him. 'Don't you understand, darling? I *want* to have a baby. It's what I've been wanting for the past twenty years.'

vii

It was like an attack of insanity. He knew what he was doing, knew the risks, knew the probable consequences – even feared, at times, the retribution of almighty God – but could not help himself. They met in Deal, in Ramsgate, in Maidstone and in Broadstairs. They were like secret agents, arranging times and places to meet and contingency plans if one or the other should be unable to make the rendezvous. They made love in her bed, in his car, in hotel bedrooms, and once in a very chilly haybarn. They lunched together at corner tables, shared an adulterous teapot in a tearoom. Once they went out shopping together in Maidstone and he bought her, under the counter, a black leather handbag and a pair of sheer nylon stockings.

Their love blossomed and flourished. Driving together along the coast roads of east Kent, he sang the latest songs to her; walking along the wintry foreshore behind the rolls of barbed wire, they played like children, throwing seaweed, running races, playing ducks and drakes – and kissing until they were breathless.

It lasted through November and on into December, and then one grey afternoon a week before Christmas when they were driving into Ramsgate they passed a dark green MG sports car coming the other way. It was Nick Massingbohm, and Christine was at his side, both in uniform.

'Damn!' said Archie softly.

'Are you sure they recognized us?' Simone said.

'Quite sure. And anyway, they could hardly fail to recognize this car.'

They arrived in Ramsgate and parked above the harbour, where small craft were aground on the mud berths.

'Well – who cares?' Simone said suddenly. 'What does it matter if Christine does know about us? She'd old enough to understand, isn't she? It's this silly bloody war that's to blame. Nobody knows who they are or where they're going any more. Besides – everyone's doing it, aren't they? Including them, I expect.' She turned to him quickly, her eyes filling with tears. 'Oh darling, I'm sorry I said that! I don't expect they are doing it at all. God! Why am I such a hateful person? And how am I going to face Christine?'

Archie was thinking of Olivia. After she died, he had told Christine that they must always remember her and be true to her memory. And now Christine had seen him with Simone, and would know that her father was a hypocrite, the sort of man who made free with his best friend's wife.

They sat side by side in the car and looked out at the drizzle. Simone said: 'It's over, isn't it?'

Yes, of course it would have to be over. It should never have started in the first place.

He turned to her. 'It doesn't make any difference to the way I feel about you, Simone.'

'I know that,' she said. 'But it's still over.'

He took her hands in his own and stared down at them. 'What are we going to do?' she asked. 'What on earth am I going to say to Christine?'

'Probably better to say nothing.'

'But if she asks, Archie? Do you want me to lie to her?'

'I just took you out for the afternoon.'

'Chrissy's not a fool, darling. She'll see through that one straight away. In fact I think she suspects something already.'

He nodded. 'Yes, I had that impression too.'

'So . . . I suppose we'll just have to stop seeing each other.' She took out a handkerchief and dabbed her eyes. 'I don't know if I can do that.'

'I don't know if I can, either,' he muttered.

He was silent for a long time. There was only one thing to do now, he knew that. He must do it for all their sakes, Griff's above all. 'I'll ask them to send me back to sea,' he said. 'They were going to anyway, sooner or later.'

viii

Nick had parked the MG outside the naval headquarters at Dover Castle. With the drizzle pattering on the canvas hood, Christine sat beside him and asked a question that was very similar to the one Simone had asked Archie.

'Do you think I should say anything?'

Nick sat with both hands on the steering wheel. 'No, I don't. Won't do any good, will it?'

'I suppose not. It makes me feel sort of . . . dirty.'

He glanced at her. 'Well it shouldn't, Chrissy.'

'It's quite irrational of me, I know that. But somehow it rubs off. And there's something –' She stopped.

'What?'

'Something awful that's only just occurred to me. About my mother. Something I've – I've sort of known about all along but have never fully admitted to myself.' She looked out at the drizzle-laden sky and the low clouds skudding over the Channel. 'Can I tell you, Nick?'

He blinked in the way he had when he was a little embarrassed. 'Yes – yes you can tell me anything, you know that.'

'Just before she died, something happened between her and Pater. Something went wrong. I think I was aware of it subconsciously even then, you know. I was twelve. We'd all spent a weekend at the Wilmots'. And I think – I don't know, but I think – that Mummy found something out. About Pater and Simone. I think she knew that there was something between them. And I can't help thinking now that – that it killed her. I know it was an accident, but somehow I know that the accident wouldn't have happened if there hadn't been something on her mind. And seeing them just now – it brought it all back, and it makes me feel all wretched inside. I suppose what really frightens me is that I'm – I'm terrified that you might think – oh, that I might be the same in some way.'

'Well I don't,' Nick said gruffly. He wasn't much of a hand at these soul-baring exercises.

'Sorry.' Christine smiled quickly. 'I'm being rather boring, aren't I? 'Nough said.' She looked at the clock on the dashboard. 'I'm on watch in twenty minutes. Must go. See you some time?'

'I'll give you a ring.'

She nearly said, 'Soon?' but managed not to. If there was

one thing Nick disliked it was women who clung to him.

She forced herself to be cheerful. 'Right-o, then. Take care. No more prangs, please.'

He shook his head and grinned. Two days before he had made an emergency wheels-up landing when the undercarriage of his Hurricane had failed to lower. 'Can't promise anything,' he said and, when she had put her hat on and collected her shoulder bag, kissed her on the cheek and watched her go up the stone steps and into the headquarters before driving off with a throaty growl from the exhaust.

ix

Two days before Christmas – which was a sombre occasion for most people that year – Archie contacted his appointing officer to arrange an interview, and the following week he put on a dark suit and a bowler hat and went up to the Admiralty to call on the Director of Naval Appointments. As soon as the interview with his appointing officer was over, he telephoned Simone and asked if he could come down to see her on New Year's Eve, as that was the only time he was free.

It was late morning when the Lagonda drew up outside the front door. Archie was in uniform and his black labrador was sitting up on the back seat looking out of the window. Christine was still on watch but due back within an hour or so.

Archie and Simone needed some time alone together to talk, so they took Blashford for a walk. They went down the narrow path between the school grounds and Reach Court, and came out in that area of scrubland just behind the cliffs.

He stopped and turned to her, taking her hands in his.

'Go on then,' she said. 'Tell me the worst.'

'They're giving me a ship,' he said.

Simone was wearing a silk scarf on her head. Only that morning, she had discovered that she was not pregnant after all.

'She's a very elderly destroyer,' Archie was saying. 'She should have been put out to grass long ago, like yours truly.'

'When do you take over?'

'Monday.'

'You mean –'

'The day after tomorrow, yes. It's what they call a pier-head jump.'

'What will you be doing?'

He shook his head. 'We don't talk about that sort of thing.'

'Can I write to you?'

'I can't stop you, Simone, but I think it would be better if you wrote to Griff.'

'So is this goodbye?'

He nodded.

'How long can you stay?'

'Not much more than an hour. You're sure it's all right about the dog? I've got a home for him with the master-at-arms at the barracks if necessary –'

'No. No, I want to have him.'

She undid his greatcoat and his reefer jacket and put her arms round him, inside. She let the tears come, and they stood like that for several minutes.

'Cheer up, old girl,' he said eventually, and it might have been Griff speaking. 'It's not the end of the world, you know. Come on, let's walk up to the cliff. That'll blow the old tears away.'

FIVE

Gwynneth Evans came from a Welsh mining village called Ystradgynlais. She was small, rosy-cheeked, black-haired, warm-hearted and sang like an angel in heaven. She was the youngest of six, three boys and three girls, the apple of her Dad's eye and the focus of attention for the lads who came to the chapel in the valley every Sunday in their best grey suits and their tight collars and their wet-brushed hair. She had attended the village school until she was sixteen and had then amazed everyone by passing the entry examination for a college of higher education. So off she went to Cardiff to study French and German (German, I ask you!), and when she stepped off the bus to spend her first vacation at home, she was a little bit more of a woman and a little bit less of a girl.

Then the war came and Gwynneth was talent-spotted by the army. When she announced that she was going to join up and do her bit, her mother was horrified, but her father, who had served four years in the Royal Welch Fusiliers, was enormously proud. They saw her off on the bus on a Saturday morning in October, and a few weeks later received a letter from her with a snap of herself in her new ATS uniform. She seemed happy enough, but she didn't say much about what she was doing, and Mr Evans remarked on the fact that she was billeted in Hampstead.

'Funny kind of a place to be, that,' he said, sitting by a lamp-blacked grate in his braces and shirtsleeves. 'Bit odd, if you ask me.'

It *was* a bit odd: Gwynneth had been recruited into the Intelligence Corps and was training at a unit in north London where she spent hours in a cubicle with headphones clamped over her ears. In addition to an intensive course in German dialects, she was also being taught how to tune radio receivers, send and read morse by WT and write shorthand; and in her spare time she shared a dormitory, personal secrets and hot cocoa with five other girls of her own age, and looked forward to the day when she would start work as a professional intelligence gatherer.

But now it was Christmas Eve, and for once Gwynneth was letting her hair down. All her friends had found themselves boyfriends since coming to London and she had decided it was time she did the same. So when a tall, dark and not entirely unhandsome young man came up to her in the public bar of Jack Straw's Castle and asked if she would care to take a drink, she said thank you very much, I'll have half a pint of stout.

'Are you Canadian?' she asked when he had struggled back through the crush of people to where she was sitting.

'American.'

She sized him up. 'You don't look like an American.'

He grinned. 'You mean I don't wear sneakers or a fancy tie? Not all Americans do, you know.'

She undid her overcoat and took her first ever sip of stout, which she thought quite revolting, and at the same time took a closer look at him. She had a feeling that he had not been out with girls much before, which was reassuring, because she had never had a proper boyfriend herself. He had a big, wide face, a snub nose, large ears and a short haircut. He was wearing a sheepskin coat over a tweed jacket, and a very long college scarf.

He said: 'Something wrong?'

She put the glass down. 'I never had this stuff before.'

'Don't you like it?'

'Not much.'

He sprang to his feet. 'I'll get you something else.'

'No – no, don't do that. It'd be such a waste!'

But he insisted, and she settled for a gin and orange. The bar filled up and someone began playing the piano. He asked how long she'd been in the army and what she was doing, but she couldn't tell him much because she wasn't allowed to.

'What is it, hush-hush?' he asked.

'Well you could say that, I suppose. Most things are these days, aren't they?'

'I guess they are.'

They almost had to shout over the noise of singing and laughter. 'So what do you do?'

'I'm a reporter.'

'A newspaper reporter?'

He laughed. '"Newspaper reporter"? Yes, I guess that's right.'

'Which newspaper?'

'None in particular. I'm freelance.'

'Are you famous? Would I recognize your name?'

He shook his head and grinned again, showing very even, white teeth. 'They haven't printed much of my stuff yet.'

'Oh but I'm sure they will,' she said.

'Well, that certainly is very kind of you to say so.'

She giggled.

'What's funny?'

'Your accent. You sound like that film star.'

'Which one?'

'I don't know his name. But he's always sleuthing and wearing his coat collar turned up and his hat over his eyes.'

'Do I look like him too?'

'Oh, no! Not at all! You're quite different to look at. You're not offended, are you? I mean because I said you had a funny accent?'

'You got a pretty funny accent yourself.'

'Ah, well I'm Welsh, see. My accent's not funny where I come from.'

'Nor's mine.'

She blushed a little. He had laughing eyes that every now and then made a little survey of her.

'So where do you come from? In America, I mean.'

'New York.'

'Oh, that's nice. I mean – I've never been there, but I expect it's nice, isn't it?'

'It's okay.' He gestured towards her glass. 'Like another one?'

'I don't know if I should really.'

'Come on! It's Christmas Eve!'

'All right then. Just one.'

She watched him elbow his way through the crush to the bar. He wasn't all that good looking, what with that scrubbing brush haircut that made his ears look so big, but she liked him all the same. He had a sort of shy way of smiling sometimes, and he looked nice and clean, too. She had always thought Americans were show-offs, but this one wasn't at all like that.

'You haven't told me your name,' she said when he arrived back with the drinks.

'You haven't told me yours.'

'Gwynneth.'

'Excuse me?'

'Gwynneth.'

'I never heard that one before.'

'There are lots of Gwynneths in Wales.'

'Perhaps I ought to go to Wales then. Are all Gwynneths like you?'

'I don't know. I don't think so. What do you think I'm like?'

He smiled whimsically. 'That'd be telling, wouldn't it?'

'So what's your name?'

'David.'

'Oh – well, that's a good Welsh name too!'

He put out his hand. 'Shake on it.'

She took his hand and didn't mind at all that he didn't let it go. She felt as if she had known him for ages.

'So. All alone for Christmas, is it?'

'I guess so.'

'That makes two of us.'

He said nothing, but she felt his hand tighten a little on hers. The evening grew noisier. People were singing round the honky-tonk piano. She asked him what it was like to be a journalist and he tried to tell her about the difficulties of writing about a war that hadn't started. He was a bit intense about it, but that was all right. They had another drink and she said, 'Come on, let's join in,' so they stood with the crowd, he with his arm round her waist, and they swayed in time to the songs and she let him kiss her on the mouth.

'You don't mind?' he shouted over the din.

She giggled. She had had three gins and she was feeling lovely. 'Not a bit. Fact, I quite liked it!'

They sang 'Roll Out the Barrel' and 'Tipperary' and the latest one, 'Wish me luck as you wave me goodbye'.

'Bit hot in here, isn't it?' she shouted in his ear.

'You want to go someplace else?'

She smiled. They hadn't said much to each other in the past half-hour, but they had had their arms round each other. 'I don't think there is anywhere else, is there?'

'We could move into the saloon.'

'No, that's for officers.' She glanced at him, hesitated, then threw caution to the winds. 'I wouldn't mind a walk outside, though.'

He looked so surprised that she almost laughed aloud.

She buttoned her coat and adjusted her little peaked cap and they went out into the chill darkness. They were at the top of Hampstead Heath. There was a pond nearby called the Leg of Mutton, upon which was reflected what little moonlight filtered through a bank of cloud. But there were no other lights anywhere. Just the pale sheen of the pond, the dark shape of the trees and buildings and the occasional vehicle creeping along at fifteen miles an hour and disappearing into the gloom.

She took his hand and led him across the road and through a gap in the railings. 'Come on,' she said. 'Let's go down this path. You can tell me the story of your life.'

He grunted. 'Not much to tell.'

81

She put her arm through his and held hands with him inside his coat pocket. 'Oh, I'm sure there is! Come on boy, talk to me! Tell me something!'

'What about?'

'Well – how would I know? Anything! I mean, you were at college, weren't you? Tell me about that. What were you studying?'

'Political science. I chucked it before I graduated.'

'That was silly. What did you do that for?'

He heaved a sigh. 'A lot of reasons. I wanted to find out things.'

'What sort of things?'

'About myself. And – and my family.'

They stopped. She was sure he wanted to talk but she didn't want to seem inquisitive. Maybe it was the gin, or Christmas Eve or even the war – suddenly she wanted to hold him, hug him. 'You don't have to tell me anything you don't want to,' she said. 'But you may feel better if you do. Everyone needs someone to lean on occasionally, don't they? And I don't mind if you lean on me a bit.' She reached up and kissed him. She could feel hurt and unhappiness in him.

They walked on in silence for a while. Then he said, quite abruptly: 'I was adopted. I came over here to try and find my real family.'

'Adopted . . . Oh. I see.'

'What do you see?'

'Well nothing, really. It was just – well, I never met anyone who's been adopted before. That must be difficult. To be adopted, I mean.' She looked up at him. 'Is it?'

He nodded jerkily. 'Yup. It certainly can be sometimes.'

'So you're looking for your family. And I don't suppose you've found them. Otherwise you wouldn't be here, would you?'

He looked away. 'Yeah,' he muttered. 'You figured that out correctly, Gwynneth.'

'Where have you looked?'

'You really want to know?'

''Course I want to know! I wouldn't ask if I didn't, would I?'

He stopped walking and kissed her. 'I like you, Gwynneth.'

'Thank you. I like you too, David.'

They walked on, and he said: 'I visited the adoption agency, but they wouldn't help. I don't even know if my mother's still alive. It — makes a guy feel kind of empty inside, you know that?'

'That's terrible!'

He laughed shortly. 'Oh, I guess I'll live.'

'So what will you do now? Go back to America?'

'Maybe. I dunno.'

She interlocked her fingers with his. 'Don't go back, boy. Not yet, anyway.'

He hugged her and undid his sheepskin coat so that she could come inside it with him. They both got better and better at kissing and she didn't want him to stop. Then they had a really long kiss — the sort of kiss her mother called sinful — and she felt herself being carried away by a new feeling, one that started exactly where it shouldn't and seemed to radiate out to every part of her body.

She opened her own overcoat and tunic as well, and when they hugged again she could feel his ribs hard against her and at the same moment they began moving back and forth against each other so that a tingling sensation went shooting from the tips of her breasts right down to her heels.

'Oh David!' she whispered. 'You're better than a teddy bear any day!'

She took his hand and put it on her breast. She began to tremble violently. She had never done anything like this before and she had a feeling he hadn't either. 'Half a mo, Kaiser Bill,' she whispered, and after a short struggle released her brassière. He sighed a great sigh and cupped her breasts in his hands; and then, after a little encouragement, fell upon them like a child who has been denied his mother's milk. He placed his cheek against them, kissed them, ran the tip of his tongue back and forth over them and finally sucked at them, sending wave upon wave of pleasure coursing through her.

'I think you'd better come up for air,' she whispered eventually, and he looked up at her, breathless, his teeth white in the darkness.

'I don't want to stop,' she said, 'but I think we ought to, don't you? I'm – I'm a virgin, see, and I want to stay that way 'til I'm married. I hope you don't mind.'

'I don't mind. I guess I feel the same way,' he said.

She really loved him for saying that.

They began walking back, their arms round each other.

She said, 'I didn't mean to go that far.'

His voice was husky. 'Nor did I.'

'I expect you think I'm a really fast piece, don't you?'

'No, I don't think that, Gwynneth.'

'It just kind of happened, didn't it?'

'I guess you could say that.'

They walked on in silence. She said, 'I feel awful about it now. What you must think of me! Some kind of a tart!'

'You're not anything of the kind,' he said. 'You're – you're a great girl, Gwynneth. You're one of the best.'

'You can't say that,' she whispered. 'That's just silly, that is. I mean – you don't know me, do you?'

'Anyway I'm glad it did happen,' he said defiantly. 'It was the most wonderful thing that ever happened in my whole life, and that's the honest truth.'

They stopped and held hands. He kissed her very gently, first on the forehead and then on the lips. She felt like crying. She didn't know why.

He said: 'I guess I'm in love with you, Gwynneth.'

She borrowed his handkerchief and dabbed at her eyes. 'That's a very nice thing to say, David. But you ought not to say it unless you mean it, see?'

'I do mean it,' he said earnestly. 'I really do.'

They had reached the road. She turned to him. 'It wasn't bad, was it? For a first try.'

He nodded in the jerky way he had.

'And it was, wasn't it?'

'Excuse me?'

'I mean it was the first time you've done anything like that.'

He smiled. 'Yup, I guess it was,' he said.

She held his hand tightly. 'Well – snap.'

'Excuse me?'

'You and your "excuse me"! I said snap! Haven't you heard of snap, David? It means – well, it means we're the same, see. Like twins.'

They crossed the road and stood outside the entrance to the public bar. She said she really ought to go and rejoin her friends.

'When do I get to see you again?'

'I don't know. We don't get much time off.'

'Can I have your address?'

'You mean in Wales?'

'No. Where you're stationed.'

The redcaps seemed to appear from nowhere. One of them, the sergeant, was fixing her with a beady stare. She tried to warn David with her eyes, but he didn't take the hint.

He grinned easily. 'Come on! Don't be shy!'

'It's – we're not allowed to –' she stammered quietly, and shot a glance over his shoulder.

'Bothering you, is he, love?' the sergeant said.

'No – not at all –'

But the sergeant wasn't prepared to take her word for it. 'I'll see your identity card if you please, young man.'

David Odell put his hand into his inside pocket. 'Oh my God!' he said. 'My wallet –'

ii

The police station at Golders Green was busy with drunks, brawlers and an assortment of no-hopers, and morning found David in a cell with two very hung-over individuals, one who had snored for the past three hours and the other who had made frequent and inaccurate use of the bucket in the corner. At eight o'clock, a breakfast of lumpy porridge, bread and margarine and a mug of tea made with evaporated milk was provided, and an hour after that a police sergeant looked in on them.

'Look, what's going on?' David protested. 'I'm an innocent citizen of the United States. When am I going to see a lawyer?'

'You won't be seeing no lawyer on Christmas Day, sonny Jim.'

'Now see here, officer, I'm a press reporter –'

'I don't care if you're Lord bloody Beaverbrook, mate, you'll not see anyone today.'

'Then will you kindly tell me why I'm being held?'

Sergeant Blenkinsop – a dour police veteran who had retired five years earlier and had been recalled for service on the outbreak of war – consulted his night report book.

'You're Odell, right?'

'Right.'

'Section 18b regulations.'

'And what the hell's that when it's at home?'

'Subversive activities.'

The cell door crashed shut.

The snorer, a grey, unshaven cockney with red, watery eyes, regarded David with unconcealed distaste. 'I fought all through the last bleedin' lot,' he said. 'From bleedin' Mons to bleedin' Wipers. One of General French's bleedin' Contemptibles, that's me. And look what I gets for me trouble. Cooped up with a bleedin' Nazi on Christmas bleedin' Day.'

iii

His cell mates were released that afternoon, and the following day he was questioned for the first time. He was marched into a bare room and made to sit at a table while an elderly civil servant stared him closely in the eye.

'Now then, Mr Odell. Perhaps we could have some personal details first, starting with your full name and address.'

Feeling relieved and confident that he would be quickly released, he gave them, and Mr Avery of MI5 wrote them down in a black loose-leaf pocket book. 'Now date of birth, if you please Mr Odell, and full names of both parents.'

'Thirty-first December, 1918. Father: Michael Patrick Odell, no apostrophe, deceased –'

'Would he have been of Irish extraction, Mr Odell?'

'That's correct. Two generations back –'

'And your mother?'

'Carlotta Odell.'

Mr Avery contained his impatience. 'The maiden name, if you don't mind, sir.'

'Weissmann.'

'And how do we spell that?'

He spelt it.

'And where was your mother born?'

'Bavaria. I'm not sure exactly where, but –'

'Bavaria? In Germany?'

'Yes, but –'

'So your mother is German.'

'Was a German. She's a naturalized American and she hasn't lived in Germany for over twenty years. And she's certainly no Nazi!'

'So you are the son of an Irish-American and a German-American, is that correct?'

David put his head in his hands. 'Yes, that's correct.'

Avery was unmoved. 'We've had your rooms searched, Mr Odell, so we know what you've been up to.'

'What's that supposed to mean?'

'I think it would be better if you told me that, wouldn't it?'

'I've told your people the whole story three times! I'm a reporter. I went out for a drink the night before last and – and lost my wallet. It may have fallen out of my pocket or some pickpocket may have lifted it, I don't know which –'

'While you were in the company, I understand, of a member of the Auxiliary Territorial Service. Yes?'

'Yes! Look, I've got nothing to hide. I'm just an ordinary guy over here to report the war.'

'There are ways and ways of reporting the war, Mr Odell. Ways and ways.'

'Are you suggesting – are you seriously suggesting –?' He broke off. 'This is just crazy!'

'It may be crazy to you, Mr Odell, but we take a more serious view. Take an example.' Avery opened a folder which contained a half-completed article David had been working on only two days before. 'Here we are. Permit me to quote a line or two: "But for the blackout and the sandbags and the little cardboard boxes slung over people's shoulders, you would hardly know that London was at war, and if that sounds illogical I make no apology, because this so-far, so-called, phoney, funny war makes about as much sense to your correspondent as half-past cheese by the village pump. Like the man said, I don't know if these people frighten the enemy, but they sure as hell frighten me."' Avery looked up. 'Do you deny that you wrote that?'

'So what if I did?'

'Very well, what about this: ". . . and hardly a day goes by when we are not reminded how scrupulously fairly the British are waging their war; and while it is painfully obvious that instead of dropping leaflets over Germany the RAF should be dropping bombs, this is not being done because, so they say, 'this would contravene international law and would be an infringement of Herr Krupp's private property'. So the kid gloves are still firmly on this side of the English Channel, and Neville Chamberlain still seems convinced that Herr Hitler can be taught how to play cricket."'

David grinned. He had been particularly pleased with that paragraph. 'Well, it's true, isn't it? And anyway, I've seen much the same sort of stuff in the *Daily Herald*.'

'Perhaps you have. But *Daily Herald* reporters carry identification papers, submit their work to the censor and are not in the habit of questioning members of the armed services about their units – as you were clearly heard to do by the military police.'

The questioning went on and on, and got nowhere at all. David made repeated demands to see the American Consul, but to no avail.

'Very well,' Avery said at last, 'I must tell you that I am not satisfied with your explanations and until we have proof of your identity you will continue to be held under Section 18b with a view to internment or prosecution, whichever is deemed appropriate by my department.'

That afternoon he was moved in a Black Maria to a commandeered apartment block in Temple Fortune, where he was to share lodgings with an assortment of undesirable aliens, IRA suspects and members of the British Union of Fascists, and it wasn't until the following day that he was at last visited by someone from the American Consulate.

'John Scott Junior,' said the official, a breezy quarterback fresh out of Yale, and shook him warmly by the hand.

'God bless America!' said David. 'Am I glad to see you!'

iv

'The problem is,' Scott said when David had told his story all over again, 'they're not letting me see those articles of yours, so I can't argue with them over the propaganda issue. And without a soul willing to vouch for you in this country, the best we can hope for is repatriation.'

'And the worst?'

'Quite a long spell in gaol if you're convicted of subversion, and the long drop if they find you guilty of spying. But it won't come to that, I'm sure.'

'Thanks very much.'

'And that's another thing. You aren't helping yourself by your manner. You've a way of putting them down, know what I mean? These Brits – they take this war of theirs seriously. Making flip remarks about it doesn't help you any, right?'

'Right.'

'Now are you sure there's no one at all who can testify on your behalf?'

'There's no one they'll listen to.' He looked up. 'Unless you go to the adoption people.'

'What adoption people?'

'The Marie Gould Agency. I was an adopted child. That's part of the reason I'm over here. Usual thing, you know. Looking for my folks.'

Scott frowned. 'Have you mentioned this before?'

'No. I . . . thought it would only complicate things. And the woman I spoke to at that agency wasn't exactly helpful. Fact is, they were plain cussed. I – I guess I lost my rag with them and we had a set to, so I doubt you'll get much change out of them.'

'Give me the address, just in case. And tell me exactly where you fired up that army girl so we can go look for the wallet.'

Another day passed, and he heard nothing at all. Then, when he was eating a midday meal of bully beef and soggy peas along with forty other internees in the canteen, he was summoned to the entrance lobby where he found Scott looking pleased with himself.

'Good news,' he said. 'We found your wallet.' He held it up and handed it over. 'If you'd care to check the contents.'

It was all there: his identity card, passport, driving licence, private pilot's licence, bank notes.

'This is incredible! Where d'you find it?'

'On Hampstead Heath, right where you dropped it, I guess.' Scott took some papers from a briefcase. 'I've talked with the security people. They're satisfied you're a bona fide citizen of the United States and not a subversive or undesirable.' He handed over a card. 'And we've fixed membership of the international press corps for you. Sign it right now, OK? It should keep you clear of trouble in the future.

Provided you don't go rolling any more army intelligence chicks in the woods.'

'I don't understand —'

'You don't need to. Just sign.'

He did so.

'They've confiscated your articles and diary, and we've guaranteed that in future you'll keep to the rules and submit all material to the censor. Otherwise you're in the clear. You can walk out the front door.'

'I don't believe it!'

Scott lowered his voice. 'Just play it cool, right? We've persuaded them you're on the level, so don't give them any cause to bring you in again. They're very jumpy about fifth columnists right now, and you might not be so lucky next time.'

David grinned ruefully. 'There won't be a next time if I have anything to do with it.'

'Great. Got any baggage?'

'Just what I stand up in.'

'Let's go then.'

'You mean right now?'

Scott held up the sheaf of papers. 'That's what it says here.'

They went to the front entrance and the papers were presented and checked. In the street, a US Embassy Buick was ticking over by the kerb.

'So what'll you do now?' Scott asked as they drove off.

'Book a passage on the first ship back to the States, I guess.'

Scott looked surprised. 'There's no need if you don't want. This war hasn't gotten itself started yet. You go back to the States now, you'll miss the action. If I was in your shoes I'd stick it out.' The Buick went under the rail bridge at Golders Green and swung left at the crossroads, past the war memorial and on up the hill between wooded banks to the Heath.

'By the way,' Scott remarked as the Buick turned left into East Heath Road. 'I found that address you wanted.'

'What address is that?'

Scott took out a pocket book. 'Your natural mother. Here – you can have this page, I've no further use for it.'

v

Mrs Wilmot . . .

Up in his third floor apartment that afternoon, he tried to construct a face to fit the name. Mrs Wilmot. So she was married. So she might have children – children who could be almost as old as himself. Maybe older. He stood at the window staring out over the Heath.

Did he really want to meet her? She might be . . . she might be anything. He didn't know how old she had been when he had been born, so she could be any age from mid-thirties to early sixties. She could be a shopkeeper, or one of those old biddies with scarves on their heads, the sort you saw scrubbing the step outside terraced houses in the London slums.

And what sort of person had she been to have given birth to an illegitimate child? Could she be the sort of person he would be ashamed to acknowledge as a mother? Was he her only bastard? Or was she a hooker, with any number of little bastards farmed out to whoever wanted them? The thought of it made him sweat. On the other hand if she was respectable and had kept her secret, what would her family have to say about the sudden appearance of an illegitimate son? What would Mr Wilmot have to say?

Suddenly the whole idea of contacting her was a far less inviting prospect than before.

But what was the alternative? To cut and run? Scuttle off home to mother and apple pie? Yes, and what would he be saying to himself when the boat went back past the Statue of Liberty and up the Hudson River?

He paced up and down the room, pausing occasionally to stare out of the window at the mist-covered Heath.

Suddenly he wanted to be with Gwynneth again.

He closed his eyes, remembered the lilt of her voice, her dark hair, her kisses – and above all her wonderful, glorious soft, warm, welcoming breasts. Things she had said echoed in his memory. 'You and your "excuse me" . . . Not a bit. Fact I quite liked it. Don't go back, boy. Not yet, anyway . . .' He sighed. She'd told him that they didn't get much time off and that she didn't normally frequent pubs. He didn't know her surname and she didn't know his. Scott had advised him to steer clear, and God alone knew what sort of trouble Gwynneth had got into because of him.

He felt depressed. It was his birthday the day after tomorrow, and there wouldn't be a soul to share it with. No presents at breakfast, no happy-birthday-to-you, no cake, no treat, no dinner, no Mom to give him a big kiss and tell him how proud she was of him.

He had to shake off these blues somehow, and the way to do that was to be positive. Take a ride down to Dover. Go and knock on Mrs Wilmot's door. After all, wasn't she the reason he'd come to England in the first place?

But he didn't feel at all enthusiastic. He still couldn't stop thinking about Gwynneth, and he wasn't sure he wanted to have this Mrs Wilmot for a mother – or anyone else, for that matter.

vi

He made an early start the next day. He packed his hold-all and Royal portable typewriter into the sidecar of the 1932 Brough Superior he had picked up for twenty-five pounds soon after landing in England; and having donned his sheepskin, wound his college scarf twice round his neck and put on his leather flying helmet and goggles and a pair of yellow gauntlets, he set out for Dover, where he arrived in the afternoon and checked into the Grand Hotel.

As it would be dark soon after four and he didn't like the idea of riding on dimmed headlights in the narrow country lanes of Kent, he decided to leave the exploring until the next day, and instead had a leisurely afternoon. In the evening, after taking a drink at the bar, he set off on foot to explore the town, and ended up at a music hall where Gipsy Rose Lee and Tommy Trinder were heading the bill and practically the whole audience was in uniform.

The following morning he got up late, read the newspapers over breakfast and, overcoming a sense of inertia that he had not experienced before, wrapped up and set off in search of Mrs Wilmot.

The village of St Margaret's-at-Cliffe, he discovered, lay just off the Deal road about three miles along the coast from Dover and consisted of the church of St Margaret, a couple of pubs, the village school, a village shop and post office and a collection of assorted houses and cottages, some with clapboard elevations that reminded him of the houses on the coast of Maine. Like most visitors who arrive in St Margaret's on wheels, he was through the village before he realized he was in it, and descended by Sea Street to St Margaret's Bay. Here he found quantities of barbed wire along the beach and an ancient mariner wielding an enormous hand net; and when he looked back up the hill he saw, perched on the cliffs, the holiday homes and guest houses whose windows had been boarded up for the winter, or the war, or both.

It was an odd feeling, actually being here and knowing that the woman he had travelled so far to find was somewhere quite close – perhaps in one of the houses he had already passed. The sense of inertia returned: he decided not to call on her just yet but use the next hour or so to get the feel of the locality.

He watched the grey waves tumbling on the shore and, becoming mesmerized by them, began mentally composing an article about this historic corner of England.

Dover Castle, that's where he'd kick off from: that bold, ancient pile of granite and stone that dominated the whole town with its Union Jack flying high over the central keep. And then Dover itself: the drab grey destroyers and minesweepers in the harbour, the anti-aircraft guns along the front, the barrage balloons tethered on dumb barges that ringed the harbour entrance; the crowds of uniformed people – sailors and soldiers mostly, but a few air force people as well, though what they might be doing here he had no idea. The feel of the place: how could he define it? It was the feeling of a garrison, a populated fortress, yes, that was the impression it made. And last night at the Hippodrome, singing along with Gypsy Rose Lee . . . that had been the first time he had sensed the fabled 'island spirit' in Britain. Why was it that he should find it here in Dover but not in London? Was it his imagination, because of the associations with the name? Or was it because the Royal Navy was here, and wherever the Royal Navy was, so they said, morale was always higher?

The cliffs, that's what he wanted to see. He couldn't go back home and admit that he had been to Dover but hadn't walked on the white cliffs.

He swung the motorbike and sidecar round and went back up the road, taking an unadopted track off to the left that led below more holiday houses, many of which looked deserted. When the track came to an end he parked the bike and set off along a path that went uphill through a wood, emerging a few hundred yards further in a shallow valley that ran parallel to the coast.

This area was deserted and windswept, with dead, flattened grass, a few stunted bushes and shrubs and plenty of rabbit holes. Overhead, seagulls wheeled and cried. He went up a steep path to his left and as he reached the top felt the wind cold and strong in his face. Fifty yards further on, England stopped abruptly at the cliff edge, and the sea lay three hundred feet below.

He stood looking out over the Channel. There was too much cloud to see France but somehow you could sense it was near. He walked to within ten feet of the edge, fascinated by the sheer drop, strangely troubled by the loneliness of the place, the sense of antiquity and the knowledge that this might be where he really belonged. For a long time he stood there looking out to sea, remembering things about his childhood: secret miseries, losses of temper, obstinacies, longings for something or someone to fill up the empty vault inside him.

A dog with a black, shiny coat came bounding up and wagged round his legs. 'Hi, boy!' he said, patting it and letting it lick his hands. 'What's your name? Are you lost?'

The dog bounded off, and he strolled on, feeling unsure, all over again, of who he was and where he was going.

He thought of Gwynneth again. He wished he had her address. He wished they could have spent a day together. He wished they could have spent the night together. And – Oh God! – why did he have to keep thinking about her goddamn tits all the time?

Nothing seemed to be working out. He still didn't know who in hell he was or where he was going, and he had a feeling that even if he met this Mrs Wilmot she was going to be the biggest let down of all time. Okay, so he'd come to England, he'd cut the apron strings and he'd found his roots. Why bother with old Ma Wilmot? He didn't owe her a thing. She hadn't even bothered to answer his letter. For all he knew, the adoption agency might have been acting on her instructions. And anyway, what point was there in trying to change himself into something he'd never been? Why bother to chase after some vague sense of identity which at best was likely to be an anti-climax and at worst might turn out to be an albatross round his neck?

He stopped in his tracks, grinned in relief, and made up his mind what to do. One more night in Dover, then back to London and straight onto the first liner bound for New York.

Feeling better already, he regained the path and started down it. But as he did so, he saw a couple of middle-aged lovers embracing by some bushes a hundred yards off.

He stopped. They hadn't seen him, but were bound to do so as soon as they quit their petting session. Not wanting to arouse suspicion he turned straight back, and gave them a few minutes in which to move on. But when he returned to the path they were coming up the hill towards him.

The man was in a dark raincoat and was wearing a naval peaked cap. An officer. Officers had a habit of challenging you and asking to see your identity card. Well, so what? He had his new international press pass on him, didn't he? So what did he have to worry about?

But his heart was hammering all the same. He didn't want to have to greet them and reveal by his accent that he was from the other side of the Atlantic. He didn't want to be quizzed all over again, whether by an officer in the Royal Navy or by some beef-faced village cop.

So when the path forked, he turned right as if he had been intending to do so all along, and was glad to put a few stunted gorse bushes between himself and the couple.

It was quite a relief to be clear of them, and it occurred to him that they were probably as relieved as he was. After all, officers didn't like to be caught necking in the bushes, did they?

He stopped to look back at them. They were standing together on the cliff, silhouetted now against a grey sky.

Suddenly he knew that he'd seen enough of England and the English. He'd had his fill of this phoney war of theirs. And he'd definitely had enough of their paranoia about German spies.

He went on down the path, found his bike and rode slowly down the unadopted track, turning left up the hill through St Margaret's-at-Cliffe to regain the main Dover road.

SIX

Sergeant Sidney Crisp turned left, stamped his foot, marched up to his unit commander, stamped to a halt, saluted stiffly and barked: 'Number four section ready for your inspection – sah!'

'Thank you, Sergeant,' replied Captain Wilmot, and tucking his ash plant under his arm proceeded along the wharf and over the mobile crane tracks to where the thirty sappers under his command were fallen in on the quayside.

He made his way down the ranks, pausing to speak to several of the men.

'You fit again, Corporal Barker?'

'Yes, sir. Thank you, sir.'

'Glad to hear it. Ward –'

'Sir?'

'Your hair needs cutting.'

'I 'ad it cut yesterday, sir. Naturally thick, sir, that's what it is, see –'

'Sergeant, see this man has another hair cut. Today.'

'Sapper Ward! Did you hear what the officer said?'

'Yes, Sergeant.'

'How's the new baby, Smith?'

'Fine, thank you, sir, last I heard.'

'Thought of a name yet?'

'Percival, sir. It was the wife's choice, sir.'

'Mmm. You can always call him Percy.'

'Yes, sir.'

'What about you, McCartney? Are you going to keep out of trouble tonight?'

'Yes, sor. Do me best, sor.'

'I certainly hope so. I don't want a repeat of your perform-

98

ance in St Nazaire. It may be New Year's Eve, but you'll be a lot happier in the coming year if you keep off the drink tonight. Understood?'

'I'll not touch a drop, so help me, sor.'

'Kingsnorth. Sergeant Crisp tells me it was thanks to a piece of very professional crane driving on your part that we avoided having a nasty accident yesterday.'

'Sir.'

'I shall mention the incident in my next report. Well done.'

'Thank you, sir.'

The inspection over, Captain Wilmot returned Sergeant Crisp's salute and told him to stand them at ease.

'Section – stand at – ease!'

Wilmot stood before his men with his feet apart, his back well braced and his hands behind his back.

'Right, pay attention, I have something important to tell you. When the Commandant Royal Engineers inspected us the other day, he was impressed by the standard of efficiency and morale he found in this unit. As you know, the battalion has already received two commendations from GO C-in-C for the rapid turn round of ships, and Colonel Dean made it clear to me that much of the credit for those commendations is due to the efforts of this section. So – well done, all of you.'

Looking up and down the ranks, Wilmot noted the effect of his words with satisfaction. It was one of his theories that if you told a man he was good, you nearly always made him even better.

'But that is not the reason for my talking to you this afternoon, nor was it the sole purpose of the Colonel's visit. Because he put a proposal to me, and it is this. He told me that he wanted me to form and train a new unit with special responsibility within the BEF for the defence of inland waterways. And when he told me that I could choose the best men for the task, I had no hesitation in telling him that provided you were willing to volunteer, I would be happy to have every single one of you as founder members of the new Waterways Defence Section which will be formed and which will, in due course, be expanded to company strength.'

He paused a moment, glanced down at his gleaming shoes and then straightened again.

'But before I call for volunteers, I think I should tell you that the unit will be relieved of stevedore duties forthwith and will be moved up to the Arras area for special weapon and demolition training to fit us for our new task. We shall be issued with the necessary transport, equipment and weapons to enable us to provide a quick-reaction unit which, if the Germans open a second front, will almost certainly put us right in the forefront of the action. So this new venture is not for the faint-hearted. Personally, that is what I want, because I firmly believe that until we are given a chance to get at Jerry and show him what we're made of, this war will drag on, perhaps for a year or more.

'So there you are, chaps. I told the CRE straight away that I would be delighted to form this important new unit, and I hope that you will want to join me in the venture. What I'm going to do now is to ask Sergeant Crisp to call for volunteers, and I want to emphasize that while I hope you will all wish to remain under my command, no one, I repeat no one, should consider himself under any obligation to volunteer.' He turned. 'Carry on, Sergeant Crisp!'

'Sah! Number four section, shun! Pay attention! You heard what the officer said! Volunteers for Captain Wilmot's special waterways defence unit will take one pace forward! Volunteers *only*, one pace forward, *march*!'

To a man, the squad took a pace forward; and having done so stood grinning happily at the thought of no more ships to unload and the delights of Arras ahead.

'Thank you,' said Wilmot. 'I am proud to have you under my command.'

He turned again to the sergeant and ordered the men to be fallen out; and as he walked away over the crane tracks to where his car was waiting, a voice – it was almost certainly Sapper Ward's – shouted, 'Good old Griff!'

Wilmot's driver and batman, a diminutive cockney with a lop-sided face who suffered under the name of Albert Hall, started the camouflaged Morris as Wilmot strode up, and they drove off through the wintry dockyard.

Griff had worked in the Military Secretary's branch for the first two months of the war with responsibility, in the words of his terms of reference, 'for the file records of the Order of Battle for the British Expeditionary Force and the pool of first grade officers available for appointment to key postings'. During that time he had worked at a headquarters at Stanmore on the outskirts of London, and by the beginning of November, when nearly half a million officers and men – as well as the tanks, artillery, transport and munitions required by a modern army – had been shipped to France, he decided that the time had come for him to play a more active role in the war.

Although technically over-age for active service, he had used his influence at the War Office to get himself back into uniform, and had had no difficulty in securing a post in the rank of acting captain on loan to the Royal Engineers, and was given command of a section with responsibility for vessels discharging cargoes for the BEF. It was not a posting for which there was great competition, nor was it exactly what Griff would have chosen for himself, but it served his purpose of getting him back in command of men, and actively involved in the preparations to meet an enemy invasion.

So Griff Wilmot was at last back in his niche. To his delight, he had been in a position to select most of the men under his command, and had chosen a mixture of brains, guts and initiative, favouring men who seemed to him to be possessed of the sort of dogged good humour and resilience which had stood the British army in such good stead twenty-five years before.

The results were surprising to all except Griff. He knew

that he had never really ceased to be a soldier and now, at last, he had the opportunity to prove his qualities as a leader of men. For two months, first at St Nazaire and now at Le Havre, his unit had unloaded a whole range of cargo vessels: ships of the Clan, Glen and City lines, special cargo ships, refrigerated store ships, ammunition ships, petrol carriers and vehicle carriers, including the heavy lifting of armoured cars and tanks. During that time, thanks largely to Wilmot's energy, enthusiasm and natural rapport with the French, the battalion had been twice commended, and by the end of the year Wilmot's confidential report had singled him out as an officer of unusual ability and drive. Griff was delighted: within a matter of months, the army had given him back his self-esteem and a reason for living. Suddenly he saw that what Archie had called a 'bloody war or a sickly season' had its advantages. If he kept going the way he had started, he could expect to be a major by the end of the year, and if or when the fighting started he would be ideally placed to move on up the ladder. Promotion could be very rapid in wartime. He might get his own battalion yet. Perhaps even his own regiment. That would make Simone sit up and take notice.

The car drew up outside the hotel where Wilmot and a few other BEF officers were billeted.

'Excuse me, sir,' said Driver Hall as Wilmot was about to get out.

'Yes, Hall?'

'Well, sir, we was wondering, the lads, that is, if you'd care to join us this evenin' at the Pomme d'Or, like, sir, bein' as how it's New Year.'

'Well, that's very kind of you –'

'Nuffink rowdy, you understand, sir, but we thought as 'ow you might care to take a drink with us, like.'

Wilmot considered. While he enjoyed commanding men and appreciated the value of getting to know his soldiers, he was less inclined to allow them to get to know him, and preferred the company of a good book to the beery camaraderie of the average British soldier. He knew, also, that there would be a New Year's Eve party in his hotel that evening, and that Madame Timonier (who made no attempt to disguise the soft spot she had for him) might take it as a slight if he failed to put in an appearance.

So he thanked Hall and, having explained that his acceptance of the invitation was on the understanding that he would be able to stay for half an hour only, he went up the steps and into the hotel to be welcomed by Madame, resplendent in black and scarlet, her mouth a red slash across her powdered face, her hair dyed orange and her watery eyes alight with menopausal adoration of this straight-backed, moustached, old-fashioned military man.

'*Monsieur le capitaine!*' she gushed, and took a letter from the rack. '*La poste est arrivée enfin. Une lettre d'Angleterre. C'est de votre femme, n'est-ce pas?*' – and she gazed fondly after him as he thanked her, took the letter from her red-nailed fingers and went up the stairs.

His room was sombrely furnished with a heavy mahogany dresser and curtains of faded green velvet. A tall window gave onto a small balcony which overlooked the main road, so there was a constant noise of traffic going by outside. The bed was double, and the feather mattress a little lumpy.

He unbuttoned his service uniform, unbuckled his Sam Browne, loosened his khaki tie and, without much in the way of pleasurable anticipation, sat in the old wicker chair by the bed to read Simone's letter, the first he had received from her in nearly a month.

Dear Griff,

This letter is a bit late, I know that, but with Peggy gone and four lodgers to look after without any help, I don't get much time for letter-writing these days. So I hope you had as good a Christmas as can be expected. Ours was not really a very happy one because Nick couldn't get away to see Christine and the others were also separate from their loved ones. The King's speech (did you hear it?) left us all very tearful, and now it's Boxing Day evening and I'm feeling lonely and desperate.

I bumped into Archie the other day in Dover – he's been working terribly hard too, and thinks he may be getting a sea job soon. He sent you his best regards. The navy certainly seems to be doing all the fighting so far, doesn't it? Also I've had a letter from my sister. Did you know that Uncle Gaston is now one of the top brass in the French army? If you need to pull strings he might be a useful contact.

Here, everything's very quiet. Every other house is up for sale and Dover is crawling with servicemen. I have to show my identity card at a road block every time I go into the town. The girls are working in watches and they go by bike down to the castle. They aren't too bad really, I suppose. Actually the one I get on with least well at the moment is Christine. I think she's impatient to marry Nick, poor girl, and takes out her frustration on me.

You asked about David. No, I haven't written to him. What's the point? He won't come to Britain with a war on. If only you had let me write when I wanted to, Griff. At least we would have made contact. When all this is over, I *will* write to him, whether you like it or not. I really wish I had been stronger over it before, now. I know you don't like arguing by letter, but I think that when you come home we must have a long talk about everything. You will have to learn that I have my own life to lead as well. That is what has always been wrong between us, Griff – you never stopped treating me like a child. If you can learn to treat me as an adult I am sure things will get better for both of us.

While I remember. There is a damp patch up behind the wardrobe in our bedroom, and the wallpaper is peeling off and going crinkly. Also, I have had to go into the red (£2.18s.9d. so far) to pay the electricity bill because the girls use so much hot water and electric light. I went to the bank last week and asked about having a joint account. They said it was perfectly easy and all you have to do is write a letter asking them to arrange it. It really would make things much easier for me, Griff.

It's getting very late and I have to be up at quarter to seven tomorrow morning to get the girls their breakfasts before they go on watch. I hope what I said about David doesn't upset you, because that wasn't what I intended. I just want a fair deal, that's all. Let's try to discuss things in a civilized way in future, without getting over-heated. After all, we are allies, aren't we?

All love as always,
Simone.

PS Here is a quotation from the King's Christmas speech which I expect you would like to see. It says it all really, doesn't it?

> I said to the man who stood at the gate of the year: 'Give me a light that I may tread safely into the unknown.' And he replied: 'Go out into the darkness and put your hand into the hand of God. That shall be to you better than light and safer than a known way.'

He sat on the bed, the pages of her letter still in his hand, and tried to fathom how sincere she had been when she had written those words 'All love as always'. Was she being faithful to him? He wished he could be sure of it and hated himself for mistrusting her. But he couldn't ignore the fact that however hard Archie was working at Chatham, he would surely have some time off, and Prowse was under an hour away in a fast Lagonda.

He closed his eyes for a moment and recalled – yet again – the sight of them asleep in each other's arms on the sofa that last morning at Eggardon. Perhaps he should have read the riot act then and there, after all. But what good would it have done? They would have been estranged completely by now – all three of them more than likely – and in time of war even this lukewarm affection of Simone's was better than no affection at all.

The trouble with Simone was that she always wanted her bread buttered on both sides – with jam on it, too. She needed him as a husband, but she wanted a secret affair with Archie at the same time. She was incapable of balancing a simple household budget, and yet wanted free access to his bank account. She was naïve and immature in her judgement over her illegitimate son, and yet demanded to be treated as an adult.

But the most ridiculous and illogical part of it all was that he still loved her, still felt guilty about her, still strove to succeed for her.

He smiled sadly to himself, remembering how he had once joked that the Channel was the biggest natural barrier in the world between logic and emotion. He had been at first surprised when Simone agreed with him, but then she had made it clear that she regarded the French as being the nation guided by logic while emotion reigned supreme north of the white cliffs of Dover. It was a typical disagreement: there were times when he was amazed how precisely they could agree on something and yet others when their viewpoints seemed diametrically opposed.

In a way, he regarded the French nation in much the same way as he looked upon Simone. Over the years, he had been enchanted by her, infuriated by her, spurned, jilted, ridiculed and now perhaps even cuckolded by her – and yet he still could not imagine a situation that would make him willing to part from her. What had she called the two nations once? 'Faithful enemies'. He could certainly agree with her there.

'Simone, my love,' he whispered aloud. 'Why must we

make life so difficult for each other?' And for the rest of the evening – while his fellow officers sang round the piano and vied with each other to kiss Madame; while his men drank cheap French beer in the Pomme d'Or and McCartney breathed over him and confided that he was a 'proper gentleman and the best commanding officer I ever 'ad, sor'; while they all sang 'Auld Lang Syne', and 1939 – that sad, incompetent year – gave way to a new, ominous decade – Griff Wilmot thought of Simone, remembered past happiness with her, wondered what she was doing, who she was with, what she was thinking, whether she was managing with her houseful of Wren officers and whether the day would ever come when he would win back her love and be confident that he shared it with no one else.

SEVEN

Christine Trendle-Home and Marjory Lane came out of the Dover naval headquarters soon after midday to find a bitter north-east wind blowing and the sky the colour of lead. They freewheeled down to the gate, showed their passes, then pushed the bikes up the hill past the Connaught Barracks before mounting to ride single file along the Deal Road towards St Margaret's-at-Cliffe.

It began to snow. Pedalling along in the lead, her shoulders hunched against the wind, Christine had neither the breath nor the inclination for conversation with Marjory. Earlier that morning, her father had rung to say he would be coming over to Prowse to deposit Blashford with Simone before joining his new ship, and hoped to see her to say goodbye.

Christine viewed the prospect of meeting him with mixed feelings. Neither he nor Simone had said anything about what they had been up to together that day on the Ramsgate road, and Christine regarded this rather childish silence of theirs as a clear indication that they had something to hide. An uneasy atmosphere had developed between herself and Simone and now she felt apprehensive that her father might try to broach the subject with her in order to clear the air or – much worse – that he and Simone might want to make some sort of joint declaration to her in order to have her approval.

If that was the case, she decided as they turned right at the corner shop and went along Reach Road, they would *not* have her approval. She was outraged that they should carry on an affair behind Captain Griff's back, and it had already taken quite a lot of self-control on her part to stop herself telling Simone so.

What terrified her most of all was that the whole sordid business might cause her to lose Nick. Having a father who had a sly affair with his best friend's wife the moment her husband's back was turned made Christine feel dirty and ashamed.

They turned into the school drive and were waved through by the sentry at the gate. And there was the Lagonda. Christine's heart sank.

Marjory – the soul of tact, as ever – said, 'I expect you'd like to have your Pa on your own, Chrissy, wouldn't you? I'll make myself scarce.'

They let themselves in and Blashford came through the hall to greet them, the snow melting on his shiny black coat and his nose muddy from burrowing in rabbit holes. Marjory went straight upstairs, and Christine went into the kitchen where Simone and Archie had just come in from their walk. Simone was taking off her headscarf. She had been crying.

Christine put on a false brightness and offered her cheek to be kissed. 'Hello, Pa! Many congrats! I saw the appointment in the CW List today. *Vagabond*'s a V and W class isn't she?'

Her father put on a similarly jolly act. 'Never thought they'd trust your old man with a ship, eh? Well, I suppose war has its compensations after all.'

The telephone rang. Simone went into the hall to answer it and Christine found herself alone with her father. All the jollity was suddenly gone. He glanced quickly at her.

'I don't really know what to say, Chrissy.'

'I don't think there is much to say, is there?'

He shook his head. 'I may not see you for some time. I – I wouldn't like to think that we'd parted on – on bad terms, so to speak. That is –'

He was dodging the issue, even now. He wanted to be reassured that she was still his loving and dutiful daughter, but no doubt still hoped to carry on this affair he was having with Simone. She despised him for that and yet, because he was her father, still loved him, still forgave him.

She tried to smile at him and failed miserably.

'We're all human, Chrissy,' he said. 'And your old Pater's more human than most.'

She turned away from him and looked out of the kitchen window at the bleak back garden and the snow falling.

'I don't know exactly what you're trying to say, Daddy, but I'm not at all sure that I want to hear it.'

'Better shut up, then,' he muttered. 'Better shut up.'

He reached out and put his hands on her shoulders. It was an unusual thing for him to do. Christine had been very close to her mother, and there had always been a part of her that instinctively blamed her father for Olivia's death. This, and Archie's long periods of absence at sea, had effectively estranged father and daughter. Christine had not become aware of it until she met Nick and saw how much warmer and closer the members of his family were with each other than she was with her father.

Now, for a fleeting moment, she expected – and wanted – to be able to turn to him as a daughter and be comforted by him. She wanted to be held tight by him, to cry on his shoulder about this beastly war as Simone had probably been doing only a few minutes before; and had her father pulled her gently to him or even whispered her name, perhaps that might have happened.

But Christine could not be aware that her poise and her maturity of judgement combined to make Archie feel at a disadvantage, and unwilling to risk a rebuff. He took his hands from her shoulders. The moment passed. He was in control again. In command again.

'You're all right I take it? I mean – at Dover.'

'Yes . . . yes, I'm fine.'

'And – er – Nick?'

'He's fine, too. Doing very well, I think.'

Archie nodded. 'I'm sure he is. Sure he is.'

They heard Simone replacing the receiver and a moment later she came back to the kitchen. She looked very pale, as if she were in shock. 'What on earth's the matter, Simone?' Archie asked.

She stood in the doorway, her mouth working. She shook her head as if she wanted to rid herself of something. 'It was my son.'

'Your *son*?'

'I don't understand,' Christine said. 'I thought –'

'I had a letter from him in the summer. He . . . must have got hold of my address somehow.' She shook her head again. 'He's staying at the Grand. I – I've invited him here. Today. It's his birthday, you see.' She turned to Archie. 'I couldn't not invite him, could I?'

'Of course not –'

'Then will you stay, Archie? Just until he arrives?'

'You mean he's coming now?'

'Yes. He's . . . got a motorbike.'

Archie looked at his watch. 'My dear – I simply can't. I'm cutting things fine as it is. I really have to go right away.'

'But he'll be here in ten or fifteen minutes, Archie! He's coming straight up from the Grand.' She took the kettle from the Aga and began filling it at the sink. 'I'll make some tea. Surely you won't say no to a cuppa, will you?'

But it was no good. He really couldn't stay. She burst suddenly into tears, but as quickly got them under control. 'I'd better phone the guardroom. Tell them he's on his way. I – I expect you two want to say goodbye to each other, don't you?'

She went quickly along the hall and a moment later they overheard her speaking on the phone again.

'Well,' Archie said. 'God bless you, Chrissy. Keep safe.'

'And you, Daddy. Better wet than duffers, remember?'

He nodded. 'Write lots. Care of GPO London.'

'Yes, of course.'

They went into the hall. Simone finished her call to the guardroom and held Blashford by the collar when Archie opened the front door. Archie gave her a peck on the cheek.

'I won't come out,' she whispered. 'Goodbye, Archie.'

He was already turning back into a naval officer. 'Right,' he said, bending to pat his dog. 'Goodbye, old fellow. Behave yourself.' He straightened up. 'Right. Let's get a move on.'

Christine went out to the car with him.

'Good luck with the new ship, Pater.'

'Thanks. I'll probably need it.'

He got in behind the wheel and slammed the door. Christine stepped back. Archie glanced at her, said, 'Cheerio, then. God bless,' and raised a hand to Simone before driving off.

They went inside. Simone went upstairs in tears. When the front doorbell rang ten minutes later, Christine answered it.

Standing in the porch stamping snow off his boots was a young man of about her own age in a heavy sheepskin coat and gauntlets, with a striped scarf round his neck and a pair of goggles pushed up onto the top of an old leather flying helmet. He had parked a motorcycle combination in the drive outside the front door.

'Hi there,' he said easily. 'You don't know me. My name's David Odell.'

ii

Simone was amazed at the size of him, the depth of his voice, the breadth of his shoulders, the extent of his appetite.

'So what do you reckon? Do I call you "Mother"?' he asked that first evening when Simone was cooking the supper.

She prodded the potatoes with a fork. 'I think perhaps "Simone" would be easier for both of us, wouldn't it?'

'Simone,' he repeated. He thought a moment. 'So – you're not English, Simone, right?'

'No, of course not. Didn't they tell you? I'm French.'

'Does that make me French?'

She stood at the stove with her back to him. 'It means you have French blood flowing in your veins, David. *Tu es un enfant de France*. You understand that?'

'I guess so.'

'But it doesn't mean that you are not an American, does it?'

'No, but – I know about my American background. What I'm interested in is my French roots.'

'Some day I shall tell you about them,' she said. 'But not just yet. How long can you stay?'

'Well, maybe a couple of days –'

She turned quickly, the fork in her hand. 'Oh, you must stay longer than that! A couple of months, not a couple of days!'

He laughed. 'Don't forget I've got a living to earn, Simone. I'm a press reporter, right? I need to be in London for that.'

'Nonsense! There are lots of reporters here in Dover. During the last war, Dover was one of the most important ports in Britain. I can clear out the boxroom for you and you can write all day up there if you want. And you can visit France more easily from Dover. You will be much closer to the war here than in London, you know.'

He thought of Gwynneth. She was the only real reason he had for going back to London, but there was small chance of finding her again.

'Well . . . I'd want to pay you a rental –'

'What do I want a rent for? You're my son, aren't you? I couldn't accept money from my son!'

'Housekeeping, then. And of course I'll give you my ration book.'

'Well, we'll see. But you will stay on?'

He relaxed. 'Okay. I'll stay on.'

'That's decided then. Now you can get the casserole out of the oven for me.' She handed him an oven cloth. 'Here you are, boy, use this, otherwise you'll burn your fingers.'

Marjory and Christine came down for the evening meal and Simone announced that as it was her son's twenty-first birthday she was going to open the bottle of champagne she had been saving for when the war ended.

'You see my war *has* ended,' she said when David had popped the cork. Then she raised her glass and proposed a toast to the birthday boy.

They listened to the nine o'clock news. The Archbishop of Canterbury had quoted Abraham Lincoln about being on the side of God; the Prime Minister's wife had spoken to the women of France, and in the war between Finland and Russia, Finland had claimed to have wiped out an entire Russian division of fifteen thousand men.

After the news, the girls went up to bed and Simone had David to herself for the first time. 'Now,' she said. 'Tell me all about yourself.'

David laughed. 'That's quite a tall order!'

'Start at the beginning. What's the very, very first thing you can remember?'

He looked at his hands. He knew already that it would be impossible to be entirely frank with Simone. With Gwynneth it would have been different. He would have been able to tell Gwynneth anything she wanted to know. He could have explained how the love, money and attention that had been lavished upon him had still left him with an empty ache inside, a feeling that he did not belong with them, that he was a stranger to them. He would have explained the anger he had felt at his natural mother, the mother who had allowed him to be adopted, and his need to seek her out, find out what sort of person she was, discover why he had been given away. He would have told Gwynneth about the time he was thirteen and went on a fishing vacation with his father up in Wisconsin, how he got lost one evening and was suddenly thrown on his own resources and forced to sleep rough and find his own way back to camp the next morning. That was the time when he first realized he was an individual with a life ahead of him, and what he made of it was down to him and him alone.

But with this French mother of his, he could only manufacture an ersatz childhood, the sort of childhood that every American boy was supposed to have, a childhood full of new bicycles and baseball gloves and Thanksgiving dinners and pumpkin pie.

'So . . . you really had a very happy childhood,' she said.

'Oh sure! My – er – parents were very good to me.'

She said nothing.

He broke the silence. 'You haven't said much about yourself. Or Mr Wilmot. Did I hear you say he was in France?'

She warmed her hands at the fire. 'Yes. He rejoined last September and he's Captain Wilmot again. He fought in the last war too, you know. But . . . he's not your father, David.'

'Can you tell me about who was?'

She avoided his eyes. 'I think we've talked enough for one day, don't you? And I have to be up early tomorrow. I'll make up a camp bed for you in here tonight, then tomorrow you can help me clear the boxroom.'

She brought sheets, blankets and a pillow down. He assembled the camp bed and she used the cushions off the sofa as a mattress. He said he could fix it quite easily by himself, but she fussed about and said she would do it. He could sense the tension rising in her all the time, and when she had finished she was on the brink of tears again.

'I still can't really believe you're here,' she said.

'It is kind of strange.'

'Will you do something for me, David?'

'What's that?'

'Just – just kiss me goodnight, will you? Kiss me goodnight and – and call me your mother. Just this once.'

He did as she asked, but felt oddly unmoved. After she had gone, he lay down and tried to sleep but found it impossible. He listened to the wind. A thousand thoughts and memories trooped in endless succession through his mind. He watched the second hand on his watch creep out of 1939 and into 1940 and wondered what the new year would bring. He thought about his mother back home, about Gwynneth, and finally about Simone.

He hadn't recognized her at first, and might not have done if it hadn't been for the dog. But Blashford had greeted him as a friend, and when Simone explained that she was looking after him for Christine's father who had gone off to take command of a destroyer, David realized with a shock that the couple he had seen kissing in the valley behind the cliff could only have been Simone and this Archie Trendle-Home, the mention of whose name, he noticed, was a sure-fire way of bringing tears to Simone's eyes.

Had Simone recognized him? He couldn't be sure and he knew better than to ask. He tried to persuade himself that perhaps their kissing had been the kissing of friends rather than lovers, but failed in the attempt. He reflected that he may have busted in on his mother's life at the most awkward possible moment.

He tiptoed into the hall, collected his sheepskin coat off the end of the bannister and put it on the bed for extra warmth. Then he needed to go to the jon, couldn't find the light switch and fell over a paraffin stove with a crash, which started Blashford barking in the kitchen.

He lifted the blind an inch or two and peered out at the falling snow. He felt as if his life had reached a high tide and that events were lapping at the dyke. He lay down again, counted to a thousand, thought again about Gwynneth — and finally gave up all ideas of sleep, put on the light and wrote a long piece in his journal.

It was still dark when he heard movement upstairs. He hadn't slept for a minute all night. He listened to Simone and the girls taking it in turns to use the upstairs bathroom.

When he looked out of the window, the world was covered in a thick blanket of snow.

EIGHT

To mark it out as the senior regiment of the German army, and because men had been specially selected from every part of Germany and from every other infantry regiment to join its ranks, the Berlin Guards Regiment had been, by special decree of the Führer, renamed the 'Grossdeutschland' or the 'Great Germany' Infantry Regiment.

The decree was read out on the Moabite parade ground by the Berlin city commander, Lieutenant General Seifert, and afterwards the officer in command, Colonel von Stock-hausen, addressed his men.

His voice echoed against the surrounding buildings as he stood straight-backed and booted on the podium. 'We shall, in our proud name, personify the German Armed Forces, and we shall perform our duty as will every other unit in the German army. But as we have been granted the honour of marching at the head of every parade, so shall we be ready, when the time comes, to be the spearhead of the attack.'

That was before the outbreak of hostilities. Soon afterwards, at the start of the Polish campaign, the regiment was sent to train as airborne troops in Silesia, but because Poland fell so easily it was not required, and the Grossdeutschlanders returned to the capital to be reorganized as one of the new fully motorized regiments. At the same time, the training regiment and a full battalion of No 92 Infantry Regiment were amalgamated into it, so making it the largest and most powerful single regiment in the German army.

There was also a new company formed: No 15 Company, which was to be equipped with very high-power weaponry and which had been given the special task of providing advance protection to the main body. In this company was a young soldier called Heinrich Lauder. Heinrich was an enthusiastic, tall, blond, powerful young Aryan who had moved straight from the Hitler Youth into the army, and along with every other member of No 15 Company, he believed that being chosen to serve in the Grossdeutschland Regiment was the highest possible honour to which he could ever aspire.

The task of re-equipping and re-training the Grossdeutschland Regiment went ahead with urgency. At the beginning of October, it transferred to Doberitz where the men were introduced to their new weapons and put through a gruelling training course to toughen them physically and train them in the new assault tactics. Three weeks later, the regiment was transferred by train to the Western Camp at Bernreuth near Grafenwohr in Bavaria, where prolonged rain and snowstorms reduced the terrain to a quagmire of clay and slush. But regardless of weather, the men marched off to exercise in Ebersberg's grim training area every morning, using live ammunition and grenades for the first time since mobilization.

A fortnight later they were off again, this time on a march westwards via Bayreuth, Bamberg, Wurzburg, Hanau and Wetzlar to the Western Forest, and it was in Montabaur, a small but picturesque health resort, that the regiment set up its provisional winter quarters – provisional because although no one knew when the great battle with France and Britain would start, everyone expected it from day to day.

There were several events that bitter winter which Heinrich and his comrades in 15 Company would always remember. There were the practice firings they did at Wahn near Cologne; the sniping competition for which Heinrich took second prize; a brief friendship with a girl called Renate who had wonderful blue eyes and flaxen hair – and the even more exciting anti-aircraft exercise they had with the Richthofen Squadron near Hirschberg. But it was on 23 December that a visit by the Führer gave the men of the Grossdeutschland

Regiment what was far and away the greatest moment of their military careers.

The speech he made during those Christmas celebrations left no further thoughts in anyone's mind that a confrontation with France and England could possibly be avoided. His words remain engraved in their memories: 'You are the bodyguard of the German people, for whose existence and protection the German nation as one man has prepared itself for battle. We shall sweep our enemies away as the storm sweeps the dust from the streets . . .'

On 29 January 1940, 15 Company left Montabaur and travelled via Koblenz to Zell on the Mosel. Their reception in the city of the 'black cat' was cool at first, but thanks to the strong wine, pretty girls and a lull in the unit's military activities, a very good relationship quickly developed between the soldiers and the locals.

Later, the relationship was further cemented by 15 Company's initiative during the Mosel floods in March.

One night, following a sudden thaw, the frozen river turned into a terrifying, surging, foaming torrent, rising to more than five metres above the emergency flood level. Enormous blocks of ice shoved against each other, piling up and causing panic in the town. With mighty rumblings, crunchings, crackings and thunderings, the massive power of the ice destroyed everything in its path. The water poured into the lower part of the town, flooding streets, filling cellars, sheds and ground floor rooms. The town was blacked out and the people of Zell were thrown into helpless confusion.

Of course there was no question of further sleep for 15 Company. Without concern for their own safety, often wading or standing up to the waist in icy water, they drove cows out of the sheds, rescued pigs, chickens and rabbits from their sties and runs and hutches and took them into kitchens or living rooms on a higher level. They sealed the wine vats, salvaged stores of potatoes and other supplies, cleared shops and workshops.

In this way it was demonstrated to the people of Zell that not only was 15 Company highly competent but that it regarded its highest duty – both now and in battle – as being the preservation of private property.

There were several other occasions on which they were able to assist the people of Zell: once when there was a fire, again during the work in the vineyard and yet again in the construction of a road.

But even in this peaceful setting, the more serious business of battle training continued uninterrupted. Though the major manoeuvres were not quite so frequent as in the autumn, the few which were carried out were all proof of the regiment's high level of efficiency.

General Guderian, the commander of the Panzer Corps to which they were attached, was able to see this for himself when the 1st Battalion practised with live ammunition and heavy weapons at Tellich. Speaking to the men afterwards, he said he was delighted with the manner in which the exercise had been conducted. But he also warned that the task which lay ahead was gigantic. It would involve driving and fighting day after day without let up, without rest and without sufficient food.

'You will have to get used to living on a bite of bread, a gulp of Coca-cola or coffee out of a flask,' he told the troops which had been fallen in on the town car park, which was used as a parade ground. 'The French are still sticking rigidly to their plans and tactics which, once thrown into confusion, will become a millstone round their necks. Already they are terrified at the very thought of our attack. They do not even begin to understand the force and dynamism that lies behind the Führer's success. But do not be complacent. Remember: once you have made the first break-through, once you have won the first battle, you must not stop or rest but must continue to hunt the enemy and stop him getting so much as a foothold. This will mean casualties on our side, yes, but they will be kept to a minimum, and only in this way can we hope to gain and hold onto the initiative. It is not the first burst of machine-gun fire that earns you the Iron Cross or the Knight's Cross – it is the last. The Führer himself does not know the exact day or hour he will call us out, but that day, that hour will surely come . . .'

A few days after the general's visit, a despatch rider rode up during the afternoon with the alarm order. It did not take 15 Company altogether by surprise because preparations had already given them warning that something like this was coming. In two hours, ammunition, equipment, kit and heavy baggage were loaded. No one knew whether this was the real thing or a practice, so no one dared leave anything behind. Everyone was more or less convinced that they were going into action and the fond farewells and kindly gifts of sandwiches from the locals made it difficult to imagine that they would be coming back this time.

At ten p.m. 15 Company took its place in the endless column of vehicles and drove in the direction of Bullay, Alf and Wittlich. Lights were severely dimmed so the drivers, who were at the wheel all night and had to cope with bad road conditions as well, needed to keep their eyes open. One or two mistook trees or the ditch for the road. Then suddenly, in the darkness, Heinrich saw a sign pointing to Cochem. So it was a practice after all: as morning came up they drove much faster back to Zell and their civilian friends, who gave them a rapturous welcome.

Such incidents helped to kill time during the oppressive calm before the storm; but all the while, hearts and minds were burning for the moment when the order would come to move westward and attack.

At last, sunshine brought the dead countryside back to life. The first spring flowers appeared in the meadows and on the lower slopes of the mountain. With every day that passed, the hour of departure drew nearer; wherever you looked, the symbols of victory were burgeoning.

NINE

Betty was small, a bit giggly, with rosy cheeks and dark hair. Elspeth was tall and angular and Scottish. Marjory was motherly and gentle and timid.

Christine was a natural enemy. She was extremely well turned out with neatly permed hair and carefully applied lipstick. She had a double-barrelled surname and had been presented to the King at Buckingham Palace. She usually appeared to David as if she had either just stepped out of, or was about to step into, the pages of the *Tatler*; and by her expression on the rare occasions when she glanced in his direction, he guessed that she regarded him as something that the cat had brought in.

'So how long will you be staying with us?' she asked a day or two after his arrival.

'I can't say for sure, Christine. Simone says a couple of months. So I guess it's indefinite, right now.'

'Oh really?' she said. 'As long as that! You've really fallen on your feet, haven't you?'

Her remark made him determined not to become a burden on Simone or the household. He had given Simone his ration book and insisted on paying rent – though Simone would only accept a very low one – and whenever possible brought presents of food or things for the house back with him when he returned from his outings to Dover or Maidstone.

Occasionally he went up to London for a couple of days and stayed at his digs in Hampstead. Whenever he was there he made a point of taking a drink in the public bar of Jack Straw's Castle, but all his enquiries after Gwynneth drew a blank.

He embarked on a series of articles for his newspaper back home about the life of ordinary people in wartime England. He sent an article off once a fortnight but never received even an acknowledgement. At least twice a week he spent the morning in Dover and mingled with the other journalists in the lounge bar of the Grand Hotel.

But short of the occasional alarm or excursion, there was surprisingly little hard news to report.

'Go and tour France,' Christine told him one day when he complained again at how little was going on. 'Go and visit the Maginot Line. Find out how much *vin ordinaire* the average *poilu* gets through in a day.'

'Excuse me? The average what?'

'*Poilu*,' Simone said. 'It's the French equivalent of what the British call a Tommy. It means hairy, or shaggy. You see, the French are able to fight with stubble on their chins, David, but the British are unable to take a good aim unless they have smooth cheeks and short hair.'

He got to know the village and some of the local personalities. St Margaret's-at-Cliffe had been practically taken over by the army. In the evenings the Hope Inn and the Carrier's were full of artillerymen from the old gun batteries that were being resurrected on the cliffs. NCOs used the saloon bars, and other ranks the public. Officers went to Dover or Maidstone. David tried both pubs, and it was in the saloon bar of the Hope Inn that he got to know the village's oldest inhabitant, a Major Hime, who had been seven years old in 1856 and could recall seeing the soldiers embarking at Dover to fight the war against Russia in the Crimea.

The queues had to be seen to be believed, and the butcher's queue always seemed to be the longest. They stood for hours, those determined English women with their frost-pinched faces and draggled stockings, and when they finally reached the head of the line they fumbled in their purses for their ration books (they never had the right one ready) and paid some crazy figure like one-and-elevenpence-halfpenny for a little parcel of flesh that was supposed to feed a family of four for a week.

The weather was an unending source of conversation. People in the village – with the exception of Major Hime – said it was the coldest winter they'd ever known, and David believed them. For weeks after the January blizzards, the whole of Kent lay under feet of drifting snow. There were nights when the moon was the colour of burnished copper, a dim disc hanging in the freezing mist. Some nights were so quiet it seemed that every tree and plant and living creature were holding its breath.

David found himself sinking slowly into a sort of frozen inertia. There were occasions when he sat in the boxroom for hours, staring at a blank piece of paper in his typewriter. He began to feel that time was grinding to a halt and he was beginning to go backwards. But at the same time, for some irrational reason he could not fathom, it seemed necessary for him to stay on at Prowse.

Whenever the subject of his possible departure date arose, Simone was always quick to postpone a discussion of it.

'But you're not thinking of leaving me already, are you, David?' she would ask.

'No, but –'

'Well then. Let's cross that bridge when we come to it.'

She made him feel he owed it to her to stay on. She made him feel that she would not be able to manage without him. He chopped firewood, cleaned grates, laid fires, replaced light bulbs and even went shopping in Dover for her. He poured kettles of boiling water over her frozen pipes, polished her car – which was seldom used now because of the fuel shortage and sat gleaming in the garage – and mended everything that needed mending. And on completion of these tasks she would turn to him and say brightly. 'You see? Now how on earth would I have managed that on my own?'

In return, he hoped he would find out more about her and about his roots but in that he was disappointed, for in spite of her promise, Simone would go to great lengths to avoid talking about what he most wanted to hear from her. Though they hit it off quite well, the passage of weeks and months did little to bring them any closer than they had been on that first evening. When they were together, he could not help feeling that she put on an act for him. And because he knew she was not being open with him, it was impossible for him to be entirely open with her.

He wanted to get to know her. He wanted to be able to say anything and everything to her, share her secrets, know the truth about his real father, her husband and the affair he was sure she had been having with Trendle-Home. But the longer he stayed, the more adept Simone became at steering the conversation round such hazards, and after a while, he found himself doing exactly the same thing.

She began mothering him more and more. He had a feeling that she knew she shouldn't do it, but couldn't help herself. It was as if she wanted to turn him into her own son again, personalize him, put her monogram on him like a fashionable garment. She wanted to make up for twenty lost years and bring him up all over again.

'Now David,' she would say, 'where did you learn table manners like that?' Or: 'My dear boy, why in the world must you have your hair cut so short?'

She also seemed to think she could take possession of him by spoiling him. She kept food back so that he could have extra bacon for breakfast or an egg for tea or an extra carrot or potato with his supper. When he protested that he wanted no special treatment, she would scold him: 'You're the only son I've got, David. Can't I spoil you just a little bit?'

Slowly, winter slackened its grip. Snowdrops and crocuses appeared on the lawn and daffodils poked up through the borders of the school drive. David took to spending more time down at Dover, and made longer expeditions into the countryside on his motorbike, sometimes staying away several nights at a time.

One day he came back with the news that he had seen a

Spitfire shoot down a barrage balloon that had broken adrift. 'First bit of shooting I've seen,' he remarked. 'Pathetic!'

Christine was eating an early supper at the kitchen table. 'Why is it pathetic, David?'

'Well . . . the allies haven't exactly taken the offensive these past months, have they? I mean, the army's done nothing but build a few more pillboxes in France, and with all due respect to your friend, all the RAF seems to be doing is flying recce missions or dropping leaflets. Or shooting down their own barrage balloons.'

Christine rose immediately in Nick's defence: 'That is quite unfair, and you know it!'

He laughed. 'You Brits are so damn touchy, aren't you? Come on, Christine! There hasn't been a single air force operation worth reporting –'

'Is that such a bad thing? We aren't fighting this war to provide newspapermen with stories, you know.'

'Strikes me you aren't fighting it at all. Look at the army – sitting out the winter on their backsides waiting to be attacked. It's only the navy that's done any real work.' He turned to Simone. 'Take Captain Wilmot for instance –'

Simone looked round from the stove. 'Griff's not a naval captain, David, surely you know that.'

His mouth opened and shut. Christine sucked her cheeks in to stop a smile. Simone took a pan off the stove and went quickly out of the kitchen.

'Shit!' he muttered, 'I think I just goofed, didn't I?'

Christine was enjoying his discomfiture. 'Yes, David, I think you probably did.'

TEN

There was some doubt now in Britain as to whether this would be a proper war after all. In the newspapers there was a discussion going on about whether horse racing should be allowed to continue. In the cities, parents were beginning to ask if their evacuated children might soon be allowed home. On the first sunny weekend in the seaside resorts, women and children with deck chairs and buckets and spades appeared beside the rolls of barbed wire, while on the radio, 'Run Rabbit Run' was popular on one side of the Channel and 'Boom!' was a hit on the other.

Nor was this optimism entirely groundless. In an interview with a prominent American journalist, General Ironside, Chief of the Imperial General Staff, had deliberately painted a rosy picture of the state of British military capability, and although his comments had been intended as background material for the American newspapers, the interview made front page news in the *Daily Express*. To bolster national morale and stiffen the national will to fight, the Ministry of Information was issuing statements to the effect that, with every passing month, new squadrons of fighters were being added to the RAF, new warships were coming off the slipways and new trenches, pillboxes and machine-gun nests were being added to the defensive line along the Franco-Belgian border.

During the long, hard winter, there had been a number of false alarms. The most important of these came in January, when a German courier aircraft carrying a staff officer of the 7th Airborne Division had lost its way in poor visibility. It had made a forced landing near Mechelen in Belgium and despite Major Reinberger's attempts to burn his papers at the military headquarters where he was taken by the Belgian police, the charred remains were snatched from the stove just in time to reveal plans of an imminent invasion on a broad front from the Moselle to the North Sea, in violation of the Dutch and Belgian neutrality which Hitler had so solemnly promised to respect.

At first the discovery was believed to be a *ruse de guerre*: it was said that Germany wanted to frighten Belgium out of her neutrality and cause her to invite French and British troops onto her soil, so giving Germany a just cause to invade; but this theory was proved wrong when the German air attaché in Belgium was allowed to visit the miserable Reinberger (who shouldn't have been carrying secret documents by air in the first place) and was heard, thanks to a hidden microphone in the cell, to seek urgent confirmation from him that he had managed to destroy the invasion plan.

There were other sources of intelligence which confirmed German intentions of an offensive: Sweden, Portugal, Italy and the Vatican were all leaking information, and one of the German anti-Nazi conspirators, Colonel Hans Oster, was supplying intelligence to the Dutch military attaché in Berlin. But because nothing came of the Mechelen scare, or several others, the rumours of an attack lost credibility and in some quarters began to cause complacency rather than watchfulness; and although contingency plans had been laid for an allied advance into Belgium in the event of an invasion of the Low Countries, the problem of Belgian and Dutch neutrality mesmerized the chiefs of staff and deafened them to warnings of an impending German attack from a quite different quarter.

All that mattered, for the time being, was that the awful winter was over: while the chiefs of staff and the war cabinets discussed secret plans to sow fluvial mines in the Rhine or cut Germany's supply of iron ore from Sweden, and while the troops at the front strengthened their lines with pillboxes disguised as cattle sheds and settled into a routine that was rather less exciting than peacetime manoeuvres on Salisbury Plain, the civilian populations of Britain and France sunned themselves on the promenades and boulevards, reassured by their leaders that they were safe behind the ever-strenghtening line of allied forces, and that if Hitler had intended to attack, he had missed the bus.

But Hitler had not missed the bus: almost within hours of Neville Chamberlain's bland assertion, German troops had broken into Denmark, and German warships were making their way through Norwegian coastal waters with orders to land troops at Narvik as the first move in the campaign to occupy and subdue another innocent nation. As a result, the First Lord of the Admiralty, Winston Churchill, was at last given the go-ahead for his plan to mine the approaches to Narvik and send the navy to oppose German operations.

Suddenly, it seemed that the major emergency, for which everyone had been waiting so long, had arrived.

ii

The Second Cruiser Squadron and fifteen destroyers sailed at action stations from the Scottish naval bases of Rosyth and Port Edgar at 2030 on 7 April.

They moved out under the Forth Bridge and formed up in column. On the bridge of HMS *Vagabond*, the midshipman of the watch peered through a Stuart's distance meter and sang out the range of the next ahead; the navigating officer bent over the dimly lit chart table on the starboard side of the bridge and put neat, pencilled fixes on the chart; the officer-of-the-watch passed wheel and engine orders down the voicepipe to the wheelhouse, while the captain – Archie Trendle-Home – stood upon the scrubbed duckboards and listened while his yeoman of signals read out a signal which had been passed down the line by means of a dimmed box lamp.

'Execute to follow, sir. Speed twenty-five knots. Ships to wheel in succession to starboard to the course oh-seven-five.'

'Thank you, Yeoman. Mid!'

'Sir?'

'Tell the engine room we'll be going up to twenty-five knots shortly.'

'Aye aye, sir!'

'Navigating officer!'

'Sir!'

'Where does oh-seven-five take us?'

Lieutenant Peter Hartley was the only regular officer in Archie's wardroom. In his early twenties, he was immensely keen, an all-round sportsman and a very promising navigator. He manoeuvred a parallel rule across the chart from the compass rose. 'Five and half miles north of May Island, sir.'

Ahead, the signal lantern was flashing again.

'Stand by!' the yeoman called, a pair of binoculars clamped to his eyes. 'Stand by . . . executive signal, sir!'

'Well come on, officer-of-the-watch!' Archie bellowed. 'What are we waiting for?'

'Revolutions two-three-oh!' the officer-of-the watch ordered down the voicepipe, and the voice of the coxswain came back: 'Revolutions two-three-oh. Two-three-oh revolutions passed and repeated, sir!'

One by one, the column of six destroyers altered, each officer-of-the-watch timing his wheel order so that the ship followed exactly in the wake of the next ahead.

When the manoeuvre was complete, Trendle-Home sent for his first lieutenant. Brian Armitage was an RNVR lieutenant who, until six months before, had been selling marine insurance. He had dark, curly hair, hooded eyes and a very pale complexion. Privately, Archie felt that he would make a better shop steward than first lieutenant. He arrived on the bridge after a ten-minute delay. There was tomato ketchup on his upper lip.

'You sent for me, sir?'

'Yes I did. Have you completed your rounds?'

'Yes, sir.'

'Why no report?'

'Sir?'

'Why have I not received your report?'

'There was nothing to report, sir.'

'That's neither here nor there, Number One. I expect a report of rounds from you every night at sea. I thought I made that clear some time ago.'

'Yes, sir, but I thought as we sailed at action stations this evening –'

'*Particularly* as we sailed at action stations.'

'Sir.'

'So – were your rounds correct?'

'Yes, sir.'

'Nothing to report at all?'

'No, sir.'

Archie stifled his impatience. 'I see you have had your supper.'

'Yes, thank you, sir.'

'You appear to have left some of it on your face, Number One.'

Armitage took out a well-used handkerchief and wiped his mouth.

'Right,' Archie said. 'Plan for tonight. We shall be remaining at action stations until further notice. I want you to pass the word round to the whole ship's company. Tell them that we shall be making passage across the North Sea towards northern Norway. A formation of German ships has been contacted moving out of the Skagerrak, and the Home Fleet has sailed from Scapa, so we've got *Rodney*, *Repulse* and *Valiant* to the north of us. With a bit of luck, we may see some action within the next twenty-four hours. Got that?'

'Yes, sir, I've got that,' Armitage said as if he too were containing his temper. 'But it occurs to me –'

Archie turned to the midshipman. 'Range of the next ahead?'

The midshipman, who had been straining his ears to catch the latest clash between the captain and first lieutenant, hurriedly put the *Stuart*'s distance meter to his eye, refocused it, found the lens was wet, dried it with the ball of his thumb and tried again.

'Er — just on two cables, sir.'

Archie took the meter out of his hands and had a look for himself. 'Damn funny two cables. More like two and a quarter. Well come on, officer-of-the-watch! We're astern of station, aren't we! Get the revs on!'

Feeling as if he were playing a one-man band, Archie turned back to find Armitage still at his elbow. 'What are you waiting for, Number One?'

'I hope you don't mind my suggesting it, sir, but as we have quite some distance to go before we reach Norwegian waters, wouldn't it make a great deal more sense to go into two watches and stand half the men down?'

In all his time in the service, Archie had never encountered an officer who irritated him as much as Armitage. 'Look, First Lieutenant — just for once — don't argue, there's a good bloke. Just do it, will you? Right?'

'Right, sir.'

'And Number One —'

'Sir?'

'Tell me, have you ever heard of the expression "aye aye, sir"?'

'Yes of course I have —'

'Well, I'd be most obliged if you'd use it to acknowledge an order. Right?'

'Right, sir,' said Armitage pointedly and, turning away, summoned the bosun's mate and began briefing him to pass the captain's message round the ship.

This was not at all what Archie had intended.

'What are you up to now, First Lieutenant? I particularly said I wanted *you* to pass the word round, didn't I? So why are you using the bosun's mate for heaven's sake?'

'Sir, I didn't think I was required to pass the word in person —'

'If I'd wanted the bosun's mate to do it I'd have told him myself.'

'In that case I stand corrected, sir.'

'You do indeed, Number One. Now kindly get on with the job.'

'Aye aye, sir,' Armitage replied sulkily, and left the bridge muttering to himself about being used by the captain as a bloody errand boy.

Archie turned back to face for'd over the dodgers. It really was extremely bad luck to get a man like Armitage for a first lieutenant. Although few captains and first lieutenants became the best of friends, in most ships the relationship was at least a tolerably easy one. It was also a widely accepted fact that one or the other had to be a disciplinarian if the ship was to be efficiently run, but Archie had never cast himself in that role. As far as he was concerned, it was the first lieutenant's job to run a taut ship and the captain's to lead and inspire the officers and men. With a first lieutenant who acted more like a trade union leader than a second in command that was impossible, and he had repeatedly found himself having to play the role of what the navy terms a 'bastard' in order to bring the ship to an acceptable level of efficiency.

But that was the war for you. With Armitage as first lieutenant and a bunch of reservists in the wardroom, you could hardly expect anything else.

He ducked as the ship buried her bows into a wave and a heavy shower of spray whipped back over the bridge. At the higher speed, the ship was plunging heavily and the wind was screaming in the lattice mast abaft the bridge. He could just make out the shape of the next ahead and could see the billow of black smoke trailing out over her port side.

'Sir?'

He turned. His steward had brought him a mug of cocoa.

'Thank you, Norman. I hope my cabin's properly secured for sea?'

'I've put your cricket cups at the bottom of the wardrobe, sir, and your gramophone's lashed down.'

'Very glad to hear it.'

He sipped his cocoa, and the ship lurched on through the

night. The guns' crews settled themselves in the lee of their guns, out of the wind; the seaboat's crew leant up against the for'd funnel to warm their backs; in the boiler rooms stokers crawled through the labyrinth of asbestos-lagged pipes to take readings of steam pressures and temperatures, and in the engine room the artificers stared up at the revolution indicators, turning the big steam control handwheels from time to time to ensure that the propellers rotated at exactly the revolutions per minute ordered from the bridge; and in every man's mind, from the captain down to the most junior rating, one thought was uppermost: perhaps tonight, or tomorrow, we shall find the enemy and fight with him.

iii

Down in the servants' basement of the Hotel de l'Univers in Arras, Private Albert Hall was not thinking about fighting. He was sitting at a long deal table rubbing tiny amounts of spit and polish into the leather of his officer's boots.

Captain Wilmot's new boots – handmade by Craig & Davies – had arrived from England only a week before, and he had been most particular about the way he wanted them polished. 'I don't want any of your hot spoon nonsense, Hall, d'you understand?' he had said. 'Spit and rub, that's the only way. Same goes for my Sam Browne. I may be meeting Lord Gort tomorrow, and Lord Gort has an eye for these things. He knows when an officer has a good batman or not.'

Hall breathed on the toe of his master's left boot for the last time and passed a yellow duster lovingly over it. Then he held the boot up and turned it this way and that to make quite sure that perfection had been achieved.

Satisfied with his work, he gave Captain Wilmot's tunic buttons a final rub before putting it and the Sam Browne over his arm and, picking up the boots carefully to avoid bumping them together, he made his way up four flights of stairs to his officer's room.

He knocked and entered, and found Wilmot sitting on the bed clipping his nails with a patent clipper.

Griff was in a state of mild apprehension. The previous day he had been out on the firing range with his Waterways Defence Section, familiarizing his men (and himself) with the Boys anti-tank rifle which he had managed to procure, when he had received orders to report forthwith to the General Headquarters in Arras, where his presence was required to assist at a briefing of the allied field commanders. Leaving his second in command, Second Lieutenant Radcliffe, in charge, he had ordered Hall to pack his best service dress uniform at the rush and they had driven the fifteen miles to Arras in the half-tonner.

He had been met in the lobby of the Hotel de l'Univers by an absurdly young-looking major on the staff of Lieutenant General Pownall, Chief of General Staff to Lord Gort.

'Ah – you must be Wilmot,' he had said after returning Griff's salute. 'I've got news for you. Giles is down with pleurisy.'

'Giles? You mean Major Giles?'

'That's right. He asked for you to assist him with the briefing, but I visited him first thing this morning and he's a lot worse and certainly in no fit state to stand up and talk to the poo-bahs. So it looks as though you'll be doing it on your own. Think you can manage that?'

'I don't see why not. Providing I can have a look at his brief.'

Major Peebles laughed gently. 'He hasn't prepared one, old boy. That's why he wanted you to assist him.'

Having set Hall to work on his uniform, Wilmot had gone along to GHQ and had worked into the small hours preparing a ten-minute review of canal defences, including a summary of key defensive points and bridges in Belgium and Flanders that, in his opinion, would require the presence of sapper units in the event of invasion. Commandeering the assistance of a young second lieutenant intelligence officer by the name of Clarke from 4th Division Royal Engineers, he highlighted the inland waterways on the wall map in the briefing room and drew up a table to show equipment available and equipment required at each key point.

The result of his preparations was a lecture that he knew would be at least disconcerting to his audience and might, if he achieved his aim, shake them out of their complacency.

'When will you be needing the truck, sir?' Hall asked when he had laid the tunic and Sam Browne over the back of a chair and Wilmot had nodded approvingly at the shine on his boots.

'We'll pack up and go as soon as the briefing's over, Hall. About midday, I should say.'

'So we are going back, definite, sir?'

Wilmot frowned. 'Of course. Why shouldn't we?'

Hall looked uncomfortable. 'Well sir – I did hear a buzz you might be staying on at GHQ, sir.'

'Oh yes, and where did you hear that?'

'One of the staff batmen, sir. He was saying as how you was acting as stand-in for an officer who's being sent back to Blighty, sir. He said the major wasn't likely to come back in a 'urry, and that you'd be getting his job permanent, sir.'

'I see,' said Wilmot, putting his nail clippers away in a leather pouch. 'Well, it sounds to me as if you're better informed than I am, Hall, because as far as I'm concerned we shall be back with the unit this afternoon.'

Hall beamed with relief. 'Very glad to hear that, sir.'

Wilmot put on a shirt and knotted his tie. Hall held his tunic for him. It carried the 1914–18 general service and victory medal ribbons – known as Mutt and Jeff to the recipients – and the former bore an oakleaf to indicate that Wilmot had been mentioned in despatches for his services at Ypres in 1917.

'I don't know why you're so anxious to get back to Douai, Hall. I'd have thought you rather enjoyed this little jaunt.'

'Well, sir, fact of the matter is, sir, I – I've become what you might call attached, sir.'

Wilmot stopped buttoning his tunic and looked back at his driver. 'Not *again*?'

Albert Hall's ears went pink. 'Very special, this one, sir.'

'But they all are!' Wilmot shook his head. 'This is no time to be getting involved with the locals, you know that.'

'I was – I was bowled over, sir,' Hall said solemnly.

Wilmot buckled his Sam Browne and stood while his servant used a bone-handled clothes brush to remove a speck of fluff from his shoulders. 'You haven't gone and popped the question, I hope?'

'As a matter of fact, I 'ave, sir.'

'Well, I can't forbid you to get yourself tied up to a local, but I can't say I'd recommend it, either. If I were you I'd wait until the war's over and you're back home before you start contemplating matrimony, right?'

With that, Griff Wilmot put on his cap, collected a canvas map case from the dresser and went off down the stairs and out into the April sunshine, striding along through Arras in his best uniform and new boots, so that passers-by glanced at him and wondered why such a distinguished-looking officer should only be wearing captain's pips.

iv

The conference was held at the C-in-C's general headquarters and had been convened for the purpose of coordinating the efforts of corps and division commanders of the 1st Army Group, which included the British Expeditionary Force. Wilmot's briefing was one of several intended to rationalize some of the conflicts of interest between French and British forces. When he arrived, the curtains were being drawn back to reveal the wall map of allied dispositions. As he was early he took the opportunity to study it once again.

The bulk of the allied armies – the forty-eight French divisions of the 2nd and 3rd Army Groups – were concentrated along the Maginot Line from the Swiss border at Basle to the end of the fortifications near Longuyon. That area was not of great concern to him: intelligence reports indicated that the German high command had chosen to oppose it with a mere nineteen divisions, so if an attack was coming from anywhere it seemed unlikely to Griff that it would come from that sector.

To the north-west of Longuyon, however, the allied troops were more thinly spread, with just twenty-two divisions of General Blanchard's 1st Army strung out along the Belgian border over a one-hundred-mile front as far as Maulde. The rest of the line was only marginally better concentrated: the nine divisions of the BEF occupied a forty-mile sector that looped northward from Maulde round Lille and Armentières to Bailleul, and the French 7th Army under Giraud guarded the last thirty or so miles to a point on the coast a few miles east of Dunkirk.

Wilmot looked at these dispositions and pondered their effectiveness. Eighty-seven divisions. It sounded a lot, but when one looked at the intelligence assessments of German strength that had been posted up on the map and examined the quality and quantity of weapons and munitions available to each side, the picture altered considerably: between them, the three army groups of Leeb, Rundstedt and Bock numbered ninety-four divisions, of which ten were armoured and six were motorized – and nearly all, unlike the allied defenders, were well equipped with modern weapons and radio communications. This force held the added advantage of being able to choose where and when to attack, and the bulk of it was positioned facing into Luxembourg, Belgium and Holland, whose armies mustered no more than twenty-six divisions between them and who had decided that a strict neutrality and faith in Hitler's promises were their best insurance against invasion.

'Ah, good man,' Major Peebles said at his elbow. 'Got your brief sorted out? You'll be on fourth, after Major Gatscombe's intelligence assessment. There's a billiard cue by the map, please leave it there when you finish. I'll give you the nod when to start.'

The brass hats began to arrive. Among the first were the three corps commanders of the BEF together with their division commanders and senior staff. Wilmot recognized one or two faces: the pinched, weasel features of Bernard Montgomery, already known to be a rising star in the British army; the tall, bespectacled Alan Brooke, in command of 2nd Corps; Generals Adam and Barker, to whom Wilmot had been briefly introduced the previous evening. They nodded good morning to their staff and leant over the backs of their chairs to talk to each other.

It's just another conference, he told himself. No need to be nervous about it. Just say what you have to and shut up.

The French were arriving now, and the hall filled with the scent of their hair oil, cigar smoke and Gauloise cigarettes. The noise of chatter rose perceptibly and was eventually brought to silence when the adjutant general barked, 'Gentlemen!' and Lord Gort, accompanied by his chief of staff and four French generals, filed in from the rear of the hall.

Wilmot recognized one of the French generals immediately, having met him socially twenty-two years before while serving as an aide-de-camp at Versailles. A large, rather flaccid man with a moustache and a shuffling way of walking that made him look flat-footed, he was the commander of the French 1st Army Group, General Billotte. He was also Simone's uncle.

v

With Generals Prioux and Giraud on his left and Billotte and Blanchard on his right, Lord Gort opened the proceedings by welcoming the French guests and announcing that, out of deference to the senior ally, the meeting would be conducted as far as possible in French. After a short reminder about the importance of security, he handed the meeting over to Major Peebles, who introduced the first speaker.

The briefings that followed covered lines of communication, anti-aircraft defences, anti-tank defences, problems of resupply, and priorities for air support. The conference broke for coffee; the intelligence briefing proceeded, and suddenly Major Peebles was saying, 'Now, in the absence of Major Giles, who is unfortunately ill, Captain Wilmot will give a short presentation on the specialized subject of inland water defences . . . Captain Wilmot.'

He walked up the three steps to the stage with his heart hammering, but almost as soon as the billiard cue was in his hand and he had spoken the first words of his carefully prepared talk, the words flowed and he found it almost as easy to lecture these staring red-tabs as it had been to teach 2b about the Norman Conquest.

Speaking quietly but persuasively in fluent French, he drew the generals' attention to the major defensive waterways across Belgium and Northern France – the Albert Canal, the Dyle, the Meuse, the Senne, the Dendre, the Scheldt, the Lys, the Yser, the Oise, the Somme and the Aa. Using actual examples of key positions which he had inspected personally, he listed what he considered to be the minimum defences required and compared these with what was actually in position. He described what might be done if Belgian cooperation could be achieved, and how coordinated cratering of roads, mining, flooding and blowing of bridges could be used to hold up the most determined advance. He showed how a company of trained sappers with the right equipment and weapons could be of better use than a battalion of inexperienced conscripts. And as he spoke, he became convinced that his listeners were giving him far closer attention than they had given the majors and lieutenant colonels who had preceded him. For a few minutes he felt that he was at last beginning to find his true potential: that this talk of his might actually influence the high command's thinking and make the difference between defeat and victory.

Convinced that he had their attention, he decided to take a risk and add an unprepared contribution of his own.

Suddenly the adrenalin flowed again: he felt his heartbeat quicken and his throat tighten.

'Finally, gentleman, permit me to make a brief comment upon the merits of Plan D. Over the past six months, the British Expeditionary Force has grown to an army of some quarter of a million front-line troops with a further one hundred and fifty thousand base and LOC troops in the rear areas. Hundreds of miles of railway lines, dozens of airfields and hundreds of pillboxes have been constructed. Huge stores of supplies and munitions have been shipped from Great Britain. And yet, under Plan D, we are committed to leave the defences we have worked so hard to establish and advance over a hundred kilometres through country which has not been reconnoitred and which, in the event of a German attack, would almost certainly be blocked by fleeing refugees. Speaking as a student of military history, this strikes me as the height of unwisdom.'

Then it was over: he was snapping to attention and Major Peebles was inviting questions. He braced himself to deal with them, hoping that perhaps Brooke or Montgomery might test him on his knowledge or invite him to expand on his opposition to Plan D. But no questions came, and when he was dismissed with a nod by Major Peebles he forgot to surrender the billiard cue and had to be called back to hand it up to the next briefing officer.

The last presentation consisted of a review of logistical plans to support an advance to the Dyle under the provisions of Plan D, and it was followed by a lengthy discussion. Listening to the French generals defending the plan that their chief, General Gamelin, had insisted upon, Wilmot was seized by a sense of intense frustration and impatience. Couldn't they see that they were in a fool's paradise? Hadn't they listened to a word he had said about the need for contingency plans to send units of trained sappers to destroy bridges, flood fields and mine crossroads in the event of a German advance into Belgium?

Billotte was speaking. He was holding the damp stub of

a cigar between thumb and forefinger, pausing now and then to place it between his lips and blow a little cloud of smoke into the already smoky room. 'The geography of France does not change, gentlemen,' he was saying, 'and because it is unchanged the enemy's strategic philosophy must necessarily remain the same. What this means is that we can expect the Boche attack to take place in the form of a wide and powerful movement through Belgium in order to establish the North Sea on their right flank, in a similar form, though on a larger scale, to the Schlieffen Plan of 1914. It is also possible that, at the same time, the enemy will attempt a strike from the north behind the Maginot Line, combined with an attack through the Saar. But, as we know, the German army now relies heavily upon armoured formations to achieve the first break-through, and this factor is curiously to our advantage, for we may be confident that the deep valleys and wooded heights of the Ardennes will rule out the possibility of a major attack from that sector. So we must not make the same mistake as Joffre made in 1914: we must beware of remaining within our fortresses or concentrating our forces too far back, and must be ready to spring forward to the Dyle the moment Hitler's armies set foot upon Belgian territory . . .'

After a while, Wilmot ceased to listen. All Billotte was doing was restating Gamelin's pet strategy, the strategy he had developed a year before and had clung to like a religious dogma. It was as if the French general staff had made up its mind what form the coming invasion would take and exactly how they would defeat it. 'Don't confuse us with details,' they seemed to be saying. 'This is how the enemy will attack. Our mind is made up.'

It was a relief when the conference came to an end. Wilmot waited with the junior staff while the brass hats withdrew for one of their sumptuous lunches, and was just about to leave when Peebles buttonholed him.

'Don't go,' he was told. 'Viscount Bridgeman would like a word.'

He waited for ten minutes while Lieutenant Colonel Bridgeman conferred with his French opposite numbers and then Peebles beckoned him over.

Bridgeman shook him by the hand. 'That was an excellent brief, Wilmot. The CGS was favourably impressed.'

'Sir.'

'I understand you're running the new SWD unit.'

'Yes, sir.'

Bridgeman looked at him. 'Does that please you?'

'It would please me a great deal more if I had the equipment I need to do the job, sir. I'm very short of transport and my allocation of landmines and anti-tank weapons is quite inadequate. As I hope I made clear in my briefing, an enormous amount more could be done if –'

'Yes, I appreciate the problems, Wilmot. Unfortunately we have to make the best of what we've got, that goes for the whole of the BEF. It may also be some small consolation to you that General Brooke is in agreement with the spirit of your criticisms of Plan D. But while we're in France we have to knuckle under and do things the French way. You're not the only one who feels frustrated, you know.'

Wilmot allowed himself a smile. 'Understood, sir.'

'Now – a proposition for you. The MO here tells me that Major Giles is unlikely to return to the staff for some time, if at all. How would you like his job?'

Griff remembered his conversation with Hall earlier that day. There had been a saying in the Lancers that a good servant was always better informed than his officer. Hall had certainly lived up to that.

Bridgeman saw him hesitate. 'Think it over,' he said. 'Give me your answer within twenty-four hours.'

'I don't think that will be necessary,' Wilmot heard himself say. 'If you don't mind, sir, I'd prefer to stay with my unit.'

'I don't think you understand,' Bridgeman said. 'You're being offered a staff job. You can put your crown up this evening if you accept and confirmation in the rank will be a mere formality – providing you don't go telling the French General Staff their plans are up the creek too often.'

'That's why I can't accept, sir,' Wilmot said. 'I'm sorry.'

Peebles looked at him in dismay. Bridgeman shook his head and shrugged. 'Well, it's your decision, old boy. I'd never force an officer onto the staff against his will, and there are plenty of others who'll be only too keen to accept the post. You're quite sure you don't want to change your mind?'

'Quite sure, sir.'

'Right – well. I wish you the best of good fortune, Wilmot. And thank you again for a first-class brief.'

Wilmot saluted and took his leave. Peebles accompanied him to the entrance, where an armed sentry sloped arms and gave a butt salute. 'You must be mad,' he said quietly. 'Stark, staring mad.'

'Maybe I am,' Wilmot said cheerfully. 'Just as well though. After all, CGS wouldn't want a raving lunatic on his staff, would he, Major?'

vi

All the way back to Douai, he wondered whether he had been a fool to turn the post down. While the truck jogged along the straight *pavé* road with poplars on either side, he tried to understand what it was inside him that had held him back – this and so many times before – from grasping success and making it his own. Why was it that he preferred the command of a handful of soldiers to a post on the staff? Was it something to do – even now – with what had happened back in 1917? Was he still trying to ease his conscience over accepting that liaison post in Paris? Did he still feel guilty about the death of so many of his comrades?

He smiled bitterly to himself. Perhaps he should have put ambition first more often. Perhaps he should have passed by on the other side that spring morning in Paris and left Billotte's niece to weep by herself. Perhaps he should have stayed in the army, transferred to a less expensive regiment and thrown himself wholeheartedly into his career. If he had done that he would have had his own battalion by now. Perhaps a regiment.

And now he'd done it all over again. A plum job, an unrepeatable opportunity turned down. Why? In the name of common sense, why?

The lorry had turned off the main road and was bumping along towards Gouy, a dirty little village with a drainage system hardly adequate for the forty sappers billeted there.

When the enlarged Special Waterways Defence Section had arrived in the new year the men had had to be accommodated in barns, stables and the unfurnished rooms of an empty house. The section headquarters had been set up in the reception rooms of the local farmhouse, and the stables and farmyard had been turned into the men's kitchen and mess hall.

Wilmot had found a reasonably comfortable billet for himself in the largest house in the village, and Driver Hall slept in the attic above his room. With the coming of spring, living conditions had improved considerably and the unit had settled into a steady routine, the typewriter clacking out reports and returns in the office every morning, the men working from eight to four-thirty every day and the amount of paperwork engendered by promotions, marriage allowances, trade gradings and the censoring of the men's letters always increasing.

But life was not unpleasant. Though Douai, four miles away, was dead in the evenings, practically everyone in the BEF made improper use of army transport at some time or other, and in this way the drivers, mail orderlies and stores parties were able to make friends with the locals in the cafés and *estaminets* on the road to Arras, and the officers went to Lille, which, although officially out of bounds, was full every night of the sex-starved officers of the British army.

As the lorry entered the farmyard, a girl in an apron came

to the back door. It was Driver Hall's intended, and the way she looked lovingly at him left Hall in no doubt as to her answer.

Beyond the farm buildings, smoke was rising from the new cookhouse which the company had built as an extension to the stables and whose outer eight feet doubled as a concealed pillbox commanding the canal.

They parked at the end of a track by the section headquarters. Freddy Radcliffe, second in command and recently promoted to lieutenant, came up and saluted. 'Good to see you back, sir!'

'Thank you, Freddy. Who won the soccer?'

Radcliffe beamed. 'Two platoon, sir. Three-one.'

'Anything else been happening?'

'Not here, sir. Norway seems to be hotting up, though.'

'Oh?'

'Some sort of naval action, I gather. I've put your mail in your room.'

He left Hall to park the lorry and unload the office stationery that had been collected in Arras and went into the kitchen to talk with Sappers Ward and Smith, the kitchen orderlies.

Ward eyed his commanding officer's gleaming boots and best uniform. 'Did you sort 'em out up at GHQ, sir? Did you get 'em organized?'

Wilmot smiled. The greatest change in the army he had noticed since joining up again – apart from the new, baggy battle dress that had recently been issued to officers and men – was the chummy attitude of these young soldiers towards their officers.

'Wish I had, Ward.'

'We weren't expecting to see you back,' continued the irrepressible Welshman. 'We reckoned you'd have red tabs by now, isn't that right, Smudge?'

'They did try to talk me into taking a staff job, Ward, but I decided I'd be more use back here with you lot than pushing bumph at GHQ.'

Ward took that as a joke and laughed loudly. 'Very glad to hear that, sir!'

He left them stirring the split pea soup and walked across the field to his quarters. There were larks singing overhead, and lambs in the field on the other side of the canal. In the distance, a barge chugged on through the afternoon.

He entered the house and went up to his room, whose window overlooked the canal. He took off his Sam Browne and sat down at the folding table to read his letters. Among them was one from Simone, but he didn't want to open it. He sat thinking of her for a while, then put the letters to one side and reached for his leather-bound pocket edition of Donne's poetry, turning to the Litany which had provided him with solace so often in the past:

> . . . My heart is by dejection, clay,
> And by self-murder, red.
> From this red earth, O Father, purge away
> All vicious tinctures . . .

He felt suddenly weary. He still loved Simone, that was the trouble, and in spite of all that had happened, Archie was still his closest friend. It was that very love, that very friendship which made this lingering suspicion of them detestable, so that if their secret liaison caused him to hate anyone, it was himself.

He didn't want to read Simone's letter because he knew it would be full of more news about her son and would leave unsaid what ought to be said and reawaken all the outrage in him. He wished he had never seen her and Archie together that morning at Eggardon, or at least that he had had the courage to confront them then and there. He wished that he could somehow have held onto Simone's love and Archie's devil-take-it companionship, and that all three of them could be back on the old, honest terms they had known before.

He wished . . . he wished that the clock could be put back twenty years, and they could all start again.

ELEVEN

Simone and her lodgers had their evening meal in the kitchen because it was the warmest place in the house and Simone was economizing on coal. Usually there were four of them at the table, two of the girls being on watch at Dover at any one time. The easiest evenings were when Elspeth and Betty were in for supper and Christine and Marjory were on watch. With Elspeth and Betty, conversation flowed easily and hackles were seldom raised, but when Christine was present the conversation tended to be forced and sometimes hostile.

Simone went to great lengths to keep the atmosphere amicable. It wasn't at all easy: Christine could be very touchy, and an ill-considered remark could bring a scathing retort from her that froze the atmosphere and left all four of them looking studiously at their soup plates.

'I wish you would contribute a bit more at supper, David,' Simone said when he had been staying a few weeks. 'Last night Marjory and I did all the work, while you and Christine just sat like dumplings.'

David took the hint. From then on, he tried to have a harmless anecdote ready to fill the awkward gaps in the table talk. But Simone's fear of silence was not lost on him, and sometimes he was tempted, at the end of a long silence, to turn to her and say, 'By the way who *was* my real father?' Or: 'Is it true that you were two-timing your husband before Archie went off to sea?'

But he resisted such temptations and stuck to recounting what he'd heard down at the Grand at lunchtime or the Hope Inn in the evenings.

'That old Major Hime, he's a real character,' he remarked one evening at the end of April. 'You know what he was saying last night? He reckons that the longbow the English used against the French at Agincourt was a better weapon than the musket they used at Waterloo.'

'I wouldn't pay much attention to that old fool,' Simone said. 'He was a Mosleyite until they locked up all the British Fascists last September. Then he changed his tune, of course. I believe he was president of some committee at that headquarters they had at Tilmanstone at one time. The only reason he wasn't interned was because of his age.'

'Is that right? Well, that makes a lot of sense, because he wasn't being very complimentary about the French last night.'

Betty looked up. 'What was he saying about them?'

'Oh – that they were a lot of Commies and that when the Germans decide to open a second front they'll make short work of them.' David laughed. 'It was the usual sort of bar talk. He even said that Britain's traditional enemy wasn't Germany but France. I said that as far as I could see every country in Europe seemed to have been someone's traditional enemy at some time or other and it all depended how far back you cared to go.'

'It's a pity Griff isn't here,' Simone said. 'He could talk to you for hours about the history of Europe.'

Elspeth and Betty excused themselves to go up for an early night. Simone and David remained at the table.

'Captain Wilmot taught history, didn't he?' David asked.

'Yes, he became head of history here at Prowse. He's an expert on the Norman Conquest, you know. Did I tell you that?'

'No, you didn't,' David said. 'Fact is, you haven't told me much about him at all, Simone.'

She smiled. 'Well. There isn't a great deal to tell.'

There was a silence. Not for the first time, David sensed that she was terrified of talking about Wilmot. 'You were married in the church here at St Margaret's, isn't that right?'

She looked up. 'How did you know that?'

'It's in the parish records. February the seventh wasn't it? Month or so after I was born.'

She nodded, and began to collect the plates. 'Well. This won't get the work done –'

But David put his hand on her arm. 'Tell me about him, Simone,' he said quietly. 'Tell me about everything. Like you said you would.'

She sat down again and looked unhappily across the table. 'It frightens me, David.'

'What frightens you?'

'The past. I'm afraid of what you might think of me.'

'There's no need.'

'Isn't there? How can you be so sure of that?'

He shook his head. 'You want to be perfect for me, isn't that it? You want to be the perfect mother for me just like I want to be the perfect son for you. But we're neither of us perfect, Simone, and I think we should stop trying to be. I don't expect you to be perfect. Fact – I don't *want* you to be. I just want – I just want to know who you are. Who I am. What happened. And why . . .'

She had known for some while that she needed to tell him the whole story, but the time had not seemed right until now. She needed to tell it because she had never told it before, carrying the whole weight of it with her down the years. Not even Griff or Archie knew the whole truth, nor had she ever confessed it to a priest, having turned her back on the Catholic faith after her mother's death.

She reached across the table and gripped his hand. 'All right, David. I shall tell you.'

ii

'I was born in May, 1901,' she began, 'so when the war came I was thirteen. My father owned a tannery, and the war made him rich very quickly. We lived in a big house on the west side of Paris near a park called the Bois de Boulogne. I was the baby of the family. Jean-Paul was the eldest and he was killed right at the beginning in that terrible September of 1914. Christophe was next and he was killed in 1916 at Verdun. All my friends at the lycée had brothers or cousins or fathers fighting, and all of them had dear ones that were killed. But I was the very first in the school to go into mourning, and it was as if the sacrifice of Jean-Paul brought my childhood to an end because he was my eldest brother and I adored him.

'I went to a school for army officers' daughters because although my father was not in the army my uncle Gaston was and ours was a well-known military family. When my brother was killed I remember being called out in front of the whole school by the head teacher, Mademoiselle Hardy. She turned me to face the school – I had my hair very long in those days and it fell in ringlets to my waist – and she told them that Simone Billotte's brother had made the greatest sacrifice of all because he had died for France. She said that already I was being brave and that my bravery must be an example to them in the months to come, because it was likely that they would have to be brave one day, too.

'For a few weeks, I enjoyed a strange fame in the school. It was as if I had some personal experience of the war that others had not. As if I were in some way involved in the war. Almost as if I were a soldier. And I liked that feeling, David because – because it made me feel important. My father was making a great deal of money selling boots and leather coats for soldiers to wear in the trenches and my elder brother had done credit to the family name by being one of the first to fall on the field of battle. I was thirteen, and already I was a little famous.

'Well. That did not last very long. Very quickly, there were other tragedies, and after a while Mademoiselle Hardy stopped announcing the deaths of near relatives to the school and instead, when a girl lost a relative, she would simply arrive at school with a black band on her sleeve. At first we would ask who it was. "My father," would come the reply. Or "my uncle" or "my brother". Later, when so many of us were wearing black bands – and some of us two or three narrower ones to show that we were in mourning several times over – we didn't even bother to ask. In those days death was a terrible creeping tide that was always at your heels, however fast you hurried over the sands. If you wanted to keep your sanity you had to ignore it. But my mother wasn't able to do that, and when Christophe was killed she died soon after of a broken heart – though the doctors said it was pneumonia.

'My elder sister Hélène had already married by now, and had moved away. My father was making thousands and thousands of francs every day, and I used to look at the smart boots the new recruits wore when they marched off to the front, and I would do sums in my head to find out how much money my father made from each boy who was killed and each new recruit who had to be given another pair of boots to take his place.

'Well. We had a big house and so many cooks and servants and gardeners and housemaids that I never had to lift a finger. My father was at his office all day and he spent a lot of evenings out as well. I was sixteen, David, and in three years I had lost my mother and two brothers. School seemed a waste of time to me, and as my father didn't mind one way or another what I did, I stopped going.

'So . . . I had to entertain myself. My father gave me a generous allowance, and I took to going into the city. I was growing into a woman, David, so please don't judge me too harshly. I put my hair up. I used to sit and drink chocolate outside the cafés along the boulevards that summer of 1917. And, of course, Paris was full of soldiers in those days. Soldiers coming back for a few days' leave, soldiers going off to the front, soldiers who had been wounded and were convalescing . . .

'At first it was innocent. Quite innocent. They would sit in a big circle with me and we would talk and laugh and I learnt how to blow cigarette smoke out of my nose and there seemed nothing wrong at all in what I was doing. I could make them laugh, you see. I could make them forget the war. It seemed to me a very good thing to do. I felt that – that I was doing the best possible thing, can you understand that?

'And something else. You see, David, I needed to – to make up for something. I knew that many of them would be killed. And I knew that each one that was killed would make more money for my father. And it was my father's money I was spending on them, when I bought them drinks and suppers. I wanted to repay them just a little of the profit that my father would make out of them. No, I don't think I thought that in so many words, but I have thought about it so much over the years, and that is the conclusion I have come to. It's my excuse, if you like, for what happened later.'

Simone looked guiltily across the table at David. 'Perhaps I have said enough already. Perhaps you don't want to hear any more?'

'Only tell what you need to tell,' he said.

She nodded. 'Well. Let me keep it as short as possible. But also let me be honest with you. I became . . .' She sighed and laughed at the same time. 'I suppose I could wrap it up in tissue paper and say I was a "good-time girl". No. I think that if you are to know the truth you may as well know the whole truth. So I shall call the shovel a spade. I became a prostitute, David. Not a streetwalker, and not a whore either. But a prostitute. There is a difference, did you know that? Some prostitutes are not whores. I didn't think at the time that I was a prostitute, but in fact that is what I was. So now you know. Do you still want me to go on? Silly question. Every man likes to hear about prostitutes, isn't that so? You want to know how I started, how I could lower myself. What was a lovely girl like me doing in a place like that? That was what they always wanted to know.

'Well, I started my apprenticeship a few weeks before the Christmas of '17. One day the landlord of one of the bars I used to go to took me into his back room and told me that if I stopped going to the place across the road and went only

153

to his, he would give me free drinks and the use of a bedroom upstairs during the day. And you know something? I did not even know why I should have need of a bedroom. Well, I learnt soon enough . . .'

She covered her face with her hands and was silent for a long time. 'I don't think I should be telling you this after all,' she whispered. 'I think perhaps I'm making a terrible mistake.'

He took her hands in his. Ever since leaving the States there had lurked at the back of his mind the thought that his mother might have been 'loose' or that he had been conceived 'by accident'. But even so, to have confirmation of his worst fears from her own lips had come like an unexpected blow in the stomach that left him winded.

'So – do you know who my father was?' he asked eventually.

She shook her head, busy with a handkerchief. 'No. I don't know.'

He gazed at her without realizing he was doing it.

'David – please don't look at me like that, with blame in your eyes!'

'It's not blame, I'm not blaming you.'

'All I can say about your father,' she said very quietly, 'was that he was young, that I – I liked him and that later, almost certainly, he was killed.'

'But I don't understand. I mean – how can you know even as much as that?'

'Well, first, I only – I could only bring myself to –' She faced him directly. 'I could choose which boys to go with, David, you understand that? There were so many, I could take my pick. So I only picked the ones I liked and they were the ones –'

'Yes?'

'Listen. There were women in Paris at that time who said they could tell whether a man was going to be killed or not. I didn't believe it when I first heard it, but I found myself looking at the men and wondering if it was possible to tell after all. And I discovered, after a while, that – that it was possible. That whenever I was attracted to a boy, later he would be killed or listed missing. It was always the same. I was very seldom wrong. In fact wrong only once, as far as I know.'

'Who was that?'

She smiled and shrugged. 'Can't you guess? Captain Wilmot, of course.'

'So you thought he –'

'Yes, I thought he was on the list. I had been right every time before. I was sure that I could tell. You can say anything you like about superstition but you won't change my mind. I really could tell. One look at a young *poilu*, and I could tell if he was going to be killed. They had a sort of . . . no, I can't even begin to explain what it was. It was like a – a halo round their heads. Not the sort I could see with my eyes so much as sense here – somewhere inside my head. Of course, some of the boys I knew came back and I used to ask them what happened to so-and-so, and always their answers proved that I had been correct. Don't misunderstand me, I didn't enjoy being able to do it, and I never told a soul about it. I was terrified of what I could do. Really terrified . . .

'And something else I must tell you, something else I never told anyone before. I was expected to earn money from those poor boys – five francs for half an hour, I think it was. I was supposed to hand it all over to the landlord to pay for the bedroom, he said. But I never asked for money. I wasn't doing it for money, you see? I was doing it . . . I was doing it because I knew it was the only thing I could do. For the war – for France too, if you like. I was giving something back, something that I believed my father had stolen. And I was giving those poor doomed boys something to take with them into the trenches that was good and gentle, something they could look back on not with shame but with love and happiness. And so, if a boy I liked couldn't pay, I used to pay the landlord out of my allowance. Yes I did!

And with a clear conscience, David, because by now I had come to hate my father and that stinking tanning factory that made him richer with every passing month of slaughter. It was a sweet, secret revenge on him. Until he found out what I was doing.'

'He chucked you out?'

'Of course. On the spot. One moment he was the doting father who thought he could buy my love with money and presents, and the next – he was calling me a whore and chucking me out, as you call it. Into the street where I belonged, of course. That is what all good fathers are supposed to say on such occasions, David. "You are no longer my daughter." That's what he said. "You are finished. I disown you and disinherit you."'

'What did you do?'

'Walked round Paris all evening. Slept under a bridge. And in the morning went and sat on a park bench until a handsome English officer came and took pity on me.'

'You mean Captain Wilmot?'

'Yes. I'd seen him before and I think he had seen me, but we had never spoken. I'd always avoided officers. It always seemed to me that officers shared some of the blame. But Griff – Griff was somehow different from other officers. He too felt guilty and – and angry about so much killing. He said there were other officers in the British army who felt the same. Some were handing back their medals and resigning their commissions because of the carnage that was being allowed by the politicians and the generals. Griff didn't go that far, but he was . . . he was a true gentleman. And although he was a cavalry officer, his boots had been made in England and – and somehow I didn't feel any need – I can't explain –'

'I think I understand, Simone.'

'Do you? Have you ever fallen in love? Truly in love?'

David grinned. 'Do I have to answer that question?'

'No of course not. But listen: if ever it should happen to you, you will know it straight away, just as I knew it with

Griff and Griff knew it with me. And if it happens, hold on to it, David, because not everyone is lucky enough to fall really and truly in love. Yes, you smile, but it does happen. You feel yourself falling, only it should not be called falling but *flying* in love. It lifts you up, David. It makes you into a new person. That is what happened to us in the summer of 1918. Griff and I . . . we flew into love.

'But I've jumped ahead. That day in the Bois de Boulogne, I threw myself on his mercy. I told him something, but not all, of what I have told you. Should I have told him I was a prostitute? I don't think so. I think he knew already, but I never asked him. And anyway, gentlemen only marry virtuous maidens, don't they? And every blushing maiden presumes that she will marry a man who has through some miracle become experienced in certain matters. It just happened that in the case of Lieutenant Wilmot and Mademoiselle Billotte, it was the other way round. He was as innocent as the day is long and I was as experienced (if that is the word one has to use) as the night is short. And being a true gentleman, Griff refrained from asking questions that might be difficult for me to answer.

'He . . . swept the past away for me. He put me in lodgings and courted me every day he was free. He gave me presents, he took me out to dinner and to dances. He was three years older than me and had been wounded at the front a few months before. He had medals on his tunic and a well-won limp. Well. Within a few weeks he had put an engagement ring on my finger. And soon after that I realized that I was going to have a baby.

'Even then, when I told him, Griff was the perfect gentleman. Other men would have thrown me away without another thought. Griff was different. He was loving and gentle. He told me he loved me and he didn't mind what had happened in the past. But he was also a cavalry officer and cavalry officers are not allowed to get married to girls who are carrying babies. It puts a tarnish on their breastplates, you see.

'Griff told me that I would have to have the baby first, then have it adopted and then we could get married. It sounds cruel now, perhaps, but then, well, it was perfectly reasonable. The regiment was very important. I had no choice in the matter. And to tell the truth . . . I didn't really mind. I didn't know whose baby I was going to have, and I was deeply in love with Griff. Also, I knew enough about men by then to understand that a man has no wish to see his wife with another man's baby at her breast, and I didn't want anything to come between us. I just left everything to Griff. That was all. We kept everything completely secret. From his mother. From the regiment. The only other person –'

'Yes?'

Simone coloured suddenly. 'No, I – I don't think I want to tell that –'

'That's OK . . . I don't mind.'

'Well. That's almost the end of the story.' She shook her head and her mouth puckered. 'No it's not, no it's not.' Her hands moved together as if they had a will of their own, and tears started to her eyes. 'I was . . . moved to England a week or two after the Compiègne armistice. I was sent as far from the regiment and Griff's family as possible. To a freezing little place in Yorkshire with a midwife with a deep voice and hairs on her chin like a man. The people there . . . they wouldn't even look at me or call me by my name. I was in disgrace. I had nobody. I felt totally unwanted.

'But when you came and I first held you . . . you became the centre of my existence. I was very lonely up there in Yorkshire, and you were my last link with my childhood, my innocence – and – and with all those poor boys I had known in Paris. Every afternoon they brought you to me and I used to hold you in my arms weeping over you and pleading with God not to let them take you from me. But they did take you. They came in a big car one afternoon and I heard them talking in the passage outside. And I watched. From the window. I saw you being carried away. My baby.

My reason for holding on to the possibility of hope and trust in a loving God . . .'

Simone clamped her mouth tight shut, battling against tears. 'So there you are, David. Now you know everything there is to know.'

He went and comforted her. He put his arms round her and wept with her. At length they got up from the table and he dried the dishes while she washed.

When they had finished she took the dishcloth from him and hung it up on the steel rail of the stove. She turned to face him. She was emotionally exhausted. 'If there's anything else you want to ask, David, ask it now, will you? And then let's never talk of this again.'

He was putting the last of the cutlery away and had his back to her. She saw him stop momentarily. '*Is* there anything?'

He turned and faced her.

'Yes there is, isn't there? I can see that there is. Well what is it? Ask me. Please do ask me . . . I'd much rather tell you everything now than have you still wondering but afraid to ask.' She smiled. 'So speak now or for ever hold your peace.'

And then, suddenly, she realized that there was something that she could not be truthful about and that in spite of her insistence she did not want him to ask any question at all.

'I guess there is something,' he said.

'Go on then.'

'It's – no.'

She knew what was in his mind, had known it for weeks. Suddenly she felt swept along by a need to scotch the rumour now, once and for all.

'You want to know about – about Christine's father; that's it, isn't it?'

He nodded.

'Yes, I thought so,' she said quietly, and her heart was going so fast now that she was sure he must notice. 'Well, I don't know why you should want to know or what Christine or anyone else may have told you, but *I* will tell you the truth, David. Archie and I are very old and close friends, but that's all. There is nothing else — nothing whatsoever — between us.' She looked him directly in the eye. 'You accept that, David? You believe me?'

He looked extremely embarrassed. 'Of course,' he said. 'Of course I believe you.'

'Good. I'm very glad to hear it. Now, then. Bedtime. I think we've had enough emotion for one night, haven't we?'

He kissed her and went upstairs. She let the dog out and warmed her back against the stove while she waited. Blashford came back into the kitchen and settled contentedly into his basket under the table. She crouched to say good-night to him, something she did every night. She held his head in her hands and fondled his velvety black ears.

'He didn't believe me,' she whispered softly. 'He t.. ks I'm a liar, Blashford.' She smiled through tears. 'Yes he docs. He thinks I'm a liar . . .'

The dog looked up at her with brown, faithful eyes, and his tail thumped softly against the side of the wicker basket.

iii

The administrative headquarters for the Royal Navy at Dover Castle was a long, imposing building of grey stone, with a wide flight of steps running up to the main entrance and a flagstaff at whose gaff flew the white ensign and from whose truck flew the personal flag of Vice Admiral Sir Bertram Ramsay, better known as 'Vice Admiral Dover.'

Inside this building the admiral's staff busied themselves daily with the task of administering that part of the Home Fleet allocated to the defence of the narrow seas. Inevitably, each staff officer had a short title: the staff operations officer was known as SOO, the staff gunnery officer as SGO and the staff navigation, torpedo, communications, intelligence and boom defence officers became SNO, STO, SCO, SIO and SBDO respectively. The more fortunate of these gentle-men, most of whom were commanders, had a small team of

Wrens to assist them, and all had offices in the administration building and messed together in a long, stately dining hall, waited upon by naval pensioners in blue serge trousers and stiff white coats.

Just down the hill from the main entrance to these offices, an inconspicuous circle of black railings and a flight of wrought iron steps led down to another headquarters which had been tunnelled into the cliff face, and admission to this secret area was allowed only to those directly involved in war operations.

This was the nerve centre. Galleries on three levels provided space for briefing rooms, operations rooms, dormitories, kitchens, bathrooms, telephone exchanges and radio rooms; and it was here that Third Officer Christine Trendle-Home stood her watches.

'What a perfectly glorious day,' she said to Nick Massing-bohm when he met her at the castle main entrance. 'You've no idea how wonderful it is to come up into the sunshine. One becomes a complete troglodyte down there after a while.'

She flopped down into the bucket seat beside him and the MG accelerated away up the steep hill, negotiating the sharp right bend at the top with a satisfying squeal of tyres. Christine kicked off her shoes and took off her uniform hat so that her bobbed hair blew back in the wind.

'Forty-eight hours!' she said, putting her head back and closing her eyes. 'I can hardly believe we've actually managed to coincide our leave for once.'

'Where would you like to go?' Nick asked.

'Anywhere you like!'

'Walk on the cliffs?'

'Wonderful!'

They sped along the Deal road between newly seeded fields.

'What news of your father?'

She opened her eyes. 'Very little, except what I see in signal traffic. I have to keep the War Narrative, which is a bit of a bore, but at least it means that one keeps reasonably abreast of things.'

Nick glanced at her. She had what was known in his squadron as a streamlined fuselage, and it was complemented by her Gieves uniform jacket, the top brass buttons of which were located in positions that seemed to him quite blatantly provocative.

'They're still tied up with this Norwegian business at the moment,' she was saying. 'Really I think we've gone and caught an awful cold over that, don't you? I mean everyone at the HQ is saying that it was a case of too little and too late.'

'Not enough air cover, that was the trouble.'

Christine sighed. 'Anyway, as far as I can make out Pater's ship's still in one piece. You know we lost the *Glowworm*?'

'No? Was she a big ship?'

'A destroyer. She lost a man overboard and got separated from her squadron. The last they heard from her was that she was engaged with a superior force. We've had absolutely nothing from her for nearly three weeks. I knew the commanding officer. He was a friend of Pater's. A splendid chap. Nick –'

'What?'

'You are being careful, aren't you?'

'How d'you mean?'

'Well – flying.'

'Nothing dangerous about flying, Chrissy.'

They were silent for a few moments, during which time Christine tried to imagine him at the control of a Hurricane.

'You *are* funny,' she said at length.

'I don't see why.'

'Well, you're so strong and silent, darling.'

'It's the way I'm made. Can't change, you know.'

'I wouldn't want you to.'

He pulled off the road.

'Now what? Why are we stopping?'

'The interests of road safety.'

'But what's the matter?'

He put on the handbrake and switched off the ignition. '*Facta non verba*,' he said. 'My family motto.' And then – to the cheers of a passing convoy of East Kents on their way to embark at Dover – he took Christine in his arms and kissed her on the lips.

iv

They lay side by side on the cliff top and looked straight up into the blue dome of the sky. 'I can't believe that it'll come to an all-out war,' she was saying. 'Not like last time, anyway. I expect we'll have a series of sideshows – like Poland and Norway and Finland – but I don't see Germany having the crass stupidity to try invading France. It just doesn't make sense, does it?'

He grunted. 'I hope you're right.'

'You don't sound very optimistic.'

She sat up and looked down into his face. He had a large, straight nose and his eyebrows were gingery. His hair was brushed straight back off his forehead, with only the suggestion of a parting, which was near the centre.

'What are you thinking?'

He smiled, and reached up to touch her face. 'What was I thinking? I was thinking, Chrissy, that the sooner we get married the happier I shall be.'

She flushed with pleasure.

'Have you any comment to make on that, Third Officer?'

'None at all, Flight Lieutenant. Those are my sentiments entirely.'

'What about next month then?'

'What about Pater?'

'Would you be terribly cut up if he couldn't be there?'

'In a way, yes,' she said slowly. 'But in another, no.' She picked a stalk of grass and chewed it thoughtfully. 'Things still aren't right between us, you know. We never really grasped the nettle. I don't want to make things any worse by – by getting married behind his back, so to speak. But on the other hand –'

'On the other hand?'

'Well, although he'd be awfully cut up to miss the wedding, poor darling, he'll be jolly pleased we're getting married, all the same. He thoroughly approves of you, you know that? Mummy would have too.'

Her eyes filled with tears, and she sought the comfort of his hand, which she held between hers, kissing the backs of his fingers, pressing it to her cheek. 'It's so silly but I still miss her, you know. I still long to be able to run to her and tell her all about what I've been doing. Even after all these years.' She sighed. 'If only we hadn't seen Pater and Simone that day! It's so hateful knowing that they – you know. And so unfair on poor old Captain Griff . . . We shan't be like that, shall we, darling? We'll be close-close-close, won't we?'

'Of course we shall.'

'Inseparable. Always and always.'

She lay across him and kissed him several times, gentle, cool-lipped kisses.

'Steady the Buffs, Chrissy,' he whispered. 'You're doing things to me –'

She jumped to her feet and pulled him up by the hand. 'Yes, you're right, we mustn't. Right-o. Let's go back and have tea, shall we? We can get the diary out and fix the day. Besides, I'm absolutely ravenous.'

v

When they got back to Prowse, they found David sitting on the floor in the drawing room surrounded by newspapers and magazines from which he was cutting articles for his scrap book.

'So how's the war reporter?' Nick asked. 'Got any good scoops?'

'Fat chance,' he said, wielding the shears. 'There's nothing to scoop.'

'Would you like some tea?' Christine asked. 'I'm making it anyway.'

'Oh – okay. Yeah.'

Christine glanced heavenward and departed to the kitchen.

Massingbohm buried himself in a newspaper for a while. At length David looked up and said: 'So what are you RAF boys up to these days? Still dropping bumph instead of bombs?'

Massingbohm laughed indulgently. 'Something like that.'

David shook his head and said, 'Crazy.'

'What's crazy?'

'The way you British are running this war, that's what's crazy.'

Christine was coming in with a tray. Nick said, 'And how do you suggest we should be running it?'

David sat back on his haunches and brandished the pair of scissors. 'Well . . . like you meant to win, for a start.'

'We do intend to win,' Christine said, and put the tray carefully down on a side table.

'You could have fooled me.'

There was a silence. Christine sat down on the sofa beside Nick and poured the tea. She said: 'It doesn't really have an awful lot to do with you, does it, David?'

'Doesn't it?'

'No. I mean – the Yanks have always sat on the fence when it comes to a fighting war. That's part of the Monroe doctrine, isn't it?'

'The Monroe doctrine's got damn all to do with sitting on fences.'

'Not in theory perhaps, but that's the effect of it, historically. You Americans never take sides until your own interests are threatened, do you? Wasn't that what happened in 1917? It was only when you realized that the war might come right up to your own front doorstep in New Mexico and Arizona that you decided it might be a good idea to join in.'

'If you believe that, Christine, you'll believe anything,' David said, and returned to the task of cutting out an article on the division of Polish spoils between the Soviets and Nazis.

Christine took a pocket diary from her bag. 'Here we are,' she said to Nick. 'What about Saturday the eighth? I can swap watches with Betty and get the whole twenty-four hours off.'

David looked up. 'Planning a vacation?'

'A vacation?' Nick said. 'I don't think that's *exactly* the right way to describe it, is it?'

It was the way she leant against him and laughed that did it. Seeing them so close, so happy, so obviously in love, David was suddenly convinced that they were laughing not just at him, but at America and Americans in general.

'Can I ask you a question, Christine?'

Christine smiled at Nick, shrugged, and said, 'Please do.'

'Where would you people have been in 1918 without the US army? You couldn't beat the Kaiser on your own, so we had to come and bail you out. And by the way you're handling things right now in Norway, it looks like we'll be doing the same thing over before long.'

Christine turned to Nick. 'Do you know what I think David's trouble is? I think he's suffering from an inferiority complex, like all the rest of his countrymen. Here he is, surrounded by people who are working flat out for the war effort, and all he can do is drink beer all day with a crowd of no-hope journalists down at the Grand or cut pictures out of the local rag.'

'Now hold on —' David started.

'No, why should I hold on? How dare you sit on your backside and tell us how to run the war, when you can't even get an article in print about it? It's a case of "them as can, do, and them as can't, write for the newspapers about it", isn't that right? If you really wanted to get a story published you wouldn't be sitting here cutting out pictures. You'd be where the fighting is. You'd be in Poland or Norway or Finland or even Germany itself. You'd be looking for first-hand news instead of trying to borrow other people's stories. At least we're doing something. At least we're in uniform and doing our bit. All you journalists – you make me sick. You're parasites, that's what you are –'

'Hey now, wait a minute, I resent that!'

'Do you? Then why don't you get out there and prove me wrong? Why don't you go and find out for yourself whether the British army is as incompetent as you seem to think? Why don't you go to France and have a look at the line? How about an article on what Tommy gets up to in the evenings when he isn't pointing a Lee Enfield into Belgium? Why not take a look at what's going on with your own eyes? The stories won't come to you, you know, David. You have to go out there and report them yourself. That's what being a reporter means, didn't anyone tell you?'

David gathered together his cuttings and magazines and left the room. Half an hour later, when Nick and Christine were enjoying a quiet afternoon on the sofa, they heard him going up and downstairs several times before banging the front door behind him and riding off on his motorbike.

vi

Simone had driven into Maidstone and had spent the day shopping for summer clothes. It was a bit extravagant of her because she could have made do with last year's, but after her heart-to-heart with David the previous evening she felt this was the best way of restoring morale.

It had been a pleasant day. The town was fuller than ever of servicemen and she had enjoyed their admiring looks and wolf-whistles. She had taken herself out to lunch at a restaurant and had drunk half a bottle of Muscadet with a nicely grilled sole; afterwards, she had strolled in the park, rejected the approaches of a Royal Marine Colour Sergeant and had then spent over an hour trying on dresses and underwear.

Now she was wearing one of her purchases: a cherry-red frock with navy blue polka-dots, fitted waist and slightly padded shoulders. Griff – if he noticed it at all – would have called it 'fast'; Archie would have swept her into his arms and told her she looked ravishing.

Archie. Walking back through the town to the car, she wondered where he was and what he was doing. When they had walked to the cliff together that wintry New Year's Eve, he had made her promise not to write to him, but that had been over four months ago and she had presumed that his ship would be in and out of Chatham and that she would see something of him. Instead, he had disappeared off to Scotland and the only information she could obtain about him was from Christine, who was disinclined to tell her very much.

In the meantime she had heard regularly from Griff, who was an excellent letter writer and who seemed to have put what had happened at Eggardon firmly behind him, taking it rather obviously for granted that she loved him, wanted him back and was being faithful to him. This made her feel uneasy. Although she liked getting his letters and found the business of writing back a useful outlet for all the anxiety she felt about both Griff and Archie, she also felt oddly guilty that she was not doing enough for the war effort.

What a strange situation hers was! She needed Griff for a husband and she needed Archie for a lover, that was the trouble. She needed two men: one to look after and provide for her and another to seduce and pleasure her. Griff and Archie performed each role to perfection. One gave her a sense of belonging and identity and was always 'there', always available to lean on, while the other refused to chain her in any way, set her free, and provided an inexhaustible source of material for her romantic daydreams and fantasies.

Was she different from other women? It didn't seem to her so very extraordinary to have this dual attachment. She didn't feel in the slightest bit sinful, nor did she want to come between Archie and Griff.

Still thinking about the complications of her love life, she put her parcels in the boot of the Standard and drove off back to St Margaret's-at-Cliffe.

When she arrived home, Nick and Christine were just about to depart by car.

'He's taking me out to dinner,' Christine said, looking radiantly happy and holding onto Nick's hand as if she had no intention of ever letting it go. She turned to Nick. 'Will you tell Simone, or shall I?'

'We've fixed the date,' Nick said.

She looked at them. 'What date?'

'For the wedding. It's to be next month.'

'When?'

Christine said: 'Saturday June the eighth. Here at St Margaret's.'

'It's very soon, Christine. Does your father know yet?'

'We're going to send him a telegram. He may not be able to come, but he wouldn't want us to hold things up for him. Simone – could we possibly hold the reception here? It'll have to be a very quiet wedding, and I don't mind making the arrangements –'

She felt suddenly happy for them. It was a glorious spring day; they were hopelessly in love with one another, and Archie, she knew, would thoroughly approve.

She kissed them both. 'Of course you can! We'll have it in the garden. I might even be able to persuade the adjutant to put up a tent on the lawn.'

Christine laughed and clung to Nick's hand. They got into the MG and Nick started the engine.

'By the way,' Christine said. 'David went out about half an hour ago.'

'Did he say if he'd be in for supper?'

'No, he didn't say anything at all.'

'He *is* a naughty boy! He knows I like to be told. I suppose you two won't be in until late?'

Christine leant against Nick's shoulder. 'No, I don't suppose we shall.'

She watched them drive off, then went ino the house. She

carried her parcels up to her room and put them on the bed. The house seemed oddly quiet. She couldn't think where David could have gone to at this time of day: he usually told her if he was going out and whether he would be in for supper.

She stood in her room looking out of the window that faced south over the lawn. It had been a mistake to tell him what she had the previous night – she knew that now. And it had been an even worse mistake to make that denial about Archie. She shouldn't even have mentioned his name. David wasn't a fool by any means, he must surely have guessed something. And in telling him a lie like that she had probably devalued everything else she had told him.

If only Archie could be here now! If only he would walk in through the door and they could rush upstairs and love each other to bits . . . !

She went onto the landing and stood there listening to the silence. Then she climbed the narrow staircase to the boxroom. She pushed open David's door – and immediately stopped dead.

All his things were gone. There was a cardboard box of books and magazines on the floor, but otherwise the room had been cleared. On the bed she found an envelope addressed simply, 'Simone'.

She opened the letter. She was hardly able to take in the words.

My dear Simone,

This is the most difficult letter I ever had to write. You see, I have decided to move on. The reason I'm doing it like this is that I know that if we talked about it we should both be upset and you might persuade me to change my mind, so I decided that as I'm going, it's best to go quickly.

The thing is, I've come to the conclusion that I can't go on watching things happen and not be personally involved any longer. I don't want anybody to say that I was content to stay on the sidelines while others were fighting. I haven't decided finally what I'll do, but I know we can't stay out of this war for ever. High on my list of options is an immediate return to the States with a view to signing up for training as a fighter pilot in the USAF.

Right now, all I want to say is thank you for all you've done for me. I shall never forget this time I spent here with you. I shall always think of you and be grateful to you for helping me find out who I am, where I came from and where I want to go.

Whatever happens, I'll keep in touch. Forgive me for walking out like this but it was the only way I could figure out that would hurt the both of us as little as possible.

From your loving son,
David.

PS: Please believe me when I say that what you told me last night has *nothing* to do with my present departure. I really appreciate the courage it took to tell me all you did. It goes without saying that I shall preserve the strictest confidentiality.

She sat down on the bed and watched David's handwriting dissolve into a mass of blots as her tears fell on the page.

'What's wrong with me?' she whispered. 'Oh, dear God! What's wrong with me, what's wrong with me?'

TWELVE

On 9 May Heinrich Lauder's company did a route march with weapons and equipment in the Briedeler Mountains. They set up practice artillery positions and dug holes for observation posts and tank hideouts. Towards midday, on the way back, they looked down over the landscape they had come to love: the silver thread of the Mosel as it wound its way down to Zell, which nestled at the foot of the mountains.

The whole world seemed to breathe a deep peace, and the soldiers were almost deceived by the tranquil atmosphere; but the political tension of recent days and the preparations of past months made it impossible to relax completely.

Their premonitions became reality at three p.m. when the call they had been expecting for so long came: Alarm!

At first nobody in 15 Company could quite believe that this was it and that they would be leaving before the Whit weekend, for which they had made all sorts of plans. But when they saw their comrades of 26 Company arriving with packed laundry bags and rucksacks they knew that this was no false alarm.

They stuffed in their last belongings and dragged everything down to the car park behind the Hotel Auling. There they waited for their vehicles which the drivers had gone to fetch from the sports ground. They came racing up and the kit was loaded in a matter of minutes. Meanwhile, all the townspeople had gathered to bid the regiment farewell and to give the soldiers their best wishes for the hard road that lay ahead.

'Fall in!' came the order from the parade ground by the river Mosel. Lieutenant Gerbener then read out a special

message from the regiment's commanding officer, Lieutenant Colonel Count von Schwerin.

'"Comrades! We are to meet the enemy! Every officer,
NCO and grenadier in the regiment will do his duty to the
last. Onwards against the enemy! With God! Long live the
Führer! Long live Great Germany!"'

ii

The Brough's tyres buzzed on the *pavé* surface, and the
handlebars vibrated heavily. The going was fast and flat: the
road went straight on into the distance with tall, narrow
trees on either side. David overtook pedestrians and cyclists,
farm labourers with handcarts and little grey motorized
tricycles with absurdly heavy loads that swayed violently
from side to side. On either hand, the fields stretched away
into a blue haze: nondescript fields, green and brown, that
were interlaced with ditches and canals. Here and there were
tumbledown farm buildings with large, red-tiled barns and
mud-spattered cattle waiting to be milked. He roared
through villages where old women in black sat making lace
at their doorsteps and men, usually in grey and black or
brown and black, smoked pipes in the shade of dusty trees.

It was what Christine had said that finally decided him to
visit France. After a few days in London, during which he
had made further unsuccessful enquiries after Gwynneth, he
suddenly realized that Christine was right. How would he
be able to live with himself if he passed up a chance like this?
What kind of schmo would people back home think him if
he just crawled back to the States without ever setting foot
in France?

Fixing it all up had been surprisingly easy. Although the
ferries to Calais and Boulogne had ceased running, the
Ostend boat was still in operation and the only condition
the customs authorities had made was that he remove the
sidecar from the Brough, which was on the wrong side for
the continent. That was quickly achieved at a local garage,

and having stocked up on Belgian and French francs and invested in a hiker's tent and sleeping bag, he embarked for Ostend. Now here he was, eating up the kilometres on some minor road that pointed like an arrow towards the heart of France.

He came to a place called Dixmude, a busy little industrial town with a canal and rail junction and a chimney belching out thick white smoke that ascended in a vertical column to the sky. He went on, parting company with the canal, and half an hour later came to Ypres. Here, he parked the bike in the central square and stretched his legs. There was a big whitestone arch nearby, so he went and looked at that.

It was quite a surprise. The whole arch – which was as big as the Washington Arch in Fifth Avenue – was covered in names. Hundreds – no, tens of thousands of names. Over fifty thousand names. He stared up at them: they were the British soldiers, grouped by regiment, who had died holding the line at Ypres against the Kaiser's army.

But he had not come to Belgium – or France – in order to look at war memorials, and when he had read enough names of fallen soldiers he rode off again, wondering as he left Ypres behind him exactly why he had crossed the Channel. To be a war reporter? Partly, yes. But not primarily. As a tourist? Not really, because he had no desire to go sight-seeing. Well then, why? Was it the risk? Was it like climbing a cliff face, something you needed to do in order to prove you could do it? He didn't know the answer. All he knew was that the noise of the engine and the wind in his face and the trees going sha-sha-sha as they flew by on either side lulled him into a state of hypnosis, made him lose track of time and distance, so that before he knew it he was at the border with France.

This is *my* country, he told himself as he accelerated away from the customs post and on along the flat road towards Armentières.

It made him feel unexpectedly emotional. He remembered Simone saying to him: 'You are French, David. Never forget that you are French,' and repeated the phrase she had taught him: '*Je suis un enfant de France.*'

He stayed that night at Lille. In the evening, he wandered into the centre of the town and visited a dimly lit bar with dark red drapes and little alcoves which was packed out with British army officers. He paid far too much for a bottle of cheap champagne, and a girl who said her name was Lulu sat on his knee and stroked his thigh. He mentally compared Gwynneth's musical voice, scrubbed cheeks and shining eyes with this woman's nasal accent, thick make-up and mascara, and felt mildly nauseated.

The next day he moved on down through Douai, and by evening was in Sedan. That night he strolled through the old city and stood on the Pont de Meuse, looking down at the fast-flowing river. This was the scene of the overthrow of the second French empire, seventy years before. Here General MacMahon had been cut off by the princes of Prussia and Saxony, and eighty thousand French soldiers had been forced to surrender.

The town seemed pretty well dead. There were few soldiers about, and the few bars that were open had a bleak, deserted look about them. He settled for an early night.

In the morning he rose at seven, intending to head south for Verdun and the Maginot Line. But fate or chance – or perhaps bad map reading – made him take a wrong turning out of the city, and within half an hour he found himself at a border post.

He consulted his Michelin and ate some chocolate at the side of the road. He was about to enter Belgium at Bouillon, and could either go back to Sedan and find the road for Montmedy and Longuyon, or go on through Florenville and into Luxembourg.

Why not have a look at the place while he was about it? After all, Luxembourg was a very small country. He could bike right across it in a couple of hours.

Another thought occurred to him. Luxembourg shared a border with Germany. He could go right on into the

'Fatherland' if he wanted – or, at least, the adoptive mother-land. Why not? Why not!

He kicked the engine into life again and swung the Brough back onto the road.

It was still early: a beautiful morning. The road led uphill, winding its way through pine forests until it brought him out on a beautiful undulating plain with picturesque farms nestling in the folds of the hills, church spires in the distance, wild flowers at the roadside, clean cows with bells round their necks – even a couple of people in national dress.

He felt suddenly – extraordinarily – free. Here in neutral Luxembourg all the absurdities of war – the shortages, the unending discussions and speculations, all that bit about blackout and talk of bombs – were far behind him. Here, for the first time since stepping ashore in England nine months before, he felt at peace.

He dawdled along, stopping frequently to admire the views, an idea forming in his mind. At midday he stopped at a road-side café and ate fresh bread, spiced sausage and white cheese. He drank a bottle of cold beer and spoke German – his only foreign language – to the proprietor.

'How far to the border?'

'Which border?'

'The German border.'

The man looked at his wife. 'Don't you know already? Aren't you German yourself?'

'No, I'm an American.'

'Is that so? We've seen so many German tourists these last few days, we naturally thought you were heading in the opposite direction.'

When he told them he was from New York, they looked at him as if he had just come out of the zoo. 'Is it easy to get into Germany from here?'

The proprietor again glanced at his wife. 'Of course. We've got no argument with our German neighbours, have we, Vera?'

He paid and went out into the sunshine. Half a dozen blond cyclists went by, heading west. There seemed no reason now why he shouldn't go into Germany. The idea fascinated and excited him. 'I'm an American citizen,' he muttered to himself as he started up again. 'I can go where the hell I please.'

He took the minor roads, still heading east. He went over to Mersch and on through Larochette to Diekirch. He was in no hurry; and if the worst came to the worst he could pitch his tent and sleep under the stars. Leaving Diekirch behind, he turned left off the Vianden road and took a narrow lane that led up to Mount St Nicholas. And it was there, on the ridge overlooking the River Our, that he had his first glimpse of Germany.

The hills were fading into a blue haze. He sat down by the bike and opened a bottle of beer. It was strange: he really felt much more at home in this part of the world than he had in the monotonous flat country of northern France or the cosy green hills of England.

A tinkle of cowbells in the distance. The last larks, twittering overhead and swooping by stages down to their nests on the hillside. A dog barking in a farmyard on the other side . . .

He sat there for a long time. A church on the German side of the valley struck the half hour and the three-quarters. His thoughts wandered about in a disorderly way. How had Simone taken his abrupt departure? How was his mother making out back home? Should he go on, or back?

Sometimes, when he was small, his mother had talked to him about her German upbringing. She used to keep a leather album of photographs in her desk, and sometimes she would take it out and show him pictures of her family. Most of them were of family occasions – weddings, bar mitzvahs, anniversaries. Severe-looking worthies, ladies in black lace and chokers, men in wing collars and spats, children in sailor suits or pinafores, stared solemnly into the camera lens. Once a year, his mother heard from her sister,

Anna, who had abandoned her Jewish upbringing in order to marry a doctor. The Lauders lived in Stuttgart with their four children. When David was sixteen a portrait photograph arrived of the eldest, Cousin Heinrich. Heinrich had joined the Hitler Youth, and in the photograph, which had been tinted to show his blue eyes and flaxen hair, he sat straight-backed in his uniform and sash, gazing in profile at some far-off, idealistic goal.

Though Carlotta was not a practising Jew and did not go to synagogue or observe any of the feasts or fasts, she knew enough about National Socialism to be aware of its tendencies; so the picture of her nephew had been hidden away in a drawer and David had not seen it since the day it arrived.

But he had not forgotten that portrait photograph and had often envied Cousin Heinrich for his idealism, his sense of identity and the burning nationalism which shone so obviously in his eyes.

So why not visit his Uncle Hans and Aunt Anna? Although his address book had been confiscated at Christmas, it should not be too difficult to trace the Lauders, and Stuttgart was only a day or so's journey away.

He had seen all he wanted to of England and the English. He had travelled through France. Now, just across this valley, here was Germany. He could go on over the border that very evening if he chose to. He could make his way by stages to Stuttgart and see the war from the German point of view.

Or . . . he could go to Paris and try to trace Simone's relations, the Billottes. Or yet again he could return to America and get on with pilot training.

His reverie was disturbed by a deep bellow from somewhere behind him, and when he looked round he found that he was being observed by a man carrying a scythe.

'Osh,' said this odd-looking individual, a man of fifty or more in heavy boots, thick corduroy breeches and a dirty flannel shirt.

'Excuse me?'

'Osh,' repeated the unfortunate, smiling and dribbling from the corner of his mouth.

'Okay, osh,' agreed David, with the result that the other threw down his scythe, grabbed David by the arm and, opening his mouth wide, pointed inside.

'No thanks, I don't want to see your – oh my God!'

Where the man's tongue should have been was a scarred stump that wiggled about at the back of his throat.

'Osh,' the mute repeated over and over again. 'Osh.' Then he started pulling at David's binocular case, nodding furiously. 'Osh, osh, osh . . . !'

'Okay, you can have a look if you want –'

But the mute did not want to look himself; he wanted David to look, and kept pointing across the valley to where a road disappeared and reappeared in a series of zigzags as it went up through a forest over the hill.

'Can't see a thing, chum,' David said.

The mute took the binoculars from him and focused them in a way that made David wonder if he was quite so mentally deficient as he had at first thought. He pointed carefully, and handed the binoculars over. David took them back, refocused and looked in the same direction.

Then he saw them: lined up at the roadside and parked right back into the trees so that they were barely visible was a line of tracked vehicles.

'Tanks!' he muttered, and lowering the binoculars turned to the mute. '*Panzerkampfwagen.*'

The mute nodded. 'Osh,' he said, but much more quietly. Then he opened his mouth and pointed again at the stump of his tongue. 'Osh,' he repeated. 'Osh.'

'Oh my God, I think I know what you're driving at. You mean Boche. Boche, right?'

The mute nodded and was silent. On the other side of the valley, the church clock was striking nine. The mute gripped David tightly by the arm and pointed, very meaningfully, first at David and then westward to the sunset. Then he picked up the scythe, nodded a goodbye and went on his way down the hill.

David remained looking out over the valley. It was getting late: he must either find a place to stay the night or pitch his tent. He trained his binoculars again on the tanks across the valley. Wouldn't it be something to cross into Germany? Of course it would. Maybe he was a news reporter after all. He could already 'hear' the opening line of his eye-witness report of the German assault on the Maginot Line. It was bound to happen, sooner or later. Would he ever be able to live with himself if he missed out?

He took a decision. From now on, he would always go where the news led him. Those tanks on the other side of the valley were news, so he would cross the border first thing in the morning. In the meantime, it would be far more interesting to sleep under canvas than in the fug of a Vianden hotel, so that was what he would do.

He unpacked the tent and his sleeping bag and prepared for the night. The whole world seemed to fall silent. He sat in the door of the tent for some while, gazing at the stars, thinking about everything and nothing. When he finally turned in for the night, he felt completely at peace with himself and the decision he had taken, and fell asleep almost immediately.

iii

It seemed as if only a few minutes had passed before he was jerked suddenly awake by the sound of aircraft engines.

He scrambled out of the tent and looked up. Several formations of German bombers were flying over, heading for Belgium and France. Without lights, they were like black double crosses against the night sky. At the same time, while he watched, he heard another sound.

On the other side of the valley, heavy-duty self-starters whined, and big six-cylinder engines began roaring into life. He looked at his watch. It was four-thirty. The peace of early morning had been shattered. More tank engines were starting up all the time. How many of them now? Fifteen? Twenty? No, far more. Fifty. A hundred – two hundred.

Suddenly the whole valley was throbbing with the noise of engines and, as he watched, sidelights came on along the road that zigzagged up the hill on the other side of the border. The first of them were already beginning to move out from the trees and head downhill. Beyond the hill he could see more lights – and over to the right, towards Bitburg and Trier, like a glimmering necklace appearing and disappearing in the hills, still more.

And then a voice, his own, joined the din. 'You bastards!' he yelled at the top of his voice. 'You fucking bastards!'

PART TWO

THIRTEEN

One by one the Grossdeutschland platoons of 15 Company were reported ready and sent on their way. A last hurried handshake and they were off – via Bullay, Alf, Wittlich, Binsfield, Speicher and Meckel, heading for Luxembourg.

As they approached the border, the main part of the regiment halted to allow 15 Company, the Advance Unit, to rush ahead. Two trucks of shock troops were the first to go and the 'Führer Group', of which Heinrich Lauder was a member, followed closely behind. It was getting lighter all the time. Heinrich could just make out the last houses of Endernach as they went through the sleeping town. Then they were out in the country again and the road ahead, wet with dew, was gleaming in the dimmed headlights. The first people ventured out of their houses. An old granny waved a handkerchief and gave the soldiers her blessing for the coming battle. Hellendorf loomed up out of the mist. The buildings stared down at the passing convoy, bleak and silent.

In the grey dawn they halted on a hill overlooking the Luxembourg border where a Stork aircraft was circling overhead. They were given coffee, but little rest. The fuel tanks had to be filled and the vehicles checked. Overhead, squadron after squadron of planes flew westward towards the enemy. Heinrich and his comrades glanced upward, silently wishing the bomber crews good luck. Then came the order to man vehicles and they drove off again.

The bunkers of the western defence line came into sight. Anti-aircraft positions pointed iron shafts skyward. They passed countless tank barriers. Barbed wire tangled down to the River Sauer, which was wrapped in mist.

Suddenly, a left turn. They had arrived at the border crossing.

The Luxembourgers had tried to blow up the bridge over the river but had been only half successful and the pioneers had no difficulty in making the crossing safe again with a few planks. The local inhabitants stared sullenly. Some distance to the south, a fierce air battle was in progress: the French were trying to stop the bombers getting through but were being driven off by the fighter escorts. To the right, still on German territory, endless cavalry and artillery units were moving past, silhouetted against the sky as they moved over a hilltop.

15 Company crossed the border and drove further and further from German territory. It gave Heinrich a strange, unfamiliar feeling in the pit of his stomach. The Advance Unit was well named: they rushed on, miles ahead, the drivers keeping their feet hard down on the gas. An idyllic landscape of woods, lakes, and deserted little villages went by. This, and the noise of the engines and rattling of slats, helped to put thoughts of battle or being in enemy territory from one's mind. New vistas opened up at the crest of every hill: all was so beautiful in this clean, well-ordered, little country that it was easy to convince oneself that this was just another exercise and they were driving through their own homeland.

Onwards, onwards! They went through Larochette, Ettelbruck and Redange to the Belgian border, which was already showing signs of the fighting. They crossed into Belgium at Niedercolpach. They charged over bumpy, dusty tracks in the midday heat. Were they really at war or was this just another exercise?

Then a sudden shout jerked Heinrich out of his daydream: 'Tank! Enemy tank to the left!'

They jumped down from the vehicles into cover. The anti-tank platoon took up position. But the tank crawled out of the way in time, apparently preferring safety to fighting.

The column moved off again. As they approached a village, Major Fost shouted an order which was passed down the line: 'Clear Attert of the enemy!' The men of 15 Company looked at each other in amazement. Attert was the place-name always used during their assault exercises and here they were in the very place itself!

'God in heaven!' someone shouted. 'Those guys knew what they were doing when they planned this!'

Attert was overrun without offering any resistance and soon afterwards 15 Company halted. A special order of the day had just been received from General von Kleist. Major Fost, the company commander, climbed onto the lid of his tank to read it out:

'The Group has been given a hard yet noble task: to force a crossing of the River Meuse in advance of the infantry. This will only be possible if every single officer and man gets every last ounce of effort both from himself and his equipment. On this side of the Meuse there will be no, repeat no, rest. Pushing forward without let up by day and by night, looking neither to left nor right, always keeping your nerve, you must take advantage of the enemy's confusion and disorder. He must be taken by surprise and never allowed to rest. Our goal is a surprise crossing of the Meuse, and if we can achieve that goal fewer losses will be necessary than if we were to allow the enemy time to think and plan his defence. The eyes of the Führer and the people are upon the tank and motorized divisions. I shall send the Führer the list of names of all those in the first group to cross to the far bank of the river. Heil to the Führer!'

And then they were off again – like devils out of hell. They left the track and cut across fields. The column kicked up a grey-brown dust and within minutes they could hardly recognize each other for the dirt. The meadows, dotted with black and white cattle, darkened as a veil of swirling dust was drawn across them.

'If they stop us now we're for it!' Falk shouted.

Heinrich laughed. 'It'll never happen! Nothing can stop us now!'

They thundered straight through villages, which looked more prepared for war now, with locked houses, barbed wire and similar diversions. But there were no serious hold-ups. Obstacles were either cleared out of the way or, to shouts of 'Keep going, keep going!' they drove straight over them.

Major Fost, a fearless old veteran from the Great War, lay on the lid of his tank, spade in one hand, automatic in the other, and thrust his arm forward in a repeated gesture that could only mean, 'Faster! Faster!'

They hurtled along a stretch of open road.

'Look! There, over there on the right!'

Their first glimpse of French troops. Just two of them. Blissfully ignorant of the danger, they were mooching about with cigarettes in their mouths. It wasn't even worth dismounting for them. They let them run off and accelerated to close up behind the next vehicle.

ii

A sudden halt.

'What's happened?'

'Over there – use your eyes!'

And then Heinrich saw them. A whole squad of French, approaching in battle order. As he watched, they too halted. They were close enough to see some of the expressions on their faces. A sort of mute bewilderment.

'They look scared,' someone muttered.

'Well, do we shoot or don't we?'

'Wait for it! Wait for it!'

They jumped down from the vehicles and there was a rattle of bolts as rifles and sub-machine guns were readied.

'Come on, come on!'

And then the order from Major Fost – given in precisely the same way as he had always given it on exercises.

'Open fire!'

The first shots went whistling off at the enemy. Quite a lot went wide just out of the sheer excitement of hearing the bangs.

But out in the field of clover, a Frenchman was writhing on the ground.

'Hey – we got one!'

'No we didn't, look, he's up again!'

But he was only up for a moment: as another bullet hit him he seemed to crumble inwards, the rifle falling from his hands, his arms crossing over his chest, his helmet tipping over his face as he went down.

Immediately, the rest of the squad threw away their weapons and put their hands up. Most of them were middle-aged men, veterans, like Major Fost, of the Great War.

They came across the field with their arms up. Their leader, an old man with several campaign medal ribbons on his blue tunic, stepped forward, *'La guerre est finie!'* he announced, and the men behind him, grey-faced with terror, nodded their agreement and kept their hands as high as they possibly could, so that there could be no mistake about the surrender.

They seemed greatly relieved that the battle had come to such a gentle end. When they had been searched and taken into custody, the inevitable Gauloise cigarettes appeared, and hands went deep into pockets. They stood around looking resigned and dejected, a fag end sticking out of each man's mouth.

iii

15 Company drove on, keeping a sharp lookout. On the roadside they saw the first corpse. At the sight of it, something cold gripped the heart and a shudder went down one's spine.

Heinrich forced himself to look. It was something they would all have to get used to, he knew that.

A town appeared up ahead. Etalle. The artillery was already in action. They were given a hot reception with some well-placed bursts of machine-gun fire. Fifty metres ahead there was an explosion. Moments later, there was a thin, high-pitched cry: 'Medic!' That was the first time it was heard. It was one of the few things they had not exercised a great deal.

One of the rifle platoons had run straight into the French defences. French tanks were advancing. The anti-tank platoon was suddenly busy. Despatch riders went roaring back on motorcycles to request the support of heavy armour.

The enemy intensified his counter-attack: shots whined past left and right, smacking into roofs and tearing holes into walls. But 15 Company was in good cover and keeping position, and the enemy's firing was wasting shells.

Major Fost came over and gave a quick briefing. 'It looks as if we're up against a division of cavalry supported by light armoured units. I want a road block built over there, just this side of the crest of the hill . . .'

The anti-tank platoon was firing rapid bursts, and quite a lot was coming in the opposite direction. Suddenly Corporal Popojewski jerked sideways and fell to the ground. Moments later, one of the auxiliaries went down too. Medics rushed to their assistance, but found it was already too late. All they could do was carry the bodies away and cover them with their greatcoats. Their boots stuck out at the bottom. Heinrich still couldn't help thinking that this was all another exercise and that they were only pretending to be dead.

Another shout: 'Medic! Medic! Major Fost's down!'

'Oh, God! That's all we need!'

Stretcher-bearers ran, doubled up, and brought back another wounded man, covered in a mess of blood.

'Who is it now?'

'Hauptmann Flesch!'

They were being pinned down. They felt utterly helpless.

'We've had it if they attack now!'

'So why don't they?'

'Probably don't realize how few we are. They could knock us out with a single blow if they wanted to.'

'Hang on, lads! We're not giving up that easily!'

Over an hour passed, and the reinforcements still didn't turn up. Then, just when it seemed that they would be able to hold on no longer, they heard a clatter of fire from the rear.

'Tanks!' someone shouted. 'They're attacking us from behind!'

'No they're not, you idiot. They're our tanks! 10th Panzers – look at the buffaloes on the turrets!'

They were only small and medium tanks, but they were very manoeuvrable and hard-hitting. They rushed up at top speed, and behind them came the remainder of 15 Company.

They moved cautiously forward. The birds had flown, but had left some valuable stuff behind them. Heinrich's platoon took great pleasure in setting a truck on fire and blowing up three tanks.

Parked at the roadside up against the wall of a house, was a private car, a Citroën. At the steering wheel sat a dead Frenchman and next to him his wife. They had both been shot through the head. No one asked how or why.

The air was heavy with the stench of death. Horses' legs were pointing skywards. On the far side of the road block, dead Frenchmen were lying in pools of blood. Round every corpse – horse and human – a cloud of flies danced attendance.

The shooting stopped. Etalle had fallen.

iv

Heinrich got a few gulps of water at a house and lay down in the shade of his vehicle. But it was only for a few minutes: despatch riders roared up with orders for 15 Company's Advance Unit to move off immediately towards a village just south of Villers-sur-Semois. All signs of fatigue gone, the men leapt to their feet and climbed back aboard the vehicles. Everyone wanted to be first on the road (you breathed less dust that way) and other companies were trying to push in. Ahead, Messerschmitts were doing good work, hedge-hopping and machine-gunning from tree-top height.

A few shells went over. White balls of light from ahead gave the signal that the spearhead troops had already entered the outlying houses.

2 Platoon was sent on a detour towards Villers itself. The fields were fenced with wire or rotten wood fences so they presented no real obstacle. They smashed, cut or pushed a way through. Sheltered behind a hedge below the level of the road, they felt comparatively secure. Suddenly, shots whipped over their heads. They grabbed their weapons, threw themselves down on the ground and sent answering fire back up the hill. For a while, it turned into a wild shooting party, then it stopped as abruptly as it started. The platoon worked its way forward, the men crawling on their bellies. The trucks came up and stopped in a dip in the road just clear of the village. Behind them more vehicles joined the queue until the approach road became blocked solid with vehicles, their engines ticking over.

Heinrich and a few others got a lift on the leading armoured car. It was just past the first houses when a burst of machine-gun fire came whining down the road. They took the safety catches off their sub-machine guns and sat on the tailgate, ready to jump.

They reached a small, open square. Suddenly it was all happening again: brakes on, jump down into cover, not a second too late. Hand grenades were exploding, shots whizzing about.

'Where on earth are they firing from?'

'It must be the church tower!'

'Oh, mother! I don't like this place!'

They crouched in the cover of a concrete shed. Machine-gun bullets rattled on the walls. In a brief lull, they dashed across the road and into another house.

The machine-gun fire was joined by something much heavier. They were firing on the house where Heinrich and half a dozen others were sheltering.

'That's our company!' someone muttered. 'Our mates are firing at us!'

They ducked as rafters, slates and chunks of concrete and plaster fell about their heads. Only 150 metres away, a light field gun was firing directly at them.

Heinrich climbed to a window and fired a flare to indicate their position. He looked cautiously out. He could recognize the gun's crew: Mulz was taking aim, Bielig was loading, Heyden was firing. While he watched, Heyden got caught by the wheel as the gun recoiled and was injured. Further up the road an assault tank of No 16 Company was backing off so as to be able to elevate sufficiently to fire at a window where an enemy machine gun was located. Shell after shell whined in directly through the window until suddenly all was still. The tank came down the lane, its tracks grinding deep into the soft surface, a moving fortress, spitting out death and destruction.

He watched. The tank had hit a house further up. The scene changed as if they were extras on an immense stage, witnessing the death throes of a village.

They left the house and moved forward. They looked over a low wall into a yard which was full of horses, all saddled. There were no French to be seen. The horses were stamping and snorting nervously. Suddenly, on the roof of the farm-house opposite, a slate came loose, then another and another and there was a glint of steel as a gun barrel was pushed through the hole.

They let fly immediately with Schmeisser machine pistols. The enemy machine gun slipped forward through the hole in the roof and clattered down over the tiles to the ground.

Another explosion: a shell had landed close to the farm, and the neighing herd began to stampede out of the gate, coming straight for them. They flattened themselves against the wall. Someone fired a short burst to halt the onrush. The leading horse stopped in its tracks, a machine gun harnessed to its back. Slowly, it spread out its legs, blood gushing from its chest. A shudder ran through its body and the head sank down, nostrils flared, eyes glazed. Blood and froth oozed from its mouth. The other horses surged and pressed forward, pushing the mortally wounded horse to the ground. Two or three others were trampled as the rest galloped away. The last twitching of these animals was terrible to see. Heinrich turned away, his mouth watering from nausea.

The battle raged on. The church tower crumbled and the people up there stopped shooting. A few last shots rang out, then all was quiet. They got back into the vehicles and moved closer. As they entered the village square they were greeted by the whinnying of riderless horses which were cantering about. Near a peacefully splashing fountain, a horse was sniffing at the corpse of its rider. In a doorway a civilian who must have been trying to escape lay dead. On the edge of the road lay a few French soldiers, some of them quite young. On a pile of straw several wounded men, covered in blood, moaned and writhed and begged for water. Wherever they turned there were new horrors – and yet it had all been the work of just a few minutes.

There was no time to worry about the fate of these people, because the next assault had to be made straight away. Machinery creaked and engines revved as the vehicles drove over the dead horses. Prisoners gaped in amazement as the column went by.

Down the road, and then back into the fields. Sporadic opposition from machine-gun fire. Cattle were bellowing to be milked. Dusk fell. Everywhere, fires against the night sky. To one side, regular explosions from a town that was already ablaze.

A motorcycle and sidecar arrived with warm coffee and something to eat. It was only cheese as there was no bread.

Night fell. Because they were so far in advance of the main

body, it was necessary to make a long, tiring drive back to Etalle, where they arrived at about midnight.

They sat in the vehicles with blankets drawn up over their heads and snatched a couple of hours' sleep. The drivers slumped over their steering wheels.

It seemed that they had been asleep for only a few minutes before the NCOs were rousing them with orders to move off.

FOURTEEN

Griff Wilmot was in the middle of a complicated dream. He was trying to round up a herd of sheep on a hillside with the assistance of Sergeant Crisp, a task made more difficult by some civilians whose random firing of shotguns was scattering the flock. 'Look – do you mind not firing while we get on with it?' he shouted across to them, and when one of the shooting party turned he saw that it was Archie, in cricket flannels, blazer and crownless Prowse boater. Then there was another report, and Wilmot woke up.

It was just beginning to get light. He heard, in the distance, a succession of explosions. He lay on his back and listened to them. Artillery? No. Bombs.

He got out of bed and went to the window. It was just light enough to see across to the line of poplars by the canal.

Another three explosions. Arras, probably. And if they were bombing Arras . . .

He debated whether to order his section to stand-to. It would be a good exercise for them even if it was a false alarm, but he wasn't a great believer in unnecessary exercises and had taken them on a fifteen-mile route march only three days before. Besides, if this was the real thing, the last thing he wanted to do was appear jumpy in front of his men.

He got back into bed. No more bombs fell, and his thoughts drifted off into more mundane matters. The day before, he had received official confirmation that his Water-ways Defence Section was to be brought up to full company strength, and that he would be promoted to the acting rank of major on the first of June. It was the best news he'd had in years.

He heard a barge chuff-chuffing along on the canal, and

the first sparrows cheeping under the eaves. Then, suddenly, three aircraft hammered overhead at high speed, the air-raid sirens wailed out over Vitry airfield, and Griff Wilmot knew that the war had begun.

ii

The bombers, nine at a time, roared off into the air, joined up in arrowhead formation, and flew north at low level over the sea before turning inland and heading for their allocated targets – Dutch airfields like Waalhaven, Valkenburg, Schipol and Bergen op Zoom. On release of their weapon loads, the squadrons split up into sections of three, some to machine-gun hangars and aircraft on the ground, some to attack railway stations or petrol dumps, others to go freelance machine-gunning over Den Haag or Amsterdam.

At the same time, the advance through the Ardennes continued. Almost unnoticed by the allies, the greatest concentration of tanks and mechanized infantry ever known was thundering along towards the Meuse. With squadrons of fighters patrolling overhead, this massive queue of moving vehicles tailed back for a hundred miles, its spearhead already well into the Belgian Ardennes, its rear still fifty miles east of the Rhine. Preceded by fifth columnists and led by motorized shock troops and tanks, it was backed up by a mighty phalanx of supply, anti-aircraft and artillery battalions, while in the rear, singing as they marched, came the full weight of the German infantry.

The bombing continued all day. Arras, where Lord Gort had his sprawling headquarters, was particularly singled out for attention, and near Rheims sixteen Blenheims of the RAF's Advanced Air Striking Force were caught on the ground and put out of action. Within the first twelve hours, the neutral Dutch and Belgian air forces were virtually wiped out. In a brilliant attack in which gliders made spot landings on the roof of Belgium's key fortress, the specially trained

Koch Storm Detachment took Eban Emael, the cornerstone of a chain of forts on the Albert Canal.

From this first day of invasion, civilians were machine-gunned indiscriminately. Right across the Low Countries the howl of Stuka dive-bombers and the stutter of their guns brought blood and despair to innocent families. Mothers huddled with their children in ditches at the roadside. Old men lay face down, dying on the cobbles and in the gutters.

Parachutists descended over Rotterdam. Disguised as tourists, policemen, priests and nuns, the fifth columnists who had been pouring into the neutral countries for the past week linked up with the invaders, spotted for artillery, passed intelligence reports by radio, secured bridges for the advancing columns – and shot anyone who tried to resist.

All the old memories of the treatment civilians had suffered in 1870 and 1914 were now re-awakened. Unwilling to wait and see whether the Nazis would prove any more gentlemanly than their Prussian or Boche predecessors, the people of Belgium tied up their belongings in tablecloths and curtains, loaded them onto bicycles, hand carts, wheelbarrows or perambulators and took to the road, heading south and west towards the protective line of the allied armies.

iii

All along the Gort Line, the BEF was packing up and preparing to move forward into Belgium. Only a few days before, Lille had been placed within bounds to officers of the 2nd Battalion, the Buffs, and when Second Lieutenant Gregory Blaxland came into the mess at La Crèche for breakfast that morning, one of the company commanders asked whether he would be taking advantage of the new order by sampling the fleshpots that evening.

Blaxland was aware that it was a loaded question. 'I did have it in mind,' he admitted cautiously.

The CO smiled. 'I don't think you will, you know. I think

you'll be marching into Belgium with the rest of us. Didn't you hear the bangs in the night? The war's started.'

The battalion was not due to move off until mid-afternoon, and as C Company, like most of the BEF, was already well-practised at moving, there was no great rush. Blaxland left the business of loading the lorries to Sergeant Skippings, making sure that there would be room for his valise of service dress for wear during any break there might be during the battle. Surplus kit – officers' and other ranks' – was stacked in the village hall, readily available to any passing looters.

One of Blaxland's fellow platoon commanders had been up since daybreak and was full of how he had seen one of the enemy aircraft brought down by the RAF. But now the skies were clear of aircraft and, after an early lunch, when he had seen the lorries properly loaded, Blaxland had an hour spare to sit in the sunshine.

There was a little garden outside the officers' messroom, and he took a chair to the French window and basked in the sun. A bee was buzzing about among the brilliant flowers. Sitting there in full equipment with his revolver and steel helmet, Blaxland cursed the fine weather. What right had the sun to shine when the thunderclouds of war were already so near? He felt suddenly queasy and began to yawn repeatedly. It came to him as something of a shock to realize that he was suffering from pre-battle nerves.

He felt better as soon as he moved off at the head of his platoon. They marched north-west, away from Armentières, for two miles along the frontier before turning right and crossing into Belgium on a newly cobbled road leading through Ploegsteert ('Plugstreet') to Menin. They marched in battle order, steel helmet on head, gas mask on chest, haversack on the back, with greatcoats, packs, Brens and tools loaded in the truck which travelled with the battalion transport column.

Platoons marched in columns of threes with intervals of fifty yards between each. Air protection was provided by the carrier platoon whose vehicles, with Brens mounted on special anti-aircraft fittings, took up stationary position by the roadside and raced on ahead to take up the new position as soon as the tail of the column passed.

In each village, the Belgians waved enthusiastically, and as the 6th Queen's were ahead and Blaxland's was the sixteenth marching platoon they had seen, they were proving the persistence of their applause. It tickled the men's pride and kept them going with heads up and arms swinging, parade-ground style, though there was a bit of tooth-sucking at these johnny-come-lately allies who until only a day before had made so much of their neutrality.

The company halted for ten minutes' rest at ten minutes to each hour, and when they stopped in Warneton the hospitality on offer from the locals became embarrassing. The men flopped down on the pavement of a crowded street, and at once glasses of beer and wine were thrust upon them. Every barman within a radius of ten miles seemed to have congregated on the spot, and every citizen of Warneton had turned out to toast the British soldiers. The ten minutes seemed to last an hour. When the whistle went giving the signal to move on, Blaxland was relieved that his men were still fit to march.

Whether it was the drink or the heat or the lack of route marching exercises in the previous months, the platoon's tread soon became laboured, and a couple of stragglers had to be helped along, their rifles carried for them by stronger brethren. Night fell and still they stumped on, until at last a guide from the advance party led the platoon into a farmyard, where cooks arrived with tea and tinned herrings for supper.

They had marched eighteen miles, which should not have troubled fit troops; but every officer and man was dog-tired and though there were only stone floors to lie on, they slept soundly.

The Supreme Commander of the Allied Forces, General Maurice Gamelin, had his headquarters behind the forbidding walls of the Château de Vincennes, just east of Paris, where Henry V of England had died of camp fever in 1422. This was the Grand Quartier Général, or GQG, the holy of holies whose hushed offices, map rooms and corridors were plunged in perpetual gloom.

Only four months before, Gamelin had ordered a complete reorganization of his general staff, and in doing so had effectively isolated himself from his subordinate commanders. His Chief of Staff, General Doumenc, had been obliged to set up a separate headquarters at the Château de Montry, and Gamelin's deputy, General Georges (whom he regarded as a rival and disliked) had, as C-in-C North East, yet another staff at La-Ferté-sous-Jouarre; and because there was no teletype link between GQG at Vincennes and the Chief of Staff's headquarters at Château de Montry, Gamelin relied upon what Captain Beaufre, a junior officer on Doumenc's staff, nicknamed the 'fiction flood'.

The fiction flood was information that was received from the Headquarters of the Armies at Doumenc's headquarters, collated and rewritten in the staff style required by Gamelin, transferred by typists to ticker-tape and finally taken by despatch riders (who had an unfortunate habit of riding into trees in the blackout) to General Gamelin at Vincennes.

The general was up early that morning. All night, news of the invasion had been building up and when Captain Beaufre arrived from Château de Montry at six-thirty Gamelin appeared to be well content with the way events were proceeding.

A small, sandy-haired man in high-laced boots and a tight tunic, he was later described as a 'button-eyed, button-booted, pot-bellied little grocer', and even Daladier, Gamelin's political minder, had once complained that when Gamelin spoke it was like having sand running through one's fingers.

Now, the 'great man' was humming one of the marches they used to play on the Sunday parades at St Cyr military academy (where he had passed out top of his term) and marching up and down the corridor outside his office, dressed as immaculately as ever in breeches and képi and highly polished boots.

Captain Beaufre had never seen him in such a perky mood.

'We have issued the general alert,' Gamelin announced, squeezing his hands tightly together and assuming a jocularity that looked like a feeble attempt to emulate Joffre. 'Everything is going like clockwork. I always said that the main thrust would be into Belgium, and I have been proved entirely correct. It is another Schlieffen Plan, as I said all along. I am confident, my dear Beaufre, that the next few days will see the complete vindication of all my arguments.'

v

In London, telegrams were pouring into the Admiralty by the boxful. The previous day, after a serious setback in the Commons caused by the crisis in Norway, Chamberlain had called the leaders of the opposition to 10 Downing Street to explore the possibilities of forming a National Government. But the Labour Party Conference was in session at Bournemouth at the time, and Mr Attlee had been reluctant to agree to a coalition without the prior consent of his party members.

Now, as Big Ben struck eleven o'clock on that Friday morning before the Whitsun weekend, Churchill and Foreign Secretary Lord Halifax sat down at a table with Neville Chamberlain for a meeting at which little was said but much transpired.

Chamberlain first announced that the response he had received from the Labour leaders the day before left him in no doubt that it was now beyond his power to form a National Government. Then, turning deliberately away from Halifax, he stared across the table at Churchill. 'The question that remains to be answered, therefore, is whom should I advise the King to send for when my resignation as Prime Minister has been accepted?'

Chamberlain's manner left Churchill in no doubt that it was he, not Lord Halifax, who was expected to provide the answer to this question; but for once he was reluctant to speak: aware that the future leadership of Great Britain hung in the balance, he did not wish to prejudice his case either by pushing himself forward or hanging too modestly back. For once, he preferred the eloquence of silence.

And it was a long silence – a silence that lasted and lasted, a silence longer than that observed in Whitehall each year at the eleventh hour on Armistice Day.

Eventually, when it was obvious that Churchill would not answer the question, Halifax spoke, and his words set Britain on a new course.

'Prime Minister, I feel that my position as a peer, out of the House of Commons, would make it very difficult for me to discharge the duties of Prime Minister in a war such as this. While I would hold responsibility for the whole course of the war, I would be powerless to guide or influence the assembly upon whose confidence the life of every government depends . . .'

He enlarged in this vein for several minutes, and by the time he had finished Churchill knew that the duty of leading the country would fall – had already fallen – upon him.

'I will have no communication with either of the Opposition Parties,' he told Chamberlain, 'until I have the King's commission to form a government.'

Half an hour or so later, Churchill returned to the Admiralty, where he found members of the Dutch cabinet in his room, having just arrived by air from Amsterdam. They were in a state of exhaustion and shock. An avalanche of steel and fire was sweeping across their country. The dykes had been opened and much of the land flooded as a countermeasure against the tanks, but the Germans were already on the causeway that enclosed the Zuyder Zee, and paratroopers were closing in on Rotterdam.

The First Sea Lord, Sir Dudley Pound, was on hand to advise. Signals poured out to the naval headquarters at Chatham, Portsmouth, Rosyth, Plymouth, Harwich and Dover. Plans were made to rescue Queen Wilhelmina; a close liasion was set up with the Royal Netherlands Navy, and an undercover operation initiated to capture urgently needed industrial diamonds and prevent them from falling into Nazi hands.

That evening, there was no crowd at the gates of Buckingham Palace when a car entered and set down its sole passenger outside a sandbagged entrance.

The King received Churchill with a glint of humour.

'I suppose . . . you don't know why I've sent for you?'

Churchill's eyes twinkled. 'Sir,' he rumbled, 'I simply couldn't imagine why . . .'

FIFTEEN

Before turning in that night, Second Lieutenant Ralph Lionel Clarke, the engineer intelligence officer who had assisted Griff Wilmot with his briefing a few weeks before and was now attached to the headquarters of the 4th Division near Lille, wrote up his diary as usual. The previous morning, he had come downstairs to find his landlady, Madame Rouzet, polishing the tiles. She was a grandmotherly sort of person who called him her '*autre enfant*', and over the past months he had become something of an honorary uncle to her grandchildren.

He had spent most of the previous day checking his monthly report to 2 Corps Headquarters and dealing with trivialities. The 18th Field Park Company had lost the bulldozer again. 30th Field Regiment, Royal Artillery, had indented for yet more sandbags. A battalion of the 10th Brigade had cut up a local dance floor for revetting material and were faced with a bill for £50. Corps wanted the return of outsize boots sent via the Despatch Rider Liasion Service and 225 Field Company had forgotten that nil returns were required.

Now, he turned the page and started the entry for the tenth of May, aware that this journal of his might at last become a little more interesting. *Gunfire rattles the windows at first light*, he began, and as he went on with his account of this first day of real war, the words flowed more and more easily.

> . . . An hour later I wake with a start to the sound of a Bren gun. Spring to the window and see a small high-winged aircraft against a pale blue sky. As I watch it drops a red flare. Towards the frontier

red dots curl slowly upwards. Excited talk from below. *'Comment, tous les deux!'* When my batman Sedgewick, an efficient but incomprehensible Geordie, brings me my morning cup of café cognac (by courtesy of Madame Rouzet) he says that the Germans have invaded Holland and Belgium.

Confirmed at breakfast that 4 Division will be moving into Belgium under Plan D, making a short disengaging move to Roubaix. This means a mass of office work, preparing hand-over documents and bringing files up to date. All files relating to local authorities to be handed over. Personnel files to be put in order and delivered to Records. Pillbox construction to be carried on by 2nd General Construction Battalion. Maps to be sorted through and a selection packed; we have them up to Brussels, but what shall we need to the west? Better take two each of Armentières and Poperinghe to be on the safe side.

At Division HQ down the road all are in ripe good humour. General Johnson looks twenty years younger having successfully warded off General Eastwood who was about to succeed him. The Duke of Gloucester has had to leave though he wants to stay. Henry Straubenzee and John Stevens in Intelligence have little news but have set up their battle map with blue marks for the enemy; parachutists at Assche and Alost, Belgians fighting in the Ardennes, a few towns bombed. Armbands are to be worn, and I proudly put on my green band with a black E for engineer intelligence officer. As I come out there is a roar of motorcycles and the Corps Commander, General Alan Brooke, sweeps up the Roubaix road, his fish flag fluttering from his car.

Company commanders arrive after lunch for a conference. Gillespie of 7th Field Company, who has taken over from Le Sauer (now Commandant Royal Engineers, 5th Division), Macdonald of 59th Field Company, Windle of 225th Field Company and Arthur Nixon of 18th Field Park Company. 3rd Division are already crossing the frontier for Louvain, and 4th Division is to move in reserve to Brussels where we are to prepare the bridges for demolition . . .

ii

The order to move reached Wilmot's headquarters near Douai a little before midnight. All day the supporting columns of the BEF had been moving up the main road. Light tanks, armoured cars, guns, motorbikes, lorries and troops went by in an endless procession. There had been a lot of enemy air activity too: in the late afternoon there had been a short, sharp dog fight over Vitry airfield, with Spitfires and Messerschmitts twisting and turning at roof-top height, their machine guns blazing.

Wilmot had anticipated the move by several hours, so the work of dumping unnecessary kit and loading the lorries was already complete by the time Second Lieutenant Tim Peterson, begrimed with dust and oil, rode up on a khaki motorbike.

The section had an allocation of four half-ton trucks. Each was to carry one NCO and twelve men complete with personal weapons and equipment, and had to be loaded with a pre-planned inventory: a winch, an earth augur and camouflet equipment; spades and picks, a Boys anti-tank rifle and Bren gun, 2000lbs of ammonal explosive (or a box of detonators, but never both), boxes of ammunition; cook's gear, petrol stove, hot boxes, fresh, dry and tinned provisions – and a strictly limited amount of personal kit.

Wilmot called his platoon commanders to a briefing as soon as he had read the movement order. They assembled in Madame Faumont's front room: Lieutenant Freddy Radcliffe, a huge second-row forward, Second Lieutenant Tim Peterson, fair-haired and fresh out of Sandhurst, and the stalwart and phlegmatic Sergeant Bill Crisp.

'Your maps, and your route cards,' Wilmot said, handing them out. 'These are the only maps of Belgium we have and they're like gold dust, so guard them with your lives.' He spread out his own on the table. 'Right, pin your ears back. I don't intend to say *any* of this twice . . .'

Their destination that night was to be the village of Normain, close to the Belgian border. Having given orders for the intended route, the order of departure and distance between sections, Wilmot dismissed them to muster their platoons and, having bade farewell to Madame Faumont, put his ash-plant under his arm and went across to the stableyard to address his men.

Standing in the dim light outside the farmhouse, he saw a face look out at him from behind the stables, and recognized Madame Faumont's nineteen-year-old daughter, Driver Hall's intended; and for a moment, he was struck by the ghastly similarity between the present situation and that of the previous war, and was tempted to draw the comparison for the benefit of the men who stood at ease awaiting his pep talk. But this was no time to play at schoolmasters.

'I just want to say this,' he told them, and in the eight months since re-joining the army, Griff's bearing and voice had regained the clipped discipline of the professional soldier. 'You all know that the sappers are the brains of the British army, and you also know that although we are only a very small section, we are as good, man for man, as any in the Corps, and probably better. Now we're going to be put to the test. We'll be moving up to the border overnight, and I expect that we shall go on into Belgium tomorrow or the day after. A few of you, I know, are old soldiers and know what to expect, but most of you are new to this game. Let me tell you this. There may be times when you are frightened. That happens to us all. But always remember that as long as we keep cool and work together, as long as we shoot straight and use our brains as well as our brawn, each man's chances of coming through are much higher. And another thing. Always remember that we are all of one company: that each individual's discipline, loyalty and courage benefits us all, and that our collective discipline and mutual loyalty benefits each individual man.'

In the pause that followed, a stifled sob was heard from somewhere behind the stables, and in the back rank Sharky Ward farted deliberately, causing a ripple of laughter.

'So there you are, chaps,' Wilmot concluded. 'I know you're good. You know you're good. Now let's go out and show Jerry just how good we are.'

With that, the sappers of the special Waterways Defence Section climbed aboard their lorries and pulled up the tailgates, and with Driver Hall at the wheel of the leading truck and Captain Wilmot beside him, the sappers moved off.

iii

By dawn of the eleventh, the Grossdeutschlanders were back on the road, and it wasn't long before 15 Company was entering Marinsart. Here, desolate, burnt-out shells of houses stared at them. The place had been completely destroyed. The bridge over the Semois on the far side of the village had been blown up so they had to ford the river. They collected bundles of brushwood to prevent the vehicles sinking. Heinrich Lauder was in the first truck to attempt the crossing. The river was about seven metres wide and seventy centimetres deep – child's play. Motorbikes and sidecars were loaded into lorries for the crossing and unloaded the other side. Armoured cars were pulled over on a tow-rope. On the far side, the armoured cars had to be towed out of a marshy field to more solid ground.

As soon as they had completed the crossing they spread out and advanced towards rising ground and the village of Rossignol. A warning came in from intelligence that a concentration of enemy cavalry was in the vicinity. But all seemed quiet, and when the platoon was allocated a position in a field where cattle were grazing everyone had a go at milking a cow. Heinrich – like everyone else – gulped the delicious liquid almost reverently. As all remained quiet, the men were allowed a long siesta, taking it in turns to keep watch while others slept. No 1 Section came up. It had to make a detour through the grounds of a stately home because the road had been cratered by a Stuka bomb. They turned off the road and continued across a field in formation. Wherever you looked, men were either sleeping or eating. All the traction vehicles had gone off to a wood beyond the village where an assault tank was stuck in the mud. In the end the tank got itself free after a bit of digging out and the placing of planks under the tracks.

Having carried out their task of providing flank defence, 15 Company reformed and hurried after the convoy. They went along a beautiful road and then through a shady wood. This area had been untouched by the war and it breathed peace and tranquillity – shattered now by the rumbling of engines and the clatter of tank tracks.

Orders came in to advance in support of the 1st Battalion. The main target for the company was a white château-like building about 2500 metres distant. A volley of machine-gun fire whined overhead and they moved quickly to get into position. One of the heavier guns was brought up and placed a little further down the hill to take direct aim. Lieutenant Marz took personal charge of laying and training the gun. The first shell fell a little short. 'Up fifty!' ordered Marz, and the next shell hit the roof, fair and square.

Just before each round was fired, one of the gun crew shouted out: 'Hearty greetings to the village of Suxy!'

On the right, marksmen were already halfway up the slope to the village. In a hollow adjacent to No 1 Section's position, No 2 Section took up position to provide extra firepower. Lieutenant General Schaal also arrived in an armoured car and watched the attack with close attention as the armoured column advanced on the village.

Across the dip and up the slope the grey 'heavies' pushed their way slowly forward over soft ground. One of the motorcycle troops right up at the front fired a flare to indicate that the white château was already taken and that the artillery could cease fire.

It was all over quite quickly. Soon they were bringing out the wounded, among them Lieutenant Kolb, who was Heinrich's company commander back in the days when the regiment was in Berlin. The French had fired from the flank, causing several casualties.

The second section had been sidestepped by about 500 metres and now shot past Suxy into the wood, clearing the way for the rest of 15 Company to advance further.

iv

The race to establish the new defensive line on the Dyle was on. The allies, confident that the fight would take place in the traditional way and on the traditional battleground between Waterloo and Charleroi, pushed on with all speed in order to get the wire up, dig trenches and tank traps and brace themselves for what General Ironside, Chief of the Imperial General Staff, expected would be a 'really hard fight all this summer'.

On the left flank, the French 7th Army under General Giraud dashed forward to secure the mouth of the Scheldt and link up with the Dutch. On the right, the French 1st Army under Blanchard headed for the Gembloux Gap between Wavre on the Dyle and Namur on the Meuse. In the centre, Lord Gort's three corps under Generals Barker, Brooke and Adam pushed forward seventy-five miles to their designated line on the Dyle from Louvain to Wavre.

And while the invasion of the Low Countries convinced the allies that this was the main thrust, the panzer divisions of General von Kleist's Army Group A continued their advance towards the River Meuse.

This was the area which Gamelin had dismissed as impassable to tanks. Defended by the 9th and 2nd Armies under Corap and Huntziger, its garrison troops were largely Parisian reservists who had been allocated the lowest priority for training and weapons. It was the rusty hinge between the iron door of the allied armies to the north-west and the concrete wall of the Maginot Line to the south-east. Not only were its men poorly trained, badly equipped and short of modern weapons and munitions, they were also the troops whose morale had suffered most during the very cold winter.

It was against these two armies, positioned on a line running down the Meuse from Namur through Houx, Dinant and Monthermé to Sedan that the cream of the German army was now pitted. In the north, the 5th and 7th Panzer Divisions were descending upon Houx and Dinant. In the centre, the 6th and 8th Panzers headed for Monthermé, while in the south, the 1st, 2nd and 10th Panzer Divisions had already routed the Belgian Chasseurs, forced the French cavalry back across the River Semois and occupied the town of Bouillon, within ten miles of the Meuse.

Seven of these panzer divisions were now attacking in the south. In the north, what the allies still believed to be the main thrust through Belgium, was supported by just three.

v

... Paul Hodgeson takes the new French liaison officer, Sauervein, resplendent in his uniform of the Chasseurs d'Afrique, to Roubaix with the Divisional Advanced Party. We are allotted two big empty houses in the Rue Gay Lussac but the keys cannot be found. This will be a change for the Section from their comfortable billet next to the office, four flats with parquet flooring. And a lift.

The telephone rings; parachutists reported above the open country east of La Madeleine. Pass the warning on to companies and set off with my pillbox files to see Lieutenant Colonel Worsfield,

2nd General Construction Battalion, RE. On my way back, remember the parachutists and think this may be an intelligence matter so head for the area. There are fields of roots and occasional dark woods, and I stand up in my 8cwt truck carrying Driver Hewitt's rifle ready loaded. Wonder whether I ought to explore the woods. Suddenly I come upon a line of men advancing towards me with fixed bayonets led by a desperado waving a revolver. In time I recognize Rollo Gillespie who is disappointed to find the parachutists to be no more than anti-aircraft puffs . . .

vi

Blaxland's platoon marched through Menin and Courtrai that day, and saw the first effects of the bombing at Wevelgem, damaged during the raids on the nearby aerodrome. There was a marked decline in the enthusiasm with which the soldiers were welcomed here, and a growing tension in the ranks as the realities of what was to come became apparent.

Going through Courtrai, they marched over cobbles and tramlines, and on the way out of the town passed a succession of heavily laden cars coming in the opposite direction. All these cars seemed to be black, all bore the look of great riches and all were driven by men with fleshy faces who gazed upon the marching soldiers from behind dark glasses with a disdainful smirk on their lips, as if sneering at the British folly of marching to meet an invincible enemy.

In one of these cars a young woman in a fur coat and turban was foolish enough to glance at the marching column as it went by, and came in for a stream of wolf-whistles and cheerful remarks.

'All right for some!' they shouted. 'Off on your 'ols are yer, darling? Will you send us a postcard?'

That night the company's billets were in a flax field just

beyond Courtrai. Early the following morning, Whit Sunday, church bells could be heard ringing in the town, and the women from a nearby farm set off in response to their call, the old and middle-aged dressed immaculately in black, the children all in white.

SIXTEEN

To the left of the BEF, the Belgian army was reeling from the shock of invasion. Beyond that, the French 7th Army under Giraud had moved far ahead along the coast towards the Dutch border, while on the BEF's right flank Blanchard's 1st Army was still catching up, so that from the start the allied line was disjointed, with dangerous gaps between troop concentrations.

Griff Wilmot's section had moved eastwards by stages, and was now in its designated position less than a mile from the River Dyle. On his way back to the section from a briefing at divisional headquarters, Griff had made a detour to survey the bridges, canals and railways which would require the attention of the sappers, and while doing so had encountered a mob of Belgian soldiers who had been dive-bombed. Their officers had left them and they were in a state of disorientation and shock.

On arrival at the section, he called an 'O' group to brief his platoon commanders on the task they had been allocated. They gathered in the farmhouse dairy which served as a section headquarters.

'First of all, General Gamelin has sent a message to all allied forces to congratulate us on a smooth and efficient move forward. That's the good news. The not so good news is that it looks as though Holland's been completely cut off. They've taken several airfields and seized the Moerdyck bridge over the Maas estuary.'

Freddy Radcliffe shook his head in disbelief. 'What's happened to the boys in blue for God's sake? We've only seen about two and a half fighters in two and a half days!'

'Division tells me they've been operating behind enemy

lines. The French air force took a bad beating on the first day. Jerry caught a lot of them on the ground, apparently.' He turned to Peterson. 'I'll be making heavy demands on you as a despatch rider, Tim. We can't set up landlines, and there's no wireless, so the BSA must be kept in tip-top working order. Right?'

Peterson beamed. 'Delighted, sir.'

'Now what about that forward recce of yours, Sergeant Crisp? Have you completed it?'

Bill Crisp looked even stonier faced than usual. 'Yes, sir. I have. And to tell the truth there wasn't much to recce, neither. I don't know what the Belgians were on about when they were talking about the defended line of the River Dyle, sir. There's no anti-tank defences. No machine-gun pits. No wire, nothing. Just a fifteen-yard ditch between us and Jerry as far as I can make out.'

'So there's plenty of work for us to do.'

'More than enough, I'd say, sir.'

After the briefing, Griff took a stroll round the section's positions. He went down the lane and across the orchard to where some of the section's camouflaged tents were pitched close to the edge of a small copse. Fifty yards further on, Sappers Ward and Smith were finishing a Woodbine prior to digging a latrine. They threw their cigarettes away as Griff approached.

'Evenin', sir!'

'Evening, Ward. What are you two up to?'

Ward gave his usual belly laugh. 'Well, sir, Smudge and me was just makin' a start on the new Maginot Line, see?'

ii

While the military leaders of Britain and France congratulated each other on the smooth execution of Plan D, the Führer was equally pleased with the progress of the battle so far. Two days before, he had arrived at his 'Felsennest' perched high in the Eifel mountains.

Wearing his personal uniform with its bright swastika armband, he sat in the sunshine on the high stone verandah and received reports from his intelligence staff.

The allies were leaving their defensive line and were rushing into Belgium. It was all happening exactly as he had intended. He could not have hoped for better news.

He felt quite overcome by the patriotic emotion of it all. Eva was at his side and his generals were dancing attendance. He could have wept for joy. How lovely Felsennest was! The birds in the early morning; the magnificent view of the road up which columns of fine young German soldiers were advancing; the brave squadrons of planes flying overhead . . .

iii

15 Company had lost contact with the field kitchen, so had done without breakfast. They had been on the move all night, a dreadful journey through forests black as pitch, the trickier corners and crossroads of which had been marked by white paint to prevent the column losing its way. Now, at daybreak, the vehicles had drawn up at the railway station in St Médard, and Heinrich was emerging from a shop with his arms full of cartons of Belgian cigarettes.

Off again, along a sandy track in the direction of Orgéo. In a meadow, a Fiesel Stork spotter aircraft was standing, and a general in helmet and goggles was holding a briefing for officers from several different units.

They arrived at Orgéo towards midday, and the vehicles spread out to occupy the village. The first requirement was a wash and shave. The men clambered wearily out of the lorries, stretched, and made their way down to a farmyard where there was an outside faucet and hand pump. They queued up for water, and while one man pumped the others collected it in any receptacle that came to hand.

The locals watched from a distance, curious but not unfriendly. They had been ordered by their mayor to evacuate the village, but had been surprised by the rapid advance of the Germans and obliged to stay. They didn't seem to regret the decision at all.

It was here that Heinrich and his comrades saw girls for the first time in enemy territory. Some of them giggled behind their hands at the sight of the soldiers washing in the nude; others could be seen peeping out from behind curtains.

After a 'shit, shave and shower' they all felt a lot better, but stomachs were rumbling. There was nothing for it but to help themselves. The farmer was invited to provide the necessary, and came up with sides of mutton and baskets of eggs.

It turned into quite a feast, and those who didn't know how to cook learned very quickly. A lump of fat into the pan, beat a few eggs up, throw in a few new potatoes and you're on your way. Wash it all down with a bottle of wine or a double mocha strong enough to stand your spoon in. Wonderful!

iv

That evening, when Erwin Rommel, the commander of the 7th Panzer Division, found himself opposite one of the most weakly defended points on the River Meuse, he decided to ignore orders from his corps commander to delay the crossing until morning and ordered a reconnaissance party of infantry and engineers across immediately.

Bridges had already been blown over that part of the Meuse, so they chose a leaky old dam just south of the Belgian town of Houx-sur-Meuse. With hand grenades slung in bundles over their shoulders, stuffed into the tops of their boots and between the buttons of their blouses, they moved forward to the river bank in short rushes, freezing every time a starshell burst overhead. Having established a machine-gun post to cover the crossing, the first man started across the weir. They went one by one, slowly, as if balancing on a tightrope. The far bank was steep, revetted and topped by a railway embankment. Dislodging stones and rocks on their way up, they alerted the Belgian defenders and the moment they put their heads up over the top they were met by machine-gun fire. Immediately, their supporting machine guns on the other bank opened up, and bullets from both sides began ricocheting off the railway lines yards from the attackers' heads.

At the same time, more men were crossing the river, either by walking the dam or in inflatable boats – some of which were shot to pieces. Gradually, the attackers spread out along the bank and brought machine guns up. A confused fight developed, with Belgian artillery pounding the approaches to the river on the opposite bank and the German reconnaissance party inching forward on their bellies and digging themselves into foxholes two hundred yards beyond the railway line.

V

. . . An early breakfast to get the mess packed up. The main divisional convoy leaves on the five-mile trip to Roubaix at 1000 hours. I lead the HQRE section of thirty men, four despatch riders and Wilkinson the MT corporal on motorcycles (four 350cc BSA and one 500cc Norton) and the rest in Morris trucks, two 8cwt, four 15cwt and one office truck which got through the garage entrance under the flats with an inch to spare. The CRE and adjutant have got the two Humber cars on their own affairs.

At Roubaix we stop near the old exhibition ground and the camp commandant Monkey Hill directs us to park the vehicles fully loaded under trees in the square. Transport is not allowed near offices or billets. I put the two Gregories on guard, and the rest lug the kit with a lot of grumbling up the slope to our houses which are at least open though without light, heat or blackout.

Locate Divisional Headquarters and A Mess where the CRE will be feeding, ready to move forward with the General in the morning. Set up the office and notify companies by DR. Wish we had wireless.

Supper at the Rue Gay Lussac is a melancholy affair in the twilight. My room at the top of an echoing staircase faces south. As darkness falls there is a distant rumbling of aircraft and the sky is white with searchlights making it light enough to write . . .

vi

The 7th Panzer Division's preparations for the river crossing near Dinant had not been greatly disrupted by Belgian artillery, and the attackers were assisted by thick fog which developed with the dawn. A footbridge was thrown across and assault boats launched, but then Belgian machine guns opened up and the crossing was abruptly halted as boats sank and infantrymen were caught in the hail of bullets.

At this moment, when the success of the operation was in serious doubt and the attackers were pinned down by Belgian machine guns, Rommel himself appeared on the scene, bounding forward, freezing and crawling on his stomach like a true professional. Seeing that supporting fire was urgently needed, he used the radio in one of the armoured cars to call up some medium tanks.

Within half an hour the tanks had taken up position and were firing their machine guns and cannon across the river; and under cover of this superior fire the crossing went ahead, the general going over on foot with one of the advance units of infantry.

Then, just at the most awkward moment of a river crossing when the engineers were in the process of launching their floating vehicle platforms, Belgian tanks appeared along the river bank from the north. These tanks could wreck the whole operation within minutes, and as yet there were no anti-tank weapons this side of the river to deal with them.

Rommel summoned the company commander and told him: 'Have your men prepare to fire red signal flares at the leading tank on my order.'

For a few moments longer the enemy tanks clattered forward. Then, suddenly, rocket projectiles with fiery tails and flat trajectories streaked towards them. To the Belgian tank commanders this meant only one thing: the Boches were firing anti-tank devices and using tracer rounds for sighting. They turned tail and fled.

vii

15 Company moved off at four in the morning, heading for Bouillon and Sedan. The men were well fed, clean, rested and in good spirits. On the way into Bertrix they passed a couple of crashed aircraft and burnt-out vehicles. A heavy armoured car lay at the roadside and as they drew closer they saw that it was German. It was completely burnt out, the metal blackened and twisted from intense heat. Immediately behind it was the grave of its crew, marked by crosses made of sticks, with their helmets on top.

The column moved on, through Bertrix to Bouillon on the steep, wooded banks of the River Semois. Here entire rows of houses had collapsed and dense smoke was rising from the still-burning town. People were standing at the roadside or sitting on the rubble of what had been their homes. The dead were lying where they had fallen, and the nauseating stench of burnt animals and human beings hung in the morning air.

With the men looking straight ahead to see as little as possible of these horrors, the column of light tanks, armoured cars, self-propelled guns and troop carriers went slowly down the hill to the river, crossed over by the pontoon bridge and up the road on the other side.

They crossed the border at the Porte de France. Here, they were joined by a large number of heavy panzer units which were to support them in the crossing of the River Meuse. The men used every available halt to break off branches and uproot bushes with which to camouflage their vehicles. After a while, the vehicles disappeared beneath the foliage and it seemed that the forest itself were moving along the highway.

They left the main road, and went down a narrow but already well-worn track into a large forest. The infantry got down from the carriers, packed up their equipment, helped each other to hoist the packs onto their backs, and set out on foot. The self-propelled guns followed close behind. The path narrowed further, falling steeply away to a swampy hollow. The French artillery had been at work here: there were shell craters in every meadow and hollow, and the way was barred by fallen trees. Pioneers set to immediately and sawed up the tree trunks, and after a short delay the troops moved on.

15 Company passed through a deserted village, pausing only to load up with beer from the shop. Moving up the hill ahead, sappers and assault troops were at work with mortars and flame throwers. For hours now, droves of aircraft – mainly Stukas and Dornier 17s – had been roaring overhead. The air was filled with the unending droning of their engines. From time to time you could see them up ahead, diving on enemy positions.

The march seemed to go on for ever, and they had only just unpacked the ammunition and set up their position when they were ordered to pack up and move to another position. This took them through Floigny which was under heavy French artillery fire, and in flames. Finally, after a trek down a narrow alleyway, past a cemetery and on to a steep slope, they halted.

Behind the bushes and shrubs were recently vacated enemy

positions. The French had obviously expected a much longer stay: the foxholes and machine-gun nests had been padded out with mattresses, feather pillows and quilts, and the place was littered with empty bottles.

While 15 Company lay ready for action in the woods above the Meuse, Heinrich was detailed off to join the infantry gun liaison detachment with Lance Corporals Tretter and von der Grun. With Sergeant Semmper in charge, they reported to the command post of 2 Battalion and were given their orders: to cross the Meuse in company with the advance units of 2 Battalion and to direct 15 Company's fire at targets in no-man's-land.

They set off with the forty-pound radio sets on their backs, over the hill with the monument and down towards Sedan itself. But within minutes they were spotted, and shells began arriving. Overhead, Stukas were screaming down, delivering their bombs two by two over enemy positions. After a check while the Frenchy artillery was silenced, the detachment set off again.

They slogged on through the heat of the day. Rivulets of sweat ran down their faces and necks, mixing with the dust and dirt of battle and rubbing the skin raw.

Close to the river, they sheltered in a cloth factory while the engineers prepared the inflatable dinghies for launching. From the skies, a deluge of bombs was falling on the French artillery positions. The sky swarmed with aircraft. Watching through binoculars, Sergeant Semmper swore in amazement: on the opposite bank the French guns' crews were tumbling out of their pillboxes and running for their lives.

The engineers ran the dinghies down to the water and the first assault troops started across. Here and there, French machine guns opened up, but these were quickly silenced, and casualties were light. Running along behind garden walls, darting across open areas, Sergeant Semmper and the liaison detachment eventually arrived at the crossing point where they took shelter while awaiting the order to embark.

Under the protection of covering fire from the riverbank, the engineers were running a shuttle service, and after a short wait Heinrich's group was called forward.

Within minutes, they were across. But immediately, there came the howl of machine-gun fire, and they had to crawl for two hundred yards across an exposed area to get to the safety of some sheds. Over and over again, they flung themselves face down to avoid the bullets that sang and whined over their heads. Around them, dead soldiers stared with distorted expressions of agony at the sky. The wounded, groaning and whimpering, dragged themselves back towards the water's edge.

After two false alarms, one of gas and the other of enemy tanks (the latter turned out to be railway carriages rolling down the slope through the station) and what seemed an eternity of crawling on their stomachs, they reached an embankment overlooking the main road from Sedan to Mézières, and for the first time were able to erect aerials and transmit a signal back to the command HQ: FRONT LINE OF 2 BATTALION HAS REACHED SEDAN TO MEZIERES ROAD. Soon afterwards, the 10.5s started a rolling barrage ahead of this line to support the consolidation of positions. By dusk, the liaison detachment's task had been completed.

For a few minutes, Heinrich was able to look around him. Overhead, the bombers continued to thunder into the enemy hinterland. Wave after wave, group after group: you could hear the thunder of their bombs falling beyond the city, and the shells from the 10.5 barrage were whistling overhead. Far in the distance, white signal flares could be seen on the banks of the Meuse: other units were crossing all the time. Nearby a village was burning, with thick black clouds rising from the houses.

The only part of the landscape that seemed to be unmarked by the battle was the River Meuse itself, which wound peacefully through the city, its waters here and there reflecting the reds and pinks of the setting sun.

David awoke that Whit Monday morning to the sound of wailing sirens, cataclysmic crashes, fire engine bells and a thunderous knocking on the door, followed by the voice of his landlady, Madame Signy. *'M'sieur! M'sieur! Les Boches sont arrivés!'*

He had got back into France by something less than the skin of his teeth, and had found himself lodgings in a comfortable guest house in the centre of Charleville-Mézières, twenty kilometres west of Sedan. This had seemed to be a safe distance back from the border and a good place from which to monitor the progress of the war – or at least the first week or two of war.

He heard running feet, shouts, screams. Going to his balcony in pyjamas, he looked down the road. A whole building had fallen into the street. Firemen and soldiers were running out hoses. A woman clad only in a nightdress, her grey hair down over her shoulders, was standing at the front door of a house, screaming hysterically. Low over the roof tops, dark grey aircraft with bent wings and undercarriages that made them look like birds of prey with claws extended were turning steeply back towards the city.

He pulled on trousers and a jacket over his pyjamas, stuffed a notepad into a side pocket, pulled shoes onto his bare feet and ran down two flights of stairs and out into the street. The raid was still in progress. He saw two aircraft wheeling overhead and then diving down in turn, almost vertically. He watched them, fascinated. He saw two bombs separate from the second aircraft. They seemed to grow bigger and bigger and bigger until he could actually make out some of the markings on one of them. Time seemed to slow to a crawl. He looked up at the bomb falling, still falling. He looked along the street. There were people lying in the gutters and behind walls. Then there was a deafening explosion and a flash that seemed to go straight through his brain – and suddenly he found himself sitting in the middle of the road twenty yards from where he had been a moment before.

He picked himself up, dazed. Quite near, a house was on fire. It was Madame Signy's guest house. Its roof had fallen in. The balcony where he had been standing only minutes before was hanging precariously off the wall.

The road was littered with chunks of stone and brick. Several cars were blazing. He looked for his motorbike. He had parked it in the road but it was not where he had left it.

He went up the street and stood opposite the wrecked pension. Then he saw his motorbike. It was on its side, close to one of the cars that was blazing. He crossed the road to retrieve it, and when people shouted at him he took no notice, but dragged the bike onto the sidewalk and wheeled it clear. As he was doing so, the car's petrol tank ignited and he smelt his hair frizzle in the hot blast of the explosion. He wheeled the motorbike further away before trying to start it up.

It started on the fourth kick. He looked back at the burning pension, and remembered that he had not paid Madame Signy. He clapped a hand to his chest to confirm that his wallet was in the inside pocket, and breathed out in relief that it was.

He rode carefully between the blocks of masonry in the road. After a hundred yards slow going, when he was almost clear of the debris, a fireman stepped out in front of him and held up his hand. He opened the throttle wide and brushed the fireman with his shoulder as he went by. He heard shouts behind him. He saw a signpost for *'Toutes directions'* and followed it. Going fast round a roundabout, the foot-rest touched the cobbles and left a trail of sparks.

An aircraft was diving behind him. What looked like a line of very heavy raindrops overtook him in the dust at the side of the road. He put his head down over the handlebars and opened the throttle as wide as it would go. He went very fast out of the town. He didn't slow until he was in the country.

Some time later he ran out of gas. He was on a stretch of dead straight road a few kilometres short of Hirson. He dismounted and started pushing the bike. It was a hot day. Traffic was overtaking him all the time. His throat was dry and his nose was streaming. He wiped it with the back of his hand and discovered that it was bleeding. He looked at himself in the motorbike's wing mirror and saw that his face was caked with blood. He propped the bike against a tree and put his head back. He sat in the shade and thought of Gwynneth. On the road, groups of people pushing bicycles and carts went by.

After a while he began to feel a bit better. He picked up the Brough and joined the procession of people trudging westward.

SEVENTEEN

Château de Montry, where General Doumenc had his head-quarters, was a huge mansion just east of Paris that was on loan to the French army from the Rothschild family. For the junior staff of which Captain Beaufre was a member, life at the headquarters was austere and boring. All the generals were over sixty, and most of them took more interest in their digestive systems than in the prosecution of war.

In time of peace and phoney war, days had been taken up in wading through the avalanche of reports, signals and staff appreciations that poured into the headquarters. Now the balloon had gone up, little had changed.

What made good staff work particularly difficult was that matters of routine and urgency were inextricably mixed in the unending flood of signals, hand messages, tele-phone calls and telegrams, so that a vast mountain of paper had to be shifted daily in order to filter out what was im-portant.

Very early on Whit Monday morning, Captain Beaufre entered the map room to place the latest information that had been sifted during the night on the wall map of Northern France.

Having been convinced for some time that the main thrust was taking place through the Ardennes, Beaufre now resorted to an extreme measure to convince the high com-mand. Taking the largest black cardboard arrow he could find in the drawer of map symbols, flags and coloured tape, he pinned it firmly to the map with its head pointing west on the Meuse in the Dinant area in order to ram home the point that the main German thrust was not in Belgium, but along the Luxembourg-Mézières axis.

Beaufre's arrow caused an immediate stir, and he was closely questioned as to the reliability of his source.

'Air reconnaissance, sir,' he told Colonel Baril, the head of intelligence. 'The evidence is quite irrefutable. We have several reports of a tail-back of sixty miles or more. They are attacking with at least six panzer divisions, possibly seven.'

Senior staff officers came in from their offices to look at Beaufre's arrow, and little groups formed to discuss its implications. Baril sent for the German plans supplied by the Deuxième Bureau, but when they were brought in there were six or seven different ones and there was no way of knowing which the OKW – the German High Command – was working to.

When General Doumenc came in for the morning briefing, he declared that the new development would be greatly to the advantage of the allies.

'Really we couldn't ask for better news,' he remarked, putting his spectacles on to look again at the wall map. 'It's impossible terrain. They'll be trapped between the Meuse and the Maginot, and Corap will be able to mop them up at his leisure. It'll also take the pressure off our tanks at Gembloux.' He turned to Beaufre. 'Be sure to make that point in our morning despatch to GQG.'

ii

Gradually, as the extent of the German break-through became clear, panic set in among the French general staff.

There were telephone delays and orders became garbled; morale drained rapidly and confusion spread. The generals lost confidence in Gamelin, field commanders lost confidence in the generals and the troops lost confidence in their officers, until cohesion was lost and chaos ensued.

A French tank unit moving back under cover of darkness was mistaken for German armour, and the rumour went straight back to army headquarters. On the strength of a single report that his front had broken, the commander of the 11th Artillery Corps passed the report on to General Georges, who personally telephoned his group commanders and ordered them to spike their guns and retreat.

Disposed in penny packets over a wide area, the French armour was unable to concentrate its forces in anything like the numbers required to meet the German advance, so that by the time the Germans had gained only a tenuous footing on the west side of the Meuse, the C-in-C North-east had been given the impression that the battle was already lost.

Late that night, when Captain Beaufre had just gone off to sleep, he was woken to take a personal telephone call from General Georges.

'Is that you, Beaufre? Listen – this is urgent. Ask General Doumenc to come here at once!'

iii

The Château des Bondons at La-Ferté-sous-Jouarre was a large villa set in the hills, and the salon had been turned into General Georges' map room, with a large trestle table in the centre at which sat a number of staff officers who answered the telephones and kept narratives of the developing situation.

Doumenc and Beaufre arrived towards three o'clock in the morning, after a hair-raising drive without lights from the Château de Montry. When they entered the headquarters, they found the map room dimly lit and in silence except for the low voice of Major Navereau, who was reading back a situation report over the telephone. Apart from this, all was quiet, and the atmosphere was one of mourning, as if there had been a death in the family.

General Roton, Chief of Staff to General Georges, was stretched out in an armchair, his eyes averted. Several other staff officers were sitting at the table with their heads in their hands.

General Georges got up quickly and came to the door. He stood swaying before Doumenc. Six years before,

Georges had been present at the assassination of King Alexander of Yugoslavia in Marseilles, and had sustained chest injuries from which he had never fully recovered. Now, his mouth was opening and shutting silently, and his fleshy face was damp and pale with shock.

'Our front has been broken at Sedan,' he whispered, and a sob overtook him. 'There's been a collapse —'

He turned quickly away and, bursting into tears, flung himself down in a chair.

He was the first senior officer Beaufre saw weeping during the campaign. The first, but not the last.

iv

General Billotte set out early that morning from his advanced headquarters at Caudry, between Cambrai and Le Cateau. He was going to visit General Giraud's 7th Army headquarters and call in at the British C-in-C's advance GHQ on the way.

The previous evening the new vice-chief of General Staff to Lord Gort, General 'Rusty' Eastwood, had called at Billotte's headquarters with a message from the C-in-C to the effect that, although Billotte had only been instructed to act as coordinator of the allied forces in France and Belgium, Gort would always be prepared and glad to receive orders from him if he thought fit to give them.

Although such command arrangements should have been ironed out months before, it had been a most cordial and pleasant meeting. Billotte had been at his best: suave and courteous, a big, shuffling, gentle man, apparently untroubled by the rapidly deteriorating situation of his 9th Army.

Accompanied by his British liaison officer, a limping rifleman called Archdale, Billotte set out in his staff car for Gort's advance GHQ at Renaix. Going north through Valenciennes, Conde, Peruwelz and Leuze, the trip was uneventful except for the unending streams of refugees.

At Renaix, Billotte had a few minutes' conversation with Gort's Chief of General Staff, Lieutenant General Pownall, before continuing his journey north. They went through Alost and Termonde (where the steel bridge had been destroyed by bombs and they had to use the wooden one alongside) to Hamme, where, after some difficulty, they found General Giraud's headquarters in the local school.

Giraud was sitting at the master's desk in a classroom. He rose to greet his superior without a smile. Billotte shuffled quickly forward, and as they shook hands Major Archdale saw in Giraud an air of command and confidence to which he and his fellow officers on Billotte's staff were strangers.

After lunch the two generals went together to call on King Leopold at the Belgian headquarters in Willbroek Fort, and as Archdale followed them in a separate car, he saw the first of the Belgian army in retreat. Most of them were bicycling, or were perched up on big wains, seeking their way to the coast. This was an army straight from the battlefield, and a draggled lot they were. An endless line, some in boots, some in carpet slippers, a few (but very few) with rifles, practically none wounded and not an officer to be seen.

At Willbroek Fort, while Billotte was with King Leopold and Archdale and Giraud were standing waiting in a crowded whitewashed office, Giraud suddenly began inveighing against the Belgians for blowing bridges before his troops had been allowed across. He stood quite still with no movement of his arms. Head and shoulders above everyone else in the room, looking straight in front of him, he just damned the Belgians.

A little while later, on leaving the fort, Archdale was joined by Lieutenant Colonel Gregson-Ellis, who had been partially responsible for planning the BEF's advance to the Dyle. As an old school friend of the King of the Belgians, he had been trying – without much success – to jerk Leopold from his depression by talking to him of the happier times they had known at Eton.

At Cambrai, the farmer who had played host to Blaxland's platoon was gesticulating angrily as the British packed up their equipment and prepared to move off.

'*Non, m'sieur! Non! Pas francs, livres! Mille livres!*'

He was demanding payment of this colossal sum for the use made of his flax as bedding. As payment was quite out of the question, an urgent message was sent to battalion headquarters asking if the representative of the relieving unit, the 4th Royal Sussex, could be sent over. This proved a happy decision, because the officer concerned was the Earl Marshal of England, Major the Duke of Norfolk, who remained quite unruffled when told that the farmer was demanding payment of a thousand pounds. The disposal of this bill was one of the last duties performed by the Duke for the BEF, as he and the Duke of Gloucester – Lord Gort's chief liaison officer – had already been ordered back to England to avoid the risk of capture.

By now, much of Sedan had been reduced to rubble. A pontoon bridge had been thrown across the Meuse to the north of the city, and the heavy armour of General Guderian's panzer corps was crossing the river.

Advancing through the city outskirts, 15 Company passed a rabble of French and Belgian prisoners, some of whom appeared completely drunk. Here, it seemed to Heinrich, the two ideologies met face to face: the one looking forward in a spirit of confidence and power to the future, while the other slouched, tail between legs, to an inevitable downfall.

Slowly, 15 Company's column advanced through the city. Encountering road blocks, wire entanglements and felled trees, they dealt with them quickly and efficiently in the way they had been trained. Here and there, huge patches of charred earth showed where the flame throwers had been at work. Shell and bomb craters, guns without wheels, spades and entrenching tools, wrecked and burnt-out vehicles were scattered wherever they looked. In the castle grounds, huge trees had been uprooted and split apart by the force of the bomb explosions.

Vast numbers of prisoners were appearing now, in all sorts of different uniforms and colours. On a slope overlooking the river, a heavy battery had been completely abandoned, their crews deserting their posts during the aerial bombing, and leaving the guns loaded and ready to fire.

But the battle for Sedan was not yet over. On the east bank, machine-gun, mortar and artillery positions were still bringing fire down on any last sign of French resistance, and as each new wave of allied aircraft came in to attack the pontoon bridge, the sky filled with tracer.

The noise was indescribable. The mortars were sending shells whistling up and over the river in high parabolas, making a boomph-boomph noise like a devilish double-bass rhythm. The shells and mortar bombs, exploding in the outskirts of the city, provided a continual series of thuds and roars. As each new air raid came in, whistles blew and orders were shouted, and the steel barrels of the anti-aircraft guns swung round to engage the new target. The harsh batt-bab-att-bab-att of the Bofors sent tracer spraying lazily into the sky, and as the attacking aircraft came into close range the faster stutter of 20-millimetre guns joined in, the whole Satanic cacophony echoing back and forth across the river.

Several plumes of water rose on either side of the pontoon as it was straddled by bombs, but when the spray subsided the bridge was still intact and a tank still crawling on, the shoulders and steel helmet of its commander visible above the hatch.

Another RAF Blenheim was diving for the attack. Fountains of tracer sought it and held onto it as it weaved and evaded. A thin stream of vapour appeared from one wing. Slowly, it rolled onto its back and the engine note rose to a scream. It was diving inverted, out of control. Its last mission ended – like so many RAF missions that day – in a sudden black explosion in the trees behind Sedan.

vii

. . . The western outskirts of Brussels are indicated by new concrete roads for unbuilt housing estates, not shown on the map. A cluster of motorcyclists is waiting at the rendezvous. As I come up, Leeming swings out ahead of me. Half a mile on he guides me to the right up a cobbled street to a village square full of apple trees. We park the vehicles underneath them, breaking a few boughs in the process.

The advanced party has a meal ready in the billet alongside. The doctor has chosen a house in the street as a mess; the lady of the house is flattered and charming. The office is in another house a few doors down marked by our sign, white 18 on a blue ground. Report safe arrival to Geoffrey Pawle who is upstairs sorting out messages. Unpack my things, get the company locations and set off on foot for Divisional HQ because no vehicles are allowed near. The street leads over the hill and I have to pick my way through piles of bicycles. The cafés are full of Belgian soldiers, drinking and singing. One shouts 'Good mornink' at me and tries to look at my mapboard. I shake him off.

Divisional HQ is established in an imposing glass-fronted building on the forward slope, probably a school. Children are playing round the feet of the military police. Back to the mess for tea where the cook, Garland, has settled down well in the kitchen and is talking fluently to Madame. Go to the office to see if Geoffrey wants relieving, but he is deep in conversation on the telephone about explosives lorries and does not want any tea. Warn

Hewitt my driver to be ready with my 8cwt truck in half an hour, and try out the piano while the kettle boils.

The centre of Brussels is full of shoppers in cotton frocks and trams are crossing the great bridge in the middle of the town. The only sign of war is a Belgian bridge guard. The map does not show all the bridges; there seems to be one every 200 yards. There is a large park of vehicles and a petrol depot on the wrong side. North of the town the canal is wider but narrows to sixty feet at the bridges, the principal crossing being the two low level steel lifting bridges at Vilvorde. I cross here and drive on to the end of our sector marked by a railway bridge which is the responsibility of the Belgian Corps on our left. I list every crossing by description, sketch, map reference and estimate of guncotton and ammonal required.

Clear moonlit night with continual red flickering to the east. The section is snoring peacefully. Nice bed with clean sheets . . .

EIGHTEEN

Christine and Marjory were late back that evening, and it was getting on for nine before they sat down to supper with Simone.

The shepherd's pie had been keeping hot in the Aga. It contained more onions and breadcrumbs than meat and tasted more of Oxo than mutton. But Marjory was as tactful as ever.

'Absolutely delicious,' she said. 'Really I don't know how you manage it, Mrs Wilmot!'

'Well, it's the last of the ration for this week, I'm afraid.'

Christine was neither as appreciative nor as tactful. Bouncing a piece of gristle determinedly between her teeth, she wondered whether she dare reject it and put it on the side of her plate. But one had to be very careful. If one so much as hinted that Simone's cooking was anything but *cordon bleu* she was inclined to become Gallic and huffy. With a supreme effort therefore, Christine swallowed the gristle whole, going pink in the process.

Simone noticed. Simone *always* noticed. 'Is it quite that disgusting, Chrissy?'

'No – no, not at all!'

There was a silence. Simone hated these suppertime silences. They made her worry and wonder about Archie and Griff. Where were they? What were they doing? Were they in danger? A great battle seemed to be imminent in Belgium, but she had no way of knowing whether Griff would be involved in it. She hoped David had had the sense to go back to America. As for Archie . . . she could hardly think of him without tears springing to her eyes. Christine had had a letter from him only a few days before but when

237

Simone asked after him all Christine had said was, 'Oh, Pater's fine. Having the time of his life by the sound of things.'

She was sure that he was not having the time of his life. He would have said that for Christine's benefit – of course he would. Or perhaps Christine had said it for hers. Whichever was the case, North Sea patrols could not by any stretch of the imagination be described as the time of anybody's life.

The BBC and the newspapers weren't much help, either. While they remained optimistic about the final outcome of the war, that optimism was already becoming guarded, and Simone was beginning to get the impression that they were hedging their bets. Even that day there had been a paragraph in *The Times* hinting that a quick victory could not be expected without the expenditure of much sweat and blood. The only really good news had been the splendid work the RAF was doing.

She turned to Christine. 'No news of Nick, I suppose?'

Christine looked up quickly, as if Simone had no right whatsoever to ask such a question.

'No. None.'

'The papers certainly seem to think the RAF is doing good work. A hundred and fifty enemy planes have been knocked out already, by all accounts.'

'Really? We don't get much time to read the papers these days, do we, Marje?'

Marjory shook her head and laughed tactfully.

Simone collected the plates the moment Christine put her fork down. Standing with her back to them while she waited for the kettle to boil, she said suddenly:

'I know you can't talk about anything that happens in the headquarters, but I do think that I might qualify for at least the occasional snippet of information. I know absolutely nothing about what's happening, do you realize that, Christine? I haven't heard from Griff for nearly a month. And I haven't –'

She stopped herself, and with a shaky hand poured water

from the kettle into the teapot and brought it to the table.

'I'm sorry. Slight loss of the stiff upper lip. I do apologize.'

Marjory said, 'Do you mind if I turn on the wireless for the news, Mrs Wilmot?'

'Of course not.'

They sat and listened. It was the evening ritual.

'Here is the news. More appointments to the Government have been announced. A great battle is beginning in front of Brussels; the Dutch have retired behind their main water defence line.

'There is a dispatch about today's action by the BEF.

'The Dutch government have arrived in London.

'The Secretary for War will speak about a new Home Front Volunteer Army.

'Allied troops have made a new landing in Narvik and more enemy transports have been sunk off the Norwegian coast . . .'

While the news proceeded, each of the listeners at the kitchen table was careful to avoid the others' eyes. Each mention of naval operations triggered off thoughts of Archie; each mention of the RAF of Nick; each mention of the BEF of Griff. Every news was the same. It was like having variations on the same nightmare, evening after evening.

'. . . It is reported from Brussels tonight that big French and British reinforcements of men and materials have been arriving steadily in many parts of Belgium. It was already known that the allied forces were taking up positions in front of Brussels for what is undoubtedly going to be a great battle and one which may be the biggest of the war . . .'

Simone closed her eyes and for a moment saw a vision of war as it had been twenty-five years before: the helmeted troops advancing into a hail of bullets, the shell craters, wrecked trees, besodden trenches; the blinded gas victims, shuffling pathetically along in line, each man with his hand upon another's shoulder.

'. . . The part of the Royal Air Force in the great battle now developing in the Low Countries has been to harass the enemy's deployment and communications. Throughout the last twenty-four hours our bombers have continued to attack columns of enemy troops, and road and rail approaches to the Dutch and Belgian battlefields . . .

'. . . Commenting on the gravity with which President Roosevelt regards this extension of the war, his secretary today said to a press conference: "The feeling here is that if there is a 'four alarm' fire up the street and the wind is blowing in the direction of your house, the issue at once becomes the protection of your house."'

Christine snorted contemptuously. 'Typical!'

'Ssh!' went Simone. She had made it a rule that no one was to speak while the news was in progress.

'. . . The Admiralty have made an order requiring all owners of self-propelled pleasure craft between thirty and a hundred feet in length to send in particulars to the Admiralty within fourteen days from today, if they have not already been offered or requisitioned.'

Simone looked quickly up, and broke her own rule. 'Pleasure craft? What on earth do they want little pleasure craft for?'

Marjory glanced quickly at Christine and shrugged. 'We've really no idea, Mrs Wilmot. Honestly.'

ii

Having been either head of the Admiralty or War Munitions throughout the Great War, Churchill had fallen into the habit, formed in the dark days of 1914 and 1915, of going to bed for at least one hour as early as possible in the afternoon, and made good use of his ability to fall at once into a deep and dreamless sleep. In this way he was able to do three days' work in forty-eight hours, and had ever since maintained that Nature had never intended mankind to work from eight in the morning to midnight without the refreshment of 'that blessed oblivion' which, even if it lasts only twenty minutes, renews the vital forces. And though he regretted having to pack himself off to bed like a child every afternoon, he was rewarded by the knowledge that when others were drooping at two and three in the morning, he was as fresh as ever and able to start the new day after only five or six hours' sleep.

He did not, however, like having his carefully rationed hours of rest disturbed, and when he was woken to take a telephone call from the French Prime Minister at seven thirty in the morning, he was not amused.

The voice of Paul Reynaud came urgently over the line. He was speaking in English.

'Prime Minister! We have been defeated!'

Winston propped himself on his elbow and blinked away the last of his sleep.

'What did you say?'

'We are beaten, we have lost the battle!'

Winston shook his head disbelievingly. 'So soon?'

'The front is broken near Sedan. They are pouring through in great numbers. Tanks . . . armoured cars –'

Churchill tried to calm him. The first offensive was always the worst, he said, and it always came to an end after a few days. 'I remember the twenty-first of March 1918. After five or six days they have to halt for supplies, and then there's an opportunity to counter-attack. I learned that from Marshal Foch himself.'

There was a pause at the other end of the line. Unlike Churchill, Reynaud was desperately short of sleep. Slowly and dejectedly he repeated: 'Mr Churchill – *we are defeated. We have lost the battle.*'

iii

15 Company had advanced right into the French lines, and had spent the night with the vehicles run up together and pickets posted. Every man was exhausted, and slept as long as he was allowed – in spite of the cold and the damp and the bombs that continued to fall during the hours of darkness.

In the morning, they crawled out of their holes, their faces pale and grey, bristly and filthy. There were dark lines round their eyes now, but the battle fervour still shone out of them and morale was as high as ever.

They drove on through a town which was still burning and then along a newly gravelled road that wound along a wooded valley. Jammed together, the soldiers sat facing ahead in the troop carriers.

'Like being back in Hunsruck!' someone shouted over the din.

'Where the hell are we anyway?'

'*La belle* France, Heinrich, didn't anyone tell you?'

'This isn't France! It's all part of Germany now!'

They clattered along through the country, singing at the tops of their voices.

After a while, the column began climbing a long, steep slope. To the left was a large bunker as yet uncompleted. The French had evidently been at work extending their Maginot Line here, by the look of the cranes and dumps of building materials. The road wound on up the hill, and just beyond the crest, on a bend, the column came to a sudden halt.

Ahead, three German tanks had fallen victim to land mines, and within moments machine-gun bullets were spraying all around. They were on the approach road to Stonne, and the enemy was clearly intent on making a stand.

Hastily, 15 Company took up position. Fields of fire were selected, guns positioned and targets detailed. But the advance, led by infantry and engineers, quickly disintegrated under enemy fire and the company fell back to the bunker to regroup.

People were shouting for the medics and wounded were lying all around. Just ahead, a tank had been stopped by anti-tank fire. Its gun barrel pointed to the sky and the whole of its front had been blown in. The legs of the driver were still in his boots and his hands still clutched the steering lever, but the rest of his body had been completely crushed.

Another attack went in, and met with considerable opposition. A fierce battle developed in the village, the infantry fighting for each house. Then the word came through: 'Enemy tanks ahead!' and the anti-tank unit really came into its own, knocking out tank after tank, including five of the 32-ton giants as well as dozens of little Renaults.

The French brought in a counter-attack with artillery, and for a while Stonne became a no-man's-land; but gradually the defence was chipped away by the mortars, grenades and machine guns of the Advance Unit, and Stonne was reoccupied.

15 Company was running short of ammunition and an urgent request for replenishments was radioed back to the command post. Minutes later, three Junker 52s flew over and dropped ammunition by parachute.

The members of 15 Company began to realize the gravity of their situation. They had advanced too far and were surrounded on three sides with enemy artillery to their front which, by firing over their heads, could cut off their retreat. During the afternoon, the platoons were moved like chessmen on a board into better positions. Every nerve was stretched to the limit.

For the second time in a week, all the enemy had to do was attack to score an important victory. But no attack came, and after a long night during which no one got any sleep, dawn found the men of 15 Company still in position and bracing themselves to continue the battle.

iv

Major Archdale, the British liaison officer on General Billotte's staff, was woken at four-thirty with orders to pack up immediately and prepare to move the headquarters. By now, the atmosphere at Billotte's 1st Army Group headquarters was one of growing tension.

The tempo of the break-through was getting too fast; the 9th Army was melting away and the reserve divisions were going to be either too little or too late to plug the gap.

Worst of all, it was becoming apparent to Billotte's staff officers that behind their general's façade of suave courtesy lurked not the calm confidence of a commander in control, but the hesitation and despair of one who had never come to grips with the situation in the first place.

At eight o'clock, General Eastwood arrived at Caudry with a message from Lord Gort bluntly stating that if Billotte intended to fulfil his role as coordinator, he must now take a decision – and take it very quickly – either to order his field commanders to hold their present positions (the Belgians on the Willbroek Canal, the British on the Dyle between Louvain and Wavre and the French from Wavre to Namur) or to retire.

After some consideration, Billotte gave his answer: the Belgians, British and French 1st Army were to withdraw in successive stages to the Scheldt.

Spirits at Billotte's headquarters were now as low as they could be. Everyone was very short of sleep, and criticism of Billotte was becoming commonplace. Although concerned at the French general's ability to command, Archdale tried not to listen to such criticism; but that afternoon, Billotte aggravated his concern by putting an extraordinary alternative proposal to him.

'I am reconsidering my decision of this morning,' he declared. 'And I shall be obliged if you would convey to Lord Gort two plans for consideration as possible alternatives to the proposed withdrawal. Firstly, that the BEF should establish an outpost position in front of Brussels and throw back their right flank to maintain contact with the French during our retirement to the Senne; or secondly that the BEF should retire to the Senne and hold that line instead of continuing back to the Dendre the following day.'

Archdale contained his impatience. He was sure Billotte's vacillation had been brought on by pleas from the Belgians to save Brussels and from General Blanchard that his 1st Army was too tired to move.

'I am absolutely certain, General,' he said, 'that the C-in-C will consent to neither alternative. However, as I cannot speak for him, I will put them to him personally, at once.'

Archdale was as good as his word, and Gort gave the message his due consideration, though it struck him as unusual that his superior officer should submit these two alternative plans for his approval.

But the decision was not a difficult one. To the left of the BEF, the Belgian army had not had the time or the will to establish a proper defensive line, and beyond them Giraud's army, having rushed forward to Antwerp, was now being forced back. On the right, the enemy had broken through at Namur, and Blanchard's exhausted and demoralized 1st Army was already falling back through the Gembloux gap. So the BEF was in danger of having both its flanks turned at the same time.

Gort's only possible course of action, if the British army was to be saved from being cut off, was to comply with Billotte's original order for a coordinated withdrawal by stages, first to the Senne, then to the Dendre and finally the reserve line on the Scheldt. His negative reply to Billotte's alternative suggestions was delivered that evening.

v

Churchill had decided to fly to Paris for talks with Reynaud. Accompanied by General Dill and Lord Ismay, he flew in a Flamingo passenger aircraft to Le Bourget, landing there at a little after four in the afternoon.

From the moment they stepped out of the aircraft it became clear to all three that the situation was immeasurably worse than they had imagined. 'We expect the Germans to be in Paris within a few days at the most,' a tight-lipped officer told Churchill as he escorted the Prime Minister to his car.

In the capital, preparations for the fall of France were

already in hand: smoke was rising from two large bonfires in the gardens at the Quai d' Orsay when the British Prime Minister arrived by car. The pensioners employed as messengers and porters were bringing out wheelbarrow loads of archives, official files, memoranda and loose-leaf documents and hurling them onto the flames.

The conference was conducted in an atmosphere of funereal gloom. Everyone remained standing. A map had been set up on an easel, upon which the German advance had been indicated by a bulging black line to the west of Sedan. Reynaud, Daladier and Gamelin were there. The latter spoke in his dry, precise manner for several minutes, and was listened to in complete silence.

'A heavy onrush of armoured vehicles is advancing with unprecedented speed towards Amiens and Arras with the apparent intention of driving straight through to the coast towards Abbeville, or thereabouts. It is possible that they may choose the alternative course of swinging left towards Paris. Behind the armour, eight or ten German divisions, all motorized, are driving onwards, making flanks for themselves as they advance against the two disconnected French armies on either side.'

There was a lengthy silence. Everyone stared at the map. Hitler's armies were on the brink not only of cutting the allied forces in two, but quite possibly of surrounding a major proportion of them, including the BEF.

Churchill turned to Gamelin.

'Where is the strategic reserve?' he asked, and to make himself entirely clear, repeated the question in French.

General Gamelin glanced quickly back and, with a shake of the head and a shrug, said simply: *'Aucune.'*

No strategic reserve. Churchill was dumbfounded. What were the British to think of the great French army and its high command? What had been the purpose of the Maginot Line but to economize on troops and provide men for reserve forces?

Why had he not known about this before?

Why had the British government and, above all, the War Office not known about it?

'We had a right to know,' he rumbled under his breath to Ismay, who stood at his side. 'We should have insisted.'

More surprised, shocked – and above all angry – than he had ever been in his political career, he turned away and went to the window. For several moments he watched the old men casting the wheelbarrow loads of state papers into the flames; then, turning back to Gamelin, he began asking questions: questions aimed as much at informing himself of what had happened and what Gamelin intended to do about it as at stopping the panic and forcing the French to think positively about a counter-attack.

Gamelin began a determined attempt to regain lost face. Assuming the air of staff officer which he had used in the Great War when he was 'Joffre's shadow', he gave forth a great torrent of words.

'It is for consideration that we should now consider the organization of a combined striking force against the Bulge. To this end, I propose to withdraw eight or nine divisions from the Maginot Line and a similar number of divisions will be brought back from Africa. These will arrive within the next two or three weeks. General Giraud will be placed in overall command of the French army north of the gap so that from now on the enemy will be forced to advance along a corridor between two fronts upon which war can be waged in the same way as it was in 1917 and 1918. It is likely that the Germans will have difficulty maintaining such a corridor while at the same time enlarging their incursion . . .'

Churchill punctured this balloon of verbiage with one question: 'When and where do you propose to attack the flanks of the Bulge?'

Gamelin faltered. He had faced similar questions in the past, but for over twenty years such questions had always been hypothetical, and high rank had bred in him an instinctive rejection of criticism from any quarter. He was used to being right – he was always right – and to silence his critics he had become adept at using the well-tried staff techniques of the bludgeon of superior rank or the dagger point of sarcasm. He was the career officer *par excellence*, the epitome of a peace-time general. Ever since making his name as the man who worked the 'Miracle of the Marne' while a major on Joffre's staff, he had pushed his way assiduously up the ladder of promotion.

Now the rocket was at last spent, and the unpleasant sensation of falling back to earth was made worse by the presence of this ferocious Briton who growled when he spoke and asked unanswerable questions.

'Inferiority of numbers,' he said quickly, glancing at Daladier to shift the blame. 'Inferiority of equipment. Inferiority of method.' And then another hopeless shrug of the shoulders.

That shrug effectively marked the end of Maurice Gamelin's career: the following day the wizened but sprightly General Weygand, aged seventy-three, was ordered back from the Sudan to take over the command of French forces, and Gamelin, piqued that he was not wanted any more, announced that he would play no further part in the war and went to live in retirement with his sister.

Daladier was similarly discredited. In a cabinet reshuffle Marshall Pétain, aged eighty-four and another old war hero, was brought out of the antique cabinet to replace him as vice-premier. It was as if France – even in her deepest crisis – was still unable to accept that this war was no longer a continuation of the last, and that new leaders and new methods were needed to fight it.

vi

A single pistol shot rang out on Le Mans railway station. Slumped at the far end of the platform, a French officer lay with his brains blown out. Pinned to his uniform was a postcard, which was addressed for the personal attention of M. Paul Reynaud.

'I am killing myself, Mr President,' it read, 'to let you

know that all my men were brave, but one cannot send men to fight tanks with rifles.'

. . . Straubenzee's map shows an ominous blue bulge to the south lined with question marks. 3 Division and our own covering troops are to fall back to avoid being cut off and need two more crossings north of Brussels. To provide these we have to use our equipment bridges, preparing them for demolition as we put them up. One bridge will be made from our folding boat equipment, the other from our small box girder resting on two barges.

I am sent off with the Camp Commandant to help recce the new site for Divisional HQ in a village six miles to the west. Am given an unpromising lane of barns and pigsties for HQRE. The only house is locked, the owner having gone to Tournai. Find a barn for the section and a tiled room for officers at the back of the house in the next street, with a feather bed and access through a ground floor window.

Coming back to Brussels on my motorcycle the sound of gunfire is persistent. Down on the canal Gus Galloway, a little dark-haired Canadian in 59 Company, is building folding rafts under the trees. He is going to run them across the road and into the water after nightfall.

Further down two barges lie alongside the farther bank being filled with gravel by a scoop under the supervision of John Macdonald to bring the decking down to the right level.

At Vilvorde a trickle of civilians crosses the bridge pushing handcarts watched by the Royal Fusiliers who are providing protection parties.

Back to the office along now-deserted roads to write my evening report. Brussels is a city of the dead, streets empty and echoing. Round the corner come troops trudging in single file along both gutters wearing the red-and-black triangles of 3 Division. At the great bridge there is glass all over the road – they must have blown the camouflets.

The news at the office is that Alan Gesty has fallen off his motorcycle and been sent to the rear, so HQ 59 Company must be shorthanded. When the CRE dismisses me, I thankfully set off for our new billet, arriving about midnight. Sedgewick has laid out my kit on the feather bed, but choose the floor as looking cleaner . . .

NINETEEN

Griff was lying on a straw paliasse in a disused dairy trying to write a letter to Simone when the German artillery opened up. It was one a.m. The first shells fell a mile or so to the north, so for the time being at least the section was not under threat.

Three hours before he had sent Peterson off on the motorbike to deliver reports and collect orders at divisional headquarters, but he had not yet returned and until he did there was little choice but to stay put in their present position.

Since moving up to the Dyle forty-eight hours before, Griff and his sappers had been demolishing bridges, building tank traps, cratering roads and laying mines. Now, with the shells beginning to fall closer and still no orders from Division, he was beginning to feel edgy.

'It's well after midnight,' he had written so far, 'and I am snatching a moment to write this as I've no idea when I shall next have time. We are somewhat in the thick of it at the moment, and things are happening so fast that it seems impossible to believe that it is now five days since we were moved forward. There is little time to eat or sleep, let alone think, which is probably for the best . . .'

He stopped writing. A motorbike was drawing up in the lane, and a moment later Tim Peterson came in, spattered in mud from head to foot and bleeding from a cut hand.

Wilmot was already on his feet.

Peterson saluted. 'We're to move immediately, sir. We were ordered back six hours ago, but the DR never got through. We're to fall back in rear of the infantry to the line of the Senne.' He handed over a message form, which confirmed his verbal message.

Wilmot studied the message by the light of a dimmed torch.

'It looks like a general retreat.'

'I think that's what it is, sir.'

'Any idea why?'

A shell whined overhead and exploded much closer – Griff estimated less than half a mile away.

'Jerry seems to have broken through on our right flank, sir. I gather the French have already begun to pull out.'

'So we have to pull out with them?'

'It looks like it, sir.'

'All right, Tim. Get over to the lorries and pass the word. We'll move off immediately. Leave the motorbike here, I'll need it to deal with the railway bridge.'

'Sir – I thought you were going to let me have a go at that –'

'Well I've changed my mind. Now get on with it.'

They went out into the lane and Peterson sprinted off into the darkness to pass the message. Moments after he had gone, another shell whizzed over, and there was a shattering explosion, very close. Having dived for cover in the ditch, Griff picked himself up and continued along the lane. More shells landed – some in the orchard where 2 Platoon were sleeping under canvas. There were two tons of ammonal explosive in the lorries, and the fall of the shells indicated that the German artillery might know what they were shooting at. He found Freddy Radcliffe, who had not heard yet from Peterson. Griff told him to take charge of loading up and moving off and then collected a toolbag and detonators and set off with Lance Corporal Kingsnorth on the pillion to deal with the railway bridge.

Leaving Kingsnorth with the motorbike concealed behind the railway embankment, Griff loped quickly along the last hundred yards of railway line to the bridge. It was an old one, single span and single track, and built of brick. Holes had already been drilled and the charges, complete with FIDs (Fuzes Instantaneous Detonating) were in position, so all that remained was to fit the gun cotton primers and detonators, connect up the electrical circuit and run the wire back to the connector box.

There were four detonators to be fitted, two on either side, and he completed one side within a few minutes. But on crossing to the other side, he managed to drop a crimping tool and within seconds of it clattering on the line, a machine gun opened fire and he was caught on top of the bridge with bullets flying round his head and pinging off the brickwork. There was a low balustrade behind which he was able to shelter, and after lying low for a few minutes the firing eased enough for him to continue.

He was much more cautious after that, keeping his head well down and working at arm's length to fit the detonators and connect the wires. Fortunately it was still completely dark, and any fire from the enemy was wildly random. But he could not ignore the uncomfortable thought that it might be covering fire for stalkers, and that at any moment he might find himself on the wrong end of a German stick grenade. When he had finished, he pulled back slowly on his stomach and tiptoed back on the sleepers, unreeling the electrical leads as he went.

'I was wondering where you'd got to, sir,' Kingsnorth remarked laconically when he arrived back on the embankment.

Wilmot inserted the wire ends into the connector box. Moments later the bridge went up, and within seconds of the last chunks of debris falling, the motorbike was bumping away along the lane, with a Spandau heavy machine gun firing into the darkness behind them.

On regaining the main road it became quickly apparent that a massive night withdrawal was taking place. Soon after dawn there were several dive-bombing attacks on the transport convoys which had not yet got into cover, and at one stage Wilmot and Kingsnorth were fired on by some stray *poilus* who seemed to have lost their way. They were very relieved, therefore, to find the section's vehicles parked under camouflage netting in a field a few miles south of Waterloo.

Wilmot was greeted by Freddy Radcliffe. 'We've lost Tim, sir,' were his first words. 'It was one of those first shells before we moved off. He was dead when we found him.'

ii

At Stonne, the Grossdeutschlanders prepared for another day's fighting. To the right of 15 Company, 13 Company began firing shortly before dawn, but almost immediately the French replied with heavy artillery, scoring direct hits on the support lines behind 15 Company's position.

An intense fire fight began, and once again the Luftwaffe had to be called up to drop replenishments of ammunition. Stukas were called up as well, but the French positions held out against their dive-bombing and after a while the advance platoons were driven back, with several gaps in their lines. Then the German artillery arrived in support, and an artillery dual began. In the course of it a hunting lodge being used as a battalion headquarters was hit and Lieutenant Marz, 15 Company Commander, was wounded. Lieutenant Gerbener took over command from him and the fight went on. The light infantry came up and started firing from the edge of the trees, and the French replied with equally heavy fire.

To support the right flank, which was coming under pressure, everyone who could move was ordered into the forest at the rush; but once again the attack that could have won the day for the French never developed, the firing became sporadic, and the men of 15 Company began to think about a bite to eat.

This time the field kitchen had driven straight through the enemy's artillery barrage; but they had only just filled the kettles and got the stoves going when they were ordered back by battalion HQ: they were considered too valuable to be put at risk. 15 Company was left with a few hunks of cheese and chocolate. The men bolted it down ravenously, without letting go of their weapons.

Cautiously, the companies started to advance again. Going along the road, the full effects of the French artillery were all too clear. Armoured vehicles, motorcycles, corpses lay everywhere. They passed one of the 14 Company vehicles whose driver was still sitting at the wheel with half his skull missing.

But in the space of a few days they had become accustomed to such sights and were hardened to them. Nothing bothered them any longer: the life or death struggle had rendered them almost feelingless.

They entered Artaise at dusk. The town was ablaze. A terrific heat radiated from the burning houses. To left and right, artillery shells still fell. Houses were torn apart; glowing beams crashed down across the street.

Then – suddenly – an uncanny silence. No more explosions; no more death rattles from machine guns. Heinrich and his comrades looked at each other in amazement.

'Drive on! Drive on!' Lieutenant Gerbener shouted, coming up from the rear on a motorcycle.

Artaise was left behind. They came to Bulson – hardly touched by battle. They joined up with some infantry who had been marching all day on foot.

And then, the blessed halt for the night. The column turned off the main road and parked under cover at the edge of a forest. The men, totally exhausted again, tumbled out of the vehicles, wrapped themselves in their blankets and fell into a deep sleep.

iii

Hampered by refugees, harried by Stukas and bewildered by the extraordinary decision to retreat, the Tommies began the long trek back, first to the line of the Senne on the night of the sixteenth, then to the Dendre the following night and, two nights after that, to the reserve line from Oudenarde to

Maulde on the Scheldt. As they went, the Sappers waited for the last platoons or convoys to cross before blowing up the bridges in their wake.

But even this withdrawal was marred by order, counter-order and disorder. The general plan of a staged retreat was almost immediately contradicted by orders from General Georges and further complicated by Billotte who was influenced by repeated appeals from General Blanchard, one moment to delay the withdrawal of the 1st Army because his troops were too tired to move and the next to expedite it because of the growing pressure on his front.

At length, Major Archdale decided that he could keep silent about Billotte's unsuitability as a leader no longer, and drove over to Gort's headquarters in the woods at Wahagnies, a few miles south of Lille.

He was received by the chief of General Staff, Lieutenant General Pownall, to whom he poured out all his misgivings.

'Frankly, sir, I believe that his inability to take decisions and improvise under stress is now leading to a situation that may imperil the BEF,' he said. 'I would rather speak out now and risk the charge of disloyalty than allow the C-in-C to remain ignorant of his . . . his malignant inaction.'

Pownall listened patiently. Archdale's outpouring was not the first he had heard that day, and he was conscious of the need for the senior staff to hold steady when things went badly. 'Isn't it quite simply a case of the French being over-fatigued? I'm sure they'll fight as soon as they're rested.' He looked closely at Archdale. 'You mustn't let their pessimism rub off on you, Major. Maybe it would be a good thing if you got a really good night's sleep yourself. You look as though you could do with one.'

Feeling chastened, Archdale returned to Douai where he was met by Billotte and asked how things were going.

'All well with us, sir,' he replied cheerfully, 'and CGS is confident that the 1st Army will soon be able to pull itself together and start fighting back.'

Billotte made no reply to this at first, but simply took out a map and spread it on the table. It was marked with the latest intelligence on the German order of battle and showed, by means of a series of red circles, the German armoured divisions confronting the allied line.

'*Un panzer,*' he said slowly, putting a thick finger down on the first red circle. '*Deux panzer. Trois panzer. Quatre . . . cinq . . . six . . . sept . . . huit panzer.*' He looked solemnly at Archdale. '*Et contre ceux-la, mon ami, je ne peux rien faire.*'

There was only one thing to be done: arrange for him to meet Gort then and there while this mood of hopeless impotence was on him. Archdale fixed up a meeting immediately therefore, and at eleven o'clock that night Billotte and Archdale arrived at Gort's headquarters.

Gort, a burly, unflappable man who had won the VC on the Hindenburg Line in 1918, greeted Billotte warmly.

'*Eh bien, mon Général! Qu'est-ce que vous avez à me dire?*'

Billotte made it quickly and abundantly clear that he had no plan, no reserves and little hope.

'*Je suis crevé de fatigue, crevé de fatigue,*' he kept repeating, and then again: '*Et contre ces panzers je ne peux rien faire.*'

iv

The men of 15 Company had found the water fountain in the village centre at Raucourt and were scrubbing each other down. A couple of dead horses lay nearby, but that didn't bother them: the important thing was to start the day with a good wash and shave.

Back at the forest's edge where the column had halted for the night, the vehicles were now thoroughly camouflaged again and stoves were being lit to prepare a midday meal of chicken, rabbit and veal, which had been foraged from the nearby farms. Each man was his own chef, and they ate well. With food inside them they were ready for anything. For the time being, they were to hold their position, so in the afternoon everyone joined in to service the vehicles. After that the company commander allowed an hour's free time for the men to write letters home, as a despatch rider was to be sent back to the rear that evening.

They fell in for roll call at six, and when they had answered their names Lieutenant Gerbener read out a special order of the day he had just received from the regimental commander:

'"After seven days of unchecked and victorious advance via Luxembourg through Belgium and into France, the regiment is now at the end of the first stage of the struggle, and at this moment I feel a deep inner need to thank every officer, NCO and private soldier for the supreme devotion to duty which each man has shown and which has undoubtedly contributed to the victory. The regiment is proud of every single one of its members . . . !"'

v

David had stopped at a crossroads in Beaumont to rest and eat some stale bread.

He had dumped his bike at Hirson and had walked by stages through La Capelle, Le Cateau and Cambrai and was now heading north, hoping to make his way back to Ostend. He was still wearing his trousers and jacket over pyjamas and had found a French army greatcoat, whose buttons he had ripped off and which he wore in spite of the blazing sun. His feet were blistered; his shoes were in holes, and he hadn't shaved for five days.

Nearby, some Tommies were lounging at the roadside, smoking cigarettes and waiting for their lorries. A British major was being harangued by an old man with a half-smoked Gauloise hanging out of his mouth.

'*C'est la même chose comme en quartorze,*' the old man was saying, the brown cigarette wagging up and down as he spoke. '*Reculer, toujours reculer.*'

'*Reculer, oui,*' replied the major with forced optimism, '*mais reculer pour mieux sauter, n'est-ce pas?*'

The old man laughed bitterly, and as the major turned

away, David stepped forward. He took out his passport and press pass.

'Excuse me, sir – I'm an American news reporter. I'm trying to get to Ostend. I lost everything back at Mézières when they broke through. I've got a cheque book but no cash and I was hoping –'

The officer looked him up and down, glanced at the passport and handed it back. 'Ostend? I doubt if you'll be getting there in a hurry. And if you want me to cash a cheque for you you can think again, old boy.'

David licked his lips. His mouth was parched and he had sores on his gums. 'What d'you reckon's my best bet then?'

The major shook his head and watched the unending stream of refugees for a few moments. 'I wish I knew the answer to that. I'd get to the coast if I were you. There are still a few trains running. Try and get on one of those.'

'Where do they go from?'

'Who knows? Lille, maybe. Or failing Lille, Armentières.'

The company lorries were arriving and the Tommies were preparing to climb aboard. David eyed them longingly. 'No hope of a lift, I suppose?'

'None whatsoever,' replied the major briskly, and strode off to take charge of his convoy.

The old man looked at David and shrugged. '*Comme j'ai dit, m'sieur. C'est exactement la même chose comme en quartorze . . .*'

vi

A week had passed since Second Lieutenant Blaxland had sat in the sunshine and suffered from pre-battle nerves. Now, on the reserve line, it was beginning to look as if his platoon might soon be involved in some fighting.

While the retreat from the Dyle was taking place, the Buffs had taken up position along the lateral road that ran parallel to the Scheldt and about a mile behind it. On the right, the 6th Queen's were taking up position around Elsegem. Just visible on the left were the towers of Oudenarde.

Preparations for the coming battle were very much in keeping with the old methods of trench warfare. Working in pairs, the men first dug their own weapon pits before expanding them to provide each section with its own continuous trench, which was in turn connected with its neighbour to form a triangle with zigzagging sides about seventy yards long.

In Blaxland's platoon were two corporals – unrelated – called Pilling, one of whom was cocky and the other melancholy.

Cocky Pilling had an idea for rigging trip wires to catch the German hordes as they stormed across the field, while Melancholy Pilling was convinced his position was vulnerable because of some dead ground he had discovered to his front.

After several hours digging, when most of the work was complete, the quartermaster sergeant (an ex-machine-gun instructor) came round with hot suppers for the men.

'You've got some fine fields of fire here, sir,' he told Blaxland breezily, 'But I can't say your weapons are sited to the best advantage.'

Blaxland thanked him for his advice, and sighed.

vii

. . . Wakened by bright sunshine at six a.m. Wash under the pump and leave a canvas bucket of water for Geoffrey and the doctor who are still snoring. Go down the road to Divisional HQ.

In the orchard outside the Field Security Office a truck is standing with a group of military police looking in the back. One says 'Look out! He's got a knife!' and there is a scuffle. On the floor of the truck somebody is squirming around wrapped in white silk. I see a bald purplish head with a gash across it. An NCO tells me it is a parachutist. From the direction of Brussels comes a distant thud followed by two more, and windows rattle. The bridges have been blown.

Back at the billet my good deed has not been appreciated because the bucket has leaked. Sedgewick is frying bacon in an outhouse. Should I go back to Brussels after breakfast or await orders? At that moment Paul Hodgeson arrives in the Humber brake with Turner, tired and hungry. He says that the CRE is remaining with the Divisional Commander and Geoffrey is to report to him. I am to take an urgent message to 12 Brigade while he gets some sleep.

Set off with Hewitt in my 8cwt; find a village, but no sign of brigade headquarters. Could they have pulled back? There is a signaller winding up wire. As I stop to ask him, a car draws up beside me with a pink Brigadier Hawksworth leaning out.

'Ah, here's a sapper!'

'Sir.'

'The bridge at Vilvorde has not been properly blown and I want it done at once. Get in touch with the Royal Fusiliers to provide a covering party.'

'Right away, sir.'

No time for me to get hold of the CRE even if I knew where he was. The Vilvorde job belongs to 7 Field Company who are in support of 12 Brigade, and their headquarters is only a mile or two away. When I arrive the second in command, Vaughan Williams, and Derek Curtis are having breakfast. Gillespie is out at the bridging site. I deliver my message. 'Afraid that was coming,' says Vaughan Williams. 'How much sleep have your section had, Derek?'

'About three hours.'

'Go yourself now and contact the commanding

officer of the Royal Fusiliers. I'll send them along in about half an hour.'

I drive off to find Gillespie, making slow progress because the road is now full of refugees observing no traffic rules and abandoning their gear whenever an aircraft appears. Gillespie's truck is standing by the roadside at the folding boat bridge. Everything is quiet. On the far side is a Tetrarch light tank of the Inniskillings who are holding the bridgehead for the benefit of stragglers. Smoke from a burning house lies low over the water.

Gillespie stands by the water's edge watching two sappers in a dinghy. I report my mission from Hawksworth and he turns on me.

'How dare you order my company out! Don't you know there's nothing between Vilvorde and the enemy? The CRE has sorted all this out already.'

'Shall I stop them?'

'Yes, and I will go and see Hawksworth.'

The only way to get back to Vilvorde quickly is along the canal bank, Germans or no Germans. I tell Hewitt to go flat out and wish my tyres did not scream so loudly. It takes me half an hour to get to Vilvorde where the road bends round away from the canal. We turn right, up the main street and stop where the 7 Field Company working party are having a smoke, their vehicles tucked into the side of the road. I walk towards the canal. At the last bend in the street a Bren carrier is parked at the ready, and opposite is the sign '67 Tac HQ' on a brown ground. Stumbling down steps into a cellar I find the CO of the Royal Fusiliers and Derek looking at a map. I report that the bridge is not to be blown after all.

'Well that's that,' says Derek, 'but we think we ought to have a shot at that last girder anyway.'

The CO is not too keen. He has withdrawn his covering party and re-establishing could cost casualties. Nobody knew what there was across there now. 'I'll check with Brigade,' he says.

Meanwhile I walk down to inspect the bridges. The main girder of one has not been properly cut but it is impassable to all vehicles. There is a rifle shot and a bullet whines overhead. I jump into a slit trench. Nothing to be seen. Return to meet Derek coming up the steps.

'All off?'

'Yes, back we go!'

The sappers stamp out their cigarettes. I follow the convoy back so I can report they are safe, and branch off to Laeken to get some more information from the 2 Corps Report Centre. Nothing there; they have pulled out. Drive on to the former Divisional HQ office and find nothing there but a rear party of military police who say that everybody has gone back to rear HQ. Something is going on and I had better get back. I postpone my tour of the blown bridges in Brussels.

The news is that we are to fall back behind the line of the Dendre now held by 3 Division. The doctor and Sauervein are to set off at once with the advance party for Resseghem, while I get some sleep and bring on the section with the HQ Division convoy after dark. We have to be across the River Dendre by first light. The adjutant and CRE are together in the Humber Snipe elsewhere so I am to take the shooting brake. The RSM, the CSM and the sergeant clerk ride in 15cwts. A tracing has been issued showing the route which avoids both Alost and Ninove. I have a torch to look at the map by but the shooting brake is not blacked out so have to be careful. We are allowed no lights.

I start badly by taking a wrong road out of the

village. Rather than face turning each truck round in the dark, I drive into a field of roots, take a wide sweep and drive out again and back; successful, but have now lost the convoy ahead. Take my direction from the flashes in the eastern sky. On the main road, Graham comes alongside on his motorcycle.

'Sir, Hodder has broken down.'

'How long?'

He goes back to find out and eight shadows behind me slush to a standstill.

'No verra bad. Ten minutes.'

Suppressing the feeling that we are well in the rear of the whole British army I decide to wait. Twenty minutes later we start. There should be a left turn soon . . .

Can hardly see the road, let alone landmarks. Turner is not much help, being so shortsighted that I have to tell him how far he is away from the edge of the road.

This could be the place, but there is no going back if it is wrong. Leeming shepherds the convoy round.

Next there should be a right turn; but I only have seven trucks instead of eight. 'Foster has gone back to look for Gregory,' says Corporal Wilkinson alongside. 'He must have gone straight on at the last turning.' I start off again. From here according to the map a beautiful wide road leads to our destination, but instead it is getting narrower and narrower. I am climbing a hill, and I feel the tyres ploughing through sand. I come to a fork. The gunfire has stopped, there is no moon and I have no idea which way I am pointing. The lanes are too narrow to turn. There is a cottage, pitch dark because it is after midnight. I knock on the door until a man emerges, his wife behind. They do not speak French. I go in and spread out the map on their table. They are excited because they have never seen a map before. I cut them short and ask the way to Resseghem but they do not seem to have heard of it. I take the right hand lane. Half a mile later it ends in a gate.

Repeating my previous performance I drive into the field and do a wide circle but this time the Humber sinks down to the axles in the soft ground. I tell the other trucks to turn round as they can, and Goddard backs over Leeming's motorcycle. The moon is now up and a mist is rising. We load up the motorcycle and offload the Humber. At last it comes free and the convoy sets off back down the lane. The other fork leads downhill between steep banks. A dark figure looms in front.

'Where does this road lead?'

'Dunno sir, but it's blocked by ammunition lor-ries up ahead.'

Four of them. They belong to Griff Wilmot, an ex-cavalryman who runs a show called the Water-ways Defence Section. We shake hands and he gives me some very welcome directions.

I squeeze past the first lorry, and turn to see the others squeezing past too; then two more, and I rouse the driver of the last one to make him pull over. We cross a stream by a grove of poplars. Up a little hill there is a hurricane lamp with the welcome sign HQRE. Inside I surprise Dick Walker, adjutant of RE 3 Division and lately 7 Field Company who puts me on the right road.

The doctor's anxious face is a cheering sight at the rendezvous where we are well overdue. Foster like a good despatch rider has already arrived, taking the sensible route by instinct. Gregory turns up later in the morning having followed an RASC convoy along the main road . . .

In the morning, the occupants of the cottage farmhouse near Wilmot's section headquarters began moving out. Two carts were brought up outside the front door and were piled high with possessions.

Some of the soldiers had volunteered to give them a hand loading up. Two were carrying a crippled old lady out who was sobbing inconsolably. She was carefully hoisted up into a chair facing backwards on top of the load. Another woman came out with a baby, which was shoved into a space in the cart. This left the farmer, two sturdy women and a boy of ten.

The farmer beckoned Wilmot into the kitchen and showed him the sides of salted pork hanging against the wall, indicating that the British could have them. Wilmot thanked him. They went outside again. The old woman was still sobbing. The man looked at Wilmot as if he were personally responsible for starting the war. 'My mother is seventy-six,' he said.

Without another word spoken by anyone they departed, the two women taking one cart and the man and the boy the other, the wheels creaking and cracking as they went down the track to the road.

ix

That afternoon on the banks of the Scheldt, Blaxland's platoon was visited by the brigadier. He walked briskly about, cast a quick eye round the positions, laughed at Cocky Pilling's trip wires, and strode off. Almost immediately there was a roar of aircraft and some German planes went overhead, pursued by British fighters. One moment the sky was full of the roar of their engines and the racket of their guns, and the next they were gone, leaving a trail of smoke rising from the horizon.

Later that day, the platoon was ordered to pack up and move to a new position commanding a crossroads on the outskirts of Oudenarde. As soon as the evening meal was over, the men started digging all over again, but now, with the expectation that daylight might bring an attack, there was no question of following the precise instructions laid down in the manual of field engineering. They just dug a trench in the shape of an arrowhead. Whether it was the softer texture of the marshy soil or the stronger sense of urgency, they sank at double the speed of the previous effort, and by daylight had mud underfoot, and Blaxland was the only man who did not have to stand on tiptoe to see over the parapet.

Vehicles arrived with anti-tank mines and coils of Dannert wire, and while Sergeant Skippings got this in position, Blaxland set about camouflaging the trench. While he was doing so, the first vehicle-loads of troops came into view along the lateral road from Oudenarde, on their way back from the Dyle.

It was Blaxland's first glimpse of the retreat, and he was shocked to see lorries laden with corpses; but after staring at them hard and seeing some movement, he realized that the bodies were not dead but asleep.

x

At a quarter past ten that night the air-raid warnings sounded in the city-port of Dunkirk, and within minutes the Luftwaffe was overhead and the bombs were falling over the docks, the oil storage tanks, the refinery and the city. For the next five hours, Dunkirk and the surrounding districts of Malo-les-Bains, Rosendael and Coudkerque came under almost constant attack.

Wave after wave of bombers – fifteen waves in all – let loose a deluge of fire and destruction. All night the fire engines went wailing through the rubble-strewn streets. Warehouses blazed; buildings collapsed; oil tankers in the harbour exploded, sending up giant cauliflowers of orange flame.

In the morning, the rescue parties counted the casualties:

sixty civilians and soldiers dead, hundreds injured. But rising into the sky above the port were four massive columns of black smoke which, while remaining for several weeks as monuments to the savagery of the bombing that night, would hinder the Luftwaffe in a way that Reichsmarschall Goering's pilots could not possibly have foreseen.

xi

. . . No time even to set up the office truck. I am to leave at once as the next advanced party with Sauervein. Divisional HQ is to move to Waregem behind the River Scheldt today as there is no time to lose.

The main road is a mass of traffic of all formations moving west with no attempt at spacing or discipline: ambulances, three ton lorries, Belgian horse drawn artillery. One horse has a flap of flesh hanging off its rump. As we draw near the Oudenarde bridge traffic becomes two then four abreast, mounting the verges in attempts to gain position. This would be a holiday for the Luftwaffe, but there is not a single aircraft in sight.

A 2 Corps staff car draws up alongside me and there is Major G. G. S. Clarke. 'About that last pillbox return of yours,' he begins . . .

After Oudenarde the road to the north-west is deserted. I stop in Kruishouten and we buy cold sausage and cheese. Waregem is a pleasant little village with a château. The road with the château is allotted to 'gunners and sappers'.

We move like lightning. While I hang the RE sign on the wrought iron gates to keep out the gunners, Sauervein marches up the front steps and bawls out a surprised Belgian family having lunch. In future they will be permitted to use the kitchen and one back bedroom. By the time he has allotted

the other bedrooms with a suite for the CRE his
interest begins to wane. But when Madame at the
house next door shows reluctance to accommodate
the section, he perks up.

'*Sale femme!* This is war you must
understand . . . Do you not hear the cannon?
Boom! Boom!'

Then he goes to sleep on the lawn while I
proceed to find a billet for the RSM. The CRE
will be pleased; he is partial to châteaux, and I have
to be firm with Monkey Hill who is having second
thoughts about a place for A Mess. Finding the
key of an empty house takes me out of the village,
but I get back at five o'clock in plenty of time to
meet the main convoy.

Sauervein is frantic. 'I have been looking for
you everywhere! Everybody has gone away. The
location has been changed to Sweveghem.' I say I
have to return the key, but Sauervein says that is a
ridiculous waste of time. We creep shamefacedly
into Sweveghem behind the convoy, but the doctor
has done wonders in the short time he was given,
finding us an office in one corner of a large classroom in the school. I balance my intelligence box
on two desks and make out my reports . . .

TWENTY

By Sunday 19 May, the fighting withdrawal from the Dyle had become a nightmare. Short of reliable maps, frequently out of touch with their headquarters, confused by orders that conflicted or were countermanded, the brigade, battalion and company commanders of the BEF struggled to prevent the retreat turning into a rout.

With the Belgian army crumbling on its left flank the 4th British Division had held the line of the Senne to the north of Brussels for a day before pulling back to the Dendre, but it was through the area to the south of Brussels – the fields of Waterloo – that the great mass of the BEF pulled back. Mile by mile, as the British forces retreated, the advance units of General von Reichnau's 6th Army came on to occupy the towns and villages that had been vacated.

Anti-tank units ordered into position by one corps were unexpectedly ordered to re-position by another. Platoons, sent out in search of neighbouring forces, became lost in the network of country lanes – some of them to be surrounded and taken prisoner, others escaping and rejoining their battalions days or weeks later.

Over a huge area of land to the west of Waterloo, men were moving on over the country. Wading through the streams, going in file through the gates, running for cover into woods and copses, coming unexpectedly face to face with the enemy, fighting, running, dodging, dying.

By Sunday morning, a great mass of men, vehicles and weapons had crossed the Dendre and were heading west towards the safety of the Scheldt. Men clambered gratefully into lorries and fell asleep on the instant. Others, not so lucky, took it in turns to march in their sleep while supported on either side by their comrades.

For the Luftwaffe, conditions were perfect. Howling down out of clear blue skies, the Stukas set the old city of Tournai ablaze before turning on the trudging columns of refugees.

The horrors of this new warfare were now evident wherever you looked: bodies were slumped in gutters and ditches; improvised casualty stations and first-aid posts echoed to the screams of the wounded and the moans of the dying; horses bolted riderless across fields; the wretched inmates of a lunatic asylum stumbled about, dribbling and undressed — and in one town the animals from a travelling circus got loose and went on the rampage.

ii

At Leuze, where the 145th Brigade was passing through on its way back to the reserve line, an immaculately dressed sapper major had stepped into the road and was marshalling the traffic. 'Close up, close up!' he shouted as each lorry-load of exhausted soldiers passed him, and the drivers, thankful that at least someone was trying to bring order to the chaos, obeyed without question. When the convoy had been closed up to his satisfaction, the major slipped away as mysteriously as he had arrived. A few minutes later nine Heinkels arrived over the horizon and bombs rained down on the traffic jam. Within minutes, dozens of vehicles were burning fiercely, and nearly two hundred and fifty men of the 2nd Gloucesters and 4th Oxford and Buckingham Light Infantry lay dead or dying.

iii

Already, Gort's senior staff were beginning to plan for the worst contingency. At the dawn staff meeting, Brigadier Leese put forward a scheme whereby, in the event of its

271

being surrounded, the BEF would form a hollow square and move *en masse* to the coast. But the situation was not yet that bad, and Gort approved a modified plan: the GHQ at Arras was to be closed down that day; 'useless mouths' were to be moved back to Boulogne for evacuation to England, and a staff nucleus was to be retained at Hazebrouk, leaving the Command Post at Wahagnies for the time being.

Later that morning, Lieutenant General Pownall telephoned the War Office and spoke to the Director of Military Operations and Plans. For the first time, he let drop that the C-in-C was considering the possibility of a staged withdrawal towards Dunkirk.

Major General Dewing was horrified and informed the CIGS, General Ironside, who in turn interrupted Anthony Eden's Sunday lunch with Lord Halifax to urge an immediate meeting of the war cabinet.

They gathered in the Admiralty 'Fish Room' – so called because of its decorative frieze of dolphins. Aware that he had the Prime Minister's full support, Ironside outlined the heated telephone calls which had taken place between Pownall and Dewing during the day and explained why he could not on any account countenance Gort's proposed withdrawal.

'My chief fear,' he told the cabinet, 'is that we may not be able to get the BEF out. The German columns are bound to push forward at top speed now and I doubt whether the French have the will or the troops to stop the thrust towards Amiens. I have already spoken to Lord Gort and have told him he must get a large proportion of his reserves down into the Douai-Béthune-Arras area.' He paused and glanced at the Prime Minister. 'But if the worst comes to the worst, I believe the whole of the BEF should be prepared to turn south and cut itself through the Abbeville-Amiens line to the Seine.'

'And the Belgians?' Anthony Eden asked quietly.

Ironside shook his head. 'All we can do is to urge them to conform, but they have the longest wheel to make and are unlikely to be willing to vacate their country. I daresay they will never get out at all. If we could rely upon French forces the manoeuvre would not be necessary. But three days have been lost as a result of Weygand's cancellation of Gamelin's proposed counter-attack, and as the French can be relied upon always to put the defence of Paris first it seems doubtful whether we can count on them for effective support on our right flank. That, in my view, leaves us only one course of action: to strike with the whole of our force southward towards Amiens. I concede that this may mean abandoning the Belgian army to its fate, but I see no alternative if the BEF is to be saved. I would like permission therefore, Prime Minister, to visit Lord Gort personally at his headquarters in order to give him our views and order him to disengage his front on the Scheldt and strike southward.'

Churchill nodded his agreement. 'Go tonight,' he said, and within hours Ironside was on board a destroyer and heading for Boulogne.

iv

. . . Aroused by a Bren carrier clattering past. As the noise dies away a muttering shuffling remains. The window is level with the loft floor so without getting out of bed I look out to see the refugees. Later there are church bells and as I go to breakfast the townspeople in their best clothes are going to church.

Take my map board to Divisional HQ. They have got the château this time and no mistake, taking it over from the Belgian Corps HQ. They had to push antique furniture aside to set up their 'tables, 6 foot' and install telephones.

We are to stand on the Scheldt which is a relief, with 44 Division on our left and 3 Division on our right. The maps are hopeless so the first task for us is to be a complete survey. Geoffrey and I divide the Division's sector between us and set out on reconnaissance.

Eastward from Sweveghem the road undulates for a mile or two and then sweeps down to the river. Beyond, tree-covered hills rise to dominate our whole forward area; but as yet there is no sign of life. The four bridges in our sector are manned and will be blown by 44 Div RE. Across the northerly one refugees are pouring, shepherded by the military police onto side roads. They are very orderly, with carts, perambulators, cars topped with mattresses, household utensils suspended, donkeys behind and dogs underneath. I get waves as I drive past. Everywhere troops are digging in, guns making use of every bit of cover. Every minute or so a ranging shot comes flip-flopping overhead.

Our right boundary is the Courtrai canal which rises by a series of locks to the watershed. Crossing the bridge at one of these locks I see to my horror that it is prepared for demolition with the detonators in position and no one on guard. In a nearby house I find the NCO who has knocked off his party for a smoke. Take him outside . . .

v

Late that evening, Gregory Blaxland went out to study the ground in the left-forward area near Petegem, where there was a stretch of marshland by the river, unsuitable for defence and glaringly exposed to view from the wooded slopes beyond, as was the whole of the forward zone.

He crept up to the towpath by the bank of the River Scheldt feeling that the enemy must already have arrived on the other side and must at that moment be taking aim on him. There was an extraordinary sense of stillness, broken only by the gentle lapping of the river, whose level had been greatly reduced and which now dawdled along between steep, high banks.

He returned to the platoon trench as darkness was falling and dossed down for the night. A few minutes later, when he was dozing off, there was a big bang and a rumble in the distance.

He heard Sergeant Skippings say, 'Up she goes!' and realized that the sappers had blown the last of the Oudenarde bridges. That meant only one thing: there should by now be no more of the British Expeditionary Force east of the Scheldt.

A lugubrious voice from a neighbouring trench broke the silence. 'What did I tell yer? We always starts orf with a bleedin' retreat in this man's bleedin' army.'

vi

Colonel von Stockhausen had let it be known in the Grossdeutschland Regiment that while the advance through enemy territory continued, troops were to be permitted to help themselves to whatever food or fuel they needed, so when 15 Company moved off after their three-day rest on the forest's edge at Raucourt, they were well fed, well rested and their vehicles were in excellent repair.

By Monday 20 May, one hundred kilometres of the French front had been broken in the southern sector, and while the spearhead thrust of the tank divisions continued westward towards Amiens, a huge mass of motorized infantry was swinging northward to guard the flank along the line of the La Bassée canal.

For a whole day, the company leapfrogged forward. Its one hundred armoured cars, troop carriers, light tanks and motorcycles rattled along past endless columns of foot regiments, and Heinrich and his comrades shouted greetings and jokes to the foot-sloggers as they sped by.

They arrived at St Quentin as dusk was falling. Just after leaving the town there was a scare: bombers circled overhead and began dropping flares to illuminate the convoy, and the anti-aircraft unit that was travelling in company loosed off tracer into the night sky. But it was only another of the enemy's reconnaissance patrols, and after another hour or two of driving through darkness the company arrived at Combles, where the men were allowed to sleep in their vehicles for two hours before moving off again.

vii

When Ironside arrived at the Wahagnies GHQ at six in the morning, Gort was waiting for him and they went straight into the C-in-C's private office and shut the door.

Both were big, burly men. The six-foot-four Ironside was known as 'Tiny'; while Gort, in his regimental days with the Grenadier Guards, had been affectionately known as 'Fat Boy'. Both were to some extent caricatures of British generals: tough, singleminded and contemptuous of 'little men' and red tape; and while Ironside wished he could be in Gort's shoes taking overall charge of the battle, Gort longed to be at the front, fighting it.

After some preliminary discussions in which it became quite apparent that Gort was not at all keen to turn his army's back on the enemy in order to drive south, Ironside summarized his views.

'Let's look at it objectively, John. You're being encircled, agree? And common sense dictates that your only hope of releasing yourself from the encirclement is to attack – right away, with all the force at your disposal – south along the line St Pol-Doullens-Amiens. Now what do you think? Do you think it's possible? If you do, I'll give you the order to go ahead right away, and I'll get on the blower to Weygand and get him to put in a similar push from the south.'

Gort was shaking his head. 'I wish I could agree with you, Tiny, but I'm afraid I can't. Seven of my divisions are in close contact on the Scheldt, and even if they could be safely disengaged – which I doubt – their withdrawal would open a yawning gap between my left flank and the Belgian army. You must realize that the Belgians have been badly shaken. Their troops are exhausted. The Germans would overrun them easily. And then they would pounce on our rearguards and simply tear them to bits.'

'All this talk of exhaustion! The Germans are probably every bit as tired as anyone else! Now if the French can only be persuaded to attack —'

'With respect, Tiny, the French are the tiredest of the lot. Everything I've seen of them in the past few days leads me to doubt whether they're capable of staging an organized counter-offensive on any worthwhile scale.'

'So what do you suggest? You have strong enemy columns on your right flank and you are in close contact to your front.'

Gort had already pondered the dilemma at length — indeed, he had thought about little else for the past twenty-four hours. And although all his instincts told him that an attack on the lines Ironside was suggesting was doomed to fail, he knew the plan had Churchill's backing and realized that his own authority might be seriously jeopardized if he did not at least appear to cooperate. 'I have plans in hand to launch a limited strike south from Arras with my two spare divisions,' he told Ironside. 'In the absence of any fresh orders from the French I shall push ahead with that.'

Ironside nodded. A limited strike wasn't at all what he or the Prime Minister had envisaged, but short of relieving Gort of his command — and that was unthinkable — he could only push him so far. He stared at the map again. 'Even if you can't break through to the Somme, you might at least narrow the gap. And if Weygand will agree to attack the German corridor from the south —'

Gort gave a chuckle of incredulity.

Ironside shot the C-in-C a quick glance. 'Is there any reason why he should not?'

'We've had no direct orders from the French high command in the last week, Tiny.'

Ironside glowered. 'Oh? So whose orders are you acting under at present?'

'In theory, General Billotte's. But I doubt if you'll get much change out of him. The man's about as much use as a jellyfish on Brighton beach.'

'First complaint I've heard of him. Where's his HQ?'

'Near Lens. Under Vimy Ridge.'

'All right. I'll go and see him. I'll take your CGS along with me, if you're in agreement. We'll beard the fellow in his lair. Put a bit of fire in his belly.'

After more discussion, Gort agreed that a spearhead force of two divisions should be sent down towards Arras forthwith, and when that had been settled Ironside set off with Pownall in a staff car to find General Billotte. This was the first time the CIGS had seen the appalling mass of refugees on the roads, and his confidence in the allies' ability to salvage the situation was shaken by the experience. Far worse, however, was the impression made on him by Generals Billotte and Blanchard, who were in a state of complete depression.

'*Nous sommes tous fatigués – très, très fatigués,*' Billotte told him, and the way he looked up at him with sad, tear-filled eyes lit the short fuse to Ironside's temper.

He seized Billotte by his tunic. 'Listen to me, General!' he boomed. 'Can't you see that the fate of France is in the balance? Are you going to be defeated by a few tanks? You must attack! There is absolutely nothing in your way! *Attaquez! Attaquez!*'

His fleshy features damp with sweat, General Billotte drew himself up to attention and clicked his heels. 'I shall make a plan immediately, *mon Général,*' he whispered.

viii

Northern France was now like an anthill which has been kicked in several places by a heavy boot. Everywhere the inhabitants, despairing of safety within their homes, were moving out. Staggering under impossibly heavy loads, they scurried in their millions from every city and town. The French authorities, having closed the Belgian border during the first few days of the battle, were now unable to prevent the flood of humanity bursting through, and a migration was taking place of dimensions unheard of since the days of Attila the Hun. Two million Dutch and Belgians were on the road and eight million French. Their numbers were swollen by thousands of defeated and demoralized French and Belgian soldiers who had thrown away their arms and were intermingled with the prams and hand carts and bicycles. Entire villages were being evacuated at a few minutes' notice. Even the mayors, priests, schoolmasters and policemen joined in. Taking their families with them in tragic little processions, they made their way along dusty lanes to join the torrent on the main roads leading south and west.

ix

On the right flank of Blaxland's position on the Scheldt, a great rumpus had broken out. Bursts of rapid fire could be heard, and tracer bullets were soaring in streams that gleamed orange-red against a darkening sky. Blaxland noted this use of tracer against infantry positions particularly: he had learnt at Sandhurst only a few months before that tracer was restricted by the Hague Convention to use against aircraft and that only one tracer round was permitted every eight shells.

The sight of this obvious disregard for the Convention, and the sound of the gunfire, gave him a sudden feeling that the BEF had little hope of competing with these demons who had obviously put so much thought and practice into the brutal business of war.

All the firing appeared to be coming from the other side. They seemed to have hundreds of light machine guns making brief staccato bursts, which were accompanied by the longer, vibrating solid bursts from the heavier machine gun whose dread name, Spandau, Blaxland had yet to learn. By comparison to this deluge of automatic fire, the occasional short and easily identifiable burst from a Bren gun seemed quite inoffensive.

As it grew dark, there were frequent firings of signal flares – white, red and green – which rose into the sky and drifted slowly down, illuminating the battlefield. Soon after one such display, a lance corporal came running across from the neighbouring trench and reported to Blaxland.

'From Corporal Pilling, sir – that was the signal for us to withdraw!'

Blaxland hauled himself out of the trench and ran across to investigate.

'It was a red followed by a green, sir,' Cocky Pilling assured him. 'That's always meant withdraw.'

'*Withdraw*, Corporal Pilling?'

'Standing orders, sir. Always used to be at Aldershot.'

'Corporal Pilling, we are at Oudenarde, not Aldershot, and the Buffs do *not* withdraw from Oudenarde.'

Blaxland was surprised at the power of his own riposte, but Pilling was quite unperturbed. Then Melancholy Pilling joined in. 'Well, sir, being as 'ow all the other lot've fallen back through our lines, I reckon it must be our turn to fall back through theirs. Besides, if this was meant to be a permanent line, they wouldn't have fallen back through it, would they, sir?'

'As far as I'm concerned this *is* a permanent line,' Blaxland told them, 'so you can forget any ideas about withdrawing unless I get positive orders to do so from a runner, in which case I shall pass the order to you by giving three blasts on a whistle.'

Feeling heroic, Blaxland ran the seventy yards back to his trench and made a spectacular leap into his own particular hole; but although he was content that he had put the two Pillings in their place, he was already converted to their expectation of a retreat, and wished he had briefed himself on the possibility more fully. Now, he had no link – telephone or wireless – with his company commander and had only the vaguest idea of the whereabouts of company headquarters.

He was just wondering whether to send a runner back when there was a very brief whistle, an orange flash, and a gigantic crash, which was followed quickly by another and another.

'Mother of Jesus!' Sergeant Skippings exclaimed. 'We're being mortared!'

Convinced that the bombs were coming from his own side, Blaxland climbed out of the trench again and ran back down the road yelling, 'Stop those bloody mortars . . . !'

Amazingly, it did the trick. The mortar bombs ceased to fall and Blaxland returned to his trench. The platoon remained at its post listening to the sound of battle and trying to ascertain whether the Germans were getting any closer.

The moon, almost full, came up. There was a lull; then a renewed spate of firing to the left. Blaxland had armed himself with a rifle; a Bren gun was returning fire and one man had hurled a grenade in the general direction of the enemy. Then, just when every man in the platoon was steeling himself to meet the enemy charge, a voice came out of the darkness.

'Fookin' 'ell!'

No German could possibly have such mastery of English dialect.

'Who are you then?' Corporal French shouted. 'Advance and be recognized!'

'South Staffs,' came the reply.

'What are you doing here?'

'We're pioneers.'

'OK, pass friends.'

Two figures came forward and revealed themselves as an officer and a sergeant, both elderly. They had been ordered to take their platoon to Petegem to prop up the defences there, which seemed ominous in itself.

'Hope no one was hit?' Blaxland enquired.

'Not a scratch,' replied the sergeant drily. 'You weren't good enough to hit any of us.'

x

. . . A dung cart goes past the window with a shovel stuck in the top. Business as usual, but not today on the forward slope. There is no going down to the river. The Germans have got across during the night on the 44 Div front and their shells are ranging on various landmarks, farms and crossroads, throwing up a cloud of pale brown dust every few minutes. Some dead animals in the fields. Nobody stirring, not even refugees.

Back to lunch having completed my reconnaissance. Sauervein plunged in gloom at the news that General Giraud has been captured. Go to Div HQ afterwards for the latest news. The map is covered with blue marks and question marks. There are fifth column scares – we shall be glad to get away from Flemish speakers who sound like Germans. Brigadier Anderson has been shot at. As I come out through the garden a padre is being marched in between two military police. Behaving in a very odd way and refusing to give his name, but is obviously British and hear later that he comes to his senses under John Stevens's steely influence.

The French have closed the frontier so the streets are now milling with refugees. No civil administration in evidence. Get talking to a girl in a blue dress and advise her not to try to get into France . . .

xi

To the west, the panzer advance had continued throughout the day. The technique of the conquerors was simple: as they approached each village, the machine guns and cannon blazed away at the roof-tops. Motorcycle troops with stick grenades and machine guns roared up and positioned themselves to cover the advance. Rumbling along, the carriers and tanks approached the village from two different directions and fired at random across the little square with its Mairie and war memorial and dusty plane trees. Loping along behind each tank, weighed down with grenades, submachine guns and pouches of ammunition, the infantry went quickly into the side streets and gardens, spraying bullets at roofs, windows, barns, sheds, chicken coops and greenhouses. If the village happened to be occupied by allied troops, the heavy and indiscriminate use of cannon and machine-gun fire quickly convinced them that they were out numbered and out-gunned. Within ten or fifteen minutes the defenders would be rounded up, their weapons would be broken and they would be taken prisoner and marched to the rear. Every village was visited at least once before the tanks moved on, and if any put up a determined defence, the tank commanders simply brought in the heavy tanks, called up air support and started systematically reducing every building to rubble.

At ten o'clock, Guderian's tanks rolled into Albert; an hour later they were at Hedauville. At midday, the 1st Division took the old city of Amiens, and by four the 2nd was at Beauquesne. Finally, a little after nine on the evening of 20 May, the first German tanks entered Abbeville, and the crews — tired out but triumphant — caught their first glimpse of the sea.

Like a piece of rotten canvas, the allied armies had been ripped apart.

TWENTY-ONE

Wilmot's convoy arrived at Armentières soon after midnight, having been ordered back from the Scheldt after a long day's fighting, during which the section had blown two small bridges and Sergeant Crisp had used a Boys anti-tank rifle to fire a gasometer. After that, pulling out under fire from German artillery, Wilmot had used a Michelin Guide to navigate the convoy along country lanes, avoiding the hold-ups at Courtrai and Menin. Now, after a frustratingly slow drive in darkness and without lights, they found the streets of Armentières silent and deserted except for the howling of stray dogs and the ghostly little groups of refugees that hurried out of town.

The section's remaining lorries (one had been overturned during a Stuka raid and abandoned) had drawn up in a side road near the station. Freddy Radcliffe had been sent to contact the Movement Control Officer and while the men snatched half an hour's sleep, Wilmot, propping his back against the wall of a cotton warehouse, was writing a report of the day's events for the official war diary.

Footsteps approached: Freddy was returning with a major whom Wilmot did not recognize. He scrambled to his feet and saluted.

'Wilmot, isn't it?'

'That's right, Major.'

'Right, well I have news for you. There's been a mix-up. You're supposed to be on your way to Festubert. Division's sending my lot back to Boulogne, not yours.'

'I've received no orders to that effect –'

'I don't give a damn what orders you haven't received,

Captain,' the other said testily. 'I'm telling you there's been a mix-up. You're in the wrong place.'

Wilmot opened up his map case and found the message Radcliffe had brought from Divisional Headquarters late that afternoon. Scribbled in indelible pencil on a piece of pink, flowered notepaper it read: WITHDRAW ON COMPLETION OF DEMOLITION OF ASSIGNED BRIDGES. REPORT MCO ARMENTIERES FOR FURTHER ORDERS.

The major looked at this note and handed it back. 'There you are then. You've been told to report for orders, and I'm giving them to you. Jerry's pushing east towards Arras and your lot's needed to make the bridges jump.'

Wilmot looked at Radcliffe. 'What about the MCO? Did you contact him?'

'He didn't know anything about us, sir. There's a train going to Boulogne but it's already full, and there's unlikely to be another one for some considerable time, if at all.'

The major looked triumphant. 'So there you are, old boy. My orders are to hand over my explosives to you, and of course you can take any other equipment you need.'

Wilmot had the strong impression that the major was pulling a fast one, but there was very little he could do about it.

'I'd like your orders in writing, if you don't mind.'

The major seemed to hesitate momentarily. 'Very well.' He took out a pad and scribbled a few lines. 'There you are. That should do it. There's a bloody nice little *estaminet* just this side of Festubert on the main road, if I remember rightly, so if I were you I'd stop there for breakfast. Best of luck!'

He turned on his heel and walked off into the station.

Radcliffe looked at the sleeping troops then at Wilmot. 'They're dead beat, sir.'

'We all are, Freddy.'

'No chance of giving them another hour before we move, I suppose?'

'None whatsoever.'

Grimly, the platoon commanders roused their men and gave their orders for loading up and transferring ammunition and stores from the lorries that were being abandoned.

There were compensations. Wilmot took over the major's staff car, which pleased Driver Hall considerably, and a couple of lorries and a quantity of weapons, explosives and equipment were commandeered, bringing the section transport back up to more than full strength.

As the convoy moved off, Wilmot, travelling in the staff car with Driver Hall at the wheel, noticed a solitary refugee hobbling along towards the station.

He was wearing a French greatcoat without any buttons, and his pyjama bottoms were showing below the turnups of his trousers.

ii

Heinrich's platoon had surrounded some British troops. They had been firing from a field of young corn just outside Doullens, but the sight of the armoured column had changed their minds, and a few well placed grenades thrown by Staff Sergeant Schwappacher had flushed them out.

Led by their officer, they came out with their hands up – about twenty of them, big blokes, and well equipped too.

The officer spoke German. 'The war will last another two years,' he told his captors while being disarmed, 'and England will win.'

Everyone thought this was very funny, and Heinrich indulged his talent for mimicry. When Lieutenant Gerbener came up most of the platoon were in fits of laughter, with the British standing glum-faced and looking into the wrong end of several Schmeisser machine pistols.

'Well done, boys,' Gerbener said. 'If all the English give in this easily they'll be as much of a walkover as the French.'

When the prisoners had been sent to the rear under guard, the company moved on and dug in on the hill overlooking Doullens. General Rommel had made another reconnaissance flight in his Feisel Stork, and word came back that strong enemy armoured forces were on the move from Arras. Not a very nice situation. The sappers began laying anti-tank mines, and overhead the Stuka squadrons flew northward on missions to attack the advancing British tanks. Not long afterwards, when they returned, they rocked their wings as a signal to the troops on the ground that their mission had been accomplished.

The British tank advance came to a rapid and ignominious end, and the men of 15 Company had time to eat a meal without rushing. The field kitchen came up trumps again and provided hot dinners for all, and the only small irritation came from a herd of cows which began helping themselves to camouflage on the vehicles. When a solitary English bomber lumbered overhead, it was quickly driven off by the anti-aircraft unit.

At evening roll call, Staff Sergeant Schwappacher was presented with the Iron Cross Second Class. After that, when pickets had been posted, the men stretched out and slept, undisturbed by the distant sounds of night bombing.

iii

Now that the French and Belgian flanks had been turned, the German divisions attacking from the north through the lowlands of Belgium came up against the BEF for the first time, and some of the bitterest fighting began. Dug in in the orchards and cabbage fields west of the Scheldt and inspired by the leadership of Brooke, Montgomery and Alexander, the British held out against an army superior in manpower, weapons, tanks, logistics and air support. Everything the defenders needed — with the exception of courage and the will to fight — was in short supply, from tanks to maps, from fire-power to food and from wireless sets to a good night's sleep.

Ammunition was running short, telephone lines were down, GHQ was being continually shifted and the tanks and reserve divisions that should have been available as reinforcements had been sent south to defend the right flank along the canal line at La Bassée. Bit by bit, the invaders gained a foothold west of the Scheldt. Once across, machine-gun nests were established in depth and Stukas made dive-bombing attacks while pontoon bridges were constructed and tanks and artillery brought across.

After thirty-six hours of almost continual fighting, some of it at bayonet point, the corps commanders were agreed that they had no alternative but to retreat to the original Gort Line on the French border.

iv

The landlady of the Dragon Vert, an *estaminet* in the village of Aulnay-sous-Bois, was cooking a very special omelette. She was using the last of her eggs, finely chopped herbs, best gammon, real butter and a hot pan. Ten minutes before, a general and his aide-de-camp had driven up in a lorry and asked to use the telephone, and Madame, who kept a picture of the signing of the Compiègne Armistice in the bar, had recognized her unexpected visitor as none other than General Maxime Weygand, the saviour of France.

So far, Weygand had had a particularly frustrating day. Having announced his intention of calling on King Leopold to discuss the progress of the war, he had invited Generals Billotte and Gort to rendezvous with him so that they could jointly discuss the plan for a counter-attack which Weygand had formulated. But Weygand had made the mistake of presuming that communications in Northern France approximated to normal, and so far his journey to meet King Leopold and the generals had been fraught with mishap.

After an infuriating delay at Le Bourget where nobody seemed to know anything about his proposed flight, he had eventually taken off, run into anti-aircraft fire east of Montreuil and Messerschmitts further on, and on landing near Béthune had found the hangars wrecked, the airfield deserted and a solitary and very dishevelled *poilu* worrying about what to do with a dump of 20,000 litres of high-octane petrol which had been left behind by the RAF who, he told Weygand, had 'all gone back to England'.

Commandeering the one remaining lorry, Weygand and his ADC had driven into the nearest village and, despairing of finding a post office open, banged on the door of Le Dragon Vert to use the telephone.

Madame bustled in with the huge omelette, which was oozing temptingly and set the platter before her hero.

'Ah, *Général*!' she exclaimed. 'We are so honoured to have you here! You have no idea what your presence means to us! Now that you are here among us, none of us have any further need to be afraid!'

Encouraged by this display of confidence in his ability to work a much needed miracle, Weygand made his telephone call, left three quarters of the omelette and returned to the airfield. He took off again, flew to St Inglevert and then made his way by road to Calais where he learned that King Leopold awaited his arrival at Ypres; so he changed cars, struggled through the unending lines of refugees and arrived at about three in the afternoon, several hours late for his audience with the King.

At the end of a long meeting with Leopold and his senior staff during which much was said but little settled, General Billotte arrived and further discussions took place, in which Billotte played down the state of abject despair both he and Blanchard were in. Blanchard, however, did not attend: he said he 'didn't think he was invited'; and Lord Gort failed to show up until after Weygand had left because he had just moved his forward HQ to Premesques and his staff had been unable to locate him in time to give him the amended rendezvous for the meeting.

The result of this goose chase was that Weygand travelled back to Paris convinced that Gort had avoided meeting him because he had made up his mind to evacuate the BEF from France; and because he had received only half the story from

Billotte and was not aware that the Arras venture was little more than a gesture and very unlikely to succeed, he went ahead with his plan for a counter-offensive – 'The Weygand Plan' – which was based on little more than wishful thinking.

But there was another, equally serious sequel to that disastrous day. Just outside Ypres that evening, a small party of British officers found some milk in a farmhouse and were about to share it out when the door burst open and a senior French general burst in.

It was Billotte. 'Ah, fresh milk, just what the doctor ordered!' he exclaimed, and, grabbing the jug, drained it to the last drop. He then smacked his lips appreciatively and departed as abruptly as he had arrived.

That was the last that was seen of the commander of the 1st Army Group. As he dozed in the rear seat of the staff car on his way back to his headquarters, a lorry without lights appeared on the wrong side of the road. Each driver swerved at the same moment; Billotte's car skidded sideways and its rear half was crushed. He never recovered consciousness.

v

Gort's latest forward HQ at Premesques was a small, well-concealed *gentilhommière* of two storeys just off the main road between Lille and Armentières. The drive up to the house was guarded by the anti-tank guns of the Welsh Guards, and for security reasons no one was allowed to walk on the terrace facing the road.

Lieutenant Colonel the Viscount Bridgeman, Gort's acting Operations Officer, arrived at the HQ late in the evening, having been summoned by the C-in-C. Gort himself had only just returned from his abortive trip to Ypres and was looking through the latest situation reports – most of which had been overtaken by events and were meaningless.

But Gort was not one to allow his impatience or anxiety to show, and having welcomed Bridgeman with old-fashioned courtesy he told him that he had an important task for him which he wanted completed as a matter of urgency.

'I want you to draw up a plan for the withdrawal of the entire British Expeditionary Force to the coast, and its evacuation from the Channel ports. I want a contingency plan that will take into account the probability of a German pincer movement along the coast westward from Ostend and eastward from Boulogne. I want to know which parts of that coast can be most readily defended, which offer the best opportunities for air cover, which are best served by roads and where anti-tank defence can be most easily secured by inundation. I want each corps of the BEF to be allocated routes and departure points, and I want a list of strong points on each flank to be held while the army withdraws between them.'

Bridgeman worked all night. By morning, his draft plan was ready.

vi

. . . Gus Galloway rings up to say that a carrier pigeon has been launched from near 59 Company office in the outskirts of Sweveghem. I take Sauervein and meet him on site where he points out the suspect house, guarded by a few sappers. As we watch, another carrier pigeon flies out from the roof. I draw my revolver and fling open the front door. Inside an elderly Belgian couple are cowering.

A policeman appears from nowhere.

'Pigeons, Monsieur? But here all the world has pigeons!'

I am conducted upstairs to the pigeon loft. The anticlimax is too much for the policeman. Struck by a happy thought he says, 'Where is your licence?'

The old man produces a dirty screw of paper. It

is out of date. He is put under arrest. Many words are spoken by all Belgians present, simultaneously.

Outside the guard is getting restive as pigeons fly out from all over the place. A crowd begins to gather and the policeman is on his mettle. Up the street he dashes into house after house, coming back proudly leading a little group of criminals.

What do I want him to do with them? Something bold is expected of me, but summary execution seems inappropriate. To play for time I bundle them into the back of my truck and drive off to the Field Security Office. I go in and ask Basil Bartlett if he is collecting pigeon fanciers. As his answer leaves no room for doubt I turn them loose hoping that the walk will teach them a lesson.

Continue on a tour of companies. 18 Field Park Company is settled in a barbed wire factory. Glorious afternoon with the fields as hard as iron. A thick column of dust rises from a group of houses half a mile away, then another and another. Harassing fire.

I get back to the office to find a panic. The adjutant has been looking for me for hours. We are to fall back to behind the French frontier, occupying as luck has it, not our old sectors but one to the left; so we take over 5 Div sector and 3 Div moves into ours. I am to leave immediately for HQ 3 Div and show them where all the engineer work is, especially pillboxes.

We have handed all our records over but I carry them in my head. Hewitt is standing by with my truck. I am not allowed to take Sedgewick because he has become too useful as mess steward, but he has packed and loaded my kit. I shall have to rough it with a batman/driver.

HQRE 3 Div are near Aalbeke and I arrive in plenty of time for dinner. They are old friends, and are interested in my account of the 4 Div war so far. They are to move next day, so Lieutenant Colonel Desmond Harrison suggests that I should go round to G(Ops) after dinner to report.

Pat Ronaldson takes me round and introduces me to the GSO1. He has received a pillbox tracing but it does not seem to be quite right. I am shown a table where I sit down and mark up their map. They do not think that 4 Div has done very much work at all. They wish they were in their old sector where they have dug a continuous fire trench from end to end as well as twice our number of pillboxes.

It is getting dark and the lighting set has not been switched on. A voice snaps, 'Who are you and what are you doing?'

A little man with a face like a weasel has come into the room, his jacket undone. I am surprised to see red tabs under his jerkin. I stand up and explain.

'All right, carry on.' He turns away. It is Montgomery, the divisional commander.

Back at HQRE Hewitt has laid out my kit on a couch in the passage . . .

vii

Heinrich Lauder dreamt a dream. The day before they had passed through some of the huge military cemeteries of the Somme, and in his dream he walked down the lines of crosses in the moonlight. And as he walked, the ghost of each soldier rose up and stood to attention behind the cross marking his resting place. Their silent presence filled him with a tremendous sense of pride and thankfulness that he had been allowed to play his part in the great German tradition of courage and duty which his forefathers had bequeathed. His, now, was a noble inheritance indeed: to ensure that the bloody sacrifice made by so many German soldiers in the

Great War should at last be crowned with victory over the jealousy of France and Britain.

He awoke feeling full of energy and ready for the new day. Before the sun was up, the column was on the move again, through Acheux, Beauval and Bernaville, heading for Calais.

They travelled now through scenes of abject misery. Interminable columns of Belgian refugees – deceived, misled and driven from their country by the British – filed past.

The armoured column forced them from the road as it swept by and they were left standing in open fields. Bicycles, chairs, tables, beds, saucepans, chicken runs, rabbit hutches, dovecots, bulging sacks and pillow cases, sofas, bundles of straw, blankets – all thrown higgledy-piggledy onto the high, overloaded carts. Cows, horses and sheep followed along behind them, often led by children. Dogs ran everywhere, sniffing and messing and whining and barking. Cowed and trembling, the womenfolk – many with babes in arms – sat miserably on the wagons. Old men and women looked on in total helplessness. They had seen all this before, and the uncertainty about sons and husbands and brothers only served to intensify their utter despair. There was no refuge for them: exposed to the elements, they were forced to live in the woods and fields. Every time planes appeared, they stopped and stared upward to see if they were going to attack. When offered a loaf of bread or a tin of meat, their gratitude was pitiful to see.

The armoured column entered Hesdin, sixty kilometres from Boulogne. The town was wrecked: the French had only just left and the streets were littered with civilian dead. Here, the refugee problem was at its worst. Thousands and thousands of people on bicycles were all trying to get to the coast. There was no end to the bicycles, and as the armoured column went through the town it did so to the ringing accompaniment of thousands of bicycle bells.

The column halted outside Hesdin for an hour's rest and clean up before moving on at midday. They reached the coast. The road followed it for a few miles. Three British Sunderland seaplanes made an attack but scored no hits. They pushed on, eastwards now, heading for the Franco-Belgian border. At Ardres, 15 Company found itself almost on the heels of the retreating allies: they must have got out at very short notice because they had left behind them huge quantities of food, condensed milk and – most precious of all – fuel.

The shouts of triumph stopped suddenly, however, when the bodies of seven German soldiers were discovered. They had been shot, probably because they got in the way of the allies' 'victorious retreat'. That was fair enough. But why had their boots been removed, and why were they bound hand and foot? For the first time, Heinrich Lauder and his comrades felt a deep hatred of the enemy, and a desire to avenge as well as to conquer.

They travelled on, very slowly, throughout the night. But the following day, much to everyone's annoyance, they were halted just short of the Aa canal and forbidden to proceed further on orders from the high command.

TWENTY-TWO

The train, which had left Armentières over twenty-four hours before, finally clanked slowly into the Gare Central at Boulogne at two-thirty a.m., its cattle trucks packed solid with British troops and its single Pullman coach equally packed with refugees.

Hollow-eyed, stiff-jointed and blistered, the troops spilled out onto the platform, and while they were fallen in and mustered by their sergeants, the refugees milled about, passing bundles and babies out of the carriage windows, dragging children along by the hand, waiting impatiently for their old folk and heading off in the direction of the quays in the hope of finding a ship to take them to safety.

David was just another refugee now. Still wearing the buttonless greatcoat he had looted from an abandoned convoy, his face was begrimed, his beard ten days old and the beginnings of starvation apparent in his gaunt look and staring eyes.

Going with the crowd, he shuffled along to a transit shed which was already packed with people. As more people surged in, those who had staked out areas of floor for their families woke up and prepared to defend them. Nobody knew if any ships were due in and no officials were to be found. Children were crying; people were arguing over territorial rights; a woman with a baby at her breast was moaning quietly in despair.

Pushing his way through the crowd, he left the shed and walked down the quayside to the town.

It was getting light. In the Commercial Basin, refugees were loading themselves in large numbers into fishing smacks. On the dockside, there was a huge jam of soldiers, vehicles and dumped stores – much of which looked like explosives or ammunition – and the refugees who had spent the night in the air-raid shelters were now pouring out into the road and pestering the troops for food, water and information.

Without any aim in mind, David walked slowly away from the docks and up the steep hill through the town. There were sandbags everywhere. Glass littered the road, and a dead horse gave off a stench so powerful that his stomach heaved. Many of the shop windows had been boarded up and some of the houses were burnt-out shells. Outside the main gates of the old fort at Haute Ville, another crowd of people was camped in the street. He stopped for a rest and sat down at the edge of the crowd. He was desperately thirsty and his head was throbbing. He had heard that the Germans tanks were already approaching the town, and he could not decide whether to try to make for Calais or stay in Boulogne in the hopes of getting a boat back to England.

ii

Further out of town, the men of No 12 Dock Section, Royal Engineers, had been given the task of preparing the defences of the centre section of the town perimeter. Their unit had been attached to GHQ at Arras until two days before, and during their forced march back to Boulogne they had narrowly escaped capture by the advancing panzers. On arrival, the section commander – an acting captain on secondment to the Royal Engineers from the Royal Dragoons – had reported to the British HQ which Lieutenant General Brownrigg had set up in Wimereux, a resort three miles up the coast from Boulogne. To his astonishment he had been ordered to take over as officer in charge of the centre section of the town perimeter.

Making their headquarters at a farm in the countryside of St Martin Boulogne, this handful of men set about using the abandoned lorries and cars as road blocks against the approaching tanks. Trees had to be felled, lanes cratered and machine-gun pits and anti-tank gun positions dug.

The section commander, Captain James Wheeler, was a family man with three children and a terraced house in Finchley. A few months before, his wife Joyce and the children – Susan, Jan and the baby, Charles – had gone to live with relations in the little seaside town of Mumbles, near Swansea. Wheeler was a man who read his Bible daily and believed firmly in the power of prayer. But as a product of Sandhurst he was also a professional soldier, and could not now ignore what he saw as very clear signs of an impending catastrophe. He had seen enough of what the enemy could do on the way back from Arras to be taken in by the reassurances emanating from General Brownrigg's HQ that the coming attack was likely to consist of 'little more than a few tanks'. The very fact that he, of all people, had been ordered to defend the centre section of the perimeter was an indication of the desperate nature of the situation, and he knew enough about warfare to be aware that his unit might be called upon to fight it out to the last man.

Standing on the high bank of a country lane, he watched as two sappers, stripped to the waist, wielded axes upon the gnarled bowl of an oak tree. A rope had been attached to its upper branches, and a dozen men awaited the word to heave. Further up the lane, a group of refugees had been stopped at gunpoint by a corporal.

It was at this moment, when the tree was teetering and ready to fall, that a despatch rider came roaring up the hill on a motorbike.

The rider, a young subaltern of nineteen or twenty, scrambled up the bank, saluted and delivered a message from General Brownrigg's headquarters. As far as Wheeler was concerned, it was a clear answer to prayer: PERIMETER DEFENCES WILL BE PROVIDED BY 20TH GUARDS BRIGADE NOW DISEMBARKING GARE MARITIME. YOU WILL PLACE YOURSELF AND NO 12 DOCK SECTION

iii

The 20th Guards Brigade, composed of one battalion each of the Irish Guards, Welsh Guards and Loyals had been training at Old Dean Common Camp in Surrey when the order to move had been received at eleven a.m. the previous day.

The orders had been passed over the telephone. The War Office had directed that the brigade was to move as quickly as possible to Dover for embarkation. Everything had to be done at short notice. Buses had to be ordered from Aldershot to transport the troops; anti-tank guns and ammunition had to be loaded up and got on the road, and companies exercising at Bisley and Lydd had to be recalled or diverted. But when the column arrived at Dover at ten o'clock that night, only two ships were ready for embarkation when three were needed and little or no preparation had been made for loading the brigade's equipment.

In spite of these difficulties, the brigade sailed aboard the SS *Biarritz, Queen of the Channel, Mona Star* and the destroyer HMS *Vimy* a little before five in the morning, and a few hours later these ships were negotiating the narrow, tortuous entrance to Boulogne and berthing at the Quai Chanzy in the Avant Port.

Though the men fell in on the quay and marched off with impressive speed and precision, the disembarkation of this force was a nightmare. Equipment had been loaded haphazardly in the rush to embark, and without its own transport, the problem of moving guns and stores out of the town and up to positions on the perimeter was acute. Without carriers, it was impossible to throw out a protective screen while positions were taken up in daylight. This meant there was no fire available to keep the enemy's heads down, with the result that the brigade's positions were quickly spotted by German reconnaissance troops.

On top of all this, the crowds of refugees and a large collection of undisciplined troops of the Pioneer Corps caused lengthy delays and incidents which, in the absence of any military police, had to be sorted out by NCOs who were urgently required elsewhere.

In the face of these difficulties, the unloading went ahead and the troops began moving out to their allotted sectors. On a perimeter line sited just outside the town, anti-tank guns and machine-gun nests were placed guarding the entrance roads, with the Irish Guards occupying the area south of the River Liane to the coast at Le Portel, and the Welsh Guards positioned along a line from St Leonard, over the heights of Mont Lambert to the coast at Wimereux.

iv

While the officers of the 20th Guards Brigade cursed the War Office brass for organizing such a shambles, the tank commanders of the XIX Panzer Corps raged with every bit as much fury against their own group commander, General von Kleist.

Instead of being allowed to take his tank columns straight on up the coast from Etaples, General Guderian had been ordered to wait on the River Canche, and for five hours the tanks had stood inactive. Each infuriating minute of that delay gave the British a little more time to prepare their defences. If only he had been given a free hand, Guderian knew very well that a rapid advance northward with his three armoured divisions would have secured not only Boulogne but Calais and the Aa canal as well, leaving only Dunkirk to be taken to draw the strings of the bag tight and capture the entire British Expeditionary Force.

At last, at twelve-forty p.m., the order came through authorizing the advance.

The carriers and motorcycle troops led the way, followed

by the tanks, the mechanized infantry and finally the tractors towing the artillery. After a little difficulty with some French opposition at Desvres, Samer and Neufchâtel, the columns moved on, making contact with the Irish Guards on the southern outskirts of Boulogne in mid-afternoon

By five o'clock the tanks were in action and the noise of machine guns, mortars and cannon could be heard clearly in the town. At six-thirty, Boulogne was bombed. By eight, the Welsh Guards were in contact. Darkness fell, but the firing continued. Road blocks were set alight by flame-throwers. Light artillery and mortars began shelling British positions. German reconnaissance platoons used stalking tactics to locate anti-tank and machine guns, which were then attacked with stick grenades. Fifth columnists mingled with the refugees that were still flooding into the town and set up signalling and machine-gun posts in the apartment blocks overlooking the harbour; and while these initial attacks proceeded, another column of tanks worked its way right round the town to the north and prepared to attack the French-held Fort de la Crèche on the coast.

v

That night, the telephone lines at the British headquarters in Wimereux went dead, and Lieutenant General Brownrigg and his staff were isolated both from the troops defending Boulogne and the War Office in London.

Something had to be done to regain control of the battle, so, taking the rear HQ staff and the chiefs of medical and provost services with him, Brownrigg crossed to Dover in HMS *Verity*, reported the worsening situation to the War Office, and asked to be taken straight back in a destroyer that would act as a floating headquarters from which he could direct the battle. But as far as the War Office was concerned, Lieutenant General Brownrigg had deserted his post and, in spite of all his protestations, he was not only forbidden to return to the battle but also informed, three weeks later, that his services on the active list of the British army were no longer required.

vi

The main German attack came in at dawn. Fort de la Crèche was captured from the French and a troop of the Anti-aircraft Regiment knocked out. At seven-thirty, attacks on the 20th Brigade came in on all sides. Further bombing attacks were made on the town, and dog-fights developed as RAF Battles, Blenheims and Lysanders came into action. The casualties mounted; lorries and ambulances hooted their way through the town. Reserves said to be marching from Calais and Desvres failed to materialize. Shells began landing in the town and around the harbour. Destroyers came and went constantly, ferrying the auxiliary troops back to England and safety: *Vimy, Venomous, Wild Swan* and *Keith* provided gunfire support from the sea. The captain of *Keith* was killed on his bridge and the captain of *Vimy* mortally wounded. The French destroyer *L'Orage* was sunk. But the screech of their low-trajectory gunfire provided tremendous moral support to the troops ashore, and delayed the advance of the panzer columns.

While the action raged, a contingent of Royal Marines took charge of the crowds of disorganized troops that were pouring into the town and got them aboard the ships. Royal Engineers worked under shellfire and dive-bombing attacks to shift tons of explosive from the quayside.

Slowly but inexorably the Welsh and Irish Guards fighting on the perimeter were forced back. They had no reserves to replace casualties, lacked anti-tank guns, were short of ammunition and out of touch with the headquarters at Wimereux.

At the same time General Lanquetot, who had received separate orders from the French high command to hold the town, set up a fortified headquarters in the fort at Haute Ville at the top of the steep hill that runs up from the docks area; but the French reinforcements promised to him had already been intercepted and he had to cobble together a defence force of lightly armed, inexperienced troops. As the Guards retreated into the town, Lanquetot's headquarters became cut off and he remained unaware of British intentions for the rest of the battle.

At about midday, when the Irish Guards had withdrawn into the buildings across the road from the docks area, an apparently French civilian came running down the street ahead of five medium tanks. 'Don't shoot! Don't shoot!' he shouted to the Guards. 'They are French!' – and then, as the leading tank came into point-blank range of the head-quarters, he darted away into cover and the panzers opened up with cannon and machine guns.

Receiving an order to evacuate Boulogne, the Irish Guards withdrew further to the cover of the sheds, warehouses and pumping stations in the dock area; but the Welsh Guards had received a quite different message, to the effect that they were to stay and fight it out. Using the destroyers' wireless to keep in contact with London, Brigadier Fox-Pitt signalled 'Situation grave' to the War Office during the afternoon, and at five-thirty p.m. HMS *Whitshed* picked up a signal ordering the 20th Brigade to evacuate immediately. This message took an hour to reach Brigadier Fox-Pitt, and it never reached General Lanquetot's garrison at all. The discovery that the British were getting out was to be a source of deep and lasting resentment among the French troops who were left behind.

vii

The destroyer HMS *Wild Swan* had transported one load of troops from Boulogne to Dover already that day and now she had been ordered back to collect another. When she arrived off the harbour, it was a calm, beautiful day, with the only cloud in the sky coming from the massive black pall of smoke that was spreading westwards down the coast from the burning oil refinery at Dunkirk.

Six French destroyers were bombarding the coast to the north of Boulogne, while a few miles to the westward HMS *Venomous* and *Venetia* were lying off the harbour entrance. *Wild Swan* joined this pair and discovered, by means of visual signalling, that two more destroyers, the *Whitshed* and *Warwick*, were in the harbour embarking troops. For a while, apart from the sound of firing in and around the town and the regular thud of the French destroyers' guns, all was reasonably quiet; then fifty Stukas appeared in arrowhead formations, and the furies of hell were let loose.

Belching smoke from their funnels, the destroyers went up to full speed, their multiple pom-poms rattling away as each aircraft dived for the attack. Using every trick of evasion, turning hard a-starboard then hard a-port, the destroyers sent up an intense barrage of fire; and when the RAF joined in, the real meaning of this new style of warfare became suddenly apparent, for all three services were now closely engaged and every weapon on shore, on water and in the air was in action.

In the town, it seemed that nothing could survive in such a storm of bombs, shells and bullets, but through it all the troops, called out in groups and marshalled by the Royal Marines, doubled out from their shelters, along the quay and down into the cover of the lower levels of the jetty, from where they went in single file aboard the destroyers, which were now bespattered by the fountains of mud thrown up by near misses in the murky waters of the harbour.

viii

There was a lull. Outside the harbour, the men on the bridge of *Wild Swan* watched as *Warwick* and *Whitshed* emerged from the Rade Carnot, low in the water from the hundreds of troops they had on board.

A signal lamp flickered. The yeoman read it aloud as it was sent. 'Your . . . turn . . . now.'

The captain turned to the navigator, who was bending over the chart table. 'In and out, pilot.'

'On a falling tide with the chart showing less than we draw,' the navigator grumbled.

Signal flags ran up to the yard of *Wild Swan* ordering *Venomous* and *Venetia* to take station astern, and the three destroyers headed for the harbour. It was flat calm. Keeping station three hundred yards apart, the warships entered the outer harbour, altering first ninety degrees to port and then almost immediately thirty degrees to starboard in order to negotiate the narrow channel that led to the Gare Maritime.

While the guns' crews kept their guns laid and trained on the lookout bearings, the torpedo crews were employed fore and aft preparing berthing ropes and fenders.

As *Wild Swan* began her final approach a stream of tracer rose – almost gracefully – into the air and then accelerated suddenly, tearing into the bridge superstructure.

'Port two-pounders – engage!' bellowed the gunnery officer, and the fight was on.

'Port side to!' shouted the first lieutenant through a megaphone, and the ship came smoothly alongside the railway quay where a crowd of troops was waiting on the lower level.

Firing her guns northward in the direction of the harbour master's office and the casino, *Venomous* came alongside on the other side of the quay, while at the same time *Venetia* started her approach to come alongside *Wild Swan*. But as she did so she suffered a direct hit on the bridge and burst into flames, heeling over and losing steerage way. All on the bridge were killed except for one midshipman.

Having failed to sink *Venetia*, the guns and tanks on shore turned their attention to the quay, and for the next forty-five minutes kept up a tornado of fire. The range was so short that direct hits were almost invariably obtained, and had not the quay been extremely well built a breach would have been inevitable, with heavy casualties among the troops sheltering on the lower level. The noise of the direct hits above their heads and the firing of the destroyers close alongside was intense. But the discipline of the guardsmen waiting to embark, many of whom could have jumped straight onto the deck of the destroyers, was such that no move of any sort was made until the order was given to do so, and when that order came it was obeyed unhurriedly and efficiently.

The troops started embarking aboard *Wild Swan* within a minute or two of the first line going ashore. First the stretcher cases, then the walking wounded and finally the fit troops. At the same time, enemy shells from artillery in the woods less than a mile away began falling round the ships, and tanks appeared on the promenade. With troops embarking all the while, the 4.7 inch fired back on the tanks, and after a few ranging rounds three direct hits were scored, forcing the last tank to withdraw into a building which promptly collapsed on top of it.

A group of armoured cars appeared, and were dealt with summarily by the two-pounders. The Stukas returned; more bombs fell; several cranes toppled – one so close to *Wild Swan* that no one knew how it missed the ship. The battery at Fort de la Crèche, captured that morning from the French, joined the bombardment of the ships, and machine guns began firing down from the windows of the flats opposite the harbour. With soldiers now leaping aboard around them, the 4.7 inch guns' crews loaded and fired, loaded and fired, shelling the flats opposite to silence the machine guns firing from the upper windows.

Whole buildings were demolished. Fires broke out and walls collapsed in clouds of dust. The number of soldiers on the upper decks and fo'c'sle grew until they were getting in the way of the guns' crews passing up ammunition, occasioning blue language from the petty officer of the quarters.

Casualties mounted. A few men fell between the ship and

the quay and were lost. On the quay, a Bren gun manned by a soldier, a seaman and a sergeant provided covering fire as each fresh squad was marched at the double out of cover, along the quay and down the iron ladders to the decks. Further along the quay, Royal Marines and sappers were fighting a rearguard action of their own to keep the enemy tanks and carriers at bay. Astern of *Wild Swan*, *Venetia* struggled to clear the harbour. Listing heavily, burning furiously, her steering out of action, the surviving officers on board managed to steer her stern first using only her main engines so that, with all guns still firing, she achieved what had seemed impossible, backing out along the narrow channel to the outer harbour and disappearing behind her own billowing clouds of smoke.

The tide was ebbing and *Wild Swan*'s bow was already aground. *Venomous* cast off, and *Wild Swan* checked her fire while the other destroyer went astern out of her berth; then it was *Wild Swan*'s turn to leave and after some juggling with the engines the captain managed to get her bows off the mud. Going astern with her for'd guns still firing, she followed *Venomous* out, and the men on board gave a cheer of relief. In a slight pause, there came a shout from the captain of 'A' gun: 'If you bloody Pongoes block my ammunition supply much longer I'm going to *desert*!'

The ship heeled suddenly and stopped. She was aground again, and while shells and tracer bullets whined around his ears the captain bellowed engine orders down the voicepipe to the wheelhouse to get her free; and then, like a squeezed orange pip, HMS *Wild Swan* came faster and faster out of the entrance, turned in her own length and – still firing back at the enemy positions in the town – headed out to sea and comparative safety.

ix

After the ships had left, the men of the Welsh Guards, Pioneer Corps and Royal Engineers who were left behind continued the battle. Ordered to withdraw from his road blocks, Lieutenant Colonel Dean found himself and his small company of Glaswegian reservists suddenly face to face with German infantry. The men – who barely knew how to fire a rifle – abandoned their weapons and ran. But they did not run away from the enemy, they ran towards them and, drawing cut-throat razors, the common currency of Glasgow slum fights, they fell on the Germans, and after a brief and bloody hand-to-hand skirmish, drove them off.

It was at about this time also that Captain Wheeler, having withdrawn from the perimeter where he and his section had been fighting alongside the Welsh Guards, ran the gauntlet on a motorbike through enemy-held positions to retrieve secret documents that had been dropped in the middle of the road during the retreat through the town. He had been a cavalry officer during the Great War and was at home on the back of a horse, but it was his first time ever on a motorbike.

Soon after sunset there was another air raid, and at ten-thirty HMS *Windsor* came alongside and took off another 600 men; but there were still hundreds of soldiers and refugees sheltering in the station, and when the destroyer backed out, it looked as if their last hope of rescue went with her.

In the lower part of the town, the shooting became sporadic. Two companies of Welsh Guards were attempting to escape to the north and a third, under Major Windsor Lewis, was fighting its way back to make a last stand in the docks area. The transit sheds had been gutted by fire, and the bridge linking the Gare Central to the Quai Gambetta had been blown up. Corpses littered the quays round the customs sheds and floated in the harbour. A big fire at the railway station lit up the sky, and there were more fires at the fort of Haute Ville, where General Lanquetot had been told by the Germans to surrender or have the whole town destroyed, building by building.

In the early hours when the firing had at last stopped and an eerie silence had settled in Boulogne, a dark shape came up the entrance channel and secured at the outer jetty. It was another destroyer: HMS *Vimiera*.

The refugees made a rush for her. French, Belgians, Dutch, Jews, Poles – even one or two Americans – all had good reason to escape the Nazis. They seethed down the quay and fought to get on board, having to be kept back at bayonet point while the troops embarked.

David was among them. Held back by a cordon of naval ratings with fixed bayonets, he watched as the soldiers filed quickly on board over the brow. When several hundred had been embarked, an officer called to the midshipman on the jetty to start embarking refugees twenty at a time.

All around him, people jostled and whimpered, prayed and pleaded to be allowed on board. Slowly – so slowly – the queue shuffled forward. At the head of the brow, the midshipman counted heads and kept looking back at the bridge. With each order of 'Another twenty,' the two ratings guarding the way raised their rifles and more heads were counted through.

Waiting his turn with the mob, David held out little hope that he would get aboard. There were eighty or more ahead of him, and the ship was already low in the water. 'Another twenty,' called the first lieutenant; and again: 'Another twenty . . .'

He was praying, now. 'O God, O God, O God!' was all he could manage. He shuffled forward, waited, shuffled forward again. He watched a young mother being helped aboard with her two-year-old son. How many ahead of him now? Forty or more. They would have to let three more twenties on board if he was to have a chance.

'Another twenty?' the midshipman asked, and when permission was given by the first lieutenant on the bridge murmured, '*Vite! Vite!*' to the refugees.

And then — as the bayonets came down again to stop the flow, David found himself fifth back in the queue. He tried to catch the eye of the midshipman. 'I'm an American citizen,' he yelled. 'For God's sake, you've got to let us on board!'

The midshipman looked up at the bridge.

'Last lot!' called the first lieutenant.

David went down the slope of the brow and onto the crowded deck of the destroyer. Moments later, as the engines went astern, one last handful of soldiers — Welsh guardsmen and a few sappers from No 12 Dock Section — broke cover from a warehouse and made a dash along the jetty, scrambling aboard over the bows.

Fourteen hundred troops and refugees were on board when HMS *Vimiera* edged gingerly away from the jetty. With shells crashing down on the quays and breakwaters and plumes of water shooting up around her, the heavily laden destroyer turned, and, churning mud up under her stern, gathered way out of the harbour.

The evacuation of Boulogne — and the dress rehearsal for a rescue of far greater dimensions — was over.

TWENTY-THREE

In the very early hours of Saturday 25 May, at about the same time that HMS *Vimiera* was embarking troops and refugees at Boulogne, General Alan Brooke, commanding 2 Corps, drove from his Corps headquarters in Armentières to visit Gort's GHQ at Premesques.

It was a call of particular urgency. The previous evening he had learnt from General Adam, the commander of 3 Corps, that while the German advance from the south had for some extraordinary reason halted on the waterline of the Aa canal between Gravelines and La Bassée, the northern flank, held by the Belgians between Menin and Courtrai, had been penetrated and was on the point of collapse; and although Brooke still had the natural obstacle of the River Lys to guard his left, any further penetration towards Ypres would put the BEF in great danger of being cut off from the sea.

Brooke's request to Gort was simple therefore. He needed reinforcements for the northern flank, and he needed them very quickly indeed.

Gort, who was still bound by his undertaking to the French to send two divisions to strike southward at the German corridor in accordance with the Weygand Plan, and who was continually plagued by the naggings and promptings and requests for information from the War Office, was at first sceptical that the danger to his left flank could be as great – or even greater – than that to his right, and at first suggested to Brooke that the nine-mile front from Comines to Ypres could be held with two machine-gun battalions. Brooke pointed out the futility of such an idea. The Belgians had all but given up: only that afternoon he had had reports from the 12th Lancers that Belgian front-line troops had abandoned their weapons and were sitting about in cafés, drinking coffee.

Having had his request virtually turned down flat, Brooke went off to visit his divisional commanders. He found Montgomery installed in a small villa, and as he walked in noticed a group of staff officers clustered round a table taking unusual interest in some papers.

'You seem to be very busy round that table,' he remarked.

One of the officers looked up. 'Yes, sir, we've got some interesting documents here. One of our patrols working across the Lys River brought them in. They shot up a Jerry staff car and found a wallet full of papers. And a bootjack, what's more, so we don't think it's a plant.'

Brooke took an interest. 'Have you got a German interpreter here?'

'No sir, but a couple of us have a smattering –'

Much to their disgust, Brooke told them to put the papers – and the bootjack – back in the wallet and give it to him to take to Gort's GHQ for proper examination.

The result of that examination, conducted by Major General Whiteford, was the discovery of two documents of almost priceless worth: the first consisted of orders to the German 6th Army to mount a concentrated attack on the Belgian front the following day, so lending enormous weight to Brooke's request for reinforcements; the second gave a very nearly complete picture of the organization of the entire German army and was a document of such high classification that only twenty copies had been issued. Its capture was to give the War Office a grip on the German Order of Battle that was never subsequently lost.

ii

General Blanchard had taken over from General Billotte, and at the headquarters his staff were by now in a state of despair, so much so that several of them had approached Major

Archdale privately to ask if it would be possible for Lord Gort to take over command of the French 1st Army Group in addition to the BEF. But when Archdale passed on this request to Lieutenant Colonel Bridgeman at Gort's headquarters in Premesques, he was informed that the C-in-C could not interfere in any internal French question of personalities.

An hour or so later, when he was working on Anglo-French coordination of the Weygand Plan, Archdale was called to the C-in-C's office. He found Gort sitting at his table looking bewildered and bitter.

Pownall, the Chief of General Staff, was also present. He told Archdale that he was to be relieved of his present duties as British liaison officer to the 1st Army Group and transferred to No 2 Military Mission at La-Ferté-sous-Jouarre, so that General Georges could be fully briefed.

'I take it you are fully conversant with the situation?' Pownall asked.

'Yes, sir, but I would like to hear it from you as well.'

Pownall glanced at Gort, who sat like an angry bear at his desk. He nodded his permission, and Pownall gave a rapid briefing, using a wall map to point out lines and positions.

'The Belgians are hard pressed at Courtrai and our only available reserves – one brigade and one machine-gun battalion – are being sent to their support. The 5th and 50th divisions are at present under orders to attack south as agreed tomorrow, but this attack will be little more than a sortie, and there will be no hope of success unless there is a strong, coordinated attack by the French from the south. Also, if the enemy breaks through on the Belgian front, we shall have to provide instant help, for obvious reasons, in which case the attack south would have to be called off. In that event there would have to be a retirement of the BEF to within the line Gravelines – Béthune – Armentières – Comines – Ypres and the sea.'

Archdale was digesting this when Gort suddenly broke his silence.

'I've had a damn raw deal from the allies,' he said. 'They've never stopped pleading to me that their troops are too tired to fight. Their staff work broke down on the first day. There's been absolutely no positive direction or information from the high command. And why did they retreat to the Scheldt when they knew that would leave a gap in the centre? Why didn't they retreat south instead of west and preserve a front and lines of communication?' He shook his head and lapsed once more into silence.

Pownall turned to Archdale. 'You'll have to make your own way,' he said quietly. 'Get a move order from Colonel Bridgeman. And come and see me before you go so that I can brief you on the very latest developments.'

Archdale stiffened to attention, saluted the C-in-C, and departed.

iii

. . . I am to recce the Lys west from Halluin making sure that the Middlesex who have joined us to guard it do not leave any barges unsunk.

My first quarry is a group of barges which the Middlesex are attending to. As I watch them at it I am conscious of a hostile presence. Behind me some very tough looking bargees are staring at me. I walk nonchalantly to my motorcycle and ride off to the next point. At Bousbecque, there is another section of Middlesex, and the corporal is worried because one barge is still occupied. I walk across the field towards it, and up the gang plank. There are lace curtains and china ornaments and an elderly couple very frightened. I give them ten minutes to pack their belongings and get out. They ask me where they are to go, and I cannot help them . . .

Immediately after his meeting with Archdale, Gort went into conference with his senior commanders to discuss the mounting crisis. During the meeting, further reports of a Belgian collapse came in. There was now little to stop General von Bock's army from advancing westward across the old Ypres battlefields and linking up with Kleist's panzer divisions which were already threatening the opposite flank at Cassel and Hazebrouck.

By five o'clock that afternoon, Gort had heard enough to know that he was faced with a decision that would either save the BEF or spell its final destruction.

He left the conference and retired to his private room to think, giving orders to his servant to refuse all requests to see him for one hour. In that hour, his military judgement, loyalty, courage and integrity were to be tested in a way that must be unique in the history of generalship.

On the one hand, he had promised Weygand, Blanchard, Ironside and Churchill that he would comply with the Weygand Plan and send two divisions – his entire reserve force – southward to attack the German corridor and link up with the French army in the hope of saving France. The risks of such a venture were now as obvious as they were appalling. Apart from General Giraud, who had been taken prisoner, not one French general had displayed the moral superiority and the will to fight that was essential if the Germans were to be repulsed, and Gort had lost all confidence in them. What guarantee had he, if he struck southward, of any determined French action? He had none. All he could expect, if his experiences of the past fortnight were any guide at all, was a plethora of orders, much talk about honour and fighting to the last man and the last bullet, followed by endless bleating that the troops were too tired to move.

There was another imponderable factor. Twenty-four hours before, a German signal had been intercepted by British

Intelligence ordering the panzer divisions to halt at the Aa canal.

He had a translation of the signal to hand:

> FORCES ADVANCING TO THE NORTH-WEST OF ARRAS ARE NOT TO GO BEYOND THE GENERAL LINE LENS—BETHUNE—AIRE—ST OMER—GRAVELINES. ON THE WEST WING, ALL MOBILE UNITS ARE TO CLOSE UP AND LET THE ENEMY THROW HIMSELF AGAINST THE ABOVE-MENTIONED FAVOURABLE DEFENSIVE LINE

Why should the German High Command have taken such an extraordinary decision when the BEF was so nearly in the bag? Why should they be talking about a defensive line, when their lightning offensive had met with such astounding success?

He tried to put himself in their shoes. They had made a phenomenal advance, and their leading units were now at the end of a very long supply train. Their tanks had been reduced in numbers – possibly by as much as forty per cent – and they would know that beyond the Aa canal the country would be inundated as a defence against tanks. Perhaps, too, they had intelligence of the Weygand Plan. Even if they had not, they must surely be expecting such a move. So . . . they would halt their armour behind this ideal defensive line and as soon as the British turned on them they would use Bock's infantry divisions – which were far more mobile than tanks on soft ground – to deliver a hammer blow from the *opposite* side, the weak Belgian flank.

This surprise blow would crush the BEF against the hard wall of armour and achieve the final break-through. It would also give the panzers a much needed rest and time to prepare themselves for what the OKW must see as the 'real' battle – the battle for Paris.

The more he thought about it, the clearer the picture became. But clarity of appreciation only intensified the dilemma. If he turned his back on the collapsing Belgian front and drove south, as Churchill was urging him to do, his link with the sea would be cut – there was no doubt of it. The Germans would swarm along the coast from Ostend to La Panne and onward to Dunkirk, where they would link up with the armoured divisions which were already close to Gravelines. The whole BEF would be sealed up in France, fighting for its life on all fronts and utterly dependent upon the French army for its salvation.

And then?

Then, Hitler, having dispensed with the BEF and conquered France as he surely would, would turn his attentions upon Britain. She would be left without her army at the moment of her greatest need. Her people would be demoralized. All her greatest military commanders, all her experienced war veterans, all her strong, courageous young soldiers would be sent to sit out the war in prison camps. The disaster for Europe and the civilized world would be as great – greater – than the fall of ancient Rome to the Barbarians. Germany, Italy, Russia and Japan would carve up the entire world amongst themselves – America included – and the rule of the jackboot would become worldwide.

He paced up and down, wrestling with the problem. He saw now that what he was having to decide was whether or not to commit an act of wilful disobedience. He had been ordered by Churchill, no less, to turn and strike south. All his training, all his instincts told him to obey, and obey without question.

The course of action he was now contemplating was the exact opposite: to ignore the orders he had received and acknowledged from Whitehall and had discussed endlessly with General Blanchard; to send his last two divisions north instead of south; to put the safety of the BEF first, renege on the French and commit his army to a hazardous evacuation by sea.

And how many of his 'brave, brown companions' would get away? Dunkirk had already been savagely bombed, and its outskirts were within range of the German artillery at Gravelines. There were a quarter of a million men to get back to England, and even at the brisk rate of ten thousand a day, evacuating them would take nearly a month. All he could hope for was two or three days. Thirty thousand men. Even that seemed to be stretching optimism too far. But thirty thousand soldiers carried back to Britain was better than no soldiers at all.

At six o'clock, one hour after going into his room, Lord Gort summoned his Chief of General Staff.

Pownall was well aware of the C-in-C's solitary dilemma. As he entered Gort's office, the latter turned, and in clipped phrases gave his decision without preamble.

'The Weygand Plan's dead and buried. The reserve divisions — 5th and 50th — are to be sent to reinforce the northern flank immediately. The BEF will withdraw down the corridor from Lille to Dunkirk. To this end, selected towns and villages are to be reinforced on either side of the British salient. These will act as stop points to keep the enemy at bay while the withdrawal takes place.'

Pownall had half expected something like this, but hearing Gort put it into words caused a dull sense of shock.

'So . . . we're committed, as I see it, to a retreat to the coast.'

'That's right,' Gort replied grimly. 'A retreat to the coast, and an evacuation from the beaches.' He turned away from Pownall and stared for several seconds at the wall map. Then, more to himself than to Pownall, he added quietly: 'Which means that we are committed to an act of military desperation.'

PART THREE

TWENTY-FOUR

Simone, in that delicious period between sleep and wakeful-
ness, was dreaming of Archie. His arms were round her, she
was his. It was so real, so blissful, that although a small
corner of her mind knew that it was only a dream, she
managed to prolong it for several minutes, sighing to herself,
her eyelids fluttering, her legs pressed tight together.

But the dream could not last: she had to let it go. She
remembered that it was her birthday. Sunday, 26 May 1940.
She was thirty-nine. Would anyone else remember? She
had had no letter from Griff for over three weeks and not a
word of news – from Christine or anyone else – about
Archie. The last letter she had had from a loved one was
the note David had left on his bed. At least he might have
remembered. But he hadn't, and she had no idea where he
was.

She lay for a while longer, listening to the sound of the
army base waking up: the clatter of pans and cooking trays
in the kitchens, the talk and laughter among the watchkeepers as they walked across the quad from their living
quarters to the dining hall. She heard the first squadron of
planes go over on their way to France and a little while later
the morning test of an alarm klaxon in the anti-aircraft gun
battery on the cliffs.

Time to get up. She went along the passage to Betty and
Elspeth's bedroom, knocked on the door and called, 'Twenty
to seven!' before going into the bathroom.

Downstairs, she let Blashford out into the back garden,
laid the kitchen table and made porridge, toast and tea.

She switched on the wireless for the first bulletin at seven
o'clock. She didn't really want to hear it, but listening to the

news had become a compulsive habit. News was like a drug: one could never get enough of it.

'. . . No important development in the situation on the Western Front has been reported during the night . . . An announcement from the office of the French Prime Minister last night gave the news that fifteen French generals had been relieved of their commands . . . The scarcity of news about the battles on the Western Front is likely to continue for some days. For reasons of security, details of new troop movements and news of places where fighting is going on are not being mentioned for the present. Self-denial in the matter of news is more than ever a contribution of importance which the general public must make towards the outcome –'

For once, Simone turned it off in mid-sentence.

'Happy birthday dear Simone,' she whispered to herself, warming her hands on the teapot. 'Happy birthday to you.'

Betty and Elspeth came down for breakfast. They said their good mornings and sat down to their porridge. Twenty minutes later she watched them depart on their bicycles. She cleared and washed up the breakfast things, went upstairs and made the beds, something she now did for her lodgers because they were working such long hours.

She wondered, as she worked, whether to attend matins that morning in answer to the call for a national day of prayer. She was not a religious person and never had been. She had formally abandoned the Catholic faith on her marriage to Griff, and had since attended church services only when the occasion – or Griff – had demanded it.

She had mixed feelings about this day of prayer. If you believed in an all-powerful God, you couldn't really deny that 'He' must have got us into this mess in the first place, so why should 'He' suddenly be expected to get us out?

No, she decided. I shall not go to matins. If I've got any prayers to say, I'll say them in private.

The telephone rang. She ran downstairs to the hall to

answer it, hardly daring to hope that Griff or Archie might be ringing to wish her a happy birthday.

But it was neither.

'Hello, Simone? It's Christine. Listen, there won't be anyone in for lunch today, and we're all going to be staying on here for the next few nights. I'm sorry about this —'

'It's all right. I quite understand.'

'One of us will pop up and collect our overnight things sometime today.'

'All right. Christine —'

'Yes?'

'Are things very bad?'

There was a short silence the other end, then: 'No, no. We're just a bit busy, that's all.'

ii

Christine's understatement was a model of sang-froid: the naval staff at Dover were considerably more than a 'bit busy'. In the last twenty-four hours, preparations had been going ahead to control the naval evacuation of the BEF from the underground headquarters, and Third Officer Trendle-Home had been involved in the preparation of a special room to be used exclusively for the purpose.

The room chosen for the command centre was the old dynamo room, which had once housed the electric generator plant that supplied heating and lighting to the headquarters. Windowless, and lit by four overhead light bulbs, it was ventilated by a fan trunking and punkah louvres. There was a large, wide, wooden table with eight chairs on either side and one at either end. A battery of telephones, back to back, ran down the centre of this table, one each for the reserve officers who were being drafted in at short notice to serve as temporary assistants to Captain Denny, the staff officer who had been put in direct charge of the operation. On the arched wall, thanks to the efforts of the Wrens, there now hung large-scale charts of the English Channel showing minefields, wrecks and other hazards; perspex tote boards, upon which would be written the names of ships involved in the operation; harbour plans for the south coast of England – and a very large plan of the port of Dunkirk and adjacent beaches.

There had been no time to write formal operation orders. Arriving by train, sometimes after long overnight journeys, the reserve officers detailed to work on Admiral Ramsay's evacuation staff were shown the austere accommodation that was theirs for the duration of the operation and then led into the dynamo room, shown which seat at the table and which telephone to use, given the briefest set of instructions upon their duties, and told to get on with it.

In the space of twenty-four hours, the dynamo room had been turned from a bare-walled, seldom-used junk room into a nerve centre, a hive of activity, where the telephones were already in constant use, the clip files filling up with pink signals and the enormity of the task ahead creating an almost tangible atmosphere of urgency and grim determination.

One officer was acting as a direct liaison link with the Ministry of Shipping and was negotiating the loan – or commandeering – of the merchant vessels that would be needed to ferry the troops back to England. Another was coordinating the efforts of minesweepers to clear a more direct channel from Dunkirk to Dover. A third was desperately ringing round to all the military training centres and requisitioning every available machine gun to provide some form of anti-aircraft defence to the unarmed ships taking part in the operation.

The telephones rang constantly; a blue haze of cigarette smoke hung permanently in the room; Wrens went to and fro, bringing cups of coffee or sandwhich meals to the staff, making up the bed in the corner for the duty officer, typing signals, orders, lists, memoranda; and from time to time Admiral Ramsay himself would look in on the preparations.

A tall, kindly man, devoted to his wife and three children,

Bertram Ramsay had sacrificed his career five years before when he tendered his resignation as Chief of Staff to C-in-C Home Fleet over what he regarded as the too rigid restriction of his responsibilities. Now, recalled for war service, he was exactly the sort of man needed to run an off-the-cuff show like this – a man with vast experience as an organizer and one who was at his best when left to get on with a job in his own way.

Adjoining his office, the admiral had a small, private balcony that was cut into the cliff face, from where he could observe the comings and goings of ships in the harbour, and it was here, sitting in the sun with his feet propped up against the iron railings, that he read his signals, interviewed his staff and, when there was a lull in the proceedings, dashed off a quick letter to his wife.

He was sitting on his balcony with a signal file open on his lap, staring out across the Channel to the coast of France, which was marked by a pall of smoke and from which came the sounds of battle. Like everyone else at the headquarters he was wondering how long the garrison in Calais would be able to hold out. The War Office had decided that this time, unlike Boulogne, there must be no evacuation: the German advance must be held up for as long as possible to enable the maximum number of allied troops to withdraw to the coast.

Only the day before, the Germans had offered terms to the encircled British Commander in Calais, which had been refused, and the Secretary of State had sent a signal to Brigadier Nicholson:

DEFENCE OF CALAIS TO THE UTMOST IS OF HIGHEST IMPORTANCE TO OUR COUNTRY AS SYMBOLIZING OUR CONTINUED CO-OPERATION WITH FRANCE. THE EYES OF THE EMPIRE ARE UPON THE DEFENCE OF CALAIS, AND HM GOVERNMENT ARE CONFIDENT YOU AND YOUR GALLANT REGIMENTS WILL PER-

FORM AN EXPLOIT WORTHY OF THE BRITISH
NAME.

and ten hours later another:

> EVERY HOUR YOU CONTINUE TO EXIST IS OF
> GREATEST HELP TO THE BEF. GOVERNMENT
> HAS THEREFORE DECIDED YOU MUST CON-
> TINUE TO FIGHT. HAVE GREATEST ADMIR-
> ATION FOR YOUR SPLENDID STAND.

Vice Admiral Ramsay turned to the Wren officer who stood beside his chair.

'You've read these signals, I take it, Christine?'

'Yes, sir, I have.'

He nodded to himself and looked across the Channel again. Then he snapped the file shut and handed it back. '"England expects". It's essentially the same message, isn't it?'

'Yes, sir,' she answered. 'I thought that, too.'

iii

After Christine rang off, Simone felt a wave of depression sweep over her. Sunday was the one day in the week when all four girls came back for lunch, and sometimes they brought friends along too. It was the day Simone looked forward to, the day when she felt she was contributing to the war effort by providing home cooking and homely surroundings for the young people to relax in for an hour or two. Today Elspeth was to have brought a new naval officer friend. Simone had managed to get a few fresh eggs from Reach Farm and had intended to make real Yorkshire pudding to go with the minuscule joint of roast beef. And though she had told none of her lodgers that it was her birthday, she had intended to make an extra special effort, to open a bottle of wine, to drink to absent friends.

326

Her chores finished, she wandered from room to room, staring out of windows, thinking, wondering.

It was the not knowing, that was the worst part. The not knowing, the waiting for news, the disappointment every morning when there was no letter, the fearful expectation of a telegram, the feeling of helpless inadequacy – and the unquenchable thirst for news, news, more news.

Last time had not been like this. Last time events had proceeded at a pace which the human brain could grasp. Last time it had been possible to understand and chart the movement of the armies, the clash, front to front, of tens of thousands of men. It had been a slow war, a war in which, after the first advances and retreats, the trench lines had remained unchanged for weeks at a time. It had been a war that was repeatedly bogged down, literally as well as figuratively. But this new lightning conflict was one which rolled on wheels and swooped in aeroplanes, in which an army advanced forty miles in a single day, and a nation was overrun in two. It was a war in which new catastrophes came so fast that the mind could not grasp the meaning of them, any more than a three-inch culvert can drain a tidal wave.

She was standing in the hall and the dog was wagging and whining round her legs. How long had she been standing there? She looked down at the black Labrador, then crouched to talk to him and pet him. She was tempted to allow the tears to come but fought them off, knowing by now how exhausting it could be if she gave way.

'Come on, old fellow,' she said to the dog – and she purposely used Archie's way of talking to it – 'Let's go for a walk.'

iv

She let Blashford off the lead as soon as they were out of the school grounds and he bounded off down into the little valley of scrub behind the cliff. It was another sunny day. There were aircraft taking off and landing at Hawkinge, and the grumble of bombs and guns from across the Channel was an incongruous accompaniment to the twittering of larks overhead. She called Blashford to heel as they approached the cliff and put him on the lead, because although Archie had claimed that the animal had enough sense not to go over the edge, she was still terrified of losing him.

She went along the cliff path. She saw a destroyer leave Dover harbour and head out into the Channel at high speed, her sharp bows cutting a long white scar in the blue water, her funnel smoke streaming away astern. For all Simone knew, that destroyer might be HMS *Vagabond* and one of those tiny figures she could see standing on the bridge might be Archie, taking his ship out to battle. In spite of herself – instinctively – she breathed a prayer for him: 'O God, keep him safe,' then added: 'And Griff. Keep them both safe, wherever they are.'

So you *do* believe in God, her alter ego whispered, and she sighed, aware that she was feeling guilty at not going to church but at the same time impatient with her own uncertainty.

As she walked on, with the cliff edge only a few yards to her left, her thoughts wandered back to a Sunday years ago when Olivia had been alive and she and Archie had come to stay at Prowse. They had tried to talk her into accompanying them to church and Griff had quoted some lines that went, 'Our God and soldiers we alike adore, ev'n at the brink of danger; not before . . .' and Archie had insisted that the lines were Nelson's and ran 'God and our *sailor* we alike adore, upon the brink of ruin, not before . . .' They had had a long, humorous discussion about it until Griff, schoolmaster to the last, had gone into the house and come out with a volume containing the epigrams of Francis Quarles, and Archie had had to concede.

How happy they had been in those days, and how quickly she had forgotten the horrors of war and taken the stability and contentment of married life for granted – had even railed at Griff for being 'dull', while all along it had been he who had made this life possible, who had plucked her from destitution and given her status and self-respect. And however dull and intellectual Griff might have been, she would never have met Archie had she not been married to Griff.

She saw now that she had fallen in love not so much with one or other of them as the two together. She had fallen in love with their sense of fair play, their openness and loyalty. It was a camaraderie that was uniquely British, something that she had never encountered among her own countrymen. In an odd way she had felt challenged by it. She wanted to be part of it, to have it for herself. After Olivia died, the campaign to capture it had provided her with a new aim in life, one that made up in part for not having children. Could she make Archie confide in her rather than Griff? Could she charm him, win his love, capture and captivate him? Yes, she discovered, she could, but what she had not realized was that in doing so she would endanger the very friendship and trust between Griff and Archie which she had wanted to share in the first place.

So if she was entirely honest with herself – and in these agonizing days of waiting and wondering one did rather a lot of this soul-searching – she had to admit that it was her own unfaithfulness to Griff that lay at the root of her present unease. In seducing Archie (yes, it had been she who had taken the lead) she had damaged something that was precious and not easily repaired. She, Archie and Griff had been like those three knives of Griff's after-dinner trick. They had supported and depended upon each other at the same time: she on Griff, Griff on Archie and Archie, after Olivia's death, on herself. But she had tried to change the pattern. She had tried to depend on Archie rather than Griff; the carefully balanced cantilever had been destroyed and their happiness and friendship – her glass of wine – was spilt and lost for ever.

So what was left? She didn't really know. War had radically changed things twenty-five years ago and was now changing them just as radically again. She was conscious of a need to regain what had been so carelessly thrown away: the peace of mind, the stability, the self-respect she had enjoyed as the wife of a schoolmaster. And however much she might shy away from the thought, she was beginning to see that the only way in which she could regain that self-respect lay in behaving as a wife should behave.

But that would be *so* dull, and how could she possibly live without the hope of making love to Archie ever again?

Away went her thoughts again, and now she deliberately re-entered the day-dream she so often had about meeting Archie unexpectedly, being held in his arms, returning his kisses, surrendering to him.

The path went down into a dip and up again. Gulls balanced on the rising air currents, floating upward as if by magic. As she came up the hill, she saw a group of people standing at the cliff edge, staring across to France.

It was a crowd of press reporters. Hordes of them had been descending on Dover in the last few days since the Germans had reached Abbeville and Boulogne had come under attack. They were a very mixed lot, mostly middle-aged men.

A few motor cars were parked in the lane behind the cliff that led to the lighthouse. In one of them, a man with a trilby tipped onto the back of his head was sitting behind the wheel scribbling in a notebook.

They had come to watch Calais burn. They were looking across the Channel at the black smoke rising from the town. The sound of explosions was like the continual rumble of a tropical storm, now growing to a crescendo, now fading to the ominous mutter of machine guns.

One of the journalists, a flashily dressed individual in knicker-bockers and a bow tie, was sitting on the turf with his legs straight out in front of him, staring at the French coast through a pair of binoculars and taking an occasional nip from a hip flask which was slung over his shoulder on a leather strap.

As Simone watched, he turned to a group behind him and made a remark that caused some laughter.

Her temper ignited. She strode over to them, confronting them while they were still laughing.

'It's funny, is it? Is that what you think of what's going on over there? Do you know something? That's my country you're laughing at, and you may be surprised to know that there are people being killed over there while you enjoy your jokes and – and drink your whisky . . .'

She ran out of words. She shook her head and walked quickly away from them; but the outburst had broken the dam of her self-control, and she gave way – at last – to tears.

She stood with her back to the reporters and wept. She wept for Archie, she wept for Griff and David and Britain and France. She wept because she felt so helpless and useless and alone . . .

'Steady there, steady,' a voice said behind her, and when she turned the knicker-bocker man was standing a few paces off.

Feeling suddenly dizzy, she had to sit down. Blashford wagged round her and licked her face. She pushed him away.

'Hey, now!' the knicker-bocker man said gently. 'Are you okay?'

'I'm just feeling a bit faint, that's all. Now please leave me alone.'

'Won't you let me apologize?'

She looked up at him. He seemed surprisingly human.

'We weren't laughing at your country, you know that? Some of us have been up here since dawn, right? Fellas get to talk about other things after a while.'

She stood up, still feeling dizzy. She had had only a cup of tea and a piece of toast for breakfast and had eaten very little the day before. It was silly of her, she knew that.

'I'm all right now, thank you,' she said, and started off down the path.

He came after her. 'Will you let me walk with you? I reckon it's the least I can do.'

She couldn't very well stop him. He paddled along at her side, a fleshy man in his fifties, rather short of breath, his whisky flask slung over one shoulder, a camera on the other and a pair of binoculars round his neck.

'So you're from France, right? What part? Paris? Is that right! And your husband? Oh, so he's English, right? Okay! And where is he now?'

It was impossible to remain silent under this barrage of questions, and as soon as she had begun to answer them she found it a great relief to talk. At the same time, she could not help being aware that she had picked up yet another man. Why was it that it always happened to her? Why was it that she could not stir out of the house without being accosted by men wherever she went? Was she marked in some way so that they knew by instinct what she was . . . or had once been?

He was like a sort of birthday present, this wheezing, expansive Aussie – the sort of birthday present which is quite a nice surprise but which you don't really know what to do with once you've opened it.

They went down into the valley behind the cliff and she let Blashford off the lead. She turned to him. 'I'll be all right now, thank you. It's no distance from here.'

'Well, if it's no distance, it's no trouble,' he said, and stuck by her. They went up the steep slope and came to the boundary of the Prowse estate, which was bordered by rolls of barbed wire and notices saying WAR DEPARTMENT – KEEP OUT. She had been required to sign an undertaking to observe security rules when the army had taken over, and she was now glad of the excuse to get rid of her sweating escort.

'This is as far as you're allowed,' she said. 'Goodbye.'

He looked very crestfallen and quite taken aback. She had the strong impression that he had been hopeful of considerably more hospitality.

'Okay,' he muttered resignedly. 'Okay.' He smiled and shrugged, then took out a billfold and produced his card. 'Ed Foxworthy,' he said, handing it over. 'If ever there's anything I can do, be sure and call me.'

He half waved, half saluted, and turned away. She put Blashford's lead on and they went up the narrow path to the wicket gate leading into the garden. As she came round the back of the greenhouse, Blashford pulled the lead out of her hand and dashed forward.

When she saw the reason she felt a cold shiver of terror: there was a man in an army greatcoat lying asleep on the bare springs of the swing seat. Blashford had stopped halfway across the lawn and was barking furiously. The man sat up, and at the same time caught sight of her. He had two weeks' growth of beard on him and was filthy dirty. The dog stopped barking and followed him, wagging, as he crossed the lawn and stood before her. He was swaying from fatigue.

'David –' she started.

He nodded in that awkward, shy way of his. 'I guess I came back after all,' he mumbled.

v

All he wanted to do was go to bed, but she said that he must have a bath first if only to relax him, and in any case she would have to make up his bed in the boxroom. She went up and ran his bath and when she came down found him nodding off in the kitchen with his head down on the table. She woke him up again and led him upstairs, and on the way he crashed from side to side as if he were drunk. She sat him down on the bathroom stool and asked him if he could manage, but his head was already back and his eyes were closing, so she helped him off with his clothes, took his arms out of the sleeves of his jacket, pulled off his worn-out shoes and trousers and took off his pyjamas. He was filthy dirty. Dust, dirt and oil were ingrained in his skin.

His feet were white and pulpy. He had bruises everywhere and a particularly large one on his thigh.

Naked, he leant on her as she helped him into the bath. Gently – almost reverently – she soaped and sponged him all over, his poor blistered feet, his scratched legs, his taut, tired body. She made him sit up and used her own flannel to wash his back and under his arms; she washed his matted hair and rinsed it with fresh, warm water whose temperature she tested first with her elbow, and when she had finished she knelt by the bath with tears streaming down her face, and held his head in her hands, and kissed him.

She helped him out of the bath and towelled him dry, every bit of him, and because she had not had time to make up the bed in the boxroom, she took him along the passage to her own bedroom and put him into the double bed.

She sat on the bed and ran her fingers gently through his hair. 'My baby,' she whispered. 'My poor baby . . .'

David heaved a massive sigh, and slept.

TWENTY-FIVE

. . . Geoffrey arrives in the small hours very cross having fallen into a ditch.

Our office is established in the stables of Div HQ's new château, and we should be very comfortable. But by the afternoon the flap is really on. We are apparently about to be attacked by two German corps, and one officer and one other rank from each unit has to get back to England to 'tell the tale'. Geoffrey Pawle has rested, and is sent off with Foster for Dunkirk with the Div HQ party.

We are to withdraw from the Lille salient tonight, but there is no mention of embarkation. I am to lead the HQRE section and rendezvous with the HQ sections of the companies led by the seconds-in-command at Beveren, the 2 Corps report Centre, travelling by Nieukerke and Poperinghe.

This time I take the Humber Snipe driven by Smith, with the section transport and doctor, Sauervein, RSM, CSM, staff sergeant, office staff, cooks and despatch riders without an advanced party. We start soon after sunset. Ahead a heavy streak of smoke lies across the horizon. Gun flashes are no guide this time because they are all around us.

The MP traffic section have marked the first part of the route with a gala of glow worm lamps, but they give out when the going gets difficult. To avoid other divisions' routes we move by a mixture of road and lane to Armentières and without lights the going is slow. A line of black shapes is standing ahead and glass lies thickly near the crossroads. We inch our way past the heavy lorries. There is a smell of death and a pile of tangled equipment. We turn right beyond the town onto a concrete surface and proceed at speed, but soon close up behind some medium gunner Scammell tractors. From now on it is stop-go . . .

ii

Major Archdale arrived in Paris that afternoon, having travelled overnight from Premesques to Dunkirk by staff car and from Dunkirk to Cherbourg aboard the French destroyer *Foudroyant*. He reported to the British military attaché, Colonel Lord Malise Graham, who was accompanied by General Sir Edward Spears, recently appointed as Churchill's personal representative in Paris.

On hearing Archdale's report, Spears said that he must go straight off and see Marshal Pétain. Archdale protested: he had been ordered by Lord Gort to report only to Brigadier Swayne, the British liaison officer on the staff of General Georges at La-Ferté-sous-Jouarre, and was sure that an interview with Pétain would far exceed his brief.

'Never mind about that, Major,' Spears said. 'Just do what you're told.'

He arrived at the Boulevard des Invalides for his interview with Pétain at six-thirty.

'You must speak very slowly,' he was told by the Chef de Cabinet before going in to meet the Vice-premier, 'otherwise the marshal will not be able to follow the conversation.'

Pétain was a very tired old man: dignified, but bowed down by cares.

After explaining that he had been ordered to report to the headquarters of General Georges, Archdale emphasized that Lord Gort had no wish to make any sort of complaint or suggestion concerning the French command. Then, at Pétain's request and speaking very slowly and clearly, he outlined the situation.

'Lord Gort has two divisions with which he might have counter-attacked in accordance with the Weygand Plan, Marshal. They were to have cooperated with the French, and the attack was due to begin tonight. But yesterday, the Belgians to the east gave way, and Lord Gort has been obliged to send one division to support them and hold another in readiness. So the attack south is unlikely to take place, and the situation of General Blanchard's army is now that of a beleaguered garrison.'

Pétain nodded to himself and there was a long silence.

'And what are your views of that army's chances, Major?'

'Sir,' said Archdale, choosing his words carefully, 'the chances of a beleaguered city without the strength to make a powerful sortie are a matter that rests with those in charge of the relieving forces.'

'And General Blanchard? What is your opinion of his competence?'

It is not often that a major of a foreign army is invited to give an opinion on the competence of a senior general. Archdale was taken aback.

'Well?' Pétain insisted.

'I – I can only speak in my own name, sir. I wish to make that quite clear –'

'I understand that. But you have been close to Blanchard, have you not? So what is your opinion?'

'He is a very tired man, sir. His army is a good one and has fought well, but he is not the man to infuse enthusiasm into overstrained forces, and what his army needs now, above all, is confidence in its commander.'

Pétain nodded in silence again.

'And . . . General Prioux?'

'He is magnificent, Marshal, and inspires confidence among his staff and his troops. And they are magnificent also.'

Pétain gave a sad little laugh. 'And will you enthuse in a similar way about the British?'

'They don't need that,' General Spears put in quietly.

'It is then the French only who need this?'

'The French have been more highly tried than we have, Marshal,' Archdale replied.

'So . . . will Lord Gort assume command of the whole force?'

Archdale glanced at Spears, then answered: 'I believe in the present circumstances that it would be impossible. To add such a responsibility to his already heavy burden —'

'And . . . the British army. I suppose it is committed, is it, to re-embark for England?'

'Marshal, if that is forced upon us, it will be for one purpose and one purpose alone: so that we can retake our place in the line and fight on, side by side, with our allies.'

Afterwards, Archdale was taken by car to La Ferté, where he was interviewed by General Georges that night; but although he tried repeatedly to extract a promise of co-operation from Georges to effect a joint Anglo-French evacuation of the encircled forces, and although Georges admitted that this was now the only possible military option open to the allies, he was still reluctant — or unable — to face up to it and issue the necessary orders.

The following day, at yet another interview, Archdale was shocked to hear General Weygand's Chief of Staff talking about the possibility of the French 'eating their way up the coast from Abbeville', a proposal that seemed to him so criminally futile that he made a faint protest and took his leave, convinced that there was little hope of the French taking constructive action, much less of agreeing to a combined evacuation.

iii

While France dithered, Britain enjoyed the sunshine. Although there had been some talk of a 'battle for the

Channel ports', the fact that the BEF was facing total defeat was known only to a few.

That afternoon, when the holiday-makers were thronging the promenade at Deal, a Spitfire came in low over the sea, its engine off, its propeller windmilling and black smoke pouring from its exhausts. Wheels up, it belly-flopped down on the beach in a hail of sand and shingle and spray, slewing round through ninety degrees before coming to a halt. The pilot – Flying Officer Lyne – had been on patrol over Dunkirk and had been caught in a dog fight with two Me 109s. His aircraft had spun out of a maximum rate turn and had been hit by several rounds of cannon fire; he had been hit in the knee but had managed to nurse his aircraft back across the Channel. Now, heaving himself out of his cockpit and onto the wing, he was amazed to see couples in their Sunday best strolling arm in arm along the beach.

iv

In the Dynamo Room of the underground headquarters at Dover, the naval staff was now working at full stretch, and the atmosphere of urgency was in stark contrast to the holiday mood on Deal beach. Over thirty merchant ships – packets, ferries, Thames barges and Dutch schuits – had already been assembled at Dover, and the operation staff were organizing the tight schedule for a shuttle service that would keep a constant stream of vessels arriving to collect passengers from Dunkirk harbour.

Everything had to be thought of in advance. Destroyers had to be detailed for anti-submarine patrols and escort duties; minesweepers had to be designated operating areas; special telephone lines to the military headquarters at Dunkirk had to be set up and manned, and arrangements made for the reception of the returning troops at ports and harbours on the south-east coast.

Remembering the shambles created by undisciplined

troops and refugees on the quays of Boulogne, Ramsay requested Admiralty to provide a special naval shore party, and word had arrived that Captain Tennant, chief staff officer to the First Sea Lord, had been appointed to take command of a group of eight officers and 120 ratings, who were in the course of being drafted. The destroyer *Wolfhound* was nominated to ferry them across as soon as they arrived at Dover.

At 1857 on Sunday 26 May, an 'immediate' signal from Admiralty chattered in over the landline teleprinter. Tearing it off the machine as soon as the final ' = + ' appeared, the chief petty officer telegraphist took it personally along the corridor to the admiral's office.

It stated simply: OPERATION DYNAMO IS TO COMMENCE.

V

The old walled town of Cassell stood at the top of a solitary knoll, thirty kilometres south of Dunkirk. Four ancient stone gates guarded the approach roads to the town, which boasted public gardens, a statue of Foch, a large windmill and the thirteenth-century church of Notre Dame. The streets were cobbled and the central square was planted with trees and provided with benches and a bandstand.

This was one of Gort's 'stop points', and it had already been turned into an armed garrison. Two infantry battalions – the 2nd Gloucesters and the 4th Oxford and Buckingham Light Infantry – had set up road blocks, anti-tank positions and machine-gun posts on the approach roads, and 'breakwater' companies had been posted to guard the villages of Zuytpene and Bavinchove to the west of the town.

On Monday morning, while the German tanks, artillery and infantry moved up the approach roads from St Omer, and Stukas began bombing the outlying positions to soften them up before the main attack, senior staff officers were arriving in the town for a high-level meeting. With shells falling only a mile or two away, the Humbers and Renaults drew up outside the Hotel du Sauvage, and the men who had come to plan the greatest evacuation ever known in history went quickly into the hotel, now stripped of its carpets, curtains and pictures. In the dining room, all that remained of the original furniture was the big table and the chairs. The tablecloths had been removed and dumped in a heap at one end of the room. In the centre of the table – a last minute gesture of hospitality on the part of the proprietor – was an opened bottle of Armagnac and a few cheap glasses.

First to arrive were Lieutenant General Adam, who had been given the task of organizing the perimeter defence of Dunkirk and was representing Lord Gort at the meeting, and General Fagalde, an old-style French soldier in puttees and beret, who had been placed in command of the Channel ports sector.

Between them, and before the main meeting began, they settled on an outline plan for the defence of the beachhead. The French, under Fagalde, would hold the area to the west of Dunkirk, establishing a line from Gravelines inland to Bourbourg, then eastward along the canal line to Bergues. The British would hold the canal line from Bergues to Furnes, and thence to Nieuport, from where it would run directly to the beach at Nieuport Bains. Fagalde agreed that all French troops should keep to the western sector and all British troops – of which there would be considerably more – to the east.

'What about the Belgians?' Fagalde asked at the end of their talk when the other officers were already filing into the room.

Adam shook his head. 'I don't think we can count on the Belgians any more, General, do you?'

The allied commanders took their seats. General Blanchard represented the French 1st Army, Admiral Abrial the French naval interests and General Koeltz the views of the supreme commander, General Weygand. On the British side, in addition to Adam, there was Lieutenant Colonel Bridgeman, armed with notepad and pencil to take notes, and Lieutenant General Lindsell, the Quartermaster General.

But while the British expected to get down to some detailed planning, the French had different ideas, Blanchard announcing that General Koeltz had a special communiqué from General Weygand.

Koeltz cleared his throat and began to read a lengthy order of the day which used all the old French rhetoric to call upon the allies to break out of their encirclement, take the offensive and drive towards Calais.

When he had finished, there was a pregnant silence. Adam turned to General Blanchard. 'What is your opinion, General?'

Blanchard shrugged and spread his hands. 'I think we must obey orders, gentlemen. For us French, there is no question of that.'

His voice echoed in the bare-boarded room. All the French nodded solemnly and looked to Adam for his agreement. But he was not prepared to give it. 'Without being in any way disloyal to General Weygand, I have to say that we are in a far better position than he is to judge what is or is not possible, and I know that I represent my C-in-C's view when I say that the very idea of mounting such an attack at this stage of our withdrawal is quite preposterous.'

'I think you misunderstand the point of General Weygand's directive,' Koeltz said. 'There comes a time when honour must be salvaged if nothing else. To withdraw all our forces to the coast without an attempt at breaking out would, for us French at least, be a shamefully dishonourable course. Like you, General, I know that I represent my C-in-C's view when I say that for us, honour must always come first . . .'

Lieutenant Colonel Bridgeman stopped taking notes, threw his pencil down on the pad in front of him and leant back in his chair. Nothing was being said that he had not heard a dozen times before.

The Grossdeutschlanders had reached the village of St Nicholas on the canal line a few kilometres west of Bergues. With the scout cars tucked away along the line of a hedge and the stalking patrols feeling their way ahead on the flanks, 15 Company's self-propelled gun was pumping rounds across the canal to force the defenders to surrender.

As soon as enemy resistance showed signs of weakening, the vehicles moved ahead under the cover of the canal embankment and then made a dash across fifty metres of open ground. One of the ammunition trucks was hit by shrapnel, but was able to keep going, and the leading platoons were soon taking up new positions much closer to the village. The self-propelled gun was brought closer, and within minutes of its being set up, it had scored a direct hit on one of the key houses, which exploded and burst into flames.

Suddenly every man was firing, and within minutes the enemy was showing signs of panic. Two lorries tried to escape but were quickly reduced to smoking wrecks, and to panic them a bit more Lieutenant Gerbener ordered the machine-gun platoon to fire on the corner wall of a building and cause ricochets into the area out of the line of fire, where enemy troops were believed to be concentrated.

It had the desired effect: all resistance stopped, and with the Spandau providing covering fire, the first stick of assault troops crossed the canal in inflatable dinghies. Further up the canal, units of 2 Battalion were also attacking: the whistling of shells and splutter of machine guns went on without a break.

Following Sergeant Semmper, Heinrich and eleven others moved forward towards the canal, picking their targets as they went. First some scrubland, then the corner of a house, then a cattle enclosure. While they were firing at the last of these, a white handkerchief tied to a stick poked up through a rooftop, and a moment later hundreds of *poilus* could be seen moving out of cover with their hands in the air.

The ammunition trucks started moving back with the wounded, and the battalion commander, Lieutenant Colonel Köhler, came up to review the situation. The enemy had destroyed the only bridge so it was not immediately possible to get the vehicles across; but it wasn't long before some boats and barges had been lashed together, boards thrown across and the first armoured cars were making their precarious way across.

The rest of 15 Company followed quickly. Within an hour they were in every part of the village and able to enjoy the fruits of victory: more fresh eggs and bacon than they could eat, and an abundance of champagne to drink to another day's victorious advance.

While they were finishing the meal, Lance Corporal Stepfansky, the despatch rider of 2 Platoon who had been missing since going ahead with the first scout cars to cross the canal, turned up on his motorbike shepherding a large number of French prisoners.

He had quite a tale to tell. On crossing the canal he had moved round the village and, losing his way, found himself walking straight into a bunch of *poilus* who had not yet surrendered. With great presence of mind, he leapt sideways into a ditch, flung a grenade, ran a short distance, threw another one, leapt back and gave them several bursts of machine-gun fire. In this way, dashing back and forth and firing from different points along the ditch, he managed to convince the enemy that they were up against a well-armed platoon.

A dozen or so of the enemy quickly surrendered, but soon after, Stepfansky was amazed to see scores more following suit. There were over a hundred, and an officer among them into the bargain. Hiding his inward amazement, and with only half a dozen rounds left, Stepfansky coolly yelled at them to form up, waved his machine gun at them and marched them off.

He was obviously very proud of his achievement. He kept laughing and grinning and shaking his fists. The incident was reported immediately to the battalion commander, and Stepfansky was presented with the Iron Cross Second Class that same evening.

vii

Within two hours of the 'Dynamo' signal being received, the first of Admiral Ramsay's fleet of merchant ships sailed for Dunkirk. The Isle of Man packet *Mona's Isle* went first, followed at intervals by *Sequacity* and *Yewdale*.

There were three routes to Dunkirk from Dover, named X, Y and Z. Route X was fifty-five miles long and went north of the Goodwin Sands, approaching Dunkirk at right angles to the coast; Route Y was eighty-seven miles long and made a huge detour to the east, swinging back in a westerly direction and converging with the coast near La Panne and Bray Dunes before reaching Dunkirk; Route Z, the shortest at thirty-nine miles, cut straight across from Dover to Calais before running eastward along the channel between the sandbanks off Gravelines.

The first ships to sail under Operation Dynamo proceeded without escort via Route Z, and after an uneventful voyage *Mona's Isle* berthed at the Gare Maritime at about midnight. When she cast off five hours later she had 1,420 troops on board.

The voyage back to Dover was not so easy. For the first twenty miles the *Mona's Isle* was within artillery range of the shore – which was now in enemy hands – and she was soon being repeatedly hit by shellfire. Luckily, the shells did not explode, and when her rudder was hit her master managed to keep going by steering with main engines. Slowly she limped out of range of short artillery – only to be attacked from the air by six Me 109s that made repeated passes, machine-gunning the decks. By the time she arrived back at Dover, twenty-three of her passengers were dead and dozens were wounded.

Mona's Isle's experience and that of the other ships using

Route Z that morning did not augur well for the success of Operation Dynamo. Admiral Ramsay had planned to run a shuttle service of ferries and merchant ships and had reckoned on the return trip to Dunkirk taking about five or six hours. But by ten o'clock that morning four ships had been turned back by enemy fire, *Sequacity* had been sunk and messages were coming in over the telephone link with Dunkirk reporting that although troops were arriving by the thousand, there were very few ships to take them off.

Reluctantly, Ramsay was forced to use an alternative route. As Route X was not yet clear of mines, that meant Route Y, which was over twice as long, and would result in a halving of the expected rate of embarkation.

viii

In London the daily meeting of the Chiefs of Staff took place in a Whitehall basement at eight o'clock each morning, and usually lasted about an hour. Seated round tables forming a hollow square, the war leaders came together to thrash out questions of strategy and decide upon priorities for contingency planning, logistics and support throughout the theatre of war.

This morning, as at every other meeting during the past fortnight, there were several pressing problems to be discussed. The question of RAF fighter support over Belgium and France was a particularly tricky one. Some time before, Air Chief Marshal Lord Dowding had told Churchill that in the event of invasion, twenty-five squadrons of fighters would be required to defend the mainland against the Luftwaffe. Now, with the BEF fighting for its life in France, the resources of Fighter Command were being stretched to the limit, and the air staff was being pressed by the army to dip into the fighter reserve and commit more squadrons to the support of the army on the beaches.

This Lord Dowding stubbornly refused to do: if Britain was to be saved from invasion, a large reserve of fighter aircraft and pilots had to be held in readiness, and could take no part in support of the evacuation.

Having dealt with the question of air support the chairman – Admiral Sir Dudley Pound – raised the question of destroyer support off the beaches, which Gort was claiming to be inadequate. Like Dowding, Pound was reluctant to release his precious reserves, and so far only four destroyers had been allocated for the support of Operation Dynamo.

While Pound enlarged on the reasons behind this decision, Group Captain Goddard, Lord Gort's air adviser, slipped into the conference room and took a seat at the bottom table. He had left Gort's headquarters at Premesques at eleven-thirty the previous evening and had taken off from a potato field in the very last serviceable RAF transport plane to be found in France. He had refuelled at Manston at four-thirty a.m., landed at Hendon at seven, taken a staff car to London and talked his way past the security guards and into this holy of holies on whose door was the uncompromising notice, CHIEFS OF STAFF ONLY.

Goddard had been sent by Gort on an unusual mission. Since taking his decision to evacuate, Gort had been plagued by fears that Whitehall would not back him with wholehearted support, and that his men would be left stranded on the beaches. So far, all the signs were that his worst fears would be justified. The RAF was still putting its biggest effort into bombing munition and fuel dumps far behind the German front, and fighter support was very thin; Whitehall was talking about the defence of mainland Britain taking priority over support of the army, and now even the navy seemed to be penny-pinching on warship allocation for Operation Dynamo. It was as if the Chiefs of Staff had not yet awoken to the enormity of the task ahead, and it was Goddard's mission, as Gort's representative, to make a personal appeal to General Ironside in the presence of the First Sea Lord, Sir Dudley Pound.

'It will be quite pointless to make any sort of appeal unless it is in the presence of the First Sea Lord,' Gort told him.

'You can't approach the admiral directly, but you can tell CIGS what I want him to get the admiral to do.'

In effect, therefore, Goddard was being sent to twist the Admiralty's arm.

Now, as he took his seat and looked round the table, his heart sank. General Ironside was not present. Unknown to Gort and Goddard, he had been relieved as CIGS the day before by General Dill.

'Right,' Pound was saying, 'unless there are any further comments I suggest we move on to the next item.'

Hardly realizing what he was doing, Goddard found himself speaking. 'Admiral –' he began. 'I have been sent by Lord Gort to say that the provision made is not nearly enough –'

There was a startled silence. The Chiefs of Staff glared down the table at this unprecedented intrusion.

Aware that he was committing a serious breach of service etiquette, Goddard felt his heart pounding in his chest. But there was no going back: he had their attention, and he must say what he had come to say.

'The troops are already pouring onto the beaches, and the number of ships provided is hopelessly inadequate. The harbours in Dunkirk are barely usable. The men will have to leave from the beaches and they will be sitting targets. We must get them off *fast* and to do that we need more than a few Channel packets. You must send everything – every available ship and boat and craft that can get across the Channel. You must send pleasure steamers, fishing smacks, barges, yachts, motorboats – everything! *Everything!*'

He looked up and down the row of faces and then back at Sir Dudley Pound. He was dead tired, and aware that fatigue and mental strain were affecting his judgement. He felt himself carried away by the desperate urgency of the situation. The fact that he might be wrecking his career no longer mattered. All that counted was that the Chiefs of Staff be made to understand the desperate situation that was developing across the Channel.

'Everything that can cross the Channel must go to Dunkirk. Lifeboats. Motorboats. Even rowing boats . . .'

The Vice-chief of Air Staff, Sir Richard Peirse, left his place and went to Goddard.

'All right, that's enough,' he whispered. 'I think you're a bit overwrought, aren't you?'

Goddard stood to attention, made a slight bow to the admiral and withdrew, feeling both ashamed of his outburst and angry that it had failed to win any sort of response.

ix

Calais had fallen; the Belgian army was crumbling; the Weygand Plan had failed to materialize; Hitler had cancelled his order holding up the panzer advance, and the tanks of Kleist's and Hoth's army groups had crossed the Aa canal and were advancing on the 'stop points' designated by Gort to guard the south-western flank of the BEF.

British and French units of every size and description were being rushed in to hold the line and buy time for the great khaki torrent that was already flowing along the lanes and over the fields and ditches and canals of the sixty-mile corridor from Lille to Dunkirk.

On the coast, the French 68th division were fighting at Gravelines, Bourbourgville and Spyckcr; inland, Prioux's divisions were holding out against Rommel's panzers south of Lille, making it possible for many thousands of British troops to join the great withdrawal. On the southern flank the BEF was fighting at Neuve Chapelle, Vieille Chapelle, Lestrem, Morbecque, Hazebrouck, Cassel, Arneke, Ledringhem, Soex and Wormhoudt – and dozens of other villages and crossroads besides. To the east, they were holding the long line of the River Yser from Boesinghe through Ypres to Comines, Halluin, Roubaix and Boiurghelles. While infantry set up their defensive positions and hurled accurate fire back at the approaching columns, and while artillery rushed from position to position to support each newly threatened strong point, the sapper field companies toiled night and day to blow bridges, crater roads, smash lock gates, sink barges, immobilize rolling stock – anything and everything to delay the advance.

At La Bassée, where the Cameron Highlanders, clad in kilts against army regulations, had been holding out for two days, the enemy stormed across the canal, burnt the town and surrounded the defenders; in the neighbouring town of Festubert, a company of the Dorsetshire regiment kept their morale up by playing 'Ramona' on an old gramophone before the attack came in. At Robecq, Cassel, St Venant and Merville, British soldiers fought until they were surrounded and then continued to fight, so that others might have a better chance of getting back to England.

'. . . At every position,' wrote a diarist in one of General von Kleist's armoured corps, 'heavy fighting has developed – especially at every village and indeed in every house. In consequence the corps has not been able to make any notable headway to the east or the north-east. Casualties in personnel and equipment are grievous. The enemy are fighting tenaciously and, to the last man, remain at their posts: if they are shelled out of one position, they shortly reappear in another to carry on the fight . . .'

Such feelings of admiration were not mutual. For the allies, it was already a commonplace to witness the Luftwaffe's machine-gunning of civilian refugees and the tactics of disguise, deception and confusion used by fifth columnists; and that day troops of the SS Totenkopf division stained the reputation of the German army further by committing an atrocity which was to set the style for many more in the months and years to come.

They had been attacking the village of Le Paradis and, after a fierce battle, took a hundred prisoners of the 2nd Royal Norfolks. Many of the prisoners were wounded and all were exhausted. When they had been disarmed they were ordered to walk in single file past a barn, and as they did so two machine guns, placed three hundred yards away, opened up on them. They fell into a ditch by the barn wall. Any that showed signs of life were shot or bayoneted.

x

While the front-line divisions of Alexander and Montgomery held off Bock's army on the eastern flank and the garrisons of Lord Gort's stop points held out on the west, the 'bag' of allied troops folded into itself as each battalion and company received the order to pull out and head for the coast.

They struggled on, hour after hour, night and day. Every road was jammed solid with trucks, sometimes three or four abreast. Nose to tail, they crawled at five m.p.h. or less, stopping and moving, stopping and moving. Every village saw the Tommies going through on foot – weary but still cheerful, still refusing to admit defeat – or even that they were getting out of France. They plodded on through ploughed fields, swam canals, waded through sewers, cut their way through barbed wire. When the Stukas came and the machine-gun bullets smacked into the ground, they threw themselves down and prayed. When each raid passed, they propped each other up, cracked jokes and started off again – little bands of men in tin hats and baggy trousers, rifles on their shoulders, arms in slings, heads in bandages, limping, hobbling, sleepwalking.

TWENTY-SIX

The pilots of Nick Massingbohm's Hurricane flight had brought the armchairs out of the crewroom so that they could enjoy the last of the sunshine. They had all flown three sorties that day and were due to fly again within the hour. In the interval, they snoozed or read or talked or listened to the wireless.

'It's a bit like a blinking cricket match really, isn't it?' Robin de Beaujeu remarked.

'Anything less like a cricket match I can hardly imagine,' Bobby Styles observed, without opening his eyes.

'Oh I don't know. I mean – here we are, sitting on the metaphorical boundary with our metaphorical pads on waiting to go into bat.'

At twenty, de Beaujeu was the youngest pilot in the flight. He had had his first brush with an Me 109 that morning and needed to talk about it.

'I suppose that's the sort of metaphorical rot they taught you at metaphorical Oundle was it, Robin?'

'Lancing, as a matter of fact.'

'Oundle, Lancing, Sherbourne – they're all the same, these provincial public schools.'

'Rugby we know, and Eton we know, but who are these?' murmured Micky Dangerman, who was sitting at the table writing up his flying log.

On the dispersal, the engine note of a fuel bowser rose as it began to pump high octane petrol into the wing tank of a parked Hurricane. In the circuit, a pair of Spitfires, in echelon, broke onto the downwind leg, flying a continuous finals turn, levelling their wings at the last second and touching down on the runway with a squeal of tyres.

De Beaujcu threw a cushion at Dangerman, causing instant retaliation. They rolled about on the grass in their mae wests and flying boots. While they did so, Flight Lieutenant Massingbohm appeared at the door of the crewroom and said, 'Right, chaps, can we have a quick pow-wow?'

De Beaujcu and Dangerman stopped wrestling. Bobby Styles opened his eyes and sat up. Apps put his detective novel aside, and Reynoldson stopped admiring the pin-up girls in *Picture Post*.

Massingbohm sat on the edge of the table and clenched a briar between his teeth.

'Right – while you chaps have been idling, your dynamic flight commander has been working his brainbox overtime on the subject of air combat, and I've come up with a short list of golden rules. As we have a couple of newcomers in our midst I thought we might run through them. I know you'll have heard most of them before, but it'll do no one any harm to hear them again. And if any of you can come up with other useful ideas let's hear from you, so that we can all benefit.'

Another three Spitfires entered the circuit and peeled off one by one to turn onto the downwind leg. Sitting in their wicker chairs and armchairs, the pilots of D Flight noted but did not comment on the fact that, so far, only five out of six had returned.

'Right then,' Massingbohm was saying. 'Here goes. Rule one – go high. No need to enlarge on that. Height equals speed and speed equals superiority. Number two: go up-sun, and always be aware that the sun is your blind spot. Number three: *always* turn towards when you're attacked. If he comes in from the right, turn right and tighten up the turn as hard and as fast as you can, and by that I mean to the verge of the high-speed stall. Forget the fancy manoeuvres and the aeros – get into a max-rate and stay there until you're on his tail. Never forget that the moment you slacken the turn, you give Jerry a chance of a squirt up your backside. Which brings me to rule four: watch your six o'clock. All the time.

Yes, Robin, even when you're on *his* tail. Sounds impossible I know, but if you want to stay alive you've got to learn to do it. Rule five: get in close, concentrate, and don't waste bullets. We've all had this drummed into us at fighter school, but it can't be said too often. I know how tempting it is to blaze away with long bursts, but it simply doesn't work. The only way is the way you were taught. Total concentration on the ring sight, two hands on the stick, short squirts of fire up his jacksy. And finally, rule six – help each other. Fly in pairs and cover each other the whole time. And remember: if you find yourself alone – *go home*.'

The first two Spitfires were taxiing in, zigzagging along the perimeter track, their engines rising to a throaty roar as they turned onto the dispersal. After closing down, the pilot of one of them stood up in the cockpit and gave V signs with both hands. It was the signal to the ground crew and the awaiting intelligence officer that he had achieved a kill.

Massingbohm looked at the pilots in his flight. Of the six who had flown to France to reinforce the Advanced Air Striking Force three weeks before, only Styles and himself remained. Now he was aware that a mightier battle was brewing, and he wondered how many of them would be left by the end of the week. 'Any comments or questions?' he asked.

'Just one,' Styles said, lighting a cigarette and looking at de Beaujeu. 'For the benefit of our new boys, it is *not* a cricket match. Nor is there anything chivalrous about it. If it's anything at all, it's a gutter fight. You stab him in the back before he stabs you. Simple as that.'

Massingbohm nodded. 'Agree entirely.' He looked at his watch. 'Okay chaps, pep talk over. Same patrol line as last time. Let's get weaving.'

ii

D Flight took off in pairs and joined up in vic formation, maintaining radio silence as they climbed out to twenty thousand feet over the North Sea before turning for the coast of Belgium.

Leading the formation, Massingbohm had little need to consult his map: visibility was excellent, and the now familiar coast of Flanders was itself like a map spread out beneath him. As they gained height, the smudges of black smoke over Dunkirk, Calais and other towns and villages in the Pas de Calais could be seen to the west.

He had been ordered to fly a thirty-mile barrier patrol on a north-south line between Ostend and Ypres. Before crossing the coast, he gave the signal to change to the pre-arranged battle formation, and the flight split up into sections of two, de Beaujeu remaining on Massingbohm's wing, Styles and Dangerman to port and slightly astern and Apps and Reynoldson to starboard and further back.

The engine droned on and the oxygen, on high flow, puffed into his face mask. All the time he kept his head moving, his eyes covering the sky systematically, left and right, back and forth, up and down. Ten minutes passed. The sky seemed ominously empty. They flew over Ypres and made a long, slow turn back to the north; and as they rolled out, a formation of enemy aircraft came into view.

There were about a dozen Ju 88s and upwards of twenty fighters in the formation, but they were a good five thousand feet below. He looked back at de Beaujeu and gave the signal to follow his lead then banked the Hurricane hard left and started a power dive.

He saw the Messerschmitts peel away, left and right, to meet the attack. One of them flashed past him going in the opposite direction. He caught a glimpse of his number two turning away to deal with him, and pressed on to attack the bombers. He came in from above and behind and caught one straight away. The aircraft juddered as the eight guns delivered forty rounds in a two-second burst. He saw spurts of flame stitching the wing as the tracer bullets found their mark, and a moment later the gratifying blossom of smoke from the bomber's wing. He came up behind a second and was about to give it the same treatment when an Me 110 swung in behind him. He turned hard right and heaved back on the stick, tensing thigh and stomach muscles as the 'g' force increased. With the throttle fully open, he clamped both hands on the control column and held the aircraft on the judder at two hundred and fifty knots, all the way round the turn, the 'g' needle hovering between five and five-and-a-half. He felt himself greying out, his vision tunnelling, the noise of the engine becoming strangely distant. The artificial horizon had gone crazy and the altimeter was winding down through five thousand feet. He shouted at the top of his voice to keep himself conscious and dragged the ring sight closer, closer, closer to the tail of the Messerschmitt. And at last, there he was, fair and square in the ring sight and the controls had a strangely gluey feel to them and he felt as though he could stay there on the hun's tail for ever and the plane juddered again as the guns spat and when the Me burst into flame he went on firing until the whole plane exploded and there was a heavy, juddering bang as his aircraft hit a piece of debris.

He tried to haul clear, but the stick went slack in his hands. He wound back on the elevator trim to come out of the dive and kicked the rudders to level the wings. Looking out to one side, he saw that he had lost the tip of his port wing; and at the same moment heard the deadpan voice of Styles in his headphones: 'Two more in your five o'clock, leader' – and almost immediately felt the thump of bullets as his aircraft was hit.

The cockpit filled with smoke. The engine coughed blood, spluttered and died. At the same time, the fire warning light came on.

What a confounded nuisance, he thought. I'm going to have to bale out.

He pressed the transmit button and said, 'I'm hopping out, chaps. See you soon.'

He opened the cockpit canopy, released his seat straps, wound the elevator trim wheel fully back and kicked on a boot-full of right rudder. The aircraft rolled lazily onto its back and he dropped out head first, his feet pointing at the sky. He scrabbled for the D ring with his right hand and pulled it hard. The chute opened with a jerk to his groin, and he heard the zip of bullets as an Me 109 fired on him. He swung in his 'chute and looked beneath him at the neat little fields and canals. Then, as the ground rushed up to meet him, he remembered just in time to put his feet together and bend his knees.

He was surprised to find himself unhurt. He released the parachute harness and looked round to get his bearings. He had landed quite close to a lake in flat, marshy land that was criss-crossed with hillocks and overgrown ditches. There was a town a couple of miles to the south-east where houses were on fire, and shells were landing on and around a group of farm buildings at a crossroads a few hundred yards away. Overhead, the dog fight was ending: it was as if each side had suddenly decided to pack up and go home. He saw an Me 109 diving steeply to evade, with a Hurricane trying to keep up. The Hurricane pulled out early; the Messerschmitt late. It came hammering over at tree-top height, and Massingbohm dived into a ditch. Then – quite suddenly – the sky was empty of aircraft and all that was left were the whorls of exhausts and the rising columns of smoke from crashed aircraft.

He climbed out of his ditch – he realized now that he had fallen among the old earthworks of the Great War – and began moving up to higher ground from which to get his bearings. But he had not reached the top of the hillock when he saw – only two fields away – a platoon of German infantry looking like black, helmeted ostriches as they loped along, bent almost double by the heavy packs they carried. He lay flat and observed them making a cautious advance in his direction. They were reconnaissance troops, almost certainly, and that meant that he had landed between the lines.

The sun was almost on the horizon, so there was no doubt about which way to run. He set off along a ditch at the side of the field, keeping low the whole time. Somewhere behind him, a heavy machine gun opened up with a succession of long, howling bursts of fire. He saw bullets smacking into poplar trees fifty yards ahead of him, and realized that they must be firing at him. He lay flat in the mud for a long time. Then, when it was almost dark, he crawled for five hundred yards, eventually reaching a narrow lane; and three hours later, after making several detours round German positions in pitch darkness, he walked slap into a column of British Grenadiers.

After the customary challenge and reply, he was ordered to advance and be recognized, and was then escorted under armed guard to the head of the column, where a young lieutenant, shaved and immaculate in clean battle dress, cap and polished boots was sitting on a shooting stick sipping tea from a Thermos.

A dimmed torch was flashed in Massingbohm's face.

'Haven't we met before?'

'Yes I think we have. You're a Wykehamist aren't you?'

'Good God!' exclaimed Lieutenant Bunberry, getting off his shooting stick. 'If it isn't the Mighty Massingbohm!'

They shook hands warmly. 'I'd offer you a hot bath and a meal,' Bunberry said, 'but we're a bit light on creature comforts at present.'

'I was rather hoping to get back across the Channel tonight –'

Bunberry laughed and shook his head. 'Not a hope, old boy. I suppose you might get a lift in one of the convoys, but they're moving at snail's pace, and you'd most probably be shot up into the bargain.'

'So what do you suggest?'

'You'd probably be just as well off to stay with us.'

'Where are you heading?'

Bunberry smiled enigmatically. 'We're plugging a gap.'

'Mind if I plug it with you?'

'On one condition.'

'What's that?'

'You carry something along with everyone else.'
'I'd be delighted.'
Bunberry turned. 'Sergeant Cummings!'
'Sir!'
'Give the flight lieutenant a Bren gun. And a cup of tea if you've any left.'

iii

. . . By the time we see Poperinghe ahead it is daylight. A solid line of transport is waiting to get through the town. Every minute a shell crashes down into the main square and a cloud of dust rises.

Bang. Crash.

The queue shifts forward a hundred yards and stops.

Bang. Crash.

Ambulances, staff cars, matadors, all mixed up like at Oudenarde. Must keep our convoy together.

Bang – Crash.

Something ahead comes loose and we all move forward, into the square and away.

To the left there is distant thunder, and tiny black dots are weaving in the cloudless sky. An hour later more black smoke rises ahead and the Stukas can be seen screaming down through it. This looks like Beveren.

Stop the convoy on the side of the road and drive on into the town with Graham on his motorcycle as soon as things are quiet. Find Bradfer Lawrence of the 18th Field Park Company who congratulates me on not having arrived a few minutes earlier when I could have shared a slit trench with him and watched his transport disintegrating. Drive on searching for 2 Corps Report Centre without success until I find myself beyond the town. Here is a track leading away from the road along a hedge offering some air cover to a field with a few poplar trees. This seems a good place for the section to rest. Leaving Graham to reserve the area I drive back to bring up the convoy.

We park under cover and the cooks serve breakfast. I post Bourner, our toughest despatch rider, as air sentry with the mounted Bren gun. The doctor sets off to Beveren to buy some fresh bread which he finds essential. The rumble of traffic on the road lulls us to sleep in the hot morning sun.

Suddenly there is a scream like splitting silk and a Messerschmitt 109 shoots over our heads a few feet above the poplars followed by another and another; a sharp turn, round and over us again. Bourner lets them have it with the Bren gun and the rest of the section falls flat. After a long minute everything is peaceful again. There are no casualties so perhaps they were firing at the traffic not us.

The doctor arrives without any bread, pink and angry having spent some displeasing moments in the 18 Field Park Company slit trench.

I set off again to look for the Report Centre and find the 59 Company sign outside a farmhouse. Gus Galloway is sitting on the verandah having breakfast. He asks me whether I am scared. He has no news. I also find Bill Hedley of 225 Company. He has no news either and we discuss what to do if we cannot make contact with anybody before the enemy arrives. I drive on to prospect an area where we can make a stand and find some convenient barbed wire defences across fields to the west indicating the Belgian frontier.

Aircraft still active as never before, but the section has not been disturbed again. They seem to knock off at meal times. Time to think about accommodation for the night, so the doctor sets off one way while I take Sauervein the other. We stop by a likely-looking asbestos barn. A Heinkel is flying about and two Belgian soldiers of the Chasseur Regiment are lying in the ditch.

'*Qu'est ce que vous chassez sous les arbres?*' says Sauervein.

The barn is full of manure, but the doctor has found something. I go back with him to have a look. It is a farmhouse with a red brick path leading up to the low door; the neat kitchen will do very well as an office. As the doctor steps outside again a Junkers 88 roars over the roof a few feet up. He lifts his arms and curses like Balaam.

Back at the section news has come via a despatch rider from the CRE. We are given the map reference of 2 Corps HQ where we are to report to the Battalion General Staff. I pick up Gus Galloway and drive to Corps where we find none other than Pepper, our late tactics instructor from the School of Military Engineering at Chatham, so we are on our mettle.

The BEF is withdrawing into the area Nieuport-Dunkirk and the bridges across the Nieuport-Bergues canal have to be prepared for demolition. We have no one-inch maps of the area so borrow one each from the limited Corps stock. We decide to divide the bridges between us; I am to take inclusive from Furnes to the Beveren-La Panne railway.

I study the map with the doctor and choose for our destination a wooded area near Adinkerke about the middle of our sector. He sets off in the Snipe with Graham as DR having fixed a road junction as rendezvous I bring on the section as soon as it has packed up, taking the main road to Furnes which is not overcrowded.

I am pleased at the sight of a line of Belgian

troops in overcoats digging in. 'Are you digging an anti-tank ditch?' asks Sauervein.

'*Non, m'sieur*,' replies the sentry. 'We are building a railway.'

Hoogstade is deserted. As we turn left down the street I see a provisions shop with the door swinging open, and rubbish on the pavement. Inside it has been ransacked. Piles of tins have been pulled off the shelves and out of the drawers, many without labels. We may need these. I bundle the lot into the back of my truck.

The road to Furnes is long and straight, running through open fields. On our left a Bofors AA gun suddenly opens up. Looking up I see a flight of Messerschmitt 109 fighters flying low towards us. As soon as they have passed overhead the leading aircraft peels away and comes screaming down. Regulations require that under air attack a convoy should proceed as if nothing were happening. In practice every vehicle has stopped and every man is lying flat in the field before the first guns start ripping.

The Messerschmitts sweep over one after the other, jerking and swerving as if they are thoroughly enjoying it. The Bofors keep firing; I keep praying. Then they are gone.

Sheepishly we walk back to our trucks; they are still there. There are no casualties either. They must have been firing blanks. We drive on.

At Furnes there is a Belgian guard on the bridge but it does not look to have been prepared for demolition. I turn left along the tarmac road which leads along the south side of the canal to Dunkirk. Graham is waiting at the road junction. He leads us up a side road to the left where we stop to wait for the doctor. There is no air cover and plenty of aircraft about, so I tell the section to leave the vehicles and get inside an old Great War German pillbox in the field alongside. When we are inside, the RSM asks me to tell the section what is happening.

'Mr Galloway,' he says, 'has told his section that the whole Royal Navy is lying off the beaches ready to take us off.'

I tell them what I know, which is not much.

'Watch it, sir,' says a voice. 'There's some civilians in here with us.'

At this moment the doctor arrives. He leads us down the road, turns right across a wooden bridge, then by grass track across a field to a wood. Inside the wood there is a large white house and a couple of empty huts. It seems perfect and nobody is there.

We are within a few yards of the Furnes-Dunkirk road having come round into the estate the back way. I tell the section to dig slit trenches and get the cooks offloaded into one of the huts. Coming back I find that the slit trenches have not been started and there is some grumbling. The RSM says the men are tired.

There is a noise of machine guns close outside the wood, and a high-winged monoplane with British markings, a Lysander, flies down the road gunning the transport. From now on all aircraft are treated as hostile. When I look round the trenches have been dug.

I explore the house. It is empty and ransacked. Rummage is piled in every room and the lavatories are clogged; no water. There is a grand piano, rather out of tune. The batmen clear out a small room and erect our camp beds.

The doctor feels the need for fresh bread so we set off on a shopping expedition leaving the section resting. There is nothing in Adinkerke. The frontier post beyond is deserted. Ahead a column of smoke fills the sky and stretches back over our heads. As we reach the Bray crossroads we hear a dull booming ahead, the sparkle of heavy AA bursts and the red five-bead strings of light AA curling slowly upwards. Over all the thunder comes the continuous whistle of falling bombs.

We decide against the fresh bread. Enjoy a pleasant late dinner of Camembert and tinned lobster . . .

iv

With the Belgian soldiers throwing down their rifles and joining the rabble of defeated soldiers and refugees on the roads, it had become clear to General Brooke that unless the gap opening up between Ypres and the coast were plugged immediately, the Germans would at last achieve their break-through, sever the British corridor to the coast and cut off the Expeditionary Force from the sea.

There was only one possible way to plug the gap, and it involved a military manoeuvre that would have daunted most generals. But in Major General Montgomery, in command of the 3rd Division, Brooke had a far from average commander. Invited to withdraw his division from its perilous position in front of Roubaix, make a twenty-five-mile flank march with eleven thousand men overnight along roads and lanes that led within four thousand yards of the front – and then set up an entirely new line to replace the crumbling Belgian defences, Monty accepted the challenge with his usual abrasive cheerfulness. What, after all, had he been exercising his 3rd Division for all these past weeks and months except for just such a march?

So saying, he hopped into his staff car and rushed off to pass precise orders to his field commanders, distributing messages at the end of a forked stick as he went by; and as dusk fell the great manoeuvre started, lorries travelling with lights out and each driver watching the rear of the vehicle ahead, whose differential was painted white and illuminated by a dimmed torchlight fixed under the chassis.

By morning, after an agonizingly slow night march along congested roads and narrow lanes, the 3rd Division had achieved the impossible and was established on a defensive line running north from Ypres.

The gap had been plugged only just in time. By midnight on Monday the twenty-seventh, the King of the Belgians had accepted defeat and his army had been ordered to cease fire. Right across Belgium, white towels, pillowcases and bedsheets were being hung out of windows, and great masses of Belgian troops were throwing down their arms and taking to the roads. This last collapse opened up a further gap on Montgomery's left. On hearing the news, he cobbled together a scratch force of machine-gunners and armoured cars to extend his line northwards and join up with the French *Division Légère Motorisée*, or Light Motorized Division, which was covering the last few miles to the coast.

Not for the first or the last time, Gort's army had been saved as much by the brilliance of its generals as the dogged stamina of its men.

TWENTY-SEVEN

HMS *Wolfhound* sailed at one forty-five p.m., and an hour later when she was halfway along Route Y, the first Stuka attacks came in. When she arrived off Dunkirk at five-thirty, the whole port seemed to be on fire, and twenty-one more bombers came in over the harbour and attacked the destroyer as she berthed.

Captain Tennant disembarked with his shore party and started through the smoking ruins of the town. Dead bodies were everywhere. Foul, oily smoke swirled about among the warehouses and fuel depots. French dogs and British soldiers prowled about, scavenging for food. From a hotel basement, the voices of a hundred men, all roaring drunk, shouted obscenities at the party of RN officers and ratings as they picked their way over the piles of glass and rubble, ducking under fallen wires, making detours round buildings that looked about to collapse.

After a forty-five-minute walk that would in normal circumstances have taken only ten, Tennant reached Bastion 32, an underground fortress between the harbour and the beaches to the east of the town, where the first of the retreating British soldiers were already assembling. This was the headquarters of Admiral Jean Abrial, the officer in command of this part of the French coast and effectively Ramsay's equivalent in Dunkirk.

Tennant was led along a damp corridor to a very small candlelit office which had been allocated to the British naval liaison officer, Captain Henderson, and the British area commandant, Colonel Whitfield.

After his experience of berthing under air attack in HMS *Wolfhound*, Tennant voiced the opinion that using the port of Dunkirk for evacuation was now out of the question. Henderson and Whitfield agreed.

'So how long have we got for the whole operation?' Tennant asked.

Henderson looked at Whitfield for the answer.

'Twenty-four to thirty-six hours. Not much more. The Germans will be in the town after that, and once they are, evacuation will be impossible.'

'In that case we mustn't waste time,' said Tennant, and reaching for a pad drafted his first signal to Dover: PLEASE SEND EVERY AVAILABLE CRAFT EAST OF DUNKIRK IMMEDIATELY. EVACUATION TOMORROW NIGHT IS PROBLEMATICAL.

That done, Tennant set about rounding up the soldiers from the cellars of Dunkirk and sending them to a collecting point above the beach at Malo-les-Bains. Smartly dressed in their number one uniforms with belts and gaiters, clean rifles and bayonets fixed, the naval patrols made a deep impression on the troops, many of whom were leaderless and demoralized; and because three naval good conduct badges looked to army eyes like the ranking stripes of a sergeant, some of the older able seamen were able to wield an authority that surprised even themselves.

Similarly, Tennant and his officers, dressed in their best brass-buttoned uniforms with gold rings on their sleeves, had an enormously powerful effect. They halted a mob trying to gain entry to Bastion 32; they rounded up scattered troops, inspired hope of rescue in the shell-shocked and jittery, and gave new confidence to those who had arrived days before and had abandoned hope of getting back to England. Over and over again, the soldiers were heard to say 'Thank God we've got the navy!'

ii

But having the navy wasn't enough. Though the first of Ramsay's fleet of destroyers, minesweepers, yachts, paddlesteamers, tugs, ferries, barges and fishing boats were by now arriving off the beaches, there were far too few boats available to ferry the troops out to them, and the process of getting men aboard was impossibly slow. Dunkirk harbour was still out of the question: although the RAF was providing a certain amount of cover, mass Stuka raids over the port were still taking place, and most of the harbour had been reduced to a jumble of sunken ships, cratered quays and blazing fuel dumps.

With every passing hour, thousands more troops were arriving within the perimeter and being directed by the military police to the collecting points on the beaches. Most of them hid in the dunes or sought shelter in the villas of Malo-les-Bains or Bray Dunes. Some waded out at low tide, hoping that by forming a queue a boat would come and take them off, half-dozen by half-dozen, to the ships that lay at anchor a mile or so offshore.

Standing on the concrete roof of Bastion 32 on that first evening of his stay at Dunkirk, Captain Tennant reviewed the scene. Something had to be done to speed up the embarkation. If it continued at this penny-packet rate, only a tiny fraction of the troops would be evacuated, and quarter of a million British soldiers would be taken prisoner when the Germans broke through.

Another raid came in. He watched the aircraft peeling off from their formations and diving steeply down on the harbour. Overhead, a mighty cloud of black smoke obliterated the evening sky. Explosions rocked the old seaport again and again; but as he stood there in his tin hat Captain Tennant noticed that there was one part of the harbour that was being ignored by the bombers. This was the slender eastern mole that ran three-quarters of a mile out to sea from Malo-les-Bains.

Something *had* to be done to speed things up, and although the east mole had never been designed to berth ships, and its wooden walkway and the concrete piles might well collapse with ships banging against them in the fast tide, there was nothing to lose: it was a straw worth clutching.

He looked back at the beaches and watched a ship's lifeboat embarking a dozen soldiers who had waded out and stood waiting, waist deep, in the surf. They were being lugged aboard one by one, over the gunwale. With fourteen on board, the boat set out, the oarsmen catching crabs, the coxswain shouting to them to get the time right, one of the soldiers shouting drunkenly to his friends who had been left behind on the beach.

Tennant turned on his heel and went back into the Bastion and along the corridor to the Bastion office. There, he drafted another signal, this time to HMS *Wolfhound*, which was acting as a communications link ship off the beaches: SEND PERSONNEL SHIP TO BERTH ALONGSIDE EAST MOLE TO EMBARK 1000 MEN.

Within an hour, one of the fast cross-channel ferries, the *Queen of the Channel*, had secured alongside and was embarking troops. They were assembled on the beach in the lee of the breakwater, and called out fifty at a time by the naval officer who was acting as piermaster. Able seamen with bayonets fixed barked orders and chivvied them along.

'Let's be 'avin' you, then! Shake it up! At the double! Come on, lads, you're goin' 'ome! Any more for any more?'

They doubled along the narrow mole, their boots thundering on the wooden planks as they went. By dawn nine hundred men had been embarked and Tennant was able to signal Dover to send all ships to embark troops from the east mole.

His gamble had paid off. There was hope yet.

iii

15 Company formed up just before dawn, when the sky was still dark, but the first streak of blood could be seen on the eastern horizon.

It was very quiet. The only sound was that of numerous burning villages and homesteads. The flames rose into the night like dancing demons – an eerie, but strangely beautiful sight. They were within five kilometres of Dunkirk now. Huge clouds of smoke welled up. Across the entire horizon, enormous tongues of fire flared, illuminating the whole area for seconds at a time. While they did so, the scene became a sharply defined silhouette, and every tree, building and vehicle threw its own long shadow.

Overhead, a flock of little birds flew nervously away, dodging and reforming as they went, as if they too expected a hail of bullets at any moment.

The column moved off along the road to Bergues. For Heinrich, there was a feeling that this next battle must be the most testing. The Company had been fighting almost continually now for three days – for the villages of St Nicolas, Capelle-Brouck and Eringhem. Fighting had been going on along a front hundreds of miles long, to encircle the allies in the Pas de Calais. Now, that encirclement had been achieved: that same morning, while the Grossdeutschlanders edged closer to Bergues, the right flank made contact with German units who had fought their way through lowland Belgium, and the armies of Kleist and Reichenau were joined up for the first time.

The scene was being set for the death blow. Bergues was an old town, heavily fortified with ramparts, walls and battlements. The French and British had been driven back into it, and were bound to make a determined stand. Until now, each town and village had been just another obstacle to be surmounted before rushing on to the next. Bergues was different. In a strange, instinctive way, Heinrich Lauder knew that Bergues was more than an obstacle. It was a destination.

iv

Since the meeting at Cassel broke up the previous day, Lord Gort had moved his headquarters to a pretentious beach-side villa, the last but one on the western outskirts of La Panne, a Belgian resort about eight miles east of Dunkirk. He had chosen it because it stood within a few hundred yards of the point where the underwater telephone cables ran from the continent across to Dover, and therefore had the best possible communications link both with the Dover and the War Office. He had placed Lieutenant General Adam in overall charge of the perimeter, and he in turn had given Brigadier Lawson the task of defending it and Lieutenant Colonel Bridgeman that of directing the troops to the beaches.

The overall plan was that 1 Corps would head for the beach at Bray Dunes, midway between Dunkirk and La Panne, 2 Corps would assemble in the La Panne area, and 3 Corps on the beach at Malo-les-Bains, on the outskirts of Dunkirk itself. The port and its suburbs and areas to the west would be defended by the French. Military police would direct the flow of traffic, and the Royal Engineers would have the job of keeping the roads clear and destroying abandoned vehicles.

As each company and battalion reported in, orders were despatched from the new GHQ at La Panne designating the position it was to take up, so that the wall map gradually filled up with the famous old names of British regiments and battalions.

Over to the east at Nieuport, the Surreys, the Royal Fusiliers and the Lancashires faced the westward advance of the German 256th Division. The Grenadier and Coldstream Guards took up positions at Furnes; the Durham Light Infantry at Bulscamp; the Green Howards, Staffords and Yorks lined the next section of the canal, and then the Borderers, Lancashires, Foresters and Leicestershires joined up to fight side by side with French units ringing Dunkirk itself. Within the perimeter, the waterlogged fields were similarly inundated with troops: practically every regiment in the BEF was represented, and supporting them everywhere were the drivers and mechanics of the Royal Army Service Corps, the telegraphists of the Royal Signals and the ubiquitious sections and companies of sappers.

Early on Tuesday morning, when Lieutenant General Adam was grappling with this vast problem of withdrawal into the perimeter, a major general arrived at GHQ looking like a man who is confident of a job well done.

It was Major General Henry Martin, the officer commanding anti-aircraft artillery. The previous night, while the bombs were falling, Bridgeman had sent word to Martin via a liaison officer to keep his guns going to the last, but to send any of his spare gunners to join up with the infantry. In the confusion of battle, the message had become garbled, and Martin had received it as an instruction to send all anti-aircraft gunners to the beaches.

Gunners don't question orders and, although it might have seemed odd that while the Stuka raids continued almost non-stop, the first men to be evacuated were the anti-aircraft guns' crews, Martin didn't question this one. Instead, he decided on his own initiative that if the AA guns were to be abandoned, they should be put out of action.

He strode into Adam's office and saluted. 'All anti-aircraft guns have been spiked, sir.'

There was a horrified silence. Lieutenant General Adam looked up from his worktable.

'You bloody, bloody fool!' he said quietly. 'Go away!'

v

HMS *Vagabond*'s estimated time of arrival at the Forth rail bridge was expressed in naval signalese as '280600' which meant six a.m. on the twenty-eighth.

For the navigating officer, Lieutenant Peter Hartley, the ship's ETA at Rosyth had become something of an obsession. Two months before, the captain had made a standing wager with him of a double horse's neck (brandy and ginger ale to the uninitiated) that he could not time their arrival so that the ship was precisely under the bridge within thirty seconds of her ETA; and Hartley, who had ambitions to make navigation his sub-specialization, was convinced that here was an easy source of drinks on the captain. But in the weeks of North Sea patrols that had followed, he had never once achieved the required degree of accuracy. Every time HMS *Vagabond* passed under the Forth bridge on her way back to her base at Port Edgar, the cry had gone up: 'Double horse's neck for the captain on the navigator's bar chit!' and when Archie had ordered 'finished with main engines' and had left his first lieutenant to double up and secure, he would descend to his cabin where Steward Norman would be waiting with a large grin on his face and an even larger horse's neck in a pony glass — served, naturally, on a silver salver.

'Looking promising, Pilot,' Archie admitted, as the old destroyer slipped along at twelve knots up the Forth Estuary and the familiar russet girders of the bridge emerged from the morning mist.

Hartley put another cross-bearing on the chart and asked for an increase of four revolutions to add half a knot to the destroyer's speed through the water.

'One-oh-four revolutions repeated, sir!' the quartermaster reported up the voicepipe from the wheelhouse, as Inchkeith Island slipped by to port.

'That was a mistake, you're going to be early,' Archie announced gleefully as the ship closed on the bridge.

But Hartley had taken the ship's chronometer from its stowage on the chart table and was checking the bridge clock against it. Calmly, and without making any attempt to conceal what he was doing, he opened the glass front of the latter and put the second hand back twenty-four seconds; and a few minutes later, when the centre span was directly overhead the open bridge of HMS *Vagabond*, the clock showed the time to be twelve seconds to the hour.

'I make that a double horse's neck you owe me, sir.'

'Not at all. You cheated, Pilot. I saw you change the clock.'

A light-hearted argument then ensued, in which Archie insisted that Hartley would not have adjusted the bridge clock had it not suited his purpose, pointing out that he had never done so before. 'What a dastardly turn, Pilot! I never imagined you would stoop to such downright trickery.'

Hartley was just rising in his own defence when a lamp began flashing from the signal tower at Burntisland, and the yeoman of signals read aloud the message from the Flag Officer as it came through.

'TURN . . . ROUND,' he read. And then: 'PROCEED DOVER WITH ALL DESPATCH.'

On the bridge of HMS *Vagabond*, there was a moment of frozen surprise.

'Can't we at least pick up fresh provisions and mail?' the first lieutenant asked from the back of the bridge.

But Archie was already passing wheel and engine orders down the voicepipe to the wheelhouse and within minutes HMS *Vagabond* had reversed course and black smoke was pouring from her funnels as she increased speed to thirty knots.

'Right, Number One,' Archie said. 'You can tell the troops we've been ordered south to Dover. I don't know the reason why, but I do know that the Pongoes are in a spot of trouble, and my bet is we're being sent south to help them out. Well don't look so bloody gloomy about it! We've got a proper job to do for a change!'

He turned back to face for'd. The wind was beginning to howl in the dodgers, and the ship was lifting gently over a low swell.

Dover . . . They would have to put in to refuel and store ship and that would mean a few hours' spare to see Simone. For nearly five months he had deliberately kept her from his mind. But now, with the prospect of seeing her again – however briefly – he was filled with a great longing for her.

But I shouldn't be thinking about Simone, he reflected. If I had any shred of decency, I'd be thinking much more about poor old Griff. What the hell would he be up to now?

Griff was blowing the wheels off a railway carriage which his section had shunted across a level crossing near Wormhoudt. Some enemy tanks were intent upon stopping him, but the fall of shot must have been unobserved, because so far all the shells had fallen in an adjacent field, killing several cows but doing no other damage.

To the section's front left, Sergeant Crisp and Sapper Smith were providing covering fire with a Bren gun from a signal box. To the right, Freddy Radcliffe and his platoon were positioned along a ditch with rifles, while three hundred yards up the approach road Kingsnorth and McCartney were dug in with an anti-tank rifle with which they proposed to deal with the approaching panzers one by one.

Griff was working with Sapper Ward who in the last few days had proved himself to be a man not only of unfailing good humour but of unshakable courage and physical stamina. Ward was carrying the explosives and Griff the detonators. They had done this before and went quickly from axle to axle firing the charges, placing the detonators, connecting up the wires. All the time they worked, the sound of Spandaus and field artillery continued.

There was a shriek and a deafening explosion as a shell landed fifty yards away. Griff taped six sticks of ammonal to the fourth axle, inserted the detonator and connected up. Another shriek and another bang, followed by a shower of dust and small stones. Bent double, he ran along the side of the railway carriage to fix the last charge. While he was doing so, a Messerschmitt came low along the line of the railway, its machine guns blazing.

'Gettin' a bit 'ot, sir,' Ward remarked.

Griff nodded and screwed the wired connector tight. 'We'll make this one the last!' he shouted over the din. 'Dump the rest of the ammonal down at the end and go back to Lieutenant Radcliffe. Tell him to get back to the lorries and withdraw them to the rallying point. Got that?'

'Got that, sir!' Ward shouted and, having dumped his load of explosives under the carriage, made a dash back along the road and across the corner of a field to Radcliffe's ditch. At the same time, the enemy artillery at last got the range of the level crossing and shells began falling uncomfortably close. Griff had wanted to place six charges but had only achieved four, but if he tried to complete all six there was a high risk that enemy shelling would cut the wires before he could detonate. Having taken the decision, he ran back ten yards and hurled himself into a ditch as another shell shrieked and exploded. Forty yards further up the ditch, Sapper Barker awaited his order to detonate. Griff saw him look up.

'Blow!' he shouted, and when the dust settled the railway carriage was lying drunkenly over on one side and the level crossing was blocked.

Kingsnorth and McCartney, acting on orders, began pulling back with the anti-tank gun on hearing the detonation, and Sergeant Crisp's Bren opened up from the signal box, covering them as they came back along the road, dodging from tree to tree, running bent double along the ditch. At the same time, the first tank appeared coming up the lane towards the railway. It came on up the road, firing at the signal box. Loping along behind it came six German infantrymen with stick grenades slung round their necks, sub-machine guns at the ready and heavy packs on their backs.

Griff heard the report of the Boys rifle and the cross fire from Crisp's Bren. Kingsnorth appeared to have stopped his withdrawal about fifty yards from the railway in order to deal with the tank, and in the signal box Crisp was maintaining his covering fire until Kingsnorth was safe.

From the ditch where Radcliffe's platoon was positioned came a splutter of rifle fire; but the tank had got the range of the signal box with its cannon and the Bren had fallen silent. Griff felt a sudden white-hot anger that his little handful of men should be expected to hold up the advance of such an overwhelming force. He watched as the tank began to move closer and then the Boys fired again, this time at almost point-blank range, and the tank stopped. Smoke was pouring from its engine. The Boys barked a third time and the tank erupted in flame.

Griff went along the ditch below the railway and made a rush over the line to the wrecked signal box. Crisp was dead, there was no doubt of that, and Sapper Smith was lying in a lake of blood. His eyes flickered at Griff's approach and he tried to say something. Griff knelt by him. Smith tried to speak again but his lips barely moved. Griff saw the life go out of him. He removed the pay book and identity disc from each of the bodies, shouldered the Bren and ran back across the railway; then, using a clump of nettles as cover, he set up the Bren and began firing diagonally across at the burning tank to cover the withdrawal of Kingsnorth and McCartney. He kept this up for some minutes then moved off again, making his way to the rear across fields to where the section's lorries were parked in a lane.

When he arrived, only the smoking wrecks of two lorries remained. He was joined by Kingsnorth and McCartney, with the Boys rifle. Together, they made their way back over fields to the rallying point. There, they found the last lorry parked under trees by a narrow canal, with a dozen men asleep on the canal bank.

Driver Hall came up with Griff's shaving kit, a tin mug of water and a towel. 'Thought you might want to freshen up a bit, sir. Sorry the water's cold.'

He was rinsing the shaving soap off his face when Radcliffe arrived with fourteen men, one of whom had a serious head wound. Radcliffe was begrimed and bruised. His eyes were pink with fatigue and his lips cracked.

Griff knotted his tie, put his battledress jacket on and jammed his hat on his head. 'We'll move off in twenty minutes, Freddy. Your lot can have first spell in the lorry. Corporal Kingsnorth is promoted to sergeant as of now. Have the men properly fallen in before we move off and impress on them that this is *not* a retreat. We'll stick together, and we'll do things properly. And Freddy –'

'Sir?'

'Get yourself smartened up a bit before we go, right?'

'Very good, sir.'

Half an hour later, the Waterways Defence Section moved off. Griff and twelve men went first on foot and Radcliffe plus fourteen travelled in the lorry, which crawled along behind. Taking the country lanes, they headed towards the four columns of black smoke that rose into the sky.

For a while, the men marched in silence. Then Sharky Ward started up.

'. . . Reminds me of our Sunday School outings this. I mean we all had to go for a country walk before tea and the teacher used to tell us Bible stories on the way, see. There was David and Goliath, and Jacob and the ladder up to heaven, and Moses and the Children of Israel with all them plagues of locusts and frogs and that. I mean – well, it's a bit similar, really, isn't it, boys? Here we are, led by a pillar of smoke by day and a pillar of fire by night . . . What d'you think, Captain Wilmot, sir? Can you make the sea open up for us, so we can all walk across to Dover?'

TWENTY-EIGHT

At Bray Dunes, where 1 Corps was collecting, discipline was breaking down. Utterly exhausted, the elderly corps commander, Lieutenant General Barker, had retired to a cellar, and his loss of grip was now filtering down through his staff and being reflected in the behaviour of his troops.

Thousands of them were arriving on the beach every hour. They were looting the villas and guest houses, befouling the cellars, drinking anything that had a semblance of alcohol in it and loosing off their small arms at every passing aircraft.

Barker's staff officers attempted to regain control, but with hundreds of leaderless men milling about on the promenade and surging down to the beach every time a boat appeared, even the threat of a service revolver seemed insignificant when compared with the Luftwaffe's attacks.

There had already been ugly scenes. A major who had tried to pull rank to get a place in a boat had been shot in the back, and numerous fights had broken out between groups claiming precedence in the queues for boats.

Into this confusion of demoralized troops strode Captain Gimson, Irish Guards. He was one of the operations officers on General Brooke's Staff, and he knew a thing or two about discipline.

'Fall in three deep!' he roared at the nearest group of soldiers, and his power of command was such that they obeyed instinctively.

Tall, straightbacked, the peak of his cap almost vertical on his nose, Gimson marched up and down smacking a swagger stick into the palm of his hand. Again and again his voice roared the order to fall in, and within seconds hundreds of men were lined up on the promenade.

Then the drill started. 'Parade – *shun*! By the right – *dress*! Slope – *arms*! Present – *arms*! Order – *arms*! Stand at – *ease*! Parade – *shun*! Move to the right in threes right – *turn*! A-bout – *turn*! Into line, right – *turn*!'

It worked like magic: as with children removed from parental care, the troops' deliquency had been a cry for the security of discipline. Captain Gimson gave them that discipline. Pacing up and down the beach he put them through all the basic parade-ground commands and rifle drill they had learnt as recruits. And having re-established control and ensured that an NCO was in charge of each unit, he dismissed the parade.

ii

Early that evening, Captain Tennant's three assistants reported in. They and the naval party had so far concentrated their efforts on the western end of the beach. Now, Tennant decided that naval organization and control was necessary at Bray Dunes and La Panne as well.

'There are upwards of five thousand men waiting at Bray Dunes alone,' he told them in the little office he had been allocated in the bowels of Bastion 32. 'So who's going to volunteer to sort them out?'

The three officers – Clouston, Richardson and Kerr – decided to draw for it, with the loser being the one to take on Bray Dunes.

They used a deck of cards. Richardson lost, but because of the size of the job they cut again and Kerr went with him. Clouston regarded himself as being lucky to be left with the charge of embarkation from the east mole.

The naval party loaded up a lorry and Kerr and Richardson set off along the beach road. It took over an hour to travel the seven miles, and by the time they arrived it was dusk. As they approached Bray, with Richardson and Kerr riding in the cab of the truck, what appeared to be gigantic break-waters running down to the water's edge came into view.

But they were not breakwaters. They were men.

'Five thousand!' breathed Richardson. 'My God, it's more like twenty-five thousand!'

iii

Along with hundreds of other units, Gregory Blaxland's platoon was on the move to the coast. Their destination and the distance to it remained unknown, but the men were drawn on now as if by a migratory instinct that told them it was time to go home. Shells were falling here and there, and the distant sound of Spandaus made one wonder if anyone was bothering to oppose them: they were in fact being shielded by French tanks of the Cavalry Corps, though they received small thanks from their British allies.

They settled down as part of a far-spread throng, with the scavengers dispersed like outriders on the flanks and in the van. Blaxland's platoon had three such: they rode on bicycles and their rare discoveries of eggs, cheese and the odd tin of food were distributed by the company sergeant major.

They avoided roads as much as possible, for the distant sounds and glimpses of air attack and the columns of black smoke that resulted from them gave added appeal to the countryside.

Blaxland discovered a horse, saddled and bridled, grazing in a field. It obviously belonged to the French cavalry, and had the quality and type of saddle to mark it as an officer's charger. It didn't mind being mounted, and Blaxland heaved himself up, weighed down by marching boots, equipment, steel helmet and greatcoat.

'Ride him, Gordon!' shouted one of the soldiers, and it gave Blaxland's morale a boost to survey his trudging men, to see their grins and hear their cheerful exhortations. He rode over to the other two companies of Buffs to discuss the route, and on meeting his General Officer Commanding limping along in front of his staff car, snapped him off a smart salute.

Soon after, the sound of automatic fire came from ahead, and Blaxland handed over his mount to a grateful French soldier. A battle was raging for a copse by the road, and he was suddenly fearful that a senior officer would come rushing up to him and order him to lead his platoon in a counter-attack. The way out – cowardly perhaps, but Blaxland was past caring – lay in a wide detour, in which the platoon became dispersed and Blaxland ripped his battledress trousers on barbed wire. Eventually the men were mustered at a rallying point, and the scavengers' takings were distributed.

Spirits rose: the columns of black smoke that marked their destination seemed nearer, and there was a strange feeling shared by all that they were taking part in a great adventure that was soon to reach its climax.

They started off again. In a field to the right, the French cavalry seemed to be assembling in force, and suddenly Blaxland saw for what purpose. They were shooting their horses. From a distance it seemed a very casual affair, with each horse patiently waiting its turn.

There was destruction on all sides here, with many blazing vehicles. They were coming to the edge of the defensive perimeter, and all stores and vehicles not required for battle were being destroyed.

They came to a wide canal. Standing on the bridge where they crossed was an officer Blaxland recognized from Sand-hurst days when he was a gentleman-cadet. His men were entrenched behind him, smartly turned out and securely ensconced behind sandbags. The marsh around them had been flooded as far back as the eye could see and every ditch, embankment and building seemed to be bristling with weapons. The knowledge that they were now within the perimeter and had behind them such highly organized de-fenders did wonders for the morale.

Darkness fell soon after crossing the canal, but they still had to keep marching, with occasional explosions, flares and blazes lighting their path.

Fatigue came like a clam, suddenly, overwhelmingly. Blaxland awoke with a start, to realize that he had been both marching and sleeping, just as had the soldiers of a former BEF during the retreat from Mons twenty-six years before. He fell asleep again and woke up again – and each time he jolted awake he found himself thinking of the men from Mons.

Then he felt sand underfoot and heard one of his fellow officers saying: 'Thank God we're all still together!' and a moment later he flopped down and slept.

When they awoke, they had a lovely view. They were on sand dunes, and barely two hundred yards away was the sea. It was a grey, overcast morning and the waves beat gently upon the sloping beach. But apart from a small motor launch which seemed to be aground, there was not a ship or a craft in sight.

TWENTY-NINE

The *Daisy Belle* was a thirty-six-foot cabin cruiser that had been custom built four years before by Tough Brothers of Teddington. Clinker-built of teak on oak, with two cabins, twin Stuart-Turner petrol engines and wheel steering, she was Geoffrey Pringle's pride and joy, and for three summers running he had taken his wife and two little girls for their fortnight's summer holiday in her.

As a schoolboy at Dulwich College, Pringle had nursed a passion to join the Royal Navy, but maternal protestations had prevailed and he had settled for the Stock Exchange instead. After making a most suitable marriage to a lovely girl called Avril, he had joined a firm of stockbrokers and for the last ten years, except for weekends, bank holidays and a fortnight each summer, had left his house in Kew Green at a quarter past eight in the morning and had returned from his office in Moorgate at a quarter to six in the evening. He had emerged relatively unscathed from the Depression, and by the outbreak of war had established himself as a prosperous and transparently honest broker who nurtured his clients' accounts as carefully as if they had been his own.

He had volunteered for military service immediately when war was declared, but was found unfit on account of a slight tendency to asthma; so he had to make do with joining the Thames River Emergency Service, an organization set up on the outbreak of war whose members were for the most part gentlemen sailors like himself. So far, membership had involved little more than the occasional training session followed by a pleasant evening in a riverside pub at Richmond, Mortlake or Kew.

The Pringles were finishing supper when the telephone

rang. Geoffrey had had a rather depressing day at the office and was a little tired, so Avril, who believed in cosseting her husband, answered it.

'For you,' she called from the hall, and when he came out of the sitting room, put her hand over the mouthpiece and said, 'Mr Tough. Isn't that the boat man?'

He took the telephone. 'Yes Mr Tough, what can I do for you?'

'Your boat,' said the cockney voice at the other end of the line. 'She's in good running order, I suppose?'

'I took her down to Greenwich only last Sunday. There's still that slight vibration on the port engine at low revs –'

'I've been contacted by the Ministry of Shipping. Admiralty are calling for small craft, and your *Daisy Belle*'s on their list. She's wanted at Southend as soon as possible. We'll be towing boats down-river at first light tomorrow, but I thought you might prefer to take her yourself.'

'I have to go to the office tomorrow. What's she needed for?'

Tough laughed without humour. 'Do I have to tell you that, Mr Pringle? Don't you never listen to the news, sir?'

Standing at his side, Avril stared up into her husband's face, and when he reached out and took her hand she gripped it tightly.

'So what you're saying is – you want skippers as well, right?'

'Are you a volunteer?'

'I could be. What does it entail?'

'Just a trip down to Southend in the first instance. The navy'll take her over from there.'

'If anyone's going to skipper her I'd rather it was me.'

'That's very good of you, Mr Pringle, I'm much obliged. Now what I suggest is you bring your boat straight down here to Teddington this evening while it's still light, and my lads'll get her fuelled up and ready for a dawn start tomorrow. Can do?'

The children – Ruth and Joanna – had come halfway

down the stairs and crouched in their dressing gowns looking scrubbed and pink after their bath. Geoffrey Pringle felt a little chill of excitement that was not entirely without fear.

'Is that definite then, Mr Pringle? Can I rely on you to bring her down-river this evening?'

'Yes. I'll be with you in under two hours.'

'And tomorrow? You'll take her on down to Southend, right?'

'Yes – yes, that'll be all right.'

They rang off.

'Well?' asked Avril. 'What was all that about?'

He kissed her and smiled. 'I'm taking *Daisy* to Southend.'

She preceded him into the sitting room. 'Why on earth should they want you to go to Southend?'

For once in his life, Geoffrey Pringle told her a barefaced lie. 'I haven't the faintest idea,' he said.

ii

. . . Paul Hodgeson arrives in the shooting brake with news. The Divisional RE have counter-attacked with the bayonet at Warneton and Mac-donald has been killed by a hand grenade, thrown when he was accepting surrender. Gus Galloway has to take over from him so I am to look after the 59 HQ Section. We have fallen back and are occupying the left of the perimeter and Div HQ is at Coxyde. I am to stay where I am and carry on preparing the bridges I have allotted myself, while 7 Field Company take over those on the other side of Furnes. I am to do the work tomorrow morning; there is an ammunition point near Moeres. Any spare effort I must put into collecting barbed wire from the hedgerows and any picks and shovels I can find. 18 Field Park Company will send a lorry. He does not want any tinned caviare.

Soon after he has gone, 59 HQ Section moves

in bringing with them a wounded man who groans in a corner of the hut under the doctor's supervision. I divide the sections up into search parties and set off on my reconnaissance.

I soon run into trouble. At Furnes when I examine the bridge a jumpy Belgian officer asks me what I am doing. When I tell him he pats his revolver and says that this is a Belgian bridge and is not to be blown up by the British. I leave immediately and go to find the Town Major. He says that liaison is tricky but he will try to sort it out. It is very quiet, and a shot rings out from across the canal. I lower the windscreen of the 8cwt truck and rest the Bren gun on the bonnet. Round the corner is a group of soldiers, John Osborne with a party from 225 Field Company. I warn him about the Belgian.

Set off driving along the towpath. First comes a lattice girder foot bridge; 20lbs of guncotton should settle that. Then comes a steep old single-arch masonry bridge which will need ammonal. There are about twelve bridges including the steel girder railway bridge at the end. I am looking at the last when the Chief Engineer Brigadier Phipps drives up with Major Boggs, both calm and cheerful. They are pleased to see that things are happening. Boggs gives me specific advice about the ammunition point. While we are talking a formation of bombers flies over towards Dunkirk so we lie on the grassy bank.

I find the ammunition point in the form of boxes dumped for a mile or so along the verges of a road with nobody in charge. Just help myself to guncotton, ammonal and accessories in liberal quantities.

Back at the section a lot of material has been brought in and the CSM of 59 Field Company has been a tower of strength. A lorry-load has already been collected. We are no longer alone. An infantry battalion wearing red shackles has occupied the field, and in our house there is a Brigade HQ. The mess staff have made a very good job of clearing the dining room, and have laid the table for dinner.

After I have called on the brigade major I work out my plans for tomorrow. There is nobody in either section who knows anything about demolitions so I allocate a party under an NCO for each bridge and will just have to tell them what to do. I give a short lecture on demolition equipment in the hut, and send them off to bed to be ready for an early start . . .

iii

The destroyer *Wakeful* sailed for Dover at about eleven p.m., having embarked troops from the beach at Bray Dunes. She followed Route Z, through the Zuydecoote Pass and North Channel. As she approached the Kwinte Whistle Buoy she began a zigzag, altering forty degrees either side of her base course every four minutes. At a quarter to one in the morning, two torpedo tracks were sighted, and the ship was hit amidships by one of them. She broke in half and sank within fifteen seconds, and all the troops on board went down with her.

Some of her crew floated clear, and within half an hour two minesweeping drifters, *Nautilus* and *Comfort*, appeared on the scene and started picking up survivors. They were joined a little while later by the minesweeper *Gossamer*. Two further ships, the destroyer *Grafton* and the minesweeper *Lydd*, stood by. After being picked up by *Comfort*, the captain of *Wakeful* warned *Grafton*, which was close alongside, that she was in danger of being torpedoed – and at that same moment *Grafton* was torpedoed. The bridge was also hit – by shell or grenade – and the captain killed instantly. *Comfort* was lifted out of the water by the explosion and the captain of *Wakeful* washed overboard. *Comfort*, going at full speed, came round in a circle back towards the other ships and was mistaken for an enemy torpedo boat. *Grafton* and *Lydd* opened fire on her, killing all but four of the *Comfort* crew and *Wakeful* survivors. *Lydd* then bore down on *Comfort*, rammed her and sank her. *Grafton* then opened fire on another vessel on her port quarter, which blew up with a bright flash. This may have been the enemy torpedo boat.

iv

For the Waterways Defence Section, it had been another long night without sleep. After the action near Wormhoudt, Griff had sent Freddy Radcliffe and the wounded ahead in the lorry and had remained with the other eighteen men to lead them to the coast on foot; but they had taken a wrong turning in the dark and had stumbled into enemy positions. Extricating themselves had been a lengthy and dangerous business, and a march of eight miles had turned into a nightmare of crawling in ditches, wading across fields and trudging in single file along cart tracks.

Now, as the sun came up, they found themselves barely a mile from the Bergues-Furnes canal, and Wilmot called a halt so that the men could use the last of the fresh water for a cup of tea and a clean up before entering the defended perimeter.

They squatted down at the side of the road, their eyes red-rimmed with fatigue. Six Woodbines were passed round, one between three men. When Sapper Ward had boiled the last of the water in the dixie, each man saved half a cup of his ration for shaving.

Wilmot had told Kingsnorth to put up sergeant's stripes. ''Scuse me, sir,' he said when Wilmot's face was still half covered with lather. 'Any chance of a loan of your tin of boot polish?'

From every direction came the staccato squabble of machine guns and the softer crump of artillery. Over Dunkirk, the black cloud from the oil storage tanks rose ten thousand feet into the sky. On either side of the road, as far as the eye could see, lorries, cars, tanks and carriers had been tipped into the ditches and abandoned.

'In my knapsack,' Wilmot told him, and watched with admiration as Kingsnorth walked over to the section and told the men, 'There you are, then. That's the officer's own boot polish. So you've no excuse for dirty boots now, have you, Sapper Ward?'

Their boots polished, their faces shaven and their tin helmets square on their heads, they picked up their weapons and set off again; and half an hour later, as they approached the canal bridge into the Dunkirk perimeter, just east of Bergues, Wilmot fell them in three deep and marched them as a squad.

'March to attention!' Kingsnorth barked. 'Heads up, swing those arms! Left-right-left-right-left . . . !'

The boots crunched over the bridge, and the squad gave a smart eyes-right to a brigadier watching from his staff car.

As they reverted to single file and went on along the straight road that ran between flooded fields towards Rosendael and the sea, Wilmot's hopes began to rise. For days he had held on grimly, determined to keep his section together and get his men back to England. And soon – only another hour or two – they would reach the coast.

He imagined his arrival at Prowse and the reunion with Simone. He imagined her running towards him, tears of happiness in her eyes. He would catch her in his arms and whirl her round. They would be happy again. All the past would be put behind them . . .

A motorbike had come up from behind and was drawing up alongside. The rider was a thickset staff major, a gunner with a bully-beef complexion and the build of a rugby second-row forward. He sat astride the bike with the engine running.

'About turn, captain,' he said. 'Your chaps are needed!'

The men had been halted, and were glancing back at the two officers, already suspicious that they were to be sent back. For a moment, Griff was tempted to tell this beet-cheeked gunner what he could do.

The major took a map case from the pannier of the motorbike and opened out a large-scale Ordnance Survey map.

'Right. The bridge you've just crossed is this one, here, Pont de Zycklin. You will turn about and march to Bergues, entering by the Ypres Gate which is on the north-east side of the town, here. Your section will be reinforced to company strength and you will place yourself under the command of the 1st Loyals, who will be holding Bergues as a strong point on the right flank. Any questions?'

'None at all, Major.'

'Right – well, get a move on, won't you? Jerry's putting on the pressure, and the Frogs haven't much to stop them with.' He revved the engine, U-turned and, with a final 'Good luck!' roared off back towards the bridge.

Wilmot called Kingsnorth over. 'Turn them about, Sergeant Kingsnorth. We've got work to do.'

Without a flicker of surprise or protest in his expression, Kingsnorth said 'Sir!', saluted, turned right and barked out the order.

That evening, the section marched into Bergues, and Wilmot took command of a mixed company attached to the 139th Brigade. Under his command – which he named 'Wilmot's Rifles' – he had men from the Welsh Guards, Lincolns, Royal West Kents, Royal Warwickshers and Royal Artillery.

On arriving at Bergues, Wilmot's Rifles were ordered to relieve some platoons of Sherwood Foresters who were in posts outside the western defences and adjacent to French positions holding the canal line west of Bergues. When they had dug weapon pits and constructed breastworks (necessary because the water level was only a couple of feet down), Wilmot made a tour of his positions before returning to the headquarters section, which was in the ramparts of the town near the Rue de la Gare.

He found Private Hall at work with needle and thread on his service dress uniform. 'Just putting your crowns up, sir,' he said. 'If you can let me have your battledress a moment, I'll do that as well.'

Sappers Ward and McCartney had been sent out foraging and had come back laden with food, including the prize of a loaf of bread. 'An' I got something else for you, sir,' Ward announced, and produced an enormous tin of Kiwi boot polish. 'There you are, sir! I got it off the Loyals CSM round the corner. He said he didn't reckon on cleaning his boots again this side of Dover.'

v

David was working in Griff's study when the staff car drew up outside. He had been trying to get something down on paper about the evacuation of Boulogne, but was finding it very heavy going. With the battle for France raging on the other side of the Channel and destroyers arriving in Dover loaded to the gunwales with soldiers, it seemed wrong to sit at a typewriter all day. He needed to get out. He needed to be involved again – however humbly – in the great rescue operation that was being mounted from the south coast ports.

There was another reason for his mind to wander, and that reason was Gwynneth.

He had a lot to thank Gwynneth for. It had been the thought of her and the hope of finding her again that had kept him going during the long hours on the road with the refugees. He had had vivid dreams of her during his thirty-six hour sleep after returning from Boulogne, and she had been uppermost in his thoughts when he woke up.

He smiled to himself, recalling her laughing eyes and shock of dark hair. What would she say if she were with him now? Something like: 'Don't sit there on your backside, boy! Get on your bike and *do* something!'

He looked up from the typewriter at the sound of tyres on gravel. There was a Wren driver at the wheel of the staff car and two naval officers in the back, one of whom was getting out.

'Ah,' said the naval officer when David opened the front door to him. 'I don't expect you know me. I'm —'

But David did know him: he recognized him instantly. 'Commander Trendle-Home, isn't it? Pleased to meet you, Commander. I'm David Odell. Simone's son.'

The dog came through from the kitchen, and on seeing his master went into paroxysms of delight.

Archie was clearly nonplussed. He looked a lot older than the photograph of him in Captain Wilmot's study.

'Ah,' he said. 'I — um — I just dropped by on the off chance that my daughter —'

'Christine? She's down at the headquarters. They all are.'

'Of course, yes —' He glanced about as if he were a total stranger. 'And — Simone?'

'In the village. Back any minute, I guess. Would you care to come in and wait for her?'

He looked at his watch and shook his head. 'I only have a minute or two.'

'Can I take a number for her to call you then?'

'No, no that's impossible. Just . . . just say I called and was very sorry to miss her.'

'That all?'

No, it was not all. HMS *Vagabond* had arrived in the early hours of the morning having made a fast passage from the Firth of Forth. She was now being refuelled at Dover and was taking on special stores — ladders, rope, scrambling nets, medical supplies — for evacuation duties. Archie had stolen ten minutes on his way to a briefing at Dover Castle. Though he tried to ignore it, he was aware of a strong premonition that if he did not see Simone now, he might never see her again.

'Perhaps you could say – perhaps you could give her my – my best regards.'

'I'll do that with pleasure, Commander.'

Archie hesitated. 'No news of Captain Wilmot I suppose?'

'Not that I know of. The last Simone heard, he was still in France. You heard about Christine's fiancé, I suppose?'

'No?'

'Oh. Well – perhaps I shouldn't have mentioned it –'

'What is it? What's happened to him?'

'He was reported shot down.'

'Where?'

'I don't know anything more than that.'

Archie turned to go, but at the same time there was a shriek of bicycle brakes and Simone appeared round the rhododendron bushes on a Rudge, practically falling off it as she came to a halt.

'Archie! What on earth are you doing here?'

She propped the bike against the porch and led the way inside, taking him through into the kitchen. 'What have you done with that ship of yours? Why didn't you tell me you were coming? How long can you stay?'

'Only a couple of minutes –'

'Nonsense! You must stay longer than that.' She searched his face, saw the strain and fatigue there. 'Archie, what *have* you been doing? No, you can't tell me, can you?' She took his hands and squeezed them tightly. 'If only you knew how much I've been thinking about you!'

He nodded, staring down at her.

'I've been thinking of you, too, Simone. But –'

'Did you get my letters?'

He was hardly able to speak. Seeing her like this – the same Simone as ever – brought home to him how desperately he needed her and yet how guilty he felt about taking her from Griff.

'My dear, I don't think you realize just how – how –'

'How much you love me?'

394

'No . . . How serious things are. Griff's the one you should be thinking about. Not yours truly.'

She turned her head and looked out of the window. 'I do think about him,' she said quietly. 'I think about you both.' She looked up at him. He was reminded of an illustration in a school history book of Jeanne d'Arc. That is what she has always been to me, he thought. A figurehead, an inspiration.

'I think about you both,' she repeated. I write to you both. I *love* you both. I know it's not supposed to be possible for a woman to love two men at the same time, but for me it is possible, Archie. It *is*.'

But even as she said it she knew it was not the complete truth. How could she tell him that she did not know which of them she loved with her whole heart? How could she tell him of her fears about the fatal effect she seemed to have on the men she loved?

'I've only got a minute,' he said. 'Literally. We're under sailing orders. I really have to go.'

'Sailing orders . . .' she echoed, and laughed sadly. 'You were always under sailing orders, weren't you, Archie? Well just hold me, then. Hold me for that one minute, and tell me that you love me, even if you don't mean it.'

He kissed her in a sort of desperation.

'I do love you, and I do mean it,' he said.

'Fight well,' she whispered. 'Fight well and bravely. For Griff as well as for me.'

They went out into the drive and said goodbye. As the staff car drove off, its roof brushed one of the lower branches of a flowering cherry, bringing down a little shower of pink petals that floated in the morning sunlight. Seeing them Simone felt a shiver go down her spine. It seemed to her that those confetti-like petals were an omen: that Archie was newly married to her oldest rival, and that very soon the marriage would reach its grim consummation.

HMS *Vagabond* sailed soon after noon with the men closed up at action stations, every gun manned, and the ship's watertight compartments closed down. As she headed out between the breakwaters and set course for Dunkirk along Route X, Archie addressed his ship's company over the new broadcast system that had been installed during the last refit.

Throughout the ship, men in tin hats and anti-flash gear gathered in little groups by the loudspeakers, listening to what he had to say.

'D'you hear there? As you know, the army seems to have got itself into a bit of a jam in France, and we've been invited to join the party and help them out. We're now on our way across the Channel to Dunkirk, and we can expect to be taking a lot of passengers on board in the next few hours. They'll be tired, some may be injured, and they'll all be relying on us to get them back safe to their mums and dads and sweethearts and wives. At the same time, Jerry is unlikely to feel inclined to make our job any easier, so we can expect a bit of excitement when we arrive off the beaches. So keep on your toes, be ready for anything and shoot straight. That's all.'

Steaming at twenty-nine knots, the destroyer made the journey across the Channel in a little over two hours. As they closed on the French coast, all on deck could hear the sound of bombs and shells bursting, and could see pillars of smoke and fire rising from the low strip of land on the horizon. When they got closer still, the queues of men on the beaches could be seen: they stretched down in zigzag patterns and extended into the sea.

On the bridge, Peter Hartley moved constantly back and forth between the chart table and the compass repeat on the bridge wing, giving the captain distances to go to the next alteration of course, depth of water, courses to steer.

'One in the bucket!' came a shout up the voicepipe to the signalman's desk, and the yeoman hauled the signal up from the WT office and read it out to the captain.

'From SNO Dunkirk, sir. "LIE OFF LA PANNE BEACH AND EMBARK TROOPS BY BOAT."'

'Thank you, Yeoman. Pilot: give me a course for La Panne beach. And find out how close we can go at this state of the tide. Number One: pass the word to the torpedo crews to stand by to lower the whaler and motor cutter and prepare scrambling nets. Officer-of-the-watch: tell the engine room we shall be manoeuvring shortly. Guns: we may have to drop the pick, so have A turret's crew prepare starboard anchor for letting go. Yes, Pilot?'

'Port to one-one-zero now, please, sir.'

'Very good, go ahead. Sub Lieutenant: you're to go in the motor cutter and take charge of embarkation on the beach. There's not much surf, but keep to seaward of it and don't on any account try to beach the boat. Your limit's twenty at a time, but they'll have to leave their weapons behind. If there's any queue-barging or panic, draw your revolver.'

'Alarm aircraft!' shouted the starboard lookout and rang his indicator bell. 'Green seven zero, angle of sight one-five!'

And there they were, nine aircraft in a dark grey formation coming out over the coast and splitting up into pairs. From the beaches came a splutter of rifle and machine-gun fire and from the ships in the harbour and alongside the east mole heavier guns pumped shell and tracer into the sky. At first it seemed that *Vagabond* would not be attacked, but then two Ju 88s circled at three thousand feet and started a dive.

'Full ahead both engines!' Archie roared down the voice-pipe to the wheelhouse and, watching over his shoulder at the first of the diving aircraft, waited for it to straighten up for the attack before ordering, 'Starboard thirty!'

'All positions, *engage*!' shouted the gunnery officer and the multiple pom-poms opened fire, with the ship heeling right over as thirty degrees of rudder took effect. Two bombs – they could be clearly seen and looked like fifteen-inch shells – separated themselves from the enemy aircraft and fell forty yards clear to port, throwing up huge fountains of spray and sending a massive judder through the whole ship.

'Check-check-check!' bawled the gunnery officer, and pressed the check-fire bell. 'Shift target right! Aircraft green one-two-zero! *Engage!*'

With the ship still turning hard and all close-range weapons firing, another two bombs fell, one of them close enough to send shrapnel spattering against the bridge and funnel, and Archie saw a sudden look of surprise on his yeoman of signals' face.

'I think I copped one, sir' the yeoman managed, and then collapsed on the bridge duckboards.

'Take cover!' the first lieutenant bawled as the Junkers came in for another attack, and only Archie remained standing, bawling wheel orders down the voicepipe to reverse the turn.

They were firing cannon and machine guns this time. Shells clanked and banged and whined on the fo'c'sle and A turret. A man screamed. The stubby gun barrels of the multiple pom-poms jerked in rhythm, swinging round fast as the aircraft went overhead, spraying tracer in a curving line into the sky.

'From the chief stoker, sir. Steam pipe fracture in number two boiler room —'

'*Get that bloody two-pounder firing!*'

'He can only give you two hundred revs, sir —'

'Another aircraft over to starboard, sir!'

And then a sight more welcome than anything anyone aboard HMS *Vagabond* had ever seen: a single Spitfire diving down into the attack, screaming into a tightening turn behind the Ju 88 and sending out a ripple of machine-gun fire that tore the bomber apart in a single explosion so that a wing, the fuselage and the tail fell into the sea in three separate pieces.

On the east mole, the piermaster, Commander Jack Clouston, assessed the damage. About thirty bombs had been aimed at the ships alongside the mole but most of them had been wide, though the personnel ship *Canterbury*, the destroyer *Jaguar* and the minesweeping trawlers *Calvi* and *Polly Johnson* had suffered near misses and all had men on board with shrapnel wounds.

After the attack *Jaguar* left harbour with a load of troops, and while the wounded were being transferred to *Canterbury* more troops started coming along the mole to embark. Clouston told Lieutenant Bill, who was in charge of the six minesweeping trawlers alongside, to fill up his ships first, and he stationed officers abreast each with instructions to get all unwounded troops aboard; but they were reluctant to go aboard what they called 'fishing boats' and made various excuses to get into the larger ships.

Lieutenant Bill ran down the mole to where Clouston was berthing a large personnel ship, the *Crested Eagle*, inshore of the transport *Fenella*.

'Submit that we've got too many ships alongside, sir! They're a sitting target if Jerry comes over again. Suggest we tell the ships on the west side of the pier to lie off while we fill up the others.'

Clouston shook his head. 'We're expecting a very large body of troops any minute. We'll need every ship we can get alongside soon.'

'Aye aye, sir.'

Minutes later, the second big raid of the day came in. All ships opened fire and no damage was done to those berthed alongside. Twenty or thirty bombs were dropped, and these were divided between *Jaguar*, now clearing the harbour, the ships on the east mole, and two French destroyers on the opposite side of the harbour.

It was *Jaguar* that suffered the worst. Repeatedly shaken by near misses and riddled with shrapnel, steam pipes were fractured and fuel tanks ruptured. With her engines temporarily out of action, she began drifting onto the beach, and was towed clear just in time by the destroyer *Express*, who took off all her troops, leaving her to limp back empty to Dover.

After this attack, troops started coming down the pier in larger numbers, their progress hampered by the wounded and the slow progress of stretcher cases, but the ships began to fill up steadily and by six o'clock Lieutenant Bill's six trawlers were nearly ready to depart.

The third raid was an even bigger one. The bombers came over in waves of six or nine every few minutes and the whole attack was concentrated on the east mole. Of the trawlers berthed in three pairs between *Canterbury* and *Grenade* on the west side of the mole, *Polly Johnson* was damaged by near misses and *Calvi* was sunk. She sat on the bottom, her funnel sticking out of the water and the red ensign flying from the foremast. The old wooden steamer *Fenella* had her hull split open by a bomb that landed between her bow and the jetty and began to sink.

Berthed at the end of the mole on the west side, the destroyer *Grenade* was hit by two bombs. The first struck close to the bridge and penetrated three decks before exploding in one of the furnace fuel oil tanks. On the bridge, everyone was thrown four feet in the air as the ship was lifted out of the water, and a huge deluge of oil and water descended. Several men – some seriously injured – were blown overboard, and the first lieutenant shouted to them to swim back and return on board. Fire broke out and dense clouds of steam and smoke ascended into the sky. When a second bomb landed aft on X turret all the stern wires securing the ship parted and the stern went under water. The torpedo gunner, Mr Clare, had already ordered all ready-use ammunition lockers to be closed, and he now supervised the closing down and flooding of the magazine. Then he joined the first lieutenant, who was trying to get for'd and destroy the secret anti-submarine 'asdic' dome, but was beaten back by a fierce fire that was raging in the canteen flat.

Without sternrope or back spring, *Grenade*'s semi-submerged stern began to swing out and a Belgian trawler came alongside to pass lines and tow her clear before she sank and obstructed the berth. She was joined by *Polly Johnson* and *Brock*, and as the ship settled the surviving crew stepped aboard the two trawlers to safety.

There was panic among the troops now. They were climbing out of one ship and into another, and a large group had decided to head back along the mole to the shore.

They were stopped by Clouston who, with Lieutenant Bill at his side, turned to face them. Clouston, or 'JCC' as he was known, was a hulking athlete of Canadian parentage whose career had been marred some years before when his ship *Isis* went aground on the Turkish coast. A gunnery specialist, he had a reputation as a disciplinarian who drove himself harder than his subordinates and who, it was rumoured, used to do without a mattress and sleep on the bare iron springs of his bunk in order to toughen himself. But underneath the steel exterior lay a family man who was one of the most straightforward, kind and understanding of persons.

Facing the mob of soldiers, he drew his revolver and ordered Lieutenant Bill to do the same.

'These ships have come here to take you back to England, and that's what they're going to do!' he bellowed. 'I have six rounds here, and the lieutenant has another six. I'm a good shot, and he's a better one. That'll take care of twelve of you. Now get back on board those bloody ships!'

They turned back, and most went aboard the *Crested Eagle* which was berthed on the east side of the mole inshore of *Fenella*. *Crested Eagle* was a wooden paddle steamer which in better times had run pleasure excursions on the River Thames. With 600 troops and survivors on board, her paddlewheels started turning and, once clear of the mole, she headed east along the coast in order to follow the northerly Route Y. But minutes later three Stukas led by Major Oscar Dinort, one of General Wolfram von Richtofen's crack pilots, screamed down, and she was hit and set on fire.

With thousands of troops on the beaches looking on in horror, *Crested Eagle* went up like a torch. Her tar-caulked wooden decks blazing, ammunition exploding and men, alight from top to toe, dancing in agony upon her decks, she drove up hard on the sands opposite the big Zuydecoote Infirmary, whose long imposing buildings of red brick dominate the beach near Bray Dunes.

Many were burned to death. Those who could escaped over the side. For one, a gunner called Chandler, it was a case of full circle. He had been in 'Clouston's Queue' on the mole since early morning, had waited his turn to embark on the *Fenella* and when she sank had transferred to *Crested Eagle*. Now, wading out of the surf and onto dry land again, he was amazed to find skin hanging from his hands in shreds from the burns he had received, and was bundled into an ambulance and taken off to the field hospital in the Casino at Malo-les-Bains.

Among the ships lying off the beaches there was more carnage. With eight landing craft on board and a hold full of four-inch shells, the 6,000-ton liner *Clan McAlister* had arrived earlier in the day and had been ordered to lie off and await orders. Having lowered six of the eight landing craft successfully, she was then attacked and hit three times. A fire started in one of her holds and the destroyer *Malcolm* came alongside and put Lieutenants Cox and Mellis aboard to fight it. Ignoring the risk of the ammunition exploding, they played hoses on the fire until it went out and *Malcolm* then took off *Clan McAlister*'s wounded and parted company. But the Stukas came back, and this time the steering gear was put out of action. A minesweeper – the *Pangbourne* – came alongside and *Clan McAlister*'s master, Captain Mackie, agreed to abandon ship – 'temporarily'. But the loss of the cargo liner turned out to be a blessing in disguise: sinking in shallow water just off the beaches, the ship remained upright and from the air appeared to be still afloat and engaged in evacuation operations, so that during the following four days *Clan McAlister* acted as a lure, drawing repeated attacks from the Luftwaffe and causing them to waste tons of bombs trying to sink her.

viii

Two of the Southern Railway ships, *Lorina* and *Normannia*, went down that afternoon, and off La Panne beach, another famous name was hit by bombs. The *Gracie Fields*, a paddle minesweeper, had 750 troops on board and in the confusion of escaping steam and a jammed rudder, she went round and round in circles with smoke and steam billowing up from her. Two Dutch schuits came to her assistance and the minesweeper *Pangbourne* – also damaged – passed a tow. Later, limping back across the Channel, *Gracie Fields* transferred the last of the troops and crew on board before the tow was let go and she was left to sink.

After working all day off the beaches to collect 600 men, the paddle minesweeper *Waverly* was attacked soon after sailing for Dover by twelve Heinkels. For half an hour she dodged and weaved her way through the rain of bombs until, after many near misses, she lost her rudder and, unable to take evasive action, suffered a direct hit that passed straight through the ship and made a six-foot hole in her bottom. Out of control and sinking, she continued to fight, with the troops on board using massed rifle fire against the aircraft, and the ship's twelve-pounder and Lewis guns pounding away to the last second. She sank within sixty seconds of the order to abandon being given, and although the Thames Special Service ship *Golden Eagle* arrived on the scene with drifters and a tug, many of the crew and over three hundred of the troops were lost.

On the beaches themselves, the work of getting men into the boats and out to the ships continued all day. Another paddle minesweeper, the *Oriole*, having no motor boat to bring men out was eventually beached in order to get the men aboard. With two hours of flood tide still to run, the captain, Lieutenant Davies RNVR, pointed her at a crowded part of the beach, sent all hands aft to lift the bows and steamed at full speed for the shore, dropping two seven-hundredweight kedge anchors astern before driving the ship hard aground on the gently shelving sand. The soldiers waded out to her with the water up to their shoulders; ropes were thrown down, five or six men would grab at it, and then it was a case of persuading some to let go so that they could be pulled aboard in twos and threes. The *Oriole* remained beached all day and over three thousand men passed over her to safety; finally, after beating off several air attacks, *Oriole* loaded up with 700 soldiers and nurses from a field hospital, floated off at high tide and got safely back to England.

x

While evacuation continued all day from the beaches, by six o'clock that evening, Dunkirk harbour was effectively out of action. Apart from a jumble of sunken and burning ships, the inner harbours were empty. On the east mole, movement of troops had stopped. The trawler *Calvi* and the passenger ship *Fenella* had sunk at their berths. The mole itself was cratered along its length and parts of the walkway were gone. Two ships, manoeuvring frantically to get clear, had rammed it and caused further damage. Corpses floated in the oily water. Stray dogs, left behind by soft-hearted Tommies who had befriended them during the retreat, barked and whined and scavenged for food.

While Clouston's shore party of naval ratings worked to clear away the debris and salvaged timber and metal from the wrecks to repair the mole, one more ship arrived along-side. This was the *King Orry*, an armed merchantmen which had been repeatedly attacked by dive-bombers during the day and was now limping in to transfer her wounded, send her crew to shelter and make herself seaworthy before attempting a return to England. Soon after midnight, having shored up sagging bulkheads with timber and stopped up the holes in her side with soft-wood wedges, she departed, but an hour or so later she rolled over and sank in the deep-water approach channel to the harbour with a loss of nine officers and men.

xi

In the Dynamo headquarters, Captain Denny had drafted the general signal issuing the plan for the night, and he now stood on the admiral's balcony while Ramsay, who sat tipping his chair back in the last of the sunlight, vetted the wording before authorizing its transmission.

'"Evacuation of troops to continue at full speed during the night,"' Ramsay read aloud, and then made a couple of small amendments. '"Evacuation of *British* troops to continue at *maximum* speed during the night. If supply of personnel vessels . . ." no, "if *adequate* supply of personnel vessels cannot be maintained to Dunkirk east pier, destroyers will be sent there as well. All other craft . . . all other craft *except hospital carriers* to embark from beach which is extended from one mile east of Dunkirk to one mile east of La Panne."'

Ramsay paused. Down in the harbour one of the old V and W destroyers was being manoeuvred by tugs to a buoy. Was it *Verity* or *Vagabond*? *Vagabond*, most probably – she had been due back about an hour before. Archie Trendle-Home. A bit slap-dash, but the morale of his ship's company was high, unlike that of *Verity*. He was particularly concerned about *Verity*. She had taken part in the Boulogne operation, and two days previously had been subjected to intensive shelling. Her captain had been seriously wounded and the morale of her ship's company had broken. One man had committed suicide and several had stated that they would refuse duty if ordered back to Dunkirk. Ramsay's old friend, Vice Admiral Sir James Somerville, had gone on board and talked to the men who, after being rested, had been persuaded to continue with the operation. Now, he had just had news that *Verity* had that day come under sustained air attack and had been repeatedly straddled by bombs.

How much longer could the destroyer crews hold out? They were under immense strain already, and the only way of keeping them going had been to reassure them that each day's operation would be the last. His own staff were similarly exhausted. They were dealing with upwards of two thousand signals a day, and nearly every single one was of high priority. In the Dynamo Room, officers were falling asleep while they worked. His flag lieutenant looked like a ghost; his secretary had suddenly become old. Every member of the staff was already strained far beyond any efficiency limit imposed in peacetime.

He forced himself to concentrate on the task in hand.

'"Whole length is divided into three equal parts referred to as La Panne, Bray, Malo, from east to west with a mile gap between each part."' He glanced up. 'Can't we be more precise? Where are the troop concentrations?'

'La Panne and Bray have troop concentration points at each end and in the middle, Malo at each end, sir.'

Ramsay wrote that in verbatim, then added, '"These points should be tended by inshore craft. Pass the message by visual signalling to ships not equipped with WT as opportunity offers."' Then he signed the signal to authorize it and Denny took it off to the signals office for encoding and transmission.

Soon afterwards, when Ramsay's signal had already gone out, the direct line telephone from the Admiralty rang in the Dynamo Room. It was answered by Third Officer Trendle-Home, who grabbed a signal pad and took down the message

as it came in: FROM LA PANNE MILITARY VIA WAR OF-
FICE AND ADMIRALTY. DUNKIRK HARBOUR BLOCKED
BY DAMAGED SHIPS. ALL EVACUATION MUST THERE-
FORE BE EFFECTED BY BEACHES.

Minutes later, another signal came in, this time from
Captain Tennant, SNO Dunkirk. Though garbled, its message was clear enough and confirmed the Dover staff's worst
fears. Dunkirk was under continuous bombing, one destroyer was sinking, one transport with troops on board was
damaged and it was impossible to embark more troops,
although the pier was undamaged.

Unable to obtain any up-to-date information on the state
of the mole, and with ships already on their way to Dunkirk,
Ramsay was faced with an agonizing decision. Feeling that
he had no option but to act on the strength of the two
messages, he ordered all ships approaching Dunkirk not to
enter the harbour but to collect troops from the shore;
and the drifters and minesweepers which were about to be
despatched to embark troops from the east mole overnight
were diverted to the beaches. Only later was it realized that
a valuable opportunity had been missed: the east mole was
in fact perfectly accessible and there were no air raids that
night.

Ten thousand troops could have been lifted from the mole
in the hours of darkness with little loss to embarkation from
the beaches. In the event, only four trawlers and a yacht
went alongside.

To prevent recurrences of this and similar muddles, a
Senior Officer Afloat had already been appointed. This was
Rear Admiral Frederic Wake-Walker, who had sailed that
evening aboard the destroyer *Esk* with a brief to take charge
of all ships arriving at Dunkirk and provide a much-needed
link between the naval shore party under Tennant, the ships
operating from Dunkirk, and the staff at Dover.

But naval operations were further handicapped that night,
and this time by the Admiralty itself. Because of the high
damage rate among destroyers and the need to retain a pool

of serviceable warships to provide defence of the British mainland against the German invasion that was now expected within a few weeks, the First Sea Lord directed that, with immediate effect, all the modern destroyers of the H, I and J classes were to be withdrawn from Operation Dynamo. With all the G class already out of action, Ramsay was therefore left with just fifteen destroyers at his disposal, and these were largely of the old war-horse variety, whose heavier anti-aircraft guns could not be elevated more than forty-five degrees and were therefore of little use against dive-bombers.

xii

. . . We set off at 0500 hours in the three vehicles. At Furnes I arrange for Bourner to cover me with the Bren gun in case the Belgian is still there. But the bridge has already been prepared for demolition and a party from 225 Field Company is standing by.

We stop at each bridge and I drop off the demolition party and the explosives, briefing the NCO on what to do. This takes time but nothing can go wrong. It is mid-morning before we reach the last bridge. Being a railway bridge the only wheeled access to it is by the road which here runs on the wrong side of the canal and upon which German troops might appear at any time. How am I going to get the demolition party away? Fortunately on my way back I find an abandoned Renault car in working order which I leave with them.

I work up the bridges again from Furnes to see how preparations are progressing. While giving a hand to evacuate an abutment, a party of Belgian troops marches up the road towards the enemy carrying a white flag – to the jeers of the British. There is a small wooden bridge for which I have no NCO so I set light to it and am duly rebuked by Brigadier Phipps who arrives at that moment for attracting the attention of the enemy. No burning is to be permitted.

Once the preparations are complete I leave an NCO and one man on each bridge as firing party with orders to fire and withdraw if the bridge is in danger of capture by the enemy. Assure them I will send out rations, but before I have to do so bridges are taken over by 225 Field Company and I pick my parties up.

The sector is now humming with activity. There is not enough room for a whole army's transport. In a field an RASC unit is having a splendid time lining up its lorries along a drainage canal and knocking them in one by one. A column of thick-armoured French tanks with tiny guns stands deserted along the verge. The Cameronians have moved into our wood. We have collected a large pile of wire and shovels which no lorry has been recently to collect. Have we been forgotten?

We entertain a stray infantry officer to dinner, and afterwards I set off on my motorcycle to report to the CRE. It is now dark and I stop to ask the way of a military policeman. His hand clamps like a vice on my shoulder, and then relaxes. 'Christ, sir; thought you were a Jerry!'

After a long search around Coxyde I find Colonel Coxwell Rogers up a dark flight of stairs and he welcomes me with courtesy. I am to keep my section in the wood and the stores will be collected. The Division will be withdrawing from the perimeter for embarkation in the next day or two and the HQ Section of 59 Field Company will revert to its own command. It will be wise to stay away from the beaches as long as possible.

Back to the wood in the small hours . . .

The telephone messages in plain language, the radio signals in encrypted groups, the cries for help made by signal lantern or loud hailer whether from beach to ship, ship to shore or ship to ship continued in a vast unabating torrent, hour after hour, night after day, day after night.

Immediate. From HMS *Hebe* to Rear Admiral Dover.

Immediate. From NOIC Ramsgate to Admiralty.

Immediate. From SNO Dunkirk to Vice Admiral Dover.

Immediate. From Vice Admiral Dover to All Ships.

There was no end to the signals. It was impossible to log and record them all. Some were overtaken by events before they were received. Some were garbled. Some were pearls of tactical wisdom. Some were cut ominously short by enemy action:

. . . Third Corps BEF and C–in–C are now at La Panne. Make every effort to concentrate all destroyers and light craft in neighbourhood with object of embarking this force as soon as possible.

Senior officers of groups at beaches are to detail ships to land adequate beach parties to assist troops to embark. Men are not to be left behind by their ships but to be relieved as necessary when ships sail.

No enemy interference at present. Embarking 2000 per hour. This can be kept up providing supply of transports is maintained. Swell prevents use of beach (corrupt group) to Dunkirk. Any air attack would be disastrous. Maximum fighter protection essential. Passenger transport, not loaded, mined and sunk about 2 miles east of Dunkirk pier light.

Tell Captain Bush in Motor Torpedo Boat 68 to use HMS *Hebe* as his headquarters. Frequent reports are necessary as to situation and requirements from beach.

Food and water should be sent to Dunkirk as soon as possible, also a guard for control of traffic. Army are quite unable to help or organize anything. Keep on sending ships. Cannot west channel be used. Good medical officer with staff required. Army unable to provide.

Twenty Thames barges in tow of five tugs expected at Ramsgate 1730/29th. For consideration that these ships might be used as piers.

Enemy troops reported north-east of Nieuport. Request destroy concentrations on roads north-east of town. Attack not to be made west of railway-coast-Nieuport-Dixmude.

SNO Dunkirk states enemy shelling pier with shore batteries from south-east. Request bombers to counter — vital.

Rear Admiral Wake-Walker is proceeding in *Esk* to *Hebe* to carry out duty of Senior Naval Officer Dunkirk in charge of all evacuation arrangements.

During present operations off Belgian coast where many small craft are present, destroyers are not to stop to render assistance to ships in distress.

Dunkirk heavily bombed at 1330. Objectives troops and transports. Request fighter protection may be increased. Embarkation being carried out normally now.

Stick it a little longer. You alone can save our army.

Investigate urgently provision of additional small craft which can be made available within 48 hours from all parts of your command for Operation Dynamo.

French troops beginning to arrive at Dunkirk and on beaches, but there are only three French destroyers and one French vessel to evacuate them. Impress on Admiral Darlan necessity for large numbers of destroyers, passenger ships and small craft.

Naval shipping plan approaching maximum efficiency. Subject to weather and reasonable immunity enemy action expect lift about 16,000 Dunkirk and 15,000 from beaches. Surf has subsided and beaches being worked today at reduced rate. Total arrivals during 12 hours to noon 29th are 13,711. Total since start of plan to 1500/29th is 39,000 disembarked and 7,500 en route for home, or 46,500 in all.

Continuous bombing for one and a half hours. One destroyer sinking, one transport with troops on board damaged. No damage to pier. Impossible at present to embark more troops.

Can you confirm harbour is blocked.

Bombing of beaches and pier Dunkirk has now commenced without evident opposition from fighters. If they hit the pier embarkation will become very slow. Beaches between La Panne and Dunkirk are covered with troops congregated in large masses. Very slow embarkation taking place from eastern beach. French authorities at Dunkirk feel strongly that they are defending Dunkirk for us to evacuate, which is largely true. Perimeter must be strongly held, food and water issued and bombing of Dunkirk pier prevented. There is no other alternative to take off more than a fifth of men now on beach before they are bombed continuously.

Danger of enemy mechanized forces working along

beach and cutting off BEF. Be prepared to engage enemy forces so encountered by day or night.

More ships and boats urgently required at west beach.

Entrance to Dunkirk harbour practicable. Obstructions exits towards outer side of east arm.

While harbour remains practicable situation at west beach would be greatly relieved if continuous stream of destroyers was available to enter Dunkirk to embark troops.

Essential to have more ships and boats as there are still many hundreds of soldiers on beach.

Channel is not blocked but large gap exists in eastern arm so that destroyers must come alongside to landward of gap. Ready for first destroyer immediately.

Destroyers can be received at Dunkirk at a higher rate.

No French craft off beach.

Following received from Captain Tennant. MTBs will be best to evacuate naval personnel except for SNO and brigadiers will probably remain to control final stage. My communications increasingly difficult.

East pier of Dunkirk practicable. All wrecks visible. East side east pier also practicable at high water.

Pass to War Office from Military Dunkirk. Absolutely imperative that minimum five hospital carriers report Dunkirk otherwise several hundred wounded cannot be accommodated or treated. Cases have occurred of carriers arriving off port and failing to enter. Can this be remedied. Essential to know time of arrival at least two hours in advance.

Am being shelled from shore batteries off Nieuport Buoy.

Opinion has been expressed to me that Germans could now take Dunkirk at any time they please but they prefer not to in order to continue their attacks on our army and fleet. I cannot of course estimate the accuracy of this view.

Try going alongside inside or outside east arm, Dunkirk pier, to embark troops. Report how things are.

Have no MTB and can only communicate to UK by French wireless station or when your destroyers are in sight if conditions remain as at present. A destroyer alongside continuously for embarkation would be a magnificent help. The moment bombing starts all must shove off.

Food scarce amongst military remaining ashore. Request 40 cases corned beef and 40 cases biscuit may be made ready for embarkation on my arrival at Dover.

Please inform Admiral Darlan that the urgent requirement for evacuation from the beaches is boats for ferrying the men from the beach to the ships.

Personal from First Sea Lord. Have you personally investigated condition on all beaches as Lord Gort has just telephoned me that there are no craft or boats of any kind off the eastern beaches where he is. Report immediately any deficiences for the rapid evacuation from Dunkirk and beaches.

Ships urgently needed abreast of La Panne.

In view of large number of vessels and boats operating tonight, fire must not be opened unless hostile character of vessels has definitely been established.

Expect arrive Margate Pier with about 500 troops on board.

Proceed, *Keith* to Bray, *Winchelsea* to Dunkirk by Route X and continue evacuation.

Expect to arrive 1600 with 450 troops.

Being shelled off Calais.

Enemy bombing off Calais.

As far as possible ensure that troops and small craft who may not have been instructed do daylight passage on Route X only.

Enemy shelling Dunkirk east pier.

Am being fired on by shore batteries off Calais.

Am on fire Dunkirk.

All ships to use Route X.

War Office have placed 7 30-knot motor launches at your disposal and are sending them to Ramsgate today. Naval crews are being sent to man them.

Crews of Tugs *Sun VII* and *Sun X* refuse to tow barges to Dunkirk. Please arrange for two new crews to be sent to Dover, crew consists of 11 men.

From interviews British officers have had with Admiral Abrial it appears that he is not aware of allied policy, particularly regarding the evacuation of British and French armies now in vicinity of Dunkirk. Please inform Admiral Darlan that we feel it would help matters if this were done.

Admiralty appreciate request, but reject. Impossible to ensure in present circumstances that foreigners are excluded from vessels evacuating personnel from France. Arrangements at landing ports are being described.

Navy are still making maximum effort, having allocated seven new destroyers today and providing six fresh destroyer crews to replace those exhausted.

Despite intense bombardment and air attack, 4000 troops have been embarked during the last hour. Every possible effort will be made as I consider Dunkirk will be untenable by tomorrow morning. Embarkation from beach will be continued until last moment but I depend on large ships and destroyers at pier tonight.

Army eastern beach being shelled and evacuation there impracticable. Evacuation from Dunkirk proceeding. Harbour being shelled at intervals. Am returning to Dover with 1400 troops. Am ordering some small craft to eastern beach.

All shore officers excepting Lt Cdr Ewing allocated to Operation Dynamo have been ordered to proceed to Tilbury for allocation between 20 motor lifeboats and 100 pulling lifeboats.

Ships meeting in bad visibility should not hesitate to use sound signals and dimmed navigation lights to avoid collision, any additional risk of contact with enemy being accepted.

25 merchant ship motor lifeboats and 46 rowing ditto in tow of six tugs leaving Tilbury from now till completely manned by volunteers and naval ratings. On arrival Southend they will be routed immediately to Ramsgate where first two should arrive about 0600 Friday. Two days fresh food and two days iron rations per man. Spare fuel and drinking water.

Dutch Government have placed following motor boats at Portsmouth at disposal of Admiralty. M73, M74 and TV speedboat. Should be sent to Ramsgate forthwith.

Small longshore motor fishing boats now being requisitioned through Ministry of Fisheries from Brixham to the Wash, to proceed to Dover or Ramsgate whichever nearer.

HM Yachts *Christobel II, Caleta, Amulree* and *Glala* sailed for Ramsgate.

Strongly recommend destroyers messdecks have at least one battleship size scuttle on each side. It is reported that many men were trapped on messdeck of *Afridi. Grenade* had two such scuttles fitted privately and they saved many of the crew.

MESSAGE ENDS = +

THIRTY

Thursday, 30 May. A grey, overcast dawn came up. Thousands upon thousands of men – dishevelled, unshaven, hungry, thirsty – huddled among the dunes. From the rubble of Dunkirk, four massive pillars of smoke ascended to the sky. As the tide ebbed, the queues of men shuffled out over the glistening beaches, many wading out to stand waist-deep in the water in order to be first in the queue for the boats.

But where were the boats? There still seemed pathetically few, and almost every one that took another load of soldiers out to the ships lying off the shore carried with it the same message: 'Tell them to send more boats!'

Many of the men had been on the beaches for two or three nights now, and though discipline and morale was still intact, fatigue was beginning to take its toll and tempers were fraying. The arrival of thousands of French troops was causing arguments over which parts of the beach belonged to which army. From the most senior generals down to the lowliest soldiers, it was firmly believed – depending on your nationality – either that the French had no right to ask to be taken off in British ships or that the British were saving their own skins at the expense of French lives.

This was the day that the last units swarmed inside the perimeter, and until their arrival few of the troops had any idea of the magnitude of the defeat. Each company or unit had believed that it was being sent back for some special reason – either because it had to prop up a less competent unit, or that its obsolete tanks or weapons were at last to be replaced or that it had already fought so bravely that it was due for a rest. All the way back – whether from Louvain or Lille, Arras or La Bassée – they had reassured themselves with rumours: that on another sector the allies had broken the Siegfried Line and advanced forty miles into Germany; that thirty thousand Royal Marines were due to be landed at Dunkirk, or that they were being taken off by the navy in order to be landed further along the French coast, supplied with new weapons and thrown back into the attack.

Now, witnessing the wreckage of so many vehicles and weapons all around them; seeing the stretcher parties collecting the dead and wounded and the ambulances going back and forth along the promenade; looking at the smoking ruins in the town; hearing the crack and thunder of artillery and diving for cover as each fresh wave of bombers approached, the reality of the situation came up as grey and sombre as the dawn. They had been defeated. The great alliance between Britain and France, the Maginot Line, the building of pillboxes through the winter, the exercises, the pep talks, the gas drills, the route marches and weapon practices – they had all been for nothing. In three short weeks Jerry had cut them in half, surrounded them and pushed them into the sea.

And there still weren't enough boats.

ii

Blaxland's division had established a control post, as it was optimistically termed, in the village of Bray Dunes, from which a vehicle jetty was being built. This seemed to provide proof that they were to be evacuated, but although everyone was confident that they were going to England, there was an ominous dearth of details about how or when. The beach controllers merely said that units would be notified when their turn came, and in the meantime they were to dig positions just in case the enemy arrived before the navy.

Bertie, one of Blaxland's fellow officers, declared that the town in the distance must be Dunkirk, and that the swarms of aircraft they had seen the day before must have been attacking it. No one knew much about Dunkirk. Blaxland asked if it was in France or Belgium. Bertie, a university man, said France.

While the three company sergeant majors set out to draw the meagre rations available from the battalion supply point, Blaxland set his men about digging with their helmets to conceal themselves from the air. This kept the men occupied and by the time they had finished the CSMs had acquired some bully beef and biscuits and had brewed tea.

Quite a large number of people could be seen strolling about the beach in a casual way, and Blaxland began to feel increasingly irritated that no one really cared how long they remained sitting on the dunes. In exasperation he decided to find out whether the motor launch, which was still rocking up and down in a few feet of water, was usable. He had waded into the water up to the knees when there was a bellow from behind him. He turned round. It was a major of the Royal Engineers.

'If you lay a finger on that launch I'll bloody well place you under arrest!' he shouted and Blaxland crept miserably back to the dunes. Mysteriously, the launch remained untouched by any finger for the rest of the day. It appeared to have been put there by the major to play the part of Tantalus.

After a further hour or so, Blaxland took another stroll. Suddenly a shell gave its evil swish and crash, landing on the beach at the water's edge. This came as a shock: weather had stopped air operations and, as there had been no other enemy interference throughout the day, it had been assumed that this part of the beach was out of range of the light artillery that must have sent this one over. Two more arrived, and Blaxland sprinted to the dunes for cover. The first hole was full, but he heard the distant poops of gunfire as he reached it and jumped in on top of two CSMs. There was a whistle, very close, and the explosion made the whole trench shudder. Blaxland felt the draught from flying splinters and was pleasantly surprised to find himself unhurt.

From the beach came a desperate cry. 'Water! I want water! Help!'

It was a revealing test of courage to see who would be first to break cover and render the wounded assistance. By the time Blaxland dared move, a war commissioned officer, Buckwell, was kneeling beside the man – a gunner – who lay on his back with a slit across his stomach. He kept yelling for water as if more in rage than in pain. Blaxland found himself despising him for making such a din. Then the gunner's jaws snapped suddenly shut. He was quite obviously dead.

Blaxland stared at him, and despised himself for his own reluctance to assist him. He had felt revolted by his agony and now shrank from feeling his pulse to confirm that he was dead. Buckwell did that and Buckwell put his hand into the man's battledress blouse and took out his paybook so that details could be reported. He then asked who would help him scoop out a grave, and at least this was something Blaxland felt able to do; but even so he was glad that others were willing to lift the body into it and fill the grave. They used his helmet as a gravestone, and Buckwell even found a piece of chalk and wrote his name on it.

Blaxland's mercury had sunk to its nadir, but an hour's digging to improve protection worked wonders and the unexpected appearance of the French liaison officer with a bottle of wine and a tin of *pâté de foie gras* improved morale considerably. The CSMs had given the officers a tin of meat and vegetable stew and this, added to *pâté* and crumbled biscuit, was cooked up by Buckwell's batman, an enterprising old soldier called Thirst whose greeting on appointment was invariably the same: 'I'm Thirst, you have me, sir.' The meal was divided into five portions and washed down with wine drunk from the bottle.

To cheer them up further, Bertie came back from the control post with news that the battalion might be called for embarkation during the night. He also said that the shells that had tormented the beach had been identified as coming from abandoned 25-pounders and that since no more had arrived it was to be assumed that the ammunition had run out.

Blaxland was by now feeling so light-hearted that he suggested they might nip into Dunkirk to see what the crumpet was up to.

'I rather doubt the crumpet's up to much, old boy,' Bertie replied.

Blaxland felt quite bucked: it was the first time Bertie had called him old boy for quite a while.

iii

Though Blaxland and thousands of others would have had difficulty in believing it, the dynamo was gathering momentum. While Ramsay's staff worked flat out to keep the flow of ships arriving at Dunkirk, the staff of the Small Ships Pool, under Admiral Preston, worked round the clock to provide the small craft Ramsay needed if his plan to take the last of the fighting troops from the eastern beaches was to work; and if any single person can be said to have masterminded the assembling of the armada of little ships, that man was Paymaster Lieutenant Commander Garrett, RNVR, the secretary to Admiral Preston.

It had been Garrett who had dealt with the flood of offers of small craft which had come in since the BBC appeal two weeks before, and his methodical indexing now made it possible to call all these craft forward at short notice. On the telephone for sixty hours almost non-stop. Garrett rang up individual yachtsmen in their clubs and fixed Admiralty cars to take them to Ramsgate, arranging special requisition forms for petrol which he signed on his own initiative so that the hundred or more boats in the upper reaches of the Thames could be fuelled from local garages and sent down-river.

Sheerness and Southend were where most of the little ships from the Thames first congregated, and the first arrivals were typical of the whole armada: a dozen or so motor yachts, nicely equipped and smartly maintained by proud, individual owners; a cluster of cheap conversion jobs, the work of amateurs who had turned old ships' lifeboats into cabin cruisers in which to take weekend trips on the quiet waters of the up-river reaches; half a dozen varnished Thames river launches with their rows of slatted seats and white-painted lifebuoys slung around the upper guardrails.

The crews and their officers were as miscellaneous a lot as the craft they manned. First arrived a group of RNVR sub lieutenants direct from training school, some of whom had been taken from a class in the middle of a lecture on practical pilotage. Many of these had never seen the inside of a naval dockyard in their lives, and yet they clambered over the little ships, bawled for their requirements of food, fuel and water and set to work on the task in hand as if they had been doing it all their lives.

Next came another group, this time of newly promoted sub lieutenants. Little more than schoolboys, they had been serving as midshipmen only a week or two before, yet each was possessed of that indescribable sang froid and cheerful discipline which are the hallmarks of the British naval officer.

Lastly – and only a matter of minutes before the time of departure – came the crews: Royal Fleet Reserve men in the first batch – tough, stout-hearted and disciplined. No time to pick and choose: stoker ratings first, one to a boat to man the engines.

Then the seamen. 'Right, you lot,' the chief petty officer in charge said as soon as they were out of the lorry and fallen in on the quayside, 'Swarm over those boats, and wherever you find an officer ask him if he needs a crew. Three men to the larger and two each to the smaller.'

Within ten minutes of the crews' arrival, the first convoy was ready for sea – manned, victualled, fuelled and equipped with all but arms. Off they went, unaware of the inferno that awaited them. Only later, when the returning troops filled the depots with sand-fouled arms, were weapons available for the protection of these craft.

Still the boats and the officers and the crews continued to arrive: fishermen, lightermen, merchant seamen. And now the civilian volunteers came in increasing numbers, too.

Many were never able to explain exactly why they volunteered. The politicians and generals had cocked it up all over again, that was the sum of it, and for once ordinary people saw that they could do something to bring the soldiers home. It was as if the Admiralty, like the Sorcerer's Apprentice, had started something it could not control: a spirit of defiance that had lurked unused for centuries.

It was this same spirit that had united the nation four hundred years before when King Philip of Spain had sent his Armada to invade England in 1588; the same that had fought with the Conqueror in 1066 and with Hengist and Horsa six hundred years before that in 455. It was perhaps the spirit that had been first forged in 43 AD when Aulus Plautius landed in Kent with forty thousand men.

Every four or five centuries, Britain had been invaded or threatened with invasion. Now it was happening again. No wonder the individuals who risked so much to take their boats across to Dunkirk could not later explain why they did what they did. It just seemed the decent thing to do.

iv

Geoffrey Pringle had set out from Teddington at dawn the previous day, in company with several other cabin cruisers and a small convoy of tugs which were taking strings of lifeboats and lighters down the Thames. He had never before experienced anything like this: sailing his own boat singlehanded gave him a tremendous sense of freedom and individuality, and sailing in company with so many other boats like his own created a sense of brotherhood and camaraderie that he had never imagined possible.

Arriving at Southend soon after midday, the private owners were told that their boats were to remain there until a naval crew arrived to take them on to Ramsgate.

'Why can't we take them to Ramsgate ourselves?' Pringle asked. 'It's only thirty-odd miles. I don't know about anyone else, but I can be there by sunset.' So they let them go, and Pringle had another happy four hours at the wheel of his beloved *Daisy Bells*.

Going alongside Ramsgate was not such a happy experience, however. The harbour was packed out, and Pringle entered without permission from Captain Wharton, who was acting as piermaster. Finding himself in the way of a coal-burning tug with a tall funnel which was manoeuvring in the harbour, and bellowed at from all sides through megaphones, Pringle became flustered and put his engines full astern. He noticed a berthing line in the water just too late, and before he could get the engine in neutral several turns of rope were wrapped round the propeller shafts. This pleased the navy not at all, and Pringle was treated to some saline language from a three-badge able seaman who looked as if he had stepped straight off a packet of Player's cigarettes. Red-faced at his own ineptitude, he was eventually pushed alongside by a harbour launch, and was told to report his arrival to Captain Phillimore, the Naval Officer In Charge.

The NOIC's offices were in a building on the seafront about a hundred yards from the inner harbour, and Pringle was dealt with by a lieutenant RNVR who gave him a chit for fuel, water and iron rations. Pringle told him about the warp round his screw.

'Send one of your crew over the side,' he was told.

'I haven't got a crew.'

'Why not? What's happened to them? Have they walked off?'

'No, I brought my boat down from Teddington single-handed.'

The lieutenant seemed less impressed than Pringle had expected. 'Well, you must have a crew. There're plenty of volunteers around, just take a couple. There's a convoy of small craft leaving at thirteen hundred tomorrow. Be ready to leave by midday.'

'Not until then? I thought this was an emergency!'

The lieutenant did not seem to hear him. 'Next skipper, please!' he shouted, and another civilian came forward with his boat's details.

Pringle went out into the sunshine and stood on the quayside. Boats were arriving and departing, lorries were unloading stores, masts were being unshipped, machine guns fitted and sandbags placed on the roofs of wheelhouses.

'Hullo there!' said a voice at his side, and he turned to find a large, amiable-looking young man in a windcheater. 'I saw you come into harbour just now. *Daisy Belle* isn't it?'

Pringle was still raw from the tongue-lashing he had received from the piermaster and wasn't feeling well disposed to anyone, least of all brash young Americans.

'I am the owner of *Daisy Belle*, yes.'

'And you're in need of a hand clearing that prop, right?'

Pringle didn't like to admit that if he tried to clear the screw himself he would almost certainly bring on an attack of asthma.

'I think I need a diver to do that.'

'A diver? You don't need a diver. I'll do it for you with a deep breath and a sharp knife!'

Pringle was about to decline the offer. 'That's very good of you –' he started, but the young man held out his hand and it seemed churlish not to accept it.

'The name's Odell,' he said. 'You just got yourself a crew.'

THIRTY-ONE

General Alan Brooke had received orders to hand over command of 2 Corps and return to England, and he spent his last morning at La Panne visiting his troops and reviewing the arrangements made for the defence of the eastern sector of the perimeter. The 3rd and 4th divisions were in good shape – twenty-five thousand men in all. But the 5th, which by its defence of the Ypres-Comines canal had saved the BEF, had been reduced to little more than a thousand fighting troops.

He visited the beaches. At Bray, the Royal Engineers were improvising a pier by driving lorries down into the water, but there were still hardly any small boats available and the chances of getting so many men to safety seemed remote. What weighed heavy on Brooke's mind was that thousands of men from the service regiments would have to be evacuated before the best fighting troops – the men most urgently needed to defend Britain against invasion – could be lifted from the beaches.

Surveying the crowds of men, the wrecks sticking up out of the water and the abandoned guns and vehicles, Brooke feared that with the evacuation going so slowly, his corps was as good as doomed.

He found Major General Bernard Montgomery in a tented headquarters among the dunes. Struggling with a sense of guilt that he was deserting his troops at a time when he was most needed, Brooke issued his final orders.

'You will take over as corps commander,' he told Montgomery, 'and Brigadier Anderson will take over your division. Lieutenant Colonel Horrocks will take over from Anderson . . .'

Suddenly it was too much: Brooke broke down and wept.

Gort was also slipping into depression. Sitting alone in the villa at La Panne, he had made up his mind to stay with the rearguard to the end. He saw it as a question of honour: the BEF had been entrusted to him, and he could not desert it. He was also very bitter: he had never had faith in Gamelin's defensive strategy, but had felt obliged to go along with it, hoping that the guts and stamina of the British soldier would make up for the BEF's lack of modern equipment. It very nearly had: wherever his troops had been properly supported on the flanks and had been supplied with enough ammunition, they had been able to resist the German attacks and even thrust them back. The field commanders had given a similarly good account of themselves, and he was proud of them. They had never wavered or lost their nerve. They had not wrung their hands or burst into tears or wailed that they were breaking up with fatigue. It had been their support and loyalty that had enabled him to stand out against the Weygand Plan, which he was still sure would have ended in a far more humiliating defeat than the present one.

How he envied the battalion and company commanders whose privilege it would be to fight the last rearguard action! How tempting it was to go now and join them, to fight alongside them as he had done in the Great War – to handle a rifle again, or lead a last charge, revolver in hand, against impossible odds!

iii

Lord Munster, one of Gort's young aides, knew what was in his C-in-C's mind and was determined to stop him. He had left La Panne beach the night before in a naval whaler. Without changing his sodden clothes he had gone straight to Whitehall to call on the Prime Minister and give a first-hand report on the situation.

Churchill had given him some dry clothes and was now

wallowing in his bath while the young peer sat on the bathstool beside him and made his report.

'For the C-in-C to be taken prisoner would be a huge propaganda coup for the Germans,' Munster was saying. 'But Lord Gort doesn't see it that way. He seems quite set on the idea of sacrificing himself for the sake of honour.'

For a while longer, Churchill lay like a massive pink baby in the soap suds; then there was a sudden tidal wave as he stood up and began to towel himself dry. Munster was bidden to follow him into the bedroom, where Churchill got back into bed and began to draft personal instructions for his C-in-C.

He directed that Gort continue to defend the present position to the utmost in order to cover maximum evacuation. He was to report every three hours through La Panne.

'If we can still communicate we shall send you an order to return to England with such officers as you may choose at the moment we deem your command so reduced that it can be handed over to a corps commander. You should nominate this commander now. If communications are broken you are to hand over and return as specified when your effective fighting force does not exceed the equivalent of three divisions. This is in accordance with correct military procedure, and no personal discretion is left to you in the matter. On political grounds,' the message continued, 'it would be a needless triumph to the enemy to capture you when only a small force remained under your orders. The corps commander chosen by you should be ordered to carry on the defence in conjunction with the French, and evacuation whether from Dunkirk or the beaches, but when in his judgement no further organized evacuation is possible and no further proportionate damage can be inflicted on the enemy he is authorized in consultation with the senior French commander to capitulate formally to avoid useless slaughter.'

Gort received the message that afternoon just before holding a conference with his corps commanders. As he listened to the estimates of numbers still to be evacuated (he was told there were 60,000, but there were in fact twice that number) he became convinced that the perimeter forces must not withdraw to the beach for final evacuation until the night of 31 May/1 June. The eastern zone, already coming under increasing enemy pressure, would have to be evacuated first, leaving 1 and 2 Corps to guard the left and centre sections, and the French the right flank.

That settled, Gort acted on Churchill's directive and nominated General Barker to succeed him. Sitting round the dining table in a room overlooking La Panne beach, the other generals avoided each other's glances as Barker gave way to histrionics. 'Why me, for God's sake?' he wailed. 'Why do I have to take the responsibility?'

'Why indeed!' muttered Montgomery, and hung back to talk to the C-in-C when the conference dispersed.

He came straight to the point.

'Look here, sir,' he said with the abrasive bluntness Gort found so irritating, 'you saw that performance! Barker's in no state to take command. The man's finished – he's completely done for. Give the job to Alexander! He's got a clear brain and he hasn't lost his nerve. With Alex we might get everyone off the beach. Under Barker we'll end up with a humiliating surrender.'

Was this Monty's Machiavellian way of getting the command for himself? A do-or-die way of becoming either a national hero or a field marshal – or both? If it was, Gort was determined that he should not have his way. He had chosen Barker because he considered him to be the most expendable of his generals, following the policy of getting the most valuable brains – like Brooke – back to England first. Alexander was another who should be got back first. He had played his part to the full – had repeatedly displayed a coolness of judgement under fire and an ability to inspire his men that were probably superior to any other serving officer, Monty included.

For the second time in three weeks, Gort found himself

faced with a decision upon which thousands of lives might depend. If he left Barker in command, there was no doubt that the chances of getting all the fighting men to safety were seriously reduced. On the other hand if he appointed Alexander, and Alexander were killed or taken prisoner, the overall loss to Britain might be even greater.

In the end he decided to follow the same policy he had adopted since the first retreat from Louvain and put the safety of his fighting troops first.

'Very well,' he said gruffly. 'I'll make the change.'

Montgomery had not doubted for one moment that he could change the C-in-C's mind. He nodded briefly and gave a quivering salute. 'Excellent! Thank you, sir!' he barked cheerfully, and marched briskly out of the head-quarters.

Gort leaned back in his chair and for a few moments closed his eyes. The trouble with Monty, he reflected, was that he was always *right*.

iv

Rear Admiral Wake-Walker's appointment as Senior Naval Officer Afloat was beginning to pay off. Gradually, the confusion of the previous night was replaced by a semblance of order. On arriving off Dunkirk, ships were now being positively directed either to go alongside the east mole or to take men off from one of the three sections of beach, so that for the first time since the beginning of the operation ships were appearing where they were most needed or could be used to best advantage.

As the day wore on, the pace accelerated. On the east mole, officers of the 44th division had organized a cordon of soldiers with fixed bayonets to control the crowd at the shore end of the mole, and the troops were called out in groups of fifty to embark. As the frequency of arrival of the ships went up, so the need for the men to move quickly along the mole increased, and to address the troops directly,

Clouston had an electric loudspeaker system rigged up along the mole.

His staccato gunnery officer's voice barked out from the speakers. 'Send another fifty! Come on lads, full speed! Think of your pals! The quicker you are the more we can take! And another fifty! Double up if you can boys! Another fifty . . . ! Send another fifty . . . ! Well done, lads, keep it up, keep it up . . . !'

Urged on from all sides, the men – many on the point of collapse – broke into a double, and for two hours without a break there were troops doubling out along the mole to the ships, clambering aboard and collapsing on deck as the ships pulled out to make room for the next to come alongside.

It was the destroyers – particularly the old destroyers of the V and W class – that did some of the best work. *Vimy, Vanquisher, Vagabond, Vivacious, Wolsey, Windsor, Worcester*: they were sometimes alongside for less than half an hour, taking up to a thousand or more at a time; while elsewhere, others were giving gunfire support to the perimeter defence force, bombarding enemy troop concentrations on the approach roads to Furnes, La Panne and Calais, maintaining anti-E boat patrols and providing anti-aircraft defence for the beaches and the unarmed transport ships.

But while the British organization swung into top gear, more and more complaints were being received from the French that they were being short-changed by their allies and that the British were deliberately preventing French troops from going aboard British ships, sometimes at gunpoint.

Neither side was blameless. Until only a day or so before the French government and the high command – Reynaud, Pétain, Weygand and Darlan – had been unwilling even to discuss evacuation. But now that they had been forced to accept that they had a responsibility towards the thousands of *poilus* stranded at Dunkirk, their response was only half-hearted. Though several small despatch boats, torpedo boats and destroyers were ordered to start collecting men from the harbour, within twelve hours the despatch boats – particularly useful because they could manoeuvre among the wrecks in the blocked harbour – were recalled for escort duties, and other French ships that could have been committed to Operation Dynamo were still being used to ferry troops from Southampton to Brest.

v

At eight o'clock that evening, Rear Admiral Wake-Walker started inshore in HMS *Worcester*'s whaler to call on Lord Gort. He took his flag lieutenant with him and a small party of signalmen who were to set up a visual signalling station at the La Panne headquarters.

There was a slight swell, and everyone was soaked to the waist on landing at the beach. They were met by Captain Tennant and General Lees, who accompanied the rear admiral to Gort's villa headquarters.

Wake-Walker found the C-in-C and his staff about to have dinner in the large dining room whose French windows opened direct onto a road running along the top of the sandy slope to the beach.

Gort shook him warmly by the hand. 'I'm delighted to meet you,' he said. 'I understand you've been sent to take charge of the embarkation. That really is excellent news. I'm sure your presence will make a huge difference to the whole operation.'

Inwardly, Wake-Walker wished he shared the C-in-C's confidence in his ability. 'Well I certainly hope so –'

'We'll discuss it after dinner. You can stay for a meal, I take it?'

'Well, that's very kind of you. But I don't want to deprive you and your staff of rations that must already be short.'

'Nonsense. I'm sure there's plenty for everyone.'

It was a quite unforgettable meal – a Last Supper. There were eight or nine present and in spite of Gort's reassurances,

433

there was very little food to go round. This was particularly obvious when it came to the dessert, which consisted of a small tin of fruit salad which had to be shared out in minuscule portions. Conversation was not easy. They sat – Wake-Walker still soaked to the waist – staring out over the sea. A servant brought in the last bottle of champagne and asked the C-in-C's permission to open it.

Afterwards, Gort, Lees, Tennant and Wake-Walker discussed the situation.

'I hope you appreciate the extraordinary achievement of my field commanders these last weeks,' Gort said. 'To fall back intact to the sea in the way they have done is no small accomplishment. My chaps have done their bit. Now we're looking to the navy to get them back to the UK.'

'And so far,' Lees added rather pointedly, 'the navy's effort doesn't seem to have been adequate to the task.'

Wake-Walker explained some of the difficulties. 'You must appreciate that an embarkation from beaches is of necessity a very slow and difficult process. We rely heavily on calm weather. It's my view that from now on the bulk of the troops should be marched westward to embark from the east pier at Dunkirk.'

Lees shook his head. 'There are far too many troops still waiting in Dunkirk already. But for the ineptitude of the navy they might all have been evacuated by now.'

'You have no business or justification for talking like that, General,' Wake-Walker said quietly. He turned to Gort. 'Perhaps we could turn to the question of your own embarkation tomorrow evening, sir?'

vi

. . . All quiet in the morning. Our infantry neighbours have left in the night. The doctor goes off with the wounded man. HQ 59 Company pull out.

By midday no lorry has arrived to pick up the material so I send Leeming off to find the CRE.

He comes back two hours later to say that he can find nothing and nobody at Coxyde. Outside the wood everybody has gone. The countryside is silent and empty except for all sorts of abandoned vehicles.

I decide to get ready to move. Destroy three of our trucks including the office truck, burn papers discreetly, put on my best service dress and boots, pocket my razor and toothbrush and throw the rest of my things with the stores down a pit in the wood. Load the food, ammunition and weapons into the remaining two trucks and the Humber Snipe, and marshal them so we can pull out at a moment's notice.

The doctor arrives, a welcome sight, to say that 4 Div HQ has moved to La Panne but we are definitely not going to embark tonight. Sauervein is to report immediately to the French Liaison Mission.

We relax and offload for supper. I tell the section that we shall not be moving tonight, but set off on a motorcycle afterwards to La Panne to prospect. I find the CRE in a house on the front. While I am there a message comes through from G Branch about embarking the following night. The sea is calm and the tide is falling revealing a long sandy beach. In the mist offshore the dark shapes of ships can be seen, blue lights winking from mastheads.

Outside I run into Brigadier Phipps. He tells me that the 2 Corps Engineers are to act under his orders to embark the Corps. I am to move my section down to the beach bringing all floating equipment possible.

Back to the wood before midnight . . .

THIRTY-TWO

The shells made a dull droning noise just before impact, and as they exploded the earth quivered and the air buzzed and whined with flying fragments. While the artillery barrage lasted, all the men of 15 Company could do was lie in their foxholes and keep their heads down.

The anti-aircraft detachment had been brought up to lend support the previous evening, and they had been firing nearly all night, so there was little rest for anyone. The British bombers made an eerie rumble as they approached, and then the night was full of the flash of exploding bombs and the ghostly parachute flares that drifted slowly down.

One bomb made a direct hit on a barn, seriously wounding Sergeant Major Jackel and Corporals Barthel and Kleinholz. The pitch blackness of the night made rescuing them and attending to their injuries all the more difficult.

The field kitchen was hit by shrapnel, too, but the chefs – Lance Corporal Oxler and Private Drincham – worked on, refusing to rest until they had provided every single man with a hot meal.

Soon after dawn on the thirty-first, it was good to see a large Stuka raid go in over Bergues. Afterwards, although the enemy kept firing, there was a noticeable fall off of the accuracy of his fire, so it was concluded that he was no longer able to observe the fall of shot. That morning, a few prisoners were taken, and under interrogation they reported that the civil population at Bergues was at breaking point and the garrison troops were being worn away as much by the stress of shelling and bombing as by the damage and casualties they caused.

Even naval guns were being used by the enemy now.

Naval guns were always more terrifying because of the shriek of their high velocity shells. One sent up a terrific fountain of earth and dirt close to 2 Platoon's position, and Heinrich Lauder was covered from head to foot in dust and cow muck. Even his mouth was full of it.

In the afternoon, the men of 15 Company set about maintaining their vehicles. Working under fire, they changed the oil, topped up fuel tanks and checked the tyres, replacing them where necessary. No one grumbled: everyone wanted to make sure that when the time came to chase after the French, the vehicles would not let them down.

Soon after dark, the insidious murmur of approaching bombers could be heard, and the bombs began falling again, bringing on more heavy showers of earth and storms of flying shrapnel. It had been a long and terrible day. The night was even worse.

ii

Wilmot's Rifles stood to at two forty-five a.m., and soon afterwards heavy shelling started. By dawn, many houses were blazing and the Bergues garrison force was taking casualties. Enemy planes were active all through the day, and the town received particular attention from the Stuka squadrons. Gradually, the old fortified town was being reduced to ruins.

Early in the afternoon, shells began landing on the 1st Loyals' battalion headquarters. As a result, spies were believed to be operating in the town and after a search two men dressed as civilians were arrested and handed over to the local French commander, who had them shot. An hour later, the first German reconnaissance parties were spotted on the outskirts of the town. They were driven back by light arms fire from the ramparts.

While Bergues held out on the western flank, the German 9th Corps massed at the opposite end of the perimeter, on the approaches to Nieuport. As at Bergues, a heavy artillery barrage opened up just before dawn. Soon afterwards, the first inflatable dinghies crossed the canal at Nieuport and assault troops mounted a determined attack on the defensive positions held by the East Surreys. While the Surreys held on, an attack was sent in two miles to the west against the British 8th Brigade, and soon after midday a sapper despatch rider arrived at the headquarters of the 2nd Grenadier Guards to report that the enemy was across the canal in strength and that the perimeter had been broken.

A detachment was immediately rushed to plug the gap. On arrival the officer in charge, Second Lieutenant Jones, found that two battalions of Guards were already withdrawing from their positions without orders, and that the few remaining officers had lost control. Jones confronted the guardsmen and had to shoot a few to stop the panic and turn them back. Others were forced at bayonet point to turn round and face the enemy. Within a couple of hours, further reinforcements in the shape of officers, guardsmen and ammunition arrived, the brigade took up its positions again, and the crisis passed.

The pressure now shifted to the old Flemish town of Furnes, which was being held by the Coldstreams and Grenadiers, but although a crossing was achieved nearby at Bulscamp it got no further, being held up by the inundated terrain and well-directed British fire. For the Germans the solution was, as usual, to saturate the area with artillery fire, and as the day wore on shells fell in increasing numbers at Moeres, Furnes, Nieuport and La Panne.

iii

While the fighting raged at Furnes and Nieuport, Lord Gort prepared to obey Churchill's directive and return to England; but first it was necessary to take leave of his French counterpart, and he drove over to Bastion 32 at ten o'clock in the morning, accompanied by members of his staff and Captain Tennant. The British officers were ushered in through the blast-proof steel door of the bunker and along candlelit corridors to the office of *l'amiral Nord*, where they were received by Admiral Abriel and Generals Fagalde and de la Laurencie.

Until now, Gort's relationship with Abrial had been one of mutual suspicion, each having a very doubtful opinion of the other's integrity. Abrial was convinced that Gort was planning to leave the French in the lurch, while Gort felt that Abrial had the wind up and was scared of emerging from the safety of his bastion.

This morning, however, possibly because each was aware that this was to be their last meeting, the atmosphere between the two men was a much happier one. In the previous twenty-four hours, Gort had had instructions from London clarifying the policy of evacuation of French and British troops, and he announced that the general who would take over command of the remnant of the BEF had orders to place himself directly under General Fagalde, and to put himself and his divisions at the disposal of the French to hold the perimeter while the French were embarked.

Abrial, Fagalde and de la Laurencie were delighted. At long last the British seemed to have decided to behave honourably. The French generals agreed that the French cavalry corps should have first place in the embarkation queue, and there were smiles all round. When General Blanchard turned up, Gort invited all three generals to return with him to England that evening, but Blanchard declined for them all. Instead, glasses were produced, heels were clicked and health drunk; but in the euphoria of these improved Anglo-French relations, the C-in-C departed without finalizing with the French a joint programme of evacuation for the troops now fighting on the perimeter.

An hour or two after Gort had left, General Alexander turned up at Bastion 32 on a bicycle. He had just taken over command of the British rearguard from Lord Gort and had come to hammer out plans for the joint evacuation of the remaining French and British troops within the perimeter, which he had already discussed and agreed with the C-in-C and Captain Tennant over lunch at the La Panne GHQ.

2 Corps were to pull back to the beaches and the east mole that night, and the final withdrawal and evacuation would take place on the night of 1/2 June. As far as Alexander's personal directive was concerned, Gort had simply passed on to him the Churchill directive, complete with the instruction that he should do nothing to imperil his army and was ultimately responsible for the safety and evacuation of his troops. But Gort had said nothing at all to Alexander about placing himself and his divisions at the disposal of the French or under the command of Fagalde.

Propping the bicycle up against the bastion wall and going in through the steel door, Alexander was perfectly clear about his orders and intentions, and as Gort had told him of the excellent meeting he had had that morning, he expected to have no difficulty in securing wholehearted agreement from the French command.

He was in for a shock. At the first mention of withdrawal and evacuation, Abrial became heated.

'My orders from Paris are to hold on to the end, General. It has all been agreed and decided. I have had Lord Gort's personal assurance that you are to place yourself and your divisions under the direct orders of General Fagalde and that from now on the British and French will fight side by side to hold the line from Gravelines to Bergues —'

'Admiral,' Alexander cut in, 'Gravelines has fallen into enemy hands. Bergues is already being defended largely by British troops —'

'— and with British assistance, the French will establish a reduced perimeter running through Uxem and Moeres to the Belgian frontier —'

Alexander was aghast. 'An attempt to hold so narrow a bridgehead with exhausted troops and limited ammunition is out of the question, Admiral. I cannot emphasize too strongly that *my* orders are to continue the evacuation, shared equally between our forces, and it is my opinion as a professional soldier that the final withdrawal must take place tomorrow night.'

Abrial shrugged and stubbed out his cigarette in an overflowing ashtray. 'In that case, General, I shall close the port. Then you and your troops will have to stand and fight just as we French have been doing for the past five days.'

iv

In Paris, another confrontation was taking place at the War Office in the Rue St Dominique. In an uneasy atmosphere of mistrust, the two Prime Ministers and their military and political advisors confronted each other across a table: Reynaud, Pétain, Weygand and Darlan on one side, Churchill, Attlee, Dill, Ismay and Spears on the other. First the situation in Norway was reviewed. With Italy likely to enter the war on Germany's side at any time, the British had decided to evacuate the 16,000 allied troops at Narvik – together with any Norwegian troops who cared to go with them – in order to carry on the fight in France. They would be useful on the Aisne or the Somme, and the warships released from the Norwegian theatre would be urgently needed in the Mediterranean.

The French agreed, and the discussion proceeded to the question of evacuation of troops from Dunkirk. It quickly became apparent that while the British had little grasp of what was happening on the front that was now advancing west towards Paris, the French were even less informed of the situation within the Dunkirk perimeter. When Churchill told them that 165,000 troops had already been evacuated, there were gasps of astonishment.

'And how many of those are French?' Weygand asked pointedly.

Churchill gave a politician's answer. 'As companions in misfortune, *mon Général*, there is nothing to be gained by recrimination.'

'Indeed there is not, Prime Minister. But I repeat: how many of those were French?'

The answer was 15,000 and the French did not like it at all.

'You must understand that many thousands of British troops were already stationed near Dunkirk at the beginning of the operation,' Churchill pointed out. 'If only the fighting divisions are counted, the disparity is far smaller –'

'Nevertheless,' Reynaud cut in, 'the fact remains that of 220,000 British troops, only 20,000 remain, and yet of 200,000 French troops, only 15,000 have been rescued. What am I to say to the people of France with figures like that? I think something must be done to evacuate more of our men, Prime Minister, don't you agree?'

Churchill could hardly do otherwise. 'I have already directed that from now on, French and British troops will be evacuated in equal numbers, and I would like to stress that the three British divisions still at Dunkirk will stand shoulder to shoulder with your troops until the evacuation is complete.'

This seemed to mollify the French a little, and Admiral Darlan was invited to draft a telegram to Admiral Abrial explaining the new policy. But when the draft was read out it stated that during the final withdrawal from the perimeter, British forces would embark first.

Churchill leapt to his feet '*Non!*' he exclaimed, and crooking his arm, mimed an arm-in-arm departure. '*Sans partage! Bras-dessus, bras-dessus!*' Becoming carried away, he went even further. 'It will be the British who form the final rearguard! I will not accept further sacrifices from the French!'

For Churchill's old friend General Spears, this was going too far, and after the meeting he spoke with Admiral Darlan and had the directive modified. Admiral Abrial was placed in overall command at Dunkirk; the evacuation would be in equal numbers, and as far as possible the British would form the final rearguard.

One more hostile exchange took place, however, and this was after the formal meeting was over when Pétain, Churchill, Spears and a few others stood talking in the bay window of the Prime Minister's room. Captain de Margerie, head of Reynaud's private office, had already spoken of the French holding out in Africa, but Pétain adopted a very much more resigned attitude towards the march of events, and his age and authority seemed to cast a spell over the others.

'In certain eventualities,' one of the French said in a neat, mealy-mouthed way, 'a continuance of military reverses might enforce upon us a modification of foreign policy.'

Grasping the implication of this statement before Churchill, General Spears turned to Pétain and said in excellent French: 'I suppose you understand, Monsieur le Marechal, that that would mean a blockade?'

'*Ah, oui, peut-etre ça serait inévitable*,' murmured another.

But Spears, who had been helping Churchill out with his French, now took the initiative entirely upon himself and rammed the point further home: 'That would not only mean blockade, but *bombardment* of all French ports in German hands.'

There was an uncomfortable silence.

Churchill set his jaw and his voice fell to a growl. 'Whatever happens,' he declared, 'and whoever falls out, the British will fight on.'

v

At Dover, Ramsay's staff were still working non-stop. The previous night, several large transports had been sailed, and by seven a.m. there were no less than nine personnel ships and three hospital ships somewhere between Dunkirk and Dover, of which the Dynamo staff had no news at all. The great danger was that they were accumulating in the confined approaches to Dunkirk and would present another easy target for dive-bombers, so in spite of the continual cries for more and yet more ships coming from Tennant's head-quarters, Ramsay ordered that, until the return of the personnel ships on passage and while the coal-burning packets were being rebunkered, sailing of transports ships would be halted.

Two special operations were also in hand. The first of these was the sailing of a very large convoy of small craft, many of them under tow, from Ramsgate. These boats had been collected and deliberately held back for the final evacuation of fighting troops, which Ramsay understood was timed for that night. They were to leave at one p.m. The Flag Officer Harwich and C-in-C Nore had been requested to provide all available motor torpedo boats as escorts, and minesweepers had been designated to anchor in selected positions to guide the boats to the collecting points on the beaches where the troops would be waiting to embark.

At the same time, in a separate operation, two MTBs were to be sailed from Dover with orders to rendezvous at 1800 off La Panne, embark Lord Gort and his staff, and bring them back to Dover.

On paper, these plans looked straightforward enough. In practice, with both the east mole and La Panne beach being shelled, communications with small craft virtually non-existent and a fresh onshore wind wrecking the pulling boats almost as quickly as they could be towed to the beaches, neither plan was going to be easily accomplished.

vi

The order 'Fall in on the beach!' was passed joyfully round Blaxland's company in the afternoon, and while it was being carried out two aircraft roared overhead, guns firing. Everyone ducked instinctively, and as they did so it became apparent that one aircraft was in pursuit of the other. When smoke appeared from one and it then crashed, the soldiers cheered; but when the winner came back they saw the German cross on his plane. Everyone dropped flat: he came fast and low overhead, machine guns blazing, but though everyone was shaken, no one was hit.

They were ordered to march eastward – away from Dunkirk – to Bray Dunes, and set off in a column of threes, two officers at the head and two in the rear. It was heavy going trudging in the sand: marching at the rear of the column, Blaxland was glad he had decided not to wear his greatcoat but had it slung over his arm. After a while the column was halted and everyone knelt down on the sand to rest. The company commander could be seen in conversation with one of the naval officers controlling this section of the beach, and a few minutes later the order was given to turn about and march in the opposite direction.

They were to march to Dunkirk, and if it was heavy going before it was hard labour now. But on they trudged – in increasing disbelief – without impediment from guns, aircraft or beach control officers.

As they drew closer to Dunkirk they were able to march on the hard causeway instead of the sand. There was a destroyer berthed on the seaward side of the harbour mole, and three more wrecks than there had been the previous day. Many palls of smoke were rising from the town, and the Luftwaffe were mounting another bombing attack. Heads down, concentrating solely on putting one foot in front of the other, they trudged along the promenade.

Where the harbour mole joined the causeway a Bofors anti-aircraft gun was in position, surrounded by sandbags. As they approached, the barrel of this gun was lowered until Blaxland – who was now at the head of the column – found he was looking straight down its muzzle. He fell flat as it let out a rapid series of deafening booms: he was convinced that had he not done so he would have had his head blown off.

While the gun was firing, Blaxland looked down into the big drainage ditch by the causeway, in which were lying ten soldiers. He was surprised and a little envious at how unconcerned and relaxed they seemed; then he realized that he had made the reverse of a mistake he had made at Petegem nearly two weeks – it seemed like two years – before. Unlike those he had seen in the lorries coming back from the Dyle and the Dendre, these soldiers were not asleep, but dead.

After prolonged firing, the Bofors stopped. Blaxland led the column up onto the narrow mole and they began jogging out towards the destroyer, HMS *Icarus*.

The destroyer captain was standing at the head of the gangway. 'Tell your men to hand over their rifles and get below decks as quickly as possible,' he ordered, and within a very short time the four officers and 150 other ranks of Blaxland's company were tightly packed in the bowels of the ship.

The officers were directed to the wardroom. A steward came up to Blaxland and asked him what he would like to drink, and he opted for a whisky and ginger ale, which was quickly produced. The ship kept vibrating and shuddering from the firing of her guns, but Blaxland had already made up his mind that the enemy could not possibly harm them.

vii

By late afternoon, *Daisy Belle* – along with hundreds of other small craft – was chugging over a calm sea, with the coast of France in sight ahead.

The previous evening, after accepting David's offer of assistance, Pringle had searched in vain for an engineer to make up a complement of three; and as the Stuart-Turners had been thoroughly serviced only a few weeks before and Odell claimed to have some engineering knowledge, he had eventually decided to make the trip without a third crewman.

David had not intended to become involved in this rescue operation. He had told Simone he was going to Ramsgate to lend a hand on shore and that he had no intention of going back to France. But the atmosphere in Ramsgate had changed his mind. An hour in the public bar of the Queen's Head had done the trick. Listening to the other press reporters talking, he had realized that if he did not at least volunteer to work as crew, he would regret it for the rest of his life.

He had walked out into the evening sunshine and watched the feverish preparations that were going on aboard every boat, and had known, then and there, that he must be a part of this. He had witnessed Pringle's ignominious arrival, had noted the neat appearance of the boat and had bluffed his way past the naval sentry on the gate by claiming he was already designated as crew of the *Daisy Belle*. Stripped to his underpants he had made repeated dives in the oily waters of the harbour to clear away the fouled screws. He had cooked up porridge on a primus stove at dawn and had helped Pringle move the boat up to the quay to be refuelled and stored for the crossing.

And now they were on their way. The varnished spokes of the wheel were in his hands; Pringle was down in the after cabin putting a fix on the chart and there were ships and boats dotted over the sea as far as the eye could see.

Daisy Belle wallowed on at seven knots in the wake of the next boat ahead. They were keeping station behind a tug with several barges in tow. Ahead, astern and on either side, motor launches, pleasure craft and paddlesteamers were streaking the sea with the froth of their wakes.

A destroyer appeared over the horizon, heading back to England. Her bow waves were like white walrus moustaches, and her funnel smoke trailed away astern like a long grey feather. Within minutes she was passing close to port, her decks crammed with soldiers, her sides filthy with oil and shrapnel damage, every gun manned by men in steel helmets, every barrel pointing at the sky.

Pringle had come up from the after cabin.

'All well?'

'Yes *sir*!'

'I reckon we're about a third of the way across.'

'Right.'

Ahead, the towering black cloud over France was extending further and further across the horizon, and the noises of war were becoming ever more distinct.

Ramsgate seemed a very long way astern.

viii

The moment *Icarus* was clear of the mole, *Vagabond* was called alongside. This was the ship's fifth trip, and Archie conned the ship expertly in, making just the right allowance for the tide and going astern on the outboard engine to take the way off the ship and bring the stern in towards the jetty so that head and stern ropes could be passed across by hand without the use of heaving lines.

As soon as the berthing ropes had been made fast and a brow and two ladders had been rigged, the soldiers started pouring on board.

Archie remained on the bridge while the loading went ahead. The battery on the western outskirts of Dunkirk was beginning to get the range of the mole now, and every ten or fifteen seconds another shell screamed in and sent up a plume of water from the harbour. Overhead a flight of Stukas was at work, at present visiting the troops on the beaches. Fountains of sand rose in the air, the sound of the explosions that had created them reaching his ears a moment after.

'Multiple pom-poms, *engage!*' the gunnery officer bellowed as one of the planes wheeled and started a low pass along the beach towards the mole, and immediately the four barrels started pumping tracer on a flat trajectory at the snub-nosed aircraft.

This one was machine-gunning. Of the three evils – bombing, shelling and machine-gunning – Archie regarded machine-gunning as the worst, not so much because of the damage it did or the casualties it caused as the effect it had on morale. It was a very terrifying thing to have an aircraft come straight at you, making that howling noise and spitting bullets at the same time. And of course wherever you happened to be at the time, it always felt as if they were aiming directly at you.

Everyone ducked as he went over. When he came back, the Bofors at the end of the mole opened up as well, and either he was hit or frightened off because he didn't come back for a third run.

'Six hundred!' sang out the sub lieutenant at the brow, counting the men as they came aboard. 'Six-fifty . . . ! Seven hundred . . . !'

It was amazing what some of the men brought with them. Many of their battledress blouses bulged with ill-concealed cartons of cigarettes or bottles of liquor. One of this lot had a canary in a cage, and dogs were everywhere. Here was yet another: a scruffy-looking mongrel scampering along the mole and leaping down the brow into the ship. They had tried to stop dogs getting aboard on the first trips, but it had caused arguments among the soldiers who had adopted them so now they were allowed on board and were landed at Dover, where they were impounded and shot.

'Eight hundred!' sang out the sub lieutenant, and a minute later the last of the batch came on board and the brow and ladders were taken inboard by the torpedomen.

'Stand by, Number One! Let go aft! Let go for'd. Half astern both engines!'

The water churned up under the quarter and the destroyer slid stern first out of the berth. Coming out fast astern, Archie stopped engines, went ahead on the starboard engine first, put on twenty degrees of port wheel, and with black smoke belching from the two funnels, set course for the Quinte Buoy, Route X and Dover.

But the danger wasn't over yet: German artillery was shelling the ships from Nieuport, and Archie kept the ship under constant helm, weaving thirty degrees either side of a base course to complicate the enemy's aiming problem. This caused the ship to heel violently from side to side, and when they were approaching the Quinte Buoy, where the shelling was heaviest, the shout went up, 'Man overboard!'

It was a soldier who, fast asleep, had simply rolled over the side; but there was no question of going back for him. If he could swim, and if he was lucky, one of the small craft would pick him up.

Between decks, the cooks and stewards were going the rounds with mugs of sweet tea. In the wardroom twenty or more army officers were already asleep, oblivious of the pounding of the ship's propellers and the harsh explosions every time her guns opened fire.

It was when the ship was halfway along Route X that the guns' crews and people on the bridge – as well as those of the soldiers on deck who were still awake – caught their first glimpse of the Little Ships. Suddenly, over the horizon came hundreds upon hundreds of them: tramps, cargo ships, barges, drifters, tugs, Dutch schuits, even ferry boats such as carried one's car across the Thames at Woolwich. Within minutes, they were passing close by on either side, their skippers waving; and soon, from the white cliffs of Dover to the monstrous black cloud over Dunkirk, an endless succession of British shipping spanned the whole scene from coast to coast.

ix

Dover. Begrimed with smoke and oil, many with gaping holes from shell and bomb damage, destroyers, paddle-minesweepers, railway ferries, hospital ships, pleasure cruisers, trawlers, schuits – they were coming in with hundreds of men standing shoulder to shoulder on their decks, and it was not an uncommon sight to see a streak of blood running down a ship's side. In the harbour, tugs worked ceaselessly, towing disabled ships, nudging others in towards the quays, transferring destroyers to fuelling berths, bringing ammunition, water and fuel lighters alongside so that ships could be turned round and sent back across the Channel to collect another load. Over on the west side of the harbour by the Lord Warden Hotel, the motor torpedo boats slipped in and out of their camouflaged berth. Every hundred yards along the waterfront, anti-aircraft gun crews – some of them mere fourteen-year-old army cadets – scanned the sky for the approach of enemy aircraft.

Waiting on the quayside were the military reception parties, the medical staff, the Women's Voluntary Service. The fit were given 'tea and wads' – a cup of tea and a thick sandwich – the wounded were taken off by ambulance to emergency reception areas and the dead were put to one side in a pile for collection and transfer to the Dover mortuary – so many of them that at one stage the men working the berthing wires asked if they could be removed more promptly because of the effect their presence was having on morale.

Some of the troops staggered off, some waved and gave the thumbs up, some limped, some collapsed, some fell in three deep and marched proudly away, their heads up to the last. When the name and unit of each man had been taken and he had handed in his rifle and ammunition pouches, he was issued with a luggage label (they had run out of post-cards) upon which he had to write the name and address of his next of kin on one side and a two word message, signed only by his Christian name on the other: 'AM SAFE.' These labels went, post free, to addresses right across the United Kingdom.

Working an endless shuttle service, buses and lorries took the troops from the harbour to Priory Station, where special trains were arriving every ten minutes to collect the returning soldiers and carry them back to their depots. After leaving Dover, the trains stopped at little Kentish halts within a few miles to coal and water, and on the sunny platforms of these country stations there were more volunteers with trestle tables and tea urns and sandwiches.

Even the local bobby joined in to hand out the tins of strong, sweet tea to the outstretched hands from the railway carriages. Some of the women volunteers worked for twenty-four hours without a break, their hands blistered from cutting and spreading sandwiches.

At Headcorn station in Kent, where many of the 'Dunkirk Specials' stopped, a train pulled in with the slogans 'Back to Blighty but not for long!' and 'Look out Hitler, we haven't started on you yet!' scrawled in chalk on the doors.

'Had a rough time, chum?' one of the porters asked as he handed up a mug of tea.

'I've ruddy well learnt how to swim, anyhow!' came the reply.

x

At La Panne, the town and beach were coming under constant and increasingly accurate fire from the battery near Nieuport, whose fall of shot was being spotted from a kite balloon placed just out of range of the last Bofors gun protecting Gort's headquarters. Troops, boats and ships were being hit, and those that were able to do so began moving westward, out of range.

GHQ was closing down now. The staff were burning the ciphers, key lists and operation orders. Wielding an axe, a corporal was destroying the radio sets. Generals were exchanging riding boots for soft shoes that would be more suited to embarkation in a small boat through surf; batmen, clerks and telephonists were being packed off to Dunkirk, many of them clutching cartons of cigarettes or other windfalls of the retreat.

On the beach, Lieutenant Commander McLelland had been given the doubtful privilege of taking over as the Senior Naval Officer at La Panne, and had received orders from Captain Tennant to report himself to Montgomery's Corps headquarters, from where he was to take charge of Lord Gort's embarkation.

Although there were still very few boats about, a large number had been promised by Dover, and these were expected to arrive from about midnight onwards. During the day McLelland coordinated the efforts of the 12th Lancers and some sappers to construct another lorry pier, so that as soon as the dusk Stuka raids were over embarkation could go ahead as quickly as possible. Working under fire, the naval shore party, under the last unwounded beach officer, Lieutenant Greatwood, set about gathering oars and repairing pulling boats that had broached to on the beach during the morning.

Gort's departure from the beach was fixed for 1800, and McLelland had specified a position two miles west of La Panne for the pick up; but as Gort prepared to depart, news of increasing pressure on the perimeter at Furnes and Nieuport came through, and he was delayed at his headquarters. He finally left by staff car at the time arranged for the beach embarkation, but unknown to McLelland his car got stuck in the sand and he had to abandon it.

After Gort had gone, McLelland reported back to 2 Corps headquarters. But he had barely arrived when an irate staff officer came in from the embarkation rendezvous.

'I don't know what the hell the navy's playing at,' he told McLelland, 'but at the present moment we have no C-in-C and no boat, and nor can we attract the attention of any of your ships.'

Taking a box signal lantern, McLelland accompanied the staff officer down to the rendezvous, where he started flashing the ships to ask for boats to be sent in, but before he had a reply the destroyer *Keith* arrived on the scene flying the flag of Rear Admiral Wake-Walker.

A boat was sent in, and all that remained was for Gort himself to show up. Then another of his staff arrived with the news that he had already embarked from a point further along the beach near La Panne.

More small craft were coming into the beach now, and it was getting dark. Enemy artillery was firing on the two lorry piers at La Panne, and some hits were scored, the damage being repaired by sappers as soon as it occurred. McLelland went back to La Panne headquarters and saw to the final destruction of equipment and confidential gear.

Two more ships arrived, and the boats, which had already been filled, set out for them. But embarkation was painfully slow – only about three hundred an hour, and when darkness fell the rate was halved. Six thousand men were to embark from that beach by first light, by which time the enemy would be so close that any remaining troops would surely be massacred. Using the telephone link from La Panne, McLelland appealed direct to Dover for more boats to be sent to this sector of beach, but none turned up; and throughout the night enemy bombers patrolled overhead, so that any light that was shown brought on an immediate rain of bombs, making communication with the ships almost impossible.

xi

At Furnes, Captain Bunberry's company had taken up residence in a seventeenth-century Flemish house overlooking the market square, and Bunberry had positioned two Bren guns in the attic from which he proposed to give the enemy a hot reception when they decided to storm the town. In the meantime, he entertained his friend Nick Massingbohm to dinner.

'Not much we can do while Jerry's shelling,' he said, 'and I don't know about you, but I don't relish the idea of sitting in the cellar with the squaddies all night.'

A card table had been brought up and Bunberry's batman had found some silver-plated cutlery. On the menu was a small tin of stuffed olives, a larger tin of asparagus tips and four army biscuits. Candles were neither available nor necessary: there were enough buildings on fire in the town to provide an eerie light through the gun ports made in the slate roof.

Massingbohm had learnt a great deal about soldiering in the past few days, and had decided that he didn't much like it. Although Bunberry had agreed that he should get back to England as quickly as possible, events had moved so rapidly since the retreat from Dixmude that he had had no option but to remain with the company, acting as a beast of burden each time it withdrew to another canal or road junction or barn. He had also had to put up with quite a lot of uncomplimentary remarks about the RAF.

'Wot's wrong with the riff-raff?' was the favourite opening line. 'They ain't done nothing!' To which the reply went, 'That's the bleedin' trouble mate, the bleedin' riff-raff ain't done bleedin' nuffink.'

Since the battle on the Yser canal, Massingbohm had been forced to admit that RAF air support did seem a bit halfhearted: explanations about turn-round times and the requirements in other sectors didn't carry much weight when a Stuka was in a power dive.

Now, the buzz had gone round the battalion that the Guards would have to fight to the last man so that others could be got back to England in safety.

'Might almost be romantic in other circumstances,' Bunberry remarked as they sat down to eat.

Massingbohm ducked involuntarily as a shell fell in the adjoining building. He knew very well his old school friend was testing his nerve. It was all part of the Guards' tradition: before an action, officers were expected to behave nonchalantly, to stroll up and down with the colours at the head of their troops as they did every day outside Buckingham Palace at the changing of the guard. It was not possible to do that here in Furnes, so Bunberry was doing the next best thing.

'I understand from the signals chappie that the BBC are saying the navy's taken two thirds of our chaps off already,' Bunberry remarked conversationally. 'Good news, wouldn't you say?'

Another salvo landed close by, and the attic filled with plaster dust. Bunberry turned to his batman, who stood waiting in attendance at his elbow.

'You can go downstairs if you want, Rogers. Flight Lieutenant Massingbohm and I have everything we need.'

'I'd just as soon wait up here, sir. It's a bit whiffy in the cellar.'

'As you wish, Rogers.'

They consumed the stuffed olives – which were of surprisingly high quality – and Bunberry divided the asparagus tips into two equal portions. As he did so, Massingbohm noticed that his hand was shaking.

'This is madness!' he said quietly.

Bunberry looked up. 'Isn't all war madness?'

'I didn't mean that, and you know it.'

Bunberry smirked and passed him his portion of asparagus.

'What did you mean?'

Massingbohm wondered if he should say what was in his mind. The trouble was, he couldn't stop thinking of Christine. What agonies of worry must she be going through now? Would he ever see her again? The possibility of that little country wedding at St Margaret's-at-Cliffe in just eight days' time seemed a wild dream now. Bunberry, a confirmed bachelor, had far less to lose; indeed, Bunberry was the sort of person who would probably welcome a hero's death. That was why people joined the Brigade of Guards, wasn't it?

But Bunberry's deliberate flirtation with danger did have its own crazy rationale. It was not entirely schoolboy bravado: Massingbohm knew that if he funked now, if he stood up and said, 'Sorry, but I'm going down to take shelter', not only would the RAF sink further in the army's esteem but, if he survived, he would carry with him the memory of his loss of nerve for the rest of his life. He would be a different man – a broken man, a man without self-respect. So he laughed and shook his head in reply to Bunberry's challenge, and stuck it out to the last army biscuit, which he was munching when a second lieutenant came up the stairs with a message from HQ that the battalion was to withdraw to La Panne.

It was essential that the enemy should not be aware of their withdrawal, so they muffled their boots with sacking. Bunberry passed the order for the men to come up from the cellar troop by troop, and with whispered commands the sergeants and corporals took charge of each handful of men and marched them in single file, over the rubble and broken glass, out of town.

It was a three-mile march, and for much of the way, shells were falling a few hundred yards ahead of the marching column, so that Massingbohm, who was carrying a mortar, felt as if they were continually moving towards the jaws of hellfire.

They marched on and on. Most of that road from Furnes to La Panne is dead straight with very little cover, and every time another shellburst lit up the sky, the men were silhouetted against it.

The entire eastern sector of the perimeter was pulling back now. As the Guards entered La Panne they found other troops doing likewise and soon, in every villa on the seafront, more men were arriving and flopping down exhausted.

xii

By ten o'clock the situation on the beach was becoming serious. Only 600 troops had been embarked and the few boats available had dwindled to three, mainly because of the mismanagement of boats by inexperienced army crews who were doing naval duties of rowing and turning the boats. By eleven o'clock, the situation was critical. Withdrawal from Furnes was in full swing and troops were piling up on the beach in their thousands. At the same time, a battery at Nieuport had started a slow, deliberate shelling of the beach, and almost every shell was causing casualties.

McLelland made another recce of the beach, and reported back to General Johnston's headquarters in a house on the seafront. McLelland was soaked to the waist from wading in surf and filthy from repeatedly hurling himself face down in the sand.

'Well?' Johnston queried. 'Have you found any boats?'

'No, sir. Apart from the three that left twenty minutes ago, we have none at all.'

'You know I have six thousand fighting troops relying on the navy to get them off the beach?'

'Yes, sir, I'm aware of that –'

'All right, Lieutenant Commander, here's a straight question for you. Are these boats of yours going to arrive or are they not?'

'General, I can't promise –'

'I'm not asking you to promise anything! I'm asking for a straight answer to a straight question. I repeat – is the Royal Navy going to provide boats for my troops or is it not?'

McLelland felt personally responsible for the navy's failure. 'I regret to state, sir, that I do not think the boats will arrive in time now.'

'That is all I wished to know,' Johnston replied and, summoning an adjutant, issued orders that all 6000 troops waiting to embark at La Panne be marched westward towards Dunkirk.

xiii

. . . Move off before dawn, leaving the wood which has served us so well and cross the canal bridge at Adinkerke, prepared for demolition by 48 Div RE. There is a lorry on fire in the road but we can squeeze past. An embarkation office has been set up at the entrance to La Panne where tickets are being handed out for the beach. As sappers we are waved past; nobody pays any attention to the tickets.

I turn along a sandy road running parallel to the beach. On my right is waste ground, on my left a line of houses standing on higher ground which slopes down to the beach beyond. I find an empty one without difficulty for the section, offload the food and the cooks' gear and park the transport opposite.

It is a fine windy morning with sand blowing along the beach. The sea is rough. A party is trying to launch a boat through the breakers but it overturns. There are several boats lying at the water's edge without oars. A pier made out of lorries parked alongside one another stretches down to the sea. Beyond there is a light AA Bofors, about half a mile up the beach. The beach is almost empty but groups of people stand around by the houses chatting. Having reported I find a warm place by a sand dune and go to sleep.

I am aroused by the arrival of Brigadier Phipps and Lieutenant Colonel Le Suer, now CRE 5 Div and formerly our 7 Field Company Commander. A second pier is to be built but no more boats are to be launched until dark. Some folding boat equipment will shortly be arriving. Meanwhile I am to search for 'runner' lorries which are difficult to find because of the rule about not bringing transport back.

I set off in the Snipe with Smith driving. Aircraft are beginning to appear in ones or twos but are met with such a terrific Bofors and small-arms fire that they veer off. Even Smith has his rifle out as soon as we stop, taking pot shots but a long way behind. I show him how to follow through.

Two aircraft are brought down, to great cheers from the sand dunes, one in flames, the other into the sea. It is quite a social gathering now that everybody seems to have arrived. CREs Harrison and Coxwell Rogers, with Gillespie, Hodgeson, Galloway, Tubby White and Derek Curtis. It is amusing to see the French liaison officers crouched in a slit trench they have dug and wearing their tin hats. Their trench is near an access road onto the beach. Across the road there is a small house where a military police post has been established. I am standing on the pavement near a glass grating, about to ask Sauervein what he thinks he is chasing down that hole when there is a mumbling which rises to a roaring whistle. I throw myself flat into a depression in the sand . . .

Dizzy with concussion I look at the grating where the glass is all shattered and conclude that the bomb has gone down there. Across the road smoke is rising from the shattered police post and people are being helped out.

Is the section all right? I find them comfortably settled in the billet. The cooks are handing out cups of tea. We shall not need the transport again now, so I get Corporal Wilkinson to drain out the oil and run the engines hard. One by one they seize up, but I keep the Snipe intact for emergencies, locking it up with the imprest box in the back.

The second pier of vehicles has now been built and the Corps Field Park Company arrives with its folding boat equipment and decking lorries. As soon as the men's dinners are finished I get them out onto the beach offloading decking and lashing it onto the tops of the lorries to make a continuous footway. It has to be tied up very firmly to resist the breakers when the tide comes up.

Rumour has it that the CRE has been killed.

'Oh my God!' says Graham, but his face lightens on hearing that it is some other CRE. It is in fact Le Suer. He, Hodgeson and Galloway were talking together on the beach when another bomb from the same stick as mine killed all three. Tubby White has been wounded.

Bill Hedley brings out a section of 225 Field Company to help with the lashing down, but we are beginning to run short of decking so I walk off along the waterline to see if there is anything useful among the flotsam. There is a young soldier floating face downwards in the surf. I pull him out and try artificial respiration but he is as cold as ice and I am wasting my time. Take one identity disc and his paybook to send in.

It is mid-afternoon when I get back to the piers. At the end of the beach towards Nieuport an observation balloon can clearly be seen. It must be German because shelling starts at about 1600 hours, falling several hundred yards away near the Bofors gun. Bill Hedley goes off in search of boats and oars while I carry on with lashing down. By 1700 I look round and find I am working alone with Bourner, so I go back to the billet where I find the section sitting. The RSM says they have come in for tea, but the billy can is still cold. I get them out again, grumbling; they can have tea when the job is finished which should not be long.

By 1800 hours we have used up all the decking and all the lashings, and the shelling has come too close to be comfortable. There is not a soul in sight, no ships, no boats, but at least the wind has dropped. There is a lot of junk near the sandhills which I prefer not to look at too closely. Embarkation from La Panne seems like a wild dream . . .

xiv

. . . Request more ships to load Dunkirk.

Every available ship will be required at Dunkirk during the next two hours to evacuate rest of army.

Embarkation proceeding satisfactorily in spite of

bombardment. I would again stress the need for more ships and constant fighter protection.

Am now receiving a number of Frenchmen. I have raised no objection to their embarking in British ships and am allowing them to do so.

Request you will inform me whether troops are now being ordered to march to Dunkirk from the beaches.

Sun is now coming through and I have a big target of ships in the harbour. Request special air protection for next two hours.

Lord Gort has agreed that 5000 French troops should be embarked here this evening after dark in British vessels. Request necessary ships may be sent to arrive at dusk.

We have been continually heavily bombarded and they are gradually finding the range of our loading berth. I would rather only enter ships as necessary for the flow of troops.

As it is vital to carry out the evacuation of troops throughout every available moment day and night it is intended to place two white lights at eastern and western pierhead as a guide to ships in the hours of darkness. It is requested that all HM ships and other vessels who are likely to enter port tonight be warned accordingly.

Slow British progress in port due to shelling, bombing and wounded French troops using quay. Weather fine and clear, sea moderate, good prospects for night embarkation.

I have felt it necessary for the operation to disregard your verbal instructions to return home, and hope you will approve. With the approval of Lord Gort

I have returned here as SNO Dunkirk and to assist the British commander.

In view of the decision (to embark rearguard the following night) request maximum number of transports and air protection tomorrow Saturday and particularly air and sea protection for the following day, when enemy will have no other occupation. Unfortunately some hours are passing tonight without a single ship entering Dunkirk for French or ourselves.

Situation report: No ships entered between 2230 and 0400. Unsuccessful dive-bombing attack has just taken place. British fighters arrive. Smoke covers pier. Embarkation recommenced.

Reported heavy shelling of beaches and improvised pier smashed. Please despatch by MTB morphia and field dressings.

MESSAGE ENDS = +

THIRTY-THREE

The night was pitch dark, with low cloud over the Channel and mist banks. The withdrawal of the troops from La Panne had been followed by an inevitable advance of enemy artillery along the coast, and it became obvious that all ships and boats operating off Bray Dunes would have to be shifted westward at first light. In the meantime, the work to get the troops into the boats and out to the ships went ahead with desperate urgency, and Ramsay's fleet of small craft were put to use as soon as they arrived off the beaches. Working in the dark and under artillery and machine-gun fire, a huge unnumbered multitude of tugs, motorboats and lifeboats went back and forth between the sands and the ships, while the queues of men shuffled slowly down into the water.

Daisy Belle arrived off the beaches a little after midnight. As they closed the coast, the ragged outline of bombed houses on the foreshore became silhouetted against the fires, and the skyline was lit by the flashes of gunfire.

When they were about two miles off the shore, a motor torpedo boat appeared out of the darkness, its engines throbbing loudly as it came up the line of small craft. The unmistakable accents of a naval officer came to them over a megaphone: 'Move – along – towards – the harbour! Move – along – towards Dunkirk – harbour!'

They waved and shouted an acknowledgement, and the MTB moved on up the line of boats repeating the message.

Pringle put the wheel over to starboard to parallel the coast then handed over the steering to David while he studied the chart by the light of a dimmed torch.

'So where are we, skipper?'

'I think that's La Panne in there,' Pringle said, pointing

at a section of coast where several buildings were on fire. 'About seven nautical miles to Dunkirk by my reckoning. We should get there within the hour.'

They fell silent. They hadn't talked a great deal during the ten-hour crossing: the thought of what lay ahead and the sheer scale of what was happening that night was not conducive to small talk.

The boat chugged on over an oily sea as part of a huge fleet of ships of every size and description. As they closed Dunkirk, they began to see the individual fires burning in the town and along the foreshore of Malo-les-Bains. Once, they collided head on with a heavy piece of timber, and after that David sat on the foredeck to keep lookout, indicating with his hand to go to port or to starboard to avoid the snakes of grassline, the swamped boats and other flotsam. There were several wrecks off the coast, and darkened ships, with pin-prick blue lights at their mastheads, slipped by, their propellers thumping rhythmically. From time to time aircraft droned overhead and bombs fell. Once, a red ball of flame broke through the clouds and for half a minute a large section of beach was illuminated by a slowly descending flare that revealed a surreal, nightmare scene of abandoned vehicles, wrecks and bombed buildings.

'Do you know your Bible?' Pringle asked suddenly, and without waiting for a reply quoted: '"I saw a star fall from Heaven unto the earth: and to him was given the key of the bottomless pit."'

A little while later, when the long, low line of the eastern breakwater of Dunkirk harbour was in sight, they were approached by a tug and told to proceed inshore and load from the beach.

Pringle became suddenly courteous. 'Would you be kind enough to get the accommodation ladder out?' he asked. 'It's down in the forecabin. And if you could perhaps sling a few fenders horizontally at the waterline they'll be able to use them as steps.' When David had obliged and they were approaching the shore he said: 'And – I wonder if you'd take soundings with the boathook? I'm particularly anxious not to put her on the putty.'

In they went, very cautiously, until they could hear the waves breaking on the beach ahead and see a line of figures wading out to meet them. Pringle got David to drop the kedge anchor over the bows and allowed the boat to move slowly astern, until David, hanging over the stern with the boathook, reported that they were in about four or five feet of water.

'Over 'ere, mate!' a voice shouted out of the darkness. 'There's bleeding hundreds of us!'

David made a rope fast to a cleat on the stern, coiled it and jumped down into the water. He waded, up to his shoulders, towards the beach and heaved the stern round until the men at the head of the queue were able to grab the fenders and ladder.

'We can only take twenty at the most,' Pringle announced as the first soldiers struggled, dripping, aboard; but no one took any notice of him and when David started pulling in on the kedge anchor some while later, there were thirty-seven men packed into the two cabins, the engine room and on deck.

Weighed down in the water, the exhaust gurgling and spluttering, the *Daisy Belle* came slowly away from the shore and headed towards the nearest ship, which moved away as they approached, so they set off for another, which did likewise. The third ship they approached – a paddle minesweeper – remained where she was. Pringle took the boat in a large circle and came alongside rather heavily. 'Sorry about that,' he murmured to no one in particular. 'Must have misjudged the increased stopping distance . . .'

The soldiers began climbing up the scrambling nets.

'Can you let us have some gasoline?' David shouted up to the minesweeper.

'Gasoline?' queried a petty officer, who leaned over the guardrail looking down at them.

'Petrol!' Pringle shouted, and a few minutes later three four-gallon cans were lowered on the end of a line.

They topped up with fuel, went back to the beach, got the propellers entangled in a greatcoat, cleared it, took another load of men out to the same ship and returned again to the beach. Each time the *Daisy Belle* reached the shallows, Pringle turned her, dropped a bow anchor and came stern first towards the beach, and as soon as it was shallow enough to stand David jumped in with the stern line and held the boat against the tug of the bow anchor.

The shelling continued almost constantly while they worked, but for some reason that he was never able to understand, David felt no fear of it. Although the soldiers were exhausted, most of them were patient and well disciplined and some were extraordinarily cheerful. Only a very few had lost their nerve. One – an officer by the sound of him – came splashing out through the surf screaming in a falsetto that he'd been waiting two days and refused to wait longer; and when someone with a thick Glaswegian accent told him to get to the back of the queue he pulled rank. There was a sudden flurry of activity in the water, and the falsetto voice was not heard again.

ii

When the sun rose, the beach at Malo-les-Bains was still covered with troops who were being lifted in lifeboats and carried out to ships of all kinds that lay offshore. Also on shore now were many tanks and armoured cars, which were being set on fire.

With the dawn, the low-level air raids began again. As the bent-winged Stukas came screaming down, the ships' anti-aircraft guns put up a terrific barrage of tracer that crisscrossed in the sky and was augmented by rifle fire from the dunes and machine-gun fire from the tugs, schuits, coasters and other small craft that had been armed.

With seventy men aboard, the tug *Sun IV*, which had

been working since midnight under fire, took two disabled vessels in tow and headed back to Ramsgate.

Tug *Tanga* took 160 troops off the beach and moved away under heavy shellfire. She picked the last six survivors of tug *St Fagan* up off Dunkirk. *St Fagan* had been bombed and sunk while towing three Thames barges. A mile further on, *Tanga* picked up the barge *Pudge* with four men on board, two badly wounded, and towed her back to Ramsgate.

The London firefloat *Massey Shaw*, manned entirely by volunteer members of the London Auxiliary Fire Service – pulled out of Dunkirk harbour at dawn with sixty men on board. Close by, the barge *Thyra* was towed home with a full load of troops.

Belgian fishing boats were at work, and Dutch schuits were everywhere, being used as go-betweens for the smaller craft and the ships anchored offshore. The naval trawlers and drifters between them carried huge numbers of men, HMS *Whippingham* estimating that between ten-thirty p.m. and one-thirty a.m. she lifted 2700 men from the beaches. With little more than twelve inches of freeboard she picked her way through the maze of wrecks and chugged slowly back across the Channel.

On the mole, even larger numbers were being embarked, with ships arriving and departing continuously. Because of the difficulty of embarking men down steep ladders and brows to the destroyer decks at low tide, the *Maid of Orleans* was ordered to remain alongside with her gangways in place so that the men could pass over her to the ships which were called in to berth outside her.

Even the bigger ships were taking some hair-raising risks now. Steaming in at twenty knots, transports and destroyers were coming alongside with the water boiling up under their sterns. Minor collisions were a commonplace, but major ones rare. At high tide, many ships took a short cut over the Goodwin Sands in order to clip half an hour off the crossing time.

At about seven-twenty a.m. – when the Thames barge

Royalty had just let go the tow line from tug *Cervia* and was setting her topsail to sail the remaining distance to the shore – an air-raid siren wailed out over the harbour. Minutes later, a huge force of Stukas and Messerschmitts arrived over Dunkirk.

For the German High Command, this was to be the death blow: synchronized with a renewed artillery barrage, the Luftwaffe was flinging everything it had into one last effort to destroy the BEF and force the Royal Navy to abandon the evacuation. There were no allied aircraft present at the time, and the destroyers, twisting and turning at full speed under the rain of bombs, were desperately short of ammunition.

Suddenly the sky was full of the smoke-bursts of exploding shells and the fountains of tracer; below, the sea was flecked white with falling bullets, splinters and debris; all round the east mole and close to every warship, bombs were sending up towers of water and smoke, so that sometimes a ship would entirely disappear from view. With Rear Admiral Wake-Walker on board and two AA shells remaining, the destroyer *Keith* was attacked repeatedly and began to sink. *Basilisk* was heavily bombed and reduced to a floating hulk which had to be scuttled. The gunboat *Mosquito* was set on fire. The French destroyer *Foudroyant* was dive-bombed and sunk with heavy loss of life.

Within the space of an hour, the navy had lost three destroyers, a fleet minesweeper and a gunboat, and almost every other warship off Dunkirk had sustained damage of some kind.

'It's too much,' Wake-Walker told Admiral Abrial in an emergency meeting in Bastion 32 an hour later. 'We can't afford to lose ships at this rate. I intend to recommend to Dover that evacuation operations cease entirely during daylight hours. It's not a question of morale or lack of willing, Admiral. Just arithmetic. They're sinking too many ships and killing too many men. Simple as that.'

In the Dynamo Room, Christine had taken on the task of keeping the tote boards up to date and writing an hour-by-hour narrative of events, so that practically every signal concerning Operation Dynamo passed through her hands.

She was aware, therefore, that her father's ship had already completed five trips and had evacuated over three thousand men; that *Vagabond* had come under repeated enemy attack and had suffered damage from near misses and flying shell splinters. She also knew that before the most recent trip one of the sub lieutenants had lost his nerve and had jumped into the water as the ship moved away from the quay at Dover. He had gone down between the ship and the jetty and had been sucked into the propeller wash and chopped to bits.

Now, after a whole sheaf of encrypted signals like 'ENEMY ARE BOMBING and 'BEING SHELLED IN POSITION . . .' came another signal, this time from the Senior Naval Officer at Dunkirk:

> THINGS ARE GETTING VERY HOT FOR SHIPS; OVER 100 BOMBERS ON SHIPS HERE SINCE 0530, MANY CASUALTIES. HAVE DIRECTED THAT NO SHIPS SAIL DURING DAYLIGHT. EVACUATION BY TRANSPORTS THEREFORE CEASES AT 0300. IF PERIMETER HOLDS WILL COMPLETE EVACUATION TOMORROW, SUNDAY NIGHT, INCLUDING MOST OF FRENCH. GENERAL CONCURS.

As the hours went by the list of destroyer losses grew. *Keith, Salamander, Skipjack* . . . Christine knew people in all of them. These were now the sort of losses incurred in a major engagement, and lingering at the back of everyone's mind at Dover was an awareness that what they were living through during these days and nights was not merely a battle but the turning point of the war: that if the losses went on mounting neither the army nor the navy nor the air force would be able to stem the Nazi onrush, and that it would be only a matter of time before German tanks were clattering along the country lanes of Kent.

Having chalked the most up to date total of British and French troops landed since midnight, she escaped for a minute's respite in the Wren's lavatory. This was the only place where she could be quite alone and where, if only for two minutes, she could think her private thoughts.

The important thing was not to give way to emotion. Nick was still missing, yes. He might have been killed, yes. But she must hold on: everyone else was holding on, everyone else was keeping their personal worries to themselves. If just one person broke down – and they all knew this – there was a danger of everyone else doing likewise.

She stood on the lavatory seat and looked out through the tiny window at the drab, explosion-pocked ships coming and going in the harbour. Surely this scene must be unique in history! Surely no evacuation on this scale had ever taken place before or would ever take place again!

She went back into the corridor, where she met Elspeth.

'Commander Ops is shouting for you, Chrissy. They're in a panic because some VIPs are visiting and they want the boards bang up to date when they arrive.'

She went down the whitewashed tunnel and back into the ill-ventilated Dynamo Room that smelt of pipe smoke, ashtrays, stale sweat and fatigue. She had been away from her desk for less than five minutes, and here was another thick wad of signals to wade through. She accepted a cigarette from an RNVR officer of whom all she knew was that he was called Ken, and began going through the signal log, sorting the messages into date-time order and writing pertinent details on the perspex board upon which was kept the running total of men landed in the UK.

One of the signals was from *Vagabond*:

RATHER WINDY WITH OCCASIONAL LEAD SHOWERS IN REGION OF NO 5 BUOY. UMBRELLA WOULD BE GREATLY APPRECIATED, PREFERABLY LIGHT BLUE.

It was entirely typical of her father. She had thought it very juvenile of him to send such signals at first, but was now beginning to change her mind: she could not imagine any German commanding officer lacing his signals with humour in such a way, and was realizing that the ability to laugh in times of crisis was perhaps the most valuable weapon of all. She put the signal into the clip file marked 'Fighter Support' and as she did so the admiral, accompanied by a civilian, looked in at the Dynamo staff working at the long table with its double row of telephones down the centre.

For a moment, seeing the bow tie and cigar, Christine mistook the civilian for Beaverbrook. Then he spoke in an unmistakably gruff voice – something about letting the workers get on with the job – and she knew it was Churchill.

He stood there in the doorway for only a few seconds, but that was enough. Having been filled with despondency and pessimism only minutes before, Christine suddenly knew that with that man leading the nation and men like her father talking about lead showers and light blue umbrellas, there was hope yet.

iv

Though evacuation operations were reduced during the day, they did not cease, and the convoy of small craft crossing from the Downs continued without interruption. At the same time, aerial convoys of RAF and Fleet Air Arm fighters went back and forth across the Channel to give air protection and harass the enemy as he closed in on the shrinking perimeter. Hurricanes, Spitfires, Defiants, Hudsons, Ansons and even the old Swordfish – Fleet Air Arm biplanes known by the aircrew as 'Stringbags' – were flung into the battle, and by the end of the day seventy-eight German aircraft had been destroyed against a loss of sixteen British; but most of these actions were fought out of sight of troops on the ground, whether above cloud or clear of the umbrella of AA fire rising from the ships at Dunkirk and lying off the beaches, and went unnoticed by the thousands who were dug in among the dunes or waiting in cellars to be called out to embark.

v

Daisy Belle was now heading for home with a mixed lot of thirty-three Tommies and *poilus* on board. The group who had come aboard last, and were sitting in the stern sheets and on the coach roof, seemed quite indefatigable. They were Royal Hussars, and in the charge of a young corporal who had organized them to provide anti-aircraft fire with rifles.

'Come on over here y'bastard!' he shouted at the wheeling Stukas and eventually one obediently came screaming straight towards them.

As the aircraft pulled out of its dive and straightened for the run, Pringle put the wheel hard over, and the gunners let fly. Whether the aircraft was hit by a single bullet no one could say, but he didn't come back, and although several shells from the shore battery at Nieuport fell within fifty yards, the *Daisy Belle* cleared Dunkirk Roads in safety and joined the procession of craft heading back to Ramsgate.

Now, two hours later, she and hundreds of other small craft were in mid-Channel. The white cliffs were in sight and the sun had broken through the haze. Sitting on the coach roof, drunk with fatigue, the Hussars were cradling their rifles and singing an old regimental song to keep themselves awake:

> 'E was saying goodbye to 'is 'orse
> 'E was saying goodbye to 'is 'orse
> And as 'e was saying goodbye to 'is 'orse
> He was saying goodbye to 'is 'orse

The tune was the same as 'Bless 'em all', and the chorus was rendered with plenty of mock tears and ad lib variations:

> Goodbye 'orse! (goodbye 'orse!)
> Ta-ta 'orse! (ta-ta 'orse!)
> I'm saying goodbye, me old 'orse! (old 'orse!)
> And being as 'ow I am saying goodbye,
> I'll just say goodbye – goodbye 'orse!

Standing at the wheel, David shook his head in disbelief. A year before, on announcing that he intended making a trip to England, one of his college pals told him that he would find the British 'kind of different'. He was beginning to understand, now, just what that meant.

Pringle looked up from the chart. 'We should have just enough fuel to make Ramsgate,' he said and then added: 'With a bit of luck.'

'Will you make another trip?'

'Oh, yes,' Pringle replied without any hesitation. 'I'm going to see this thing out now. What about you?'

THIRTY-FOUR

Inland, the rearguard troops were coming under increasingly heavy pressure. Major General Alexander had already told Admiral Abrial that the front could not be held much more than a further twenty-four hours, and it was as if the German High Command had overheard him and were determined to finish off the BEF and the French 1st Army within the space of twelve hours.

To the west of Dunkirk, the enemy had penetrated along the coast from Gravelines and were now in possession of Mardyck Fort, only three miles from Dunkirk's east mole. To the west, the shrunken perimeter now ended just east of Bray Dunes. To the south, the old fortified town of Bergues, which was in some ways the key to Dunkirk, still held out, manned by the 1st Loyals and a few 'ad hoc' companies of mixed troops.

At mid-morning, the corps commander issued his orders for the withdrawal to his divisional commanders:

INTENTION
To embark the remains of the BEF tonight 1/2 June, and if not completed to continue embarkation until all are evacuated or till as long as the enemy allows.

METHOD
Present Forward Defence Lines will be denied until 2200 hours, mobile Rear Guards finally withdrawing from FDLs at 2359 hours.

During 1 June up to 2200 hours all available personnel not essential for above intention will be withdrawn and sent to place of embarkation.

Place of embarkation will be the MOLE and between the MOLE and west end of MALO LES BAINS.

Troops waiting embarkation will be dispersed in small bodies on sands.

Route to place of embarkation: by shortest way to sea and thence to MOLE area.

Commands are responsible for the withdrawal of all troops in their area.

Commands will report, as far as possible, progress of withdrawal and embarkation.

When approximately three quarters of a formation is embarked, the Command himself will embark.

All personnel will embark armed.

TIMINGS
(a) *On receipt of this order*
2/5 Leics, 2/5 Forresters, direct to beach at once and as inconspicuously as possible. 1 Loyals less one company to COUDERKERQUE. One company of 1 Loyals to line of CANAL DE BERGUES.

(b) At 2130 hours 6 Lincolns will move to occupy CANAL DE DUNKERQUE. 6 Yorks and Lancasters direct to beach.

(c) 1 Loyals, one company 1 Royal Warwicks and 9 Foresters less mobilized rear parties on trucks or cycles, direct to beach.

Artillery. Field and anti-tank guns south of Dunkerque Canal will be withdrawn at discretion of CRA to positions north of canal at 2200 hours.

Guns which Commandant, Royal Artillery decides to leave will be destroyed. All dial sights, sight clynometers and ammunition will be either expended or withdrawn.

Orders for destruction of guns north of DUNKERQUE CANAL will be given by Commander 46 Division.

Even if troops come under shell fire or machine-gun fire or bombing on the beaches, the progress of embarkation must not be impeded.

French troops may be embarking on the same ships as British troops.

ii

For Wilmot and his company of a hundred men in the Bergues garrison, time had lost its meaning. Three minutes waiting for another box of ammunition could become like three hours, while fifteen minutes of intense action could pass as if they were as many seconds.

After each bomb or shell whined in and the world filled with brick dust and flying splinters, Griff was repeatedly convinced that he must be the only survivor of his group – and repeatedly amazed at how many of his comrades came out of it unscathed.

Just before first light, he received orders to take up a new position in support of D Company on the north-east ramparts near the Ypres Gate. The enemy was within small-arms range now, and their infantry was moving forward over open country in waves. Tanks had been brought up to bombard the west gate and their cannon and heavy machine guns were beginning to make life increasingly difficult in the town, much of which was on fire.

Soon after midday, large bodies of enemy troops were seen to be moving across the front in the vicinity of Klaphoeck village, and an hour or so later an urgent message was received from Brigade Headquarters:

ENEMY HAVE BROKEN THROUGH AT LES MOERES AND HAVE WORKED UP NOTRE DAME DES NEIGES ROAD TO A POINT ABOUT 600 YARDS FROM THIS PLACE. SEND TWO COMPANIES TO A POINT ABOUT 287782 AND SEIZE OPPORTUNITY TO COUNTER-ATTACK ENEMY FORCE ON LEFT FLANK. YOU ARE SUPPORTED BY A TROOP OF DIV CAV AT A POINT ON THE ROAD 600 YARDS SOUTH OF NOTRE DAMES DES NEIGES. HOLD WATERLINE IMMEDIATELY NORTH OF BERGUES WITH REMAINDER OF BERGUES GARRISON.

Messages were sent by runner to the company commanders. The orders for the withdrawal to the beach had now been received and, to cover the withdrawal and comply with this new order from Brigade, A and C Companies were ordered to take up positions to the north of the town, while the rest of the battalion withdrew by stages. As part of the plan, Wilmot was ordered to provide two rifle platoons, one each in support of A and C Companies. When he called for volunteers there was no shortage of them – especially from the remnants of his original section – and although it was not strictly necessary for him to do so, he decided to take personal command of one of the platoons, leaving the remainder of his company to withdraw under the command of the 1st Loyals.

iii

15 Company had worked its way round to the east of Bergues and 2 Platoon had reached the embankment of the Bergues-Furnes canal. Because of the inundated terrain, the armoured cars had been left at the rear, and the heavy machine guns and mortars had to be lugged forward by hand.

While in previous days most of the fire had been high-calibre stuff, the Grossdeutschlanders were now within small-arms range of the fortified town, and the enemy had defensive positions all round it, so that now the fields and marshes were crisscrossed with rifle and light machine-gun bullets, and movement could only be made in safety on the flat of the stomach.

Sergeant Semmper and Corporal Falk set up the Spandau on the lip of the canal bank with the gun barrel sticking through long grass. This gave an excellent enfilade over the enemy positions on the far side.

When they had fired off several belts the firing from the other side appeared to lessen. Inflatable boats were brought up and 2 Platoon was called forward to make the crossing. They assembled under cover behind the embankment, and while they waited more belted ammunition was brought up so that they would not be short of covering fire.

Lance Corporal Heinrich Lauder, who had been put in charge of one of the dinghies, crouched tensely, awaiting the order to go. Each man carried a sub-machine gun and four stick grenades, two stuck into his belt and two slung round his neck.

As the Spandau opened up, they ran down the bank, threw the dinghies in and jumped after them, and their momentum was enough to take the boats most of the way across, so that only a few strokes of the paddle were necessary to get them to the other side.

There was still plenty of cover in the dip of the canal, and Heinrich and the four with him doubled a hundred yards along the bank to the left.

Cautiously, Lauder crawled up the bank and peered through a clump of grass. Only about fifty yards away, two of the enemy − British by the shape of their helmets − were running across a stretch of open ground. Heinrich acted instinctively. With no thought for his own safety, he crouched on one knee and fired a long burst on his Schmeisser machine pistol. But while he did so, he saw − out of the corner of his eye − a third figure bob up and heard the repeated heavy bark of a revolver. Still firing, Lauder swung the stream of bullets round at this new target; but as he did so a bullet caught him in the throat and he fell backward down the embankment with a strangled cry.

iv

Wilmot left the town with his platoon by the Ypres Gate under covering fire from D Company and after a few hundred yards on the road struck out over flooded fields to a farm a mile north of the town. There, they came under intense machine-gun fire. Two of Griff's men were killed and four wounded, but they pushed slowly on, wading across a flooded field, struggling in mud up to their knees, flopping down on their bellies in ditches and behind hedges, hastily setting sights and firing the Bren and the Enfields across the besodden land; and while this and many similar gutter-fights went on all along the line of the Bergues-Furnes canal, enemy aircraft continued to dive-bomb and machine-gun the troops on the ground.

The counter-attack put in by A and C Companies made progress: the enemy was subjected to accurate small-arms fire and although the canal bank had not yet been re-established, the enemy advance had been checked and the withdrawal from the town was being adequately covered.

Acting on orders from C Company, Wilmot led his platoon out towards the right flank to provide covering fire while the Brens and mortars were leap-frogged forward. He and eight others were now lying in a foot of muddy water with bramble bushes for cover, firing at any German infantryman who failed to keep his head down.

They had accounted for nine of the enemy in this way when, weaving and splashing across the field to their right, a young French ensign arrived, very out of breath.

'We are being . . . pushed,' he managed. 'Machine guns . . . Our – er – *officier* –'

'*En français*,' Wilmot cut in. '*Je comprendrai*.'

The boy looked relieved and launched into a spate of rapid French. All his officers had been killed; his unit was being pinned down by intense machine-gun fire; enemy infantry were beginning to outflank him; they were running out of ammunition and desperately needed covering fire if a break-through was to be avoided.

Wilmot had made up his mind what had to be done before the ensign had finished.

'I want two volunteers,' he said, and of the five that came forward he picked the two Welshmen: Sapper Ward and a thickset, red-headed guardsman known as Taff.

Taking a Bren gun and as much ammunition as they could carry between them, Griff led the way, moving diagonally across a waterlogged field to a point beyond the extremity of the company's right front. This movement in itself was hazardous enough, but the last twenty-odd yards to the ditch he was heading for were commanded by the canal embankment about forty yards distant and were without cover.

'That ditch,' he said, and pointed. 'Go on my order. Wait for it . . . Now!'

The sub-machine gun opened fire when they were halfway across. Wilmot, who had remained behind to give covering fire, stood up, steadied his service revolver over the crook of his arm and fired three deliberate shots.

Sapper Ward and Guardsman Taff had crossed the gap and were safe in the ditch. Ward looked back to see what had happened to the officer.

'All right, sir?' he shouted.

But it was not all right. Griff Wilmot was gritting his teeth and clutching his side, and a moment later he pitched forward into the mud.

V

CHURCHILL TO WEYGAND, 6.45 PM.

CRISIS IN EVACUATION NOW REACHED. FIVE FIGHTER SQUADRONS ACTING ALMOST CONTINU-

OUSLY IS MOST WE CAN DO, BUT SIX SHIPS, SEVERAL FILLED WITH TROOPS, SUNK BY BOMBING THIS MORNING. ARTILLERY FIRE MENACING ONLY PRACTICABLE CHANNEL. ENEMY CLOSING IN ON REDUCED BRIDGEHEAD. BY TRYING TO HOLD ON WE MAY LOSE ALL. BY GOING TONIGHT, MUCH MAY CERTAINLY BE SAVED, THOUGH MUCH WILL BE LOST. SITUATION CANNOT BE FULLY JUDGED ONLY BY ADMIRAL ABRIAL IN THE FORTRESS, NOR BY YOU, NOR BY US HERE. WE HAVE THEREFORE ORDERED GENERAL ALEXANDER COMMANDING BRITISH SECTOR OF BRIDGEHEAD TO JUDGE IN CONSULTATION WITH ADMIRAL ABRIAL WHETHER TO TRY TO STAY OVER TOMORROW OR NOT. TRUST YOU WILL AGREE. MESSAGE ENDS = +

THIRTY-FIVE

Number 12 Casualty Clearing Station in Rosendael – which was the biggest at Dunkirk and effectively a field hospital – had been set up in a large, ostentatious mansion whose principal feature was a large tower of red brick, from which hung the Red Cross flag. There were about two acres of grounds, including a long, sweeping drive leading between shrubs and bushes which served as good camouflage for the ambulances that came and went almost continually. In front of the house was a large lawn, with an ornamental pond, and an expanse of shrubbery that ran down to the south bank of the Calais canal. To the left was a huge kitchen garden, which gave onto open fields.

Inside the building, which was called Chapeau Rouge because of its distinctive red roof, everything was very spacious and solid. A flight of white stone steps led up to the front door, and an impressive staircase dominated the entrance hall.

All the rooms, all the landings and halls and vestibules were taken up by wounded men, some on stretchers, a few on beds, but the majority were made as comfortable as was possible on the floor. The whole building buzzed constantly with flies. Down in the double cellars, the surgical teams worked non-stop, stitching wounds, removing splinters, setting bones, while out in the gardens stray dogs sniffed and scavenged among the heaps of bloody dressings.

In the afternoon the officer commanding, Colonel Pank, assembled his staff of seventeen surgeons in the main cellar, which had been reinforced with sandbags and oildrums filled with gravel.

'You all know why I've called this meeting,' he told them.

'We're still hopeful of some more hospital ships being able to take the stretcher cases, but there is a large number of cases too ill to be moved, and I have orders that for every hundred casualties left behind, one medical officer and ten orderlies must also remain.'

He looked round at the haggard faces, the blood-stained coats. In the not-far distance a Bofors gun was firing. From time to time, the house shook from bomb explosions.

'What I propose to do is get the chaplain and Father O'Shea here to draw names out of a hat. I estimate that the maximum number of wounded remaining will be three hundred, so the last three officers' names out of the hat will stay, and the last thirty orderlies. Does anyone have any objection to that method?'

Heads shook, and someone mumbled, 'Let's get on with it then.' The slips of paper were thrown into two hats, the C of E chaplain drawing for the officers and Father O'Shea for the other ranks.

Later, there was a short valedictory service in the cupola. Catholics and Protestants joined together to sing a few hymns and say a few prayers. After the service, Father O'Shea gave his crucifix to Major Newman, whose name had been last out of the hat and who would be in command of the medical team staying on. Then it was time for the last handshakes and wishes of good luck; and that evening the medical team, less three officers, thirty orderlies and one courageous man – Private Gaze – who chose to remain behind and face capture, embarked for England.

ii

With his commanding officer on his back, Sapper Ward waded waist deep across flooded fields and marshland, bullets whipping all around him. When he got back to the rallying point he asked for transport to get his officer back to the casualty clearing station, but as none was available he found a wheelbarrow in the farm buildings, lowered Griff into it and set off along the cratered lanes and cart tracks as calmly as if he were taking a sack of potatoes down the valley to the market at Ystalyfera.

Weak from loss of blood, Wilmot slipped in and out of consciousness as the wheelbarrow bumped along. They were overtaken by other troops making their way back to the coast, but the only ambulance that came past was full up. Shells fell ahead, behind and on either side. Aircraft came over at tree-top height, spattering bullets along the road. Just after dusk, they met a unit of French infantry marching in single file to take up positions being vacated by British troops. They were in perfect formation: bayonets fixed, totally silent, every man in step. Light-headed and half-conscious, Griff raised a hand in salute from the wheelbarrow, and the French officer in command returned it smartly as he went by.

It was after midnight when Ward finally pushed the wheelbarrow up the gravelled drive of Chapeau Rouge and handed his charge over to an orderly.

Griff was lifted onto a table. He was dimly aware of his uniform being cut away and the haggard face of a surgeon examining him. 'All right, old chap,' a voice said. 'We'll do something to ease the pain right away.'

He felt a stab with a needle, and almost immediately experienced a sensation of floating rapidly upward to a great height.

iii

Simone had decided to dig up the back lawn. For over a week now she had been haunted by the sound of gunfire from across the Channel and, with the girls still away at the headquarters and everyone else in Kent feverishly engaged in voluntary work, she felt she needed to do something positive to take her mind off what was happening – or what might be happening – to the men in her life.

Apart from planting a few bulbs in pots for Christmas she

485

had never done any serious gardening before. Determined to do things properly, she had tied up her hair in a silk scarf, donned an elegant pair of summer slacks, pegged out a square with string and, while Blashford watched in canine amazement, set about lifting the turf.

She quickly discovered that it required every ounce of her strength even to make the spade penetrate the grass, let alone sink to any depth, and after fifteen minutes she had succeeded only in making herself hot and angry. She was just debating whether to persevere or give up, when a uniformed figure appeared at the side gate.

'Major Pearce,' he said, saluting as he advanced across the lawn. 'I wonder if I might have a word, Mrs Wilmot?'

She dropped the spade and put her hands to her mouth. 'Oh God – no. It isn't Griff, is it?'

He shook his head and smiled. 'No, no. Not bad news at all.'

Blashford was being a nuisance so she put him inside the house. When she returned, the major was examining her earthworks. 'You probably don't remember me, but we met a long time ago,' he said. 'I was at school here at Prowse in '25.'

She took off her headscarf and shook out her hair. 'Really?'

'I remember your husband well, Mrs Wilmot. He taught me all the history I know.'

Why was it that people always had to speak of Griff as if it had been a privilege to know him? 'Is that what you came to tell me?'

'No, not at all. I've come to ask a favour.'

'What sort of favour?'

He hesitated, then shot her a quick glance. 'We need French interpreters, Mrs Wilmot. To act as liaison officers.'

'I don't want to be any sort of officer,' she said quietly.

'There would be no need at all for you to be,' he assured her. He turned away and looked southward at the cloud over France. When he turned back to face her, he was much more businesslike. 'I don't know if you're aware of it, but large numbers of French troops are now arriving in England. We have a number of French interpreters, of course, but not enough, and it would be an enormous help if we could have the assistance of someone like yourself who is not only fluent in both languages but who is actually French.'

'I see.'

'Would you like to volunteer?' He glanced at her efforts with a spade. 'I'm quite sure, if you were prepared to, we might be able to arrange a couple of men to come in and give you a hand with the digging . . .'

She smiled. 'Are you bribing me to work for you, Major?'

'Not at all. It would simply be . . . one of the perks that goes with the job.'

'So what exactly is it you want from me?'

'First and foremost, your cooperation. I'm not at liberty to give you very much more information until I have your agreement. I'm sure you understand the reasons for that. But I think I can guarantee that you would be doing interesting work – work for France every bit as much as for Britain. There are men returning now who have been in the thick of the fighting. To be received and welcomed by a person such as yourself, who can speak to them in their own language, would be invaluable.'

Simone turned away. This was the sort of request she had always dreaded. It was the call to arms essentially, the call of her country, the call to be involved again, the call of duty. And she hated 'duty'. She hated the 'my country right or wrong' attitude, the 'all pull together and we'll get the job done' approach that one read so often in British newspapers and heard continually on the BBC. It had been that very attitude that had caused her scorn of Griff when she found him trying on his uniform hat that day they arrived back from Eggardon.

But perhaps, she reflected now, her scorn had been a cover-up for a deeper-seated emotion that was neither hatred nor fear so much as a sensation of nausea. War and authority – they went hand in hand, and were the root cause of every unhappiness she had ever known. The thought of being involved with them all over again caused a sickness in her stomach, a gut rebellion.

But wasn't she already involved? Wasn't everyone? And wasn't it this same refusal to face up to reality which had given Hitler the confidence to walk into Austria and Poland and Belgium and Holland? Though she had not known what form the request – or call to duty or whatever it was – would take, she had always known secretly, in the bottom of her soul, that if ever it came, she would not be able to refuse it. She had known it that morning a year before when she lay in bed with Griff after listening to the nightingale. She had been aware then that there was no avoiding what was coming, no escape from the white water as it went over the cliff. One might cling to the banks for a while, as she had done these past nine months, but eventually the tide of events won, and you were swept along with everyone else.

Even now she sought desperately to hang on a little longer. Surely she had done enough – lost enough – to be excused a second involvement?

But what was the alternative? To shut her eyes to it all? To dig up her lawn and grow potatoes? To try to put the clock back and make David into her little boy again? To go on aimlessly through life, wondering what she was trying to do, where she should be going, where she belonged?

'I would appreciate an early decision, Mrs Wilmot,' Pearce said quietly. 'We need your services now, not in a week's time.'

She had almost forgotten he was still there. She turned back and smiled, shrugging. 'In that case, Major, what are we waiting for?'

iv

. . . Another group joins us led by an officer with a flashlight. Some way along there is a ship lying close in and somebody suggests using it to signal for help. It works. There is an answering signal from the deck and within a few minutes a boat appears in the surf. This time we hold it well out and make people wade waist deep.

A rough queue is formed and the whole party is embarked in three trips. Nobody breaks queue and an officer goes with each boatload.

Kind hands help us up the companionway of a minesweeper and give us hot cocoa. They take away my uniform to dry it and I collapse exhausted on the floor of the wardroom. I hear vaguely through my dreams the diving of a Stuka and the shout 'They've got *Grasshopper*!'

When I wake it is light and I look outside; we are still horribly close inshore, engaged in pulling a destroyer off the sand. Rumour comes that we have been ordered to proceed to Dunkirk. I am woken up next by people pouring into the wardroom. We are alongside a mole packed with troops wearing French helmets.

At last we put to sea to the accompaniment of five bomb crashes and the deafening noise of the ship's anti-aircraft cannon firing above our heads.

At Sheerness I am given back my uniform nearly dry, minus my silver cigarette case and wallet – without money I cannot make my way home and have to deliver myself to the troop train. We are given a very welcome lunch at the naval barracks but I feel somewhat ill-dressed, covered in tar. The rail transport officer gives us cards to write our telegraph messages on, but in the event they are sent by post which causes my family some anxiety.

In the train someone says that to win back what we have lost will take many years of bitter fighting. We feel ashamed of our 'also-ran' performance, but are much moved by the sight of every road as we come into London packed with cheering people waving Union Jacks as if we had won a splendid victory . . .

THIRTY-SIX

Sunday, 2 June. The early hours: huge flames are rising from Dunkirk. The eastern arm of the harbour is lit up in silhouette against the flames. The stream of soldiers continues to move out along the mole. Many of these are French now, and because of conflicting orders some of them refuse to be parted from their units or to give up their arms, and confusion results.

Sometimes they are urged by the naval shore party to hurry into a tired run, but for the most part they just plod blindly on towards safety. Sometimes the queue stops moving altogether and the troops are packed stationary on the narrow walkway waiting for the next ship to come alongside. These are men who have borne the brunt of the battle, men who have been fighting rearguard actions all the way back from the Dyle. They are men who have been holding out on the perimeter at Nieuport and Furnes and Bulscamp, Les Moeres, Galghoeck, Bergues, Coudekerque and Ghyvelde. There are heroes among them: men like Captain Ervine-Andrews who only hours before held up a German advance singlehanded, picking off no less than seventeen of the enemy with an Enfield rifle from the roof of a blazing barn. They include the best of the British army who, along with the French regiments still in position to cover the withdrawal, have made possible what was believed to be impossible.

'Wounded to the front! Gangway! Gangway! Make a gangway for the stretchers! Mind the hole in the walkway! It's no good, he's dead, chum. Push him out the way . . .'

Here and there a company or platoon arrives in parade ground order. A Guards officer, his battledress blackened and charred and his head roughly bandaged, salutes the quarterdeck as he steps aboard HMS *Shikari* and apologizes to the captain for his appearance. Every man carries a rifle or light machine gun: many have spent part of their day scouring the dunes for spare ammunition. But the ships are taking such huge numbers of troops now that every pound of unnecessary topweight has to be discarded, and on arrival at the ships they are told to throw all weapons into the sea.

Some of them sing. One platoon comes onto the jetty to the tune of 'Tipperary' on a mouth organ. And while they wait patiently on the mole, moving slowly forward as each ship fills up and is replaced by another, the guns bark on, the shells whistle overhead and the bombs continue to thunder and crash into the sea, the harbour, the town, the dunes.

ii

Loaded to the gunwales with troops, the small craft were arriving at Ramsgate in an unending stream. Normal life in the town had virtually ceased: everyone was in some way or other involved in welcoming the men back home. The fit had to be loaded onto buses and lorries and driven off to the station; the injured had to be transferred to hospital; the dead had to be identified, labelled and removed to the mortuary. Working round the clock – and in some cases twice and three times round the clock – parties of women stood at trestle tables making hundreds of gallons of tea and spreading margarine on tens of thousands of sandwiches so that the troops could have their tea and wads as soon as they stepped ashore.

For a few days, the heart and soul of Britain was to be found at this cheap and cheerful little seaside resort, the resort of domineering landladies, henpecked husbands and naughty postcards. For a few days, people mattered more than regulations. For a few days – and especially for the eighty thousand allied troops who landed in the little harbour

– Ramsgate came to mean Britain, and Britain Ramsgate.

Soon after dawn, Nick Massingbohm arrived alongside aboard a forty-foot motor cruiser called *Lady Petronella*. He was one of about fifty passengers, mostly French, having lost touch with the Grenadiers in the confusion of the arrival at Malo-les-Bains. His RAF uniform singled him out immediately from the rest, and he was directed to a reception area where army officers assisted by clerks and interpreters sat behind trestle tables taking details of each arrival.

'Name and unit?' an army captain barked.

He gave them, and produced his identity disc. 'Any chance of a lift to Manston?'

'My God!' sneered the captain. 'You bloody Brylcreem boys want it with jam on, don't you? It's only a couple of miles! Do what everyone else has been doing for the past three weeks. Walk!'

If he had felt less exhausted he might have hit back. As it was, he turned away from the table in disgust and made his way past the line of soldiers that were getting aboard buses. But he had not gone more than a few yards when a familiar voice called his name. He turned.

'Simone! What on earth are you doing here?'

She made a throw-away gesture towards the trestle tables. 'Oh, just interpreting, you know. I saw what happened back there. Some of these people are animals, you know. Does Christine know you're safe?'

'Not yet.'

'Do you want to send a telegram?'

'Rather!'

'Come with me, I'm sure it can be arranged.'

He followed her back to the reception area, carefully ignoring the glower from the captain who had taken his details.

Simone was a different person now that she had something positive to do. She was working alongside some French liaison officers, and obviously had them all eating out of her hand.

'You can have five words,' she told him, so he wrote, 'SAFE BACK MARRY ME SATURDAY', and addressed it to Christine at the Wren officers' mess in the Lord Warden Hotel at Dover.

'Now what about transport?' Simone asked, and within a few minutes had talked a major into dropping Nick off at RAF Manston.

When he arrived, an elderly hall porter glanced up as he paused in the lobby of the officers' mess, where the royal portraits hung. 'Oh, Mr Massingbohm,' he said. 'Will you be dining in the mess this evening, sir?'

iii

Rear Admiral Wake-Walker arrived alongside the depot ship *Sandhurst* at Dover in a motor torpedo boat that morning, and having borrowed a clean shirt and flannels to replace those he had borrowed from Captain Allison in the *Worcester*, took his flag lieutenant with him up to the castle, where a conference was to be held in the underground headquarters.

He was greeted by Admirals Ramsay and Somerville, who had just heard that HMS *Keith* had been hit on the bridge and were relieved to see that he was unhurt.

He was taken down a steep road with a fine view of the harbour, and then by a tunnel into the hill. First down a steep slope with floor and walls of concrete, then into a wide passage through walls of chalk with layers of huge flints, dimly lit by an occasional lamp. This opened at the end into a larger oblong chamber at right angles to the passage which was divided up by boarding into a number of offices. Past these a narrow passage led to the vice admiral's office. Here the chamber finished in a large window and door onto a narrow railed-in platform on the sheer face of the cliff. Immediately below, you looked down three hundred feet into the chimney pots and gardens of houses on the foreshore. Beyond, the harbour spread out: no naval officer could ever have had a better overall view of his command than the Vice Admiral Dover.

The conference assembled. Ramsay presided, and all the key areas of interest were represented: Admiral Somerville, who acted as Ramsay's assistant; Captain Vaughan Morgan, the Chief of Staff and one of Ramsay's old shipmates; his assistant Captain Bisset; Captain Denny, in charge of the Dynamo team; Commander Jack Clouston, who had returned overnight from Dunkirk to brief Ramsay on conditions ashore in Dunkirk and collect an augmented shore party; the army and RAF liaison officers; the representatives of the Board of Trade; the sea transport officers; the specialist staff officers, and finally the Wren writer who sat with pad and pencil taking the minutes of the meeting and recording the admiral's decisions and directives.

Ramsay began without preamble as soon as the meeting had been called to order.

'I intend that embarkation tonight will take place between 2100 and 0350,' he told his staff. 'Because the enemy is now advancing westward from La Panne, it will be necessary to use the piers in the Nouveau Avant Port as well as the east mole for embarkation. For this purpose, a large number of small craft have been assembled and they will tonight make a massed descent, arriving at nightfall and working throughout the hours of darkness. Personnel ships and destroyers will be sent to the east mole, and careful coordination will be required to ensure that the alongside berths remain vacant for the shortest possible time. Naval officers are being sent to act as advisors to the masters of personnel ships, and parties of naval ratings are being drafted to stiffen the morale of their crews. The RAF are being requested to concentrate their fighter effort to provide maximum air protection at dusk and dawn, when ships and boats will be at greater risk from dive-bombers . . .'

After the meeting, Wake-Walker lunched with Ramsay at his house in the castle grounds before taking a nap on Admiral Somerville's bed. Halfway through his snooze, he was awakened by two naval officers, their uniforms blackened with oil and smoke. It was the captain and first lieutenant of *Keith*, who had called in to reassure him that they were safe.

iv

HMS *Vagabond* was being moved by tug to the fuelling buoy when the general signal to all ships involved in Operation Dynamo arrived from Vice Admiral Dover. Half an hour before, after the last of nearly a thousand soldiers had disembarked and marched off along the quay to the station, Archie had ordered that as soon as the ship had been secured at the fuelling buoy and rum had been issued, Sunday routine would be worked for the rest of the day. In this way, all hands except watchkeepers and dutymen would be stood down to grab a few hours' sleep.

While the first lieutenant took charge of moving the ship, Archie was trying to catch up on the paperwork, and when the new yeoman of signals knocked on his door the correspondence officer was standing beside his desk keeping him supplied with letters for signature, correspondence from Captain D and a welter of other reports and returns that make it difficult for captains of HM ships to improve their golf handicaps.

'Come in, Yeoman,' Archie said tiredly, and held out his hand to take the signal clipboard. He read:

> FINAL EVACUATION IS STAGED FOR TONIGHT, AND THE NATION LOOKS TO THE NAVY TO SEE THIS THROUGH. I WANT EVERY SHIP TO REPORT AS SOON AS POSSIBLE WHETHER SHE IS FIT AND READY TO MEET THE CALL WHICH HAS BEEN MADE ON OUR COURAGE AND ENDURANCE.

He pondered this signal for several minutes. He knew Admiral Ramsay personally and had a great deal of respect for his judgement: he would not make such a signal without good reason.

So why had he made it? Why had he thought it necessary to receive reports from every ship? Why should the Dynamo staff not do as it had done on every previous day of this operation, and simply promulgate sailing orders in the usual way?

He was at first inclined to send the reply straight off – something like READY AYE READY, or FIT, READY AND EAGER TO OBEY YOUR ORDER. But if Ramsay had had the wisdom to call for reports from his captains shouldn't he call for a similar report from the men under his command?

'Thank you, Yeoman,' he said. 'Ask the first lieutenant to come and see me as soon as we've shifted berth, will you?'

Armitage appeared at his door a few minutes later.

'You wanted to see me, sir.'

'Yes. Come in.' Archie nodded to the correspondence officer to dismiss him. 'Now,' he continued when the sub lieutenant had withdrawn. 'Read this and tell me what you think I should say in reply.'

Armitage read the signal. 'We're having our arm twisted, aren't we? We have no option but to report in the affirmative.'

'And what if we aren't fit or ready?'

'Sir, you know as well as I do that the ship's company's just about all in. Half of them are already asleep on the messdecks as it is –'

Archie looked up quickly. 'Why's that? I haven't heard Pipe Down. Who gave them permission?'

Armitage shook his head and looked sulky.

'Well?'

'No one, sir. It – it just happened –'

'But with your knowledge and tacit approval, right?'

'If you want someone to blame, yes, sir. Right.'

'Are there any watchkeepers among the men turned in?'

'Probably, yes.'

'What the hell do you mean, "probably"? You're supposed to *know*, First Lieutenant! That's why you wear two rings on your sleeve!'

Armitage sighed deeply. 'Some of the men have been secured by the captains of tops, sir. The chief boatswain's mate came to me and told me they'd be more use to him in their bunks than wandering about like ghosts. I can't answer for the stokers, but I should imagine Chief will be refuelling with a skeleton crew.'

'So what you're saying is you've lost control. Right?'

'No, sir, that is not right. What I am saying is that the ship's company is on the point of exhaustion, and if you'll permit me to say so, I think both you and I and all the wardroom officers are as well.'

Archie stared down at Ramsay's signal. For five months now he had put up with Armitage's lack of cooperation. He had given him his head, allowed him to organize the ship's company and lead the wardroom in his own way. He had not liked that way very much, and Armitage had made it clear to him that he did not approve of his style of captaincy. It was a personality clash, that was all. There was nothing very wrong with Armitage as an officer, a seaman or first lieutenant. It was just that when Their Lordships appointed Armitage as Archie's second in command, they put a square peg in a round hole.

'You still haven't answered my question. Is this ship fit and ready for operations tonight?'

'I think I have given you the fullest possible answer to that question, sir.'

'Well, I won't argue with you, Number One. I'll just take another opinion.' Archie lifted a sound-powered telephone from its hook and wound the handle. It was answered immediately.

'Coxswain!'

'Captain. Come and see me in my cabin please, Coxswain.'

'Aye aye, sir.'

Armitage moved to go, but was stopped by a peremptory, 'Wait!' A minute later the coxswain appeared at the door, knocked at the lintel and entered. He was a man in his mid-thirties, a cheerful, ruddy faced man from Liverpool. He was also the senior rating on board and the man who had his ear closest to the ground in matters of morale and discipline.

'A question for you, Coxswain,' Archie said. 'We're being invited by Flag Officer Dover to make one last effort tonight. Does that present any problems?'

Chief Petty Officer Bennett looked taken aback. 'Problems, sir? What sort of problems?'

'On the messdecks. Would you say the chaps are fit and ready?'

Bennett broke into a wide grin. 'Ready, willing and able, sir,' he said without any hesitation.

'There you are, Number One,' Archie said quietly when the coxswain had departed back to his office to sort the mail. 'That's the sort of answer I would have expected from you. I think they call it "the fighting spirit", don't they?'

Half an hour later, *Vagabond*'s signalled reply to the vice admiral's appeal was logged by Christine in the Dynamo Room. It read: 'READY, WILLING, ABLE.'

v

But among the many other signals from destroyers and minesweepers that rang with the same self-confidence came a quite different one from Dunkirk, one that presented Ramsay and his staff with yet another difficult decision. Unlike all Captain Tennant's other signals, this one had been intentionally transmitted uncoded, so that it was bound to have been picked up by German intelligence and passed to the high command. 'WOUNDED SITUATION ACUTE,' it read, 'AND HOSPITAL SHIPS SHOULD ENTER DURING THE DAY. GENEVA CONVENTION WILL BE HONOUR-

ABLY OBSERVED AND IT IS FELT THAT THE ENEMY WILL REFRAIN FROM ATTACKING.'

As the entire harbour facilities at Dunkirk would be required for the final evacuation that night, Ramsay agreed to send the hospital ships over in daylight, presuming that the Germans would take the hint and allow them to cross unmolested.

Accordingly, the Southern Railway steamer *Worthing* – which had been converted to a hospital ship on the outbreak of war – was ordered to sail at one p.m. and the *Paris* at five. Both ships were painted white with bold red crosses on their sides and funnels, so there was no possibility of German pilots mistaking them for anything other than hospital ships.

vi

As it was Sunday, there was a church service on the beach at Malo-les-Bains soon after dawn, and it continued to the end in spite of five interruptions from enemy fighters that swept at low level over the sands, machine-gunning the troops.

No ships were due to arrive in daylight hours, so the rest of the day was spent waiting for darkness. One of the largest battalions was the 1/6 South Staffordshires. They had reached the sea at four that morning to find thousands of French troops milling about on the east mole and confusion everywhere. The brigadier had ordered that the battalion was to remain on the sands until nightfall, so the troops dispersed and dug in. Soon afterwards the beach was bombarded by enemy artillery using air-burst shells, but the fuses had been set too high – just as they had been in the closing months of the Great War – and casualties were light.

No troops left cover without orders, but when there was a bit of heat in the sun, some of the troops paddled in the sea or practised trick riding on abandoned motorcycles.

At times the scene resembled Blackpool Sands on a bank holiday: some men played cards; some gambled on where the next shell would fall; some just snoozed in the sun. One company commander insisted that his men clear up the beach, saying that if they left a tidy beach it would be less of a coup for Goebbels's propaganda photographers. Another officer had his hair cut on the orders of a senior officer – who happened to be his father. And while the hours passed, the raids came in with monotonous regularity. One minute the sands would be black with men; the next, as the aircraft started diving and the bombs falling, the ants went scurrying back into the cover of the sand hills.

vii

Because of the large scale of the coming night's operation (which included the sinking of block ships in the harbour entrance) it had been agreed that Commander Clouston should return to Dunkirk in advance of the main fleet, taking with him an augmented naval pier party to ensure that this last phase of the evacuation proceeded as smoothly as possible.

They set out at three-thirty p.m. in two RAF crash boats, Clouston in Crash Boat 243 and Sub Lieutenant Roger Wake in Crash Boat 270. Three hours later, after a calm, uneventful crossing, they were set upon by eight Junkers 87s off Gravelines.

It was as if the German planes knew which boat to attack, and within minutes of the first bombs falling Clouston's boat had been swamped by near misses.

On board Crash Boat 270 the French liaison officer, Lieutenant de Vaisseau Roux, brought one aircraft down with the Lewis machine gun – in spite of having the foresight shot off while he was firing – while Sub Lieutenant Wake evaded repeated attacks by violent manoeuvres.

When the attack had passed, Wake took his boat over to Clouston's, and found that it was now almost submerged, with the crew in the water.

Aware that more enemy planes might arrive at any second,

Clouston waved the other boat away. 'Don't wait around!' he shouted from the water. 'Get on to Dunkirk!'

'I think I ought to pick you up at least, sir!'

But Clouston was still very much the senior officer. 'You're a sitting target, Sub! Get on to Dunkirk!'

After Crashboat 270 had moved off, the French liaison officer heaved himself up onto the swamped wreck and reported a lifeboat adrift a mile or two distant.

'Permission to swim over and collect it, sir?' Sub Lieutenant Solomon asked.

Two people would be needed to row the lifeboat, and as Clouston had always prided himself on his physical fitness, a two-mile swim did not seem a great challenge. He decided to go with Solomon himself.

They began swimming, but Clouston had not reckoned on the effect the past week had had on him and he soon realized that he was becoming exhausted. Telling Solomon to go on without him, he turned back to join the rest of his party who were still clinging to the wreck, swapping stories and singing to keep up their spirits while they waited. But although Sub Lieutenant Solomon reached the lifeboat and managed to get aboard, he never returned with it – there was only one oar and he too was exhausted. The hours passed, and one by one the officers and men of Crash Boat 243 slipped beneath the waves. Only one – an RAF aircraftsman – survived long enough to be picked up by a passing destroyer; and Commander Clouston, under whose guidance over two hundred thousand men had made their way along the east mole to safety, was never seen again.

THIRTY-SEVEN

Wilmot was lying on a camp bed in the garden at Rosendael when the stretcher party came to collect him.

'Good news for you, Major,' said the orderly. 'You're goin' 'ome!'

He was very weak and drowsy. Everything he said sounded to himself as though someone else had said it. 'Home?' he echoed. 'I thought – I thought . . .'

They lifted him onto a makeshift stretcher that had been made out of two broomhandles and a greatcoat.

'They're sending a 'ospital ship after all, sir.'

'How many of us are they taking?' he managed.

'Couldn't tell you that, sir, but the more of you as go, the fewer of us 'as to stay be'ind and meet Jerry when he arrives.'

'I – I think . . . surely there are others who should go before me –'

'Don't bother your 'ead about that, Major. Just count yourself lucky.'

They loaded him into an ambulance with several other stretcher cases, and after a delay while they waited for another air attack to finish, the lorry set out through the port.

The driver of the leading vehicle in the convoy was Private Gaze, who had driven his town volunteer ambulance before the war and who had agreed to work as a driver at Rosendael on learning that several of the regular ambulance drivers had deserted to get themselves back to England. He had already led several convoys of ambulances through the city to the west quay and probably knew the safest routes as well as anyone at Dunkirk. Threading his way round craters, sheltering by the bastions during air raids and making detours round areas where the roads were blocked, he led the six lorries to the western end of the harbour where the hospital ships were expected to berth.

After several lengthy stops, they came to a final halt and when the wounded had been unloaded, the ambulances left to collect another load of casualties. While it was gone, Griff lay on his back looking up at the billowing cloud of oily smoke above him and trying to ignore the nearer of the shells that were arriving with uncomfortable regularity.

He felt curiously detached from the whole scene now, and his thoughts wandered. He tried to recite a sonnet by Donne to himself, but the lines became mixed up, so instead he tried to repeat to himself the accession date of every English monarch from Egbert to George VI. It had been one of the great feats he had been able to perform at the blackboard in his days as Head of History at Prowse.

Prowse . . . He went back there in his imagination. He walked up the gravel drive past the rhododendrons and smelt the smell of furniture polish. He heard the shouts of boys playing Rugby football, the distant voices of the choir at practice. While the sirens wailed and another Stuka raid came in, he remembered some of those old jokes he reserved for the new fourth form at the beginning of the school year. 'You have tasted a whole worm. You may leave by the town drain . . .' Would he ever tell that one again?

He had not fully appreciated the extent of what was happening until he had marched into the perimeter with his section a few days before. But now . . . he struggled to view events as an historian rather than a participant, and could only feel pessimistic. All those abandoned tanks and weapons . . . all those aircraft destroyed . . . and if France fell into German hands . . .

It was too depressing to think about. He watched the enemy aircraft wheeling and diving, and his thoughts turned to Simone.

Images of her came like the flickering pictures of an early cinematograph: the waif-like girl, beret pulled down over her ears, he had found weeping in the Bois de Boulogne;

the beautiful young woman with her hair up who, over coffee and liqueurs at the Coq d'Or, lifted a slender hand for him to slip the engagement ring on her finger; the pale, defiant Simone only a few weeks later who told him she was to have another man's child.

What would she have been up to? Had she been seeing Archie? Had they turned him into a complete cuckold?

He heard the sound of tyres on glass and rubble and a moment later a convoy of ambulances drew up. The same stretcher-bearers who had brought him began lifting him back into the ambulance.

'Where are we going?'

'Back where you came from, sir.'

'You mean England?'

'No, sir. I mean the 'ospital.'

'But . . . what happened to the ships?'

The stretcher-bearer laughed. 'Never got 'ere, sir. Nobody told Jerry about the Geneva Convention, seemingly.'

ii

Nerves were beginning to fail now. On board the mine-sweeper *Hebe*, which had acted as headquarters ship off the beaches through the fiercest attacks, a sub lieutenant had collapsed in convulsions, and several members of the crew, many of whom had been without sleep for the best part of a week, suffered the same symptoms the following day. The skipper of the Hythe lifeboat refused to take his boat to Dunkirk and deliberately ran it aground, persuading the skippers of the Dungeness and Walmer boats to follow his lead.

The destroyer *Verity* still had severe morale problems, with six men listed as deserters and the rest of the ship's company loth to return to the hellfire on the other side of the Channel. Some of the small craft turned back in mid-Channel without collecting a single man from the beaches. Even some of the tugs were refusing duty: in one case a tugmaster had to be threatened with gunfire before obeying Admiral Wake-Walker's order to assist a stranded ship.

On board the hospital ship *Tynwald* the crew were in a virtual state of mutiny. Armed naval ratings had been used to prevent the men from deserting, the master had been relieved and fresh officers drafted in. The *Malines* and *Ben-My-Chree* had followed *Tynwald*'s dubious example and had lain idle all night while signal after signal came in urgently requesting that hospital ships be sent. Their reluctance to sail was to be reinforced, however: that afternoon the hospital ship *Worthing* was set upon by enemy bombers and turned back after several near misses, and a few hours later *Paris* was sunk by an almost identical raid.

But in spite of the fear and the fatigue, Ramsay's 'massed descent' went ahead that afternoon as planned, hundreds more small craft setting out from Ramsgate. Among them went *Daisy Belle*, with Pringle and Odell now assisted by an elderly Scottish garage mechanic called Sid Imrie.

'You know something?' Sid remarked when they were clear of the breakwater, 'I always wanted to go to sea as a lad. I wanted to be a stoker. Now just think o' that!'

'So why didn't you?' David asked.

Sid gazed ahead at the line of little ships wallowing their way across the Channel. 'Me mum wouldnae have it, God rest her. Said no son of hers was goin' into the navy and learnin' the sort of tricks sailors get up to.'

David grinned. 'Didn't you ever wonder how she knew?'

'How she knew what?'

'What they get up to.'

Sid lifted the peak of a very greasy cap and scratched his balding head. 'Come to think of it, I never looked at it that way before!'

iii

Soon after darkness fell, a despatch rider arrived at Chapeau Rouge and reported to Major Newman that if there were any walking wounded, there was a chance that they could be evacuated that night, provided they could make their own way down the mole, and when this message was passed to the inmates there was an almost general effort to qualify, with some men literally crawling from their stretchers to the awaiting lorries.

An hour or so before, the French had brought in from Zuydecoote Infirmary about seventeen terrible cases of men who had been burnt out of recognition in the *Crested Eagle*. Some of them had great swollen heads, blackened and blistered by the fire.

One of these had been placed on a stretcher next to Griff, and when he learnt that there was a chance of evacuation he began trying to undo the bandages which covered his eyes; but in doing so, he peeled chunks of skin away at the same time, and screamed out in agony, finally falling back, sobbing and whimpering.

Wilmot leant across and replaced the man's bandages as best he could. He spoke to the man in French and tried to comfort him.

'I've got a wife and new baby,' the man whimpered. 'A wife and new baby!'

A mop and a broom were propped up against the back of an outhouse nearby. Wilmot dragged himself over to them and, more by willpower than anything else, managed to hoist himself up and use them as a crutches. Slowly, he made his way back to the blinded *poilu*.

'On your feet, soldier!'

'I can't! I can't . . . !'

'Yes you can. Come on, make an effort! Try!'

'I can't see!'

'I'll guide you.'

The man stood up, holding his bandaged hands out before him.

'That's the way! Now, turn to your left. A bit more. Three paces forward . . .'

Slowly, with the *poilu* obeying Griff's directions and Griff leaning heavily on his mop and broom, they picked their way out of the garden to an awaiting lorry.

On the way down to the east mole, the lorry went into a hole in the road, which jerked it violently and threw Wilmot off the bench. There was no orderly, and none of the other casualties was able to help him. As the lorry bumped and swayed slowly along, he rolled back and forth on the floor. After a while he realized dully that the blood he was lying in was his own.

Quite suddenly, while the lorry continued slowly down towards the harbour, the pain went right away. It was as if he had been given another shot of morphia: he felt himself floating upward again, but far higher than before; and he was aware of a voice saying, 'Would you like to go on further?' and his own replying, 'Yes! Yes!' – and it didn't matter any more whether or not he saw England or Simone again.

iv

Commander Maund had stepped into the breach as piermaster in the absence of Commander Clouston, and as darkness fell and the ships began to arrive he directed them to the beach, the mole, or the harbour to collect troops. Afloat, Rear Admiral Wake-Walker coordinated the berthing of the larger ships, using his speedboat as a tug, water ambulance and despatch boat as the need arose.

On Malo beach, parade for the South Staffords was ordered for 2100 hours. A portion of the beach had been staked off, and into this area the troops filed two deep. There was a small degree of confusion for a while as no order of march had been issued, but this was overcome by the company commanders and platoon sergeants, and at 2140 about four thousand men began to move off along the beach and onto the mole in an orderly column of route. Discipline was admirable and there was no attempt to hurry unduly on anyone's part. Two destroyers took off the leading units, but the two cross-Channel packet boats for the remainder had difficulty securing to the jetty against the wind and tide, and the half-hour wait for them seemed a very long time.

Because of the high morale of the battalion, dozens of stragglers had attached themselves to it, and if these were counted, the battalion was stronger when it left France than it had been on arrival from England some months before.

The last few thousands of the BEF were making their way along the mole now, and among them, sharing the weight of a heavy suitcase with a staff colonel, came General Alexander and one or two other senior staff officers. The beaches, field hospitals and the town had been checked, and as no more complete units of the BEF had been found, its Commander-in-Chief was returning to Britain.

Venomous was lying alongside and the captain was on the bridge when a voice hailed him from the jetty.

'Can you take some senior officers and staff?'

The officer-of-the-watch, Lieutenant Angus Mackenzie, went aft to the brow on the starboard side of the quarterdeck and a few minutes later reported back to the bridge.

'Two generals, sir,' he told the captain. 'Alexander and Percival. And there's a colonel asleep in your bunk with his boots on.'

As she pulled away from the jetty, *Venomous* was so overloaded with men that she nearly turned turtle, so she stopped and the men were ordered to move lower down in the ship to trim her before making passage back to Dover.

Half an hour after her departure, Commander Maund saw that there were only French left on the mole, and he too decided that his job was done. He embarked in the destroyer *Winchelsea*, leaving Sub Lieutenant Wake in charge of the pier.

v

A little before midnight Third Officer Trendle-Home hurried along the tunnel from the Dynamo Room with a pink message form in her hand. When she entered Ramsay's office, the admiral was in conference with Captain Denny.

'We've just received this, sir,' she said.

Ramsay took the signal from her. It was from the Senior Naval Officer at Dunkirk and read: BEF EVACUATED.

THIRTY-EIGHT

When HMS *Vagabond* came alongside in the early hours of Monday, 3 June, the east mole was all but deserted of troops and coming under steady but not very accurate artillery fire from La Panne.

'Where the hell are the French?' Archie bellowed down to a sub lieutenant standing on the jetty.

It was Roger Wake, who had been presented with a megaphone by the departing Commander Maund and told to take over as piermaster. 'No idea, sir!' he shouted back, and ducked instinctively as a shell whistled overhead.

Astern of *Vagabond* the destroyer *Codrington* was coming alongside, and the *Malcolm* was lying off. On the other side of the jetty the modern car ferry *Autocarrier* lay alongside, empty.

Archie stormed up and down the bridge duckboards. 'Sod the bloody French! What the hell are the buggers up to?'

Aircraft – night bombers – droned overhead, and a stick of bombs fell on the port. Archie felt a great ache of tiredness. He had lost count how many trips the ship had done and he didn't know how much longer he could last. But he was even more concerned about his first lieutenant. He glanced back at him. Armitage seemed to be drunk with fatigue: he was standing with his eyes closed, steadying himself with one hand on the Pelorus to stop himself swaying.

'What's wrong with you, Number One? Missing your beauty sleep?'

Armitage's eyes snapped open but took a moment to refocus. 'Nothing wrong, sir.'

'You were asleep on your feet, man,' Archie muttered. 'Now for God's sake brace up.'

'Sir.'

Five minutes passed, then ten, then thirty, but no troops showed up. Then a motor torpedo boat came throbbing by at slow speed.

'*Vagabond!*' a voice shouted and, seeing that it was Admiral Wake-Walker himself, Archie scrambled to the bridge-wing to raise a hand in acknowledgement. 'You may have to wait some time!' Wake-Walker bellowed. 'Stay alongside until ordered to move.'

'Aye aye, sir!' Archie bellowed back, and saluted as the MTB engines revved and the boat moved seaward along the mole.

Archie stepped down from the bridge-wing and returned to the Pelorus. Armitage's eyes were closed again.

'Did you hear that, Number One?'

Again the eyes snapped open. 'Sir?'

'I said did you hear that? Did you hear what the rear admiral said?'

Armitage stared at him. 'Er –'

Archie turned abruptly away to prevent himself exploding with anger. What did you do with a first lieutenant like this? Something had to be done about him certainly, because if they had to stay alongside under fire much longer Armitage would either collapse or crack. Somehow the man had to be propped up, forced into carrying on. And there was a well-tried way of doing that: heap a lot more responsibility on his shoulders. Make or break.

'Right. Bugger this for a game of darts. Take over the ship, Number One. I'm going ashore.'

It did the trick. Armitage was suddenly wide awake. 'You're what, sir?'

'I said, I'm going ashore. Stretch my legs, buy a few picture postcards. You know the sort of thing.' He looked at his wristwatch. It was one-thirty a.m. 'If anyone asks, say I'm hunting Frogs. Back within an hour. You have the ship, First Lieutenant.'

While there were plenty of ships but few troops on the east mole, less than a mile away on the west quay of the Nouveau Avant Port there were plenty of French troops but few ships to take them off.

Some French units had been told to go to the right place but had been delayed in extricating themselves from the rearguard action on the perimeter; some had been told to go to the wrong place; some had mistaken their orders and some had received no orders at all. The result was confusion, anger and recrimination on a huge scale. To make matters worse, thousands of men who had been sheltering for days in the cellars and basements of the city had now emerged and were crowding onto the quays and landing stages in the harbour and taking places in the boats that had been intended for the fighting troops. So while the British fumed at the French for failing to turn up as agreed on the east mole, in the Nouveau Avant Port, thousands of officers and men of the French army became more and more convinced that, having fought gallantly to enable the British to escape, the British were now failing to keep to their side of the agreement and they were being left in the lurch.

It was in this nightmare of falling shells, boats without lights and floating wreckage that Pringle now found himself, *Daisy Belle* having been directed to enter the port by the sub lieutenant on the end of the east mole.

With no chart of the harbour, all Pringle could do was follow in the wake of a tug until he found himself in a position to go alongside one of the quays. Here, he found a huge crush of men waiting to jump into the boat, all pushing and shoving and ordering each other about at the same time.

'But those behind cried "Forward" and those before cried "Back"!' he muttered as he stopped engines and allowed *Daisy Belle* to drift the last few yards, then shouted to Odell, who stood on the foredeck with a boathook: 'Count thirty of them and then shove off regardless!'

The boat listed heavily as a dozen *poilus* jumped aboard and tried to remain on the coach roof. Sid, swearing volubly, tried to get them to go below. Most of these were unarmed, but nearly every man carried a huge pack of personal belongings. One insisted upon bringing his accordian.

'Make them sit down!' Pringle shouted, and then, as more hobnailed boots crashed down on what a few days before had been immaculate varnish, '*Asseyez-vous, tous, s'il vous plait!*'

'Okay that's thirty!' David yelled, and waved the soldiers back. '*C'est tout!*' he shouted. '*Fini!*' but as Pringle went hard astern a *poilu* with a heavy pack on his back tried to jump the gap, missed, caught his chin on the gunwale, hung suspended for an agonized moment and then disappeared overboard.

Pringle stopped engines and swung the boat round to starboard. All the French were shouting and cursing and getting in his line of vision. 'Can you see him?' he yelled to Odell, who was peering down into the oily water.

'I guess he went right under with the weight of his backpack!' David shouted, and as the skipper of one of the War Department boats was shouting at him to clear the quay, Pringle abandoned the search and began feeling his way out of the harbour by keeping close to the quay where he had just embarked his passengers.

'This is not my idea of fun,' he muttered to himself, but almost at the same time David turned to look aft, and on doing so immediately bawled 'Look out!' – following which there was a heavy jolt as the bluff bow of an Admiralty motor fishing vessel tore into *Daisy Belle*'s starboard quarter.

'You're on the wrong side of the fucking channel!' an exasperated voice bawled at them out of the darkness, and then: 'Any damage?'

Pringle tried to put the wheel amidships but found that it was jammed solid. 'Lost my steering!' he shouted.

'Ay, an' we're taking water aft an' all!' Sidney added.

'Stand by to take a tow!' the voice bellowed. 'I'll be back for you as soon as I've collected a load.'

Ten minutes later the MFV returned and a heavy coil of two-inch rope was hurled across, hitting David squarely in the chest. 'Lead it through the bullring and make it fast to a Samson post!' the sub lieutenant skipper shouted. 'No, not like that, through the bullring first – the ring on the bow, for God's sake . . . Now take it to the Samson post . . .'

David turned to Pringle. 'What's a Samson post when it's at home?'

'Here, give me the end. I'll take it to the mast.'

He made a round turn and two half-hitches and shouted to the MFV that they were ready; and minutes later *Daisy Belle* left harbour under tow, while Sid Imrie used Pringle's Bourne & Hollingsworth pyjamas to bung up the leaks down aft.

iii

Archie stepped off the for'd brow and paused a moment to glance back at the dark outline of his ship before setting out along the deserted mole. Walking along with the flashes of artillery fire lighting up the horizon ahead of him and the whine and whistle of shells all around, he became aware of a strange sense of unreality, as if his spirit was not entirely present in his body. It was the effect of fatigue, doubtless, but it was a strange sensation all the same – as if body and soul had been forced slightly apart, and he was able to watch himself walk on towards the shore.

It was quite a long walk, and from time to time he took cover when the shelling seemed to be getting close. On arriving at the shore he turned left onto the promenade of Malo-les-Bains and turned right at what remained of the casino into the suburbs. Many of the houses had been reduced to rubble and some were burning. The sound of machine-gun fire and artillery was coming from the countryside only a mile or two away and from time to time shells fell a little way to the west, nearer the city centre. He looked into some of the undamaged houses and shouted, 'Anyone here? *Il y a quelqu'un?*' but received no reply.

He found an abandoned bicycle and rode it over broken glass and rubble into the suburb of Rosendael. Smoke – acrid, oily smoke – was billowing along through the streets, which were deserted except for a few stray dogs and cats.

Hearing a cry from outside a wrecked café, he investigated and found a little girl lying against the wall, still alive.

There was a huge bruise on her temple, and a globule of blood from her nose had clotted and dried on her cheek and neck. When he bent over her, her eyes opened and she regarded him in a way that seemed to lay blame upon him personally for all the bloodshed and misery that had ever been in the world.

He lifted her in his arms, left the bicycle and set off on foot again through the smoke and flames; but he had not gone more than a hundred yards when his burden seemed suddenly heavier, and he knew she was dead.

He set her down in the street and put her hands together and closed her eyes. He shuddered: for a terrible moment a picture of Christine at the same age came to mind.

He resumed his search of the gutted buildings, calling out and shining a torch into cellars that were full of fallen beams and plaster. As he emerged from one of these, a few stray dogs attached themselves to him, loping silently along at his heels.

It seemed a long way back, and he must have taken a wrong turning somewhere because when he came out on the shore he found himself on the beach about half a mile east of the mole. He went down onto the sands and began walking along the beach past the litter of abandoned vehicles, wrecked boats, spiked guns. He could just make out the line of the breakwater: *Vagabond* and a paddle mine-sweeper were still alongside, but the other ships appeared to be leaving.

He looked at his watch. Twenty past two. He would just

about make it if he hurried. He broke into a trot along the sands, weaving between the empty ammunition boxes, the shell cases, the abandoned vehicles.

There was a large drainage ditch with a sloping concrete embankment adjacent to the mole, and he was halfway up it when he saw, laid out along the dried-out ditch, several corpses of British and French soldiers. Something about one, which had obviously been treated for injuries, caught his eye. He stopped and bent over the body, and gently rolled it over to identify it.

As he did so Griff's eyes looked up at him and he could almost hear him say, 'It's all right, Archie old boy. It's only me.'

iv

Time was very short: his hands trembled as he searched the pockets of Griff's battledress. He had been terribly injured. He found no wallet, identity card or disc, but in a breast pocket of the battledress he discovered a single, faded snapshot of himself, Griff and Simone. They had taken it with a timer one afternoon in the garden at Prowse fifteen or twenty years before, in the days when Griff and Simone were newly married and all three had shared a friendship that had seemed unique and indestructible.

He didn't know how long he remained crouching there in the drainage ditch, staring at that sepia-tinted photograph; all he knew was that suddenly he could hear the crunch of many boots and when he looked up a long column of French soldiers, fully laden with packs and weapons, was moving down the mole.

He pocketed the photograph and climbed up the embankment, but the French troops were already pouring along the mole in such numbers that it was difficult to take his place among them. Certainly there was no question of getting to the head of the queue.

Forcing his way into the crowd of shuffling men, he began

to move slowly down the jetty with them until a shell fell very close to the mole and the whole mass of men came to a complete halt.

Somewhere ahead Sub Lieutenant Wake was sounding a hunting horn in an attempt to rally the French, but its repeated braying only served to infuriate them. Archie tried to force his way on to the front.

'*Je suis capitaine de ce vaisseau-là*,' he told a burly-looking sergeant, and pointed at *Vagabond* two hundred yards further down the mole.

'*Et ta soeur*,' the sergeant replied sullenly, and he and his comrades closed ranks to bar the way.

When he came nearly abreast the paddle minesweeper that was alongside, there were *poilus* streaming off the ship and back onto the mole, and a slanging match was taking place between a French officer and the minesweeper captain. Archie forced his way on through the crowd and reached the officer. 'In the name of God!' he managed in French. 'Why aren't your men embarking?'

The officer turned to him and spoke English as if he felt sullied by it. 'You try to break our company in different boats and tell us to throw our weapons, Lieutenant. But I have orders to hold my company in one part and in our army soldiers are forbidden to throw their rifles in any circumstance.'

'If you want to get off this jetty you'll have to take *our* orders!' Archie yelled back at him over the din. 'Now get these men back on board right away!'

The other shook his head. '*Non, M'sieur*. It's not possible –'

Archie put his hand to his revolver. 'Do I have to threaten you, Major?'

The other shrugged. 'I too have a revolver. My company will wait to embark in the next ship.'

Archie turned and shouted up to the minesweeper captain. 'You may as well clear off! He says he'll take the next ship!'

'There won't be a next ship!' the lieutenant shouted back.

'And if they'd only ditch their packs I could take the whole company!'

Archie raised his hands palms upward and shrugged a mock-Gallic shrug which the minesweeper skipper understood perfectly. He grinned and replied with a thumbs up, and minutes later the minesweeper cast off and backed away into the darkness.

Archie forced his way on up the mole towards where *Vagabond* was berthed. There was just as much confusion here, with the embattled Roger Wake shouting '*Vite! Vite! Allez-vous* bloody *vite*, God-damn it!' and blowing his hunting horn – until the sergeant Archie had encountered earlier snatched the offending instrument from him and stamped it flat under the heel of his boot.

Vagabond was now one of the last ships still alongside. The ferry *Autocarrier* and the destroyers *Malcolm*, *Codrington* and *Express* had all gone, and apart from a few schuits the only other warship alongside was the minesweeper *Speedwell*.

Standing in the queue fifty yards from *Vagabond*'s bow, Archie took his hat off and waved it frantically above his head to attract the attention of those on the bridge; but it was no use: his way was again blocked by a solid mass of men, and he was powerless to do anything but watch as the headrope splashed into the water and, with Armitage in command and Hartley acting as his first lieutenant, *Vagabond* pulled away from the mole. But it was as well that she went when she did: less than a minute after she had gone, a shell landed right in the berth she had vacated, sending up a massive fountain of water and leaving several dead and injured on the jetty.

v

Christine was standing on a ladder in the Dynamo Room making up the evacuation tote board when Third Officer Lane brought her the signal. Some hours before, she had received Nick's telegram and although she was very tired she felt strangely elated. At the beginning of Operation Dynamo a week before, all at Dover had been pessimistic of getting even a quarter of the BEF back to England: fifty thousand had seemed a wildly optimistic figure to hope for. Now, the fact that somewhere in the region of three hundred thousand men had been brought back, and nearly a hundred thousand of those French, seemed beyond explanation: it was a quite phenomenal number – perhaps a miracle.

Marjory handed the message form up to her. 'I think you ought to see this one, Chrissy.'

It was from *Vagabond*. Christine had to read it twice to take in the full meaning of the clipped signalese: SAILED DUNKIRK 0248 WITHOUT COMMANDING OFFICER WHO LANDED TO SEARCH FOR TROOPS ASHORE BUT DID NOT RETURN. HAVE APPROX 650 FIT TROOPS AND 3 STRETCHER CASES ON BOARD. ALL FRENCH.

It was as if she had been given a wonderful birthday present earlier that day and had now received an impossibly high demand for payment.

'Thanks,' she said very quietly. 'Thanks for showing it to me.'

'I'm sure he'll be all right –' Marjory started, but Christine had already turned back to the tote board and was writing the latest totals of men evacuated in neat, black capitals.

THIRTY-NINE

When the sun rose into a clear sky, no ships were moving in Dunkirk Roads. The moles and quays were once again deserted. The French troops in the city who had been left behind had taken shelter again in the cellars and among the dunes. The attempt to sink blockships in the harbour entrance had not been a success, but it had been made all the same, and the British had gone. For thirty thousand French troops within the bridgehead it seemed unlikely that they would be coming back.

The German forces began closing in for the kill. At first light a strong attack was mounted from Spycker, the spearhead thrusting north-east between the lines of the Bergues and Bourbourg canals. This attack met stubborn resistance from the French 68th Infantry Division, and for the time being made little progress. A mile or so to the east, a French attack by the 137th Regiment – four battalions and the last of the tanks – was sent from Teteghem towards Galghoeck and Notre Dame des Nciges; but it only got as far as the Galghoeck crossroads before being subjected to superior artillery fire and was forced back.

Colonel Menon's 1st Battalion bore the brunt of this battle, and regrouped in the village of Teteghem to meet the inevitable counter-attack; at the same time he sent urgent messages to Admiral Abrial and General Barthelemy in Bastion 32 requesting reserves, but the only answer he got was an order to hold the position at all costs. This he did, and when Teteghem fell towards evening only fifty of Colonel Menon's battalion remained.

Guarding the central route to Dunkirk from Bergues, French naval forces had moved two heavy guns from Fort

Vallières – which had been subjected to repeated Stuka attacks – to the bridge of Sept-Planètes. All day, these two guns kept up a steady bombardment of the advancing enemy columns, and when they had fired their last rounds the crews used vehicles to build a road block which they held to the last man.

So, at bitter cost, the French hung on for another day; but as the light began to fade no one was in any doubt that it would be their last.

ii

After seeing his ship leave the mole, Archie had caught a lift back to Dover in a schuit, and had snatched an hour's sleep in the skipper's bunk on the way over. On landing at Dover he first went to the reception authorities to make a confirmatory report of Griff's death, and when he had done that he made his way past the crowds of disembarking troops to the destroyer berths, and was relieved to find *Vagabond* berthed outboard of *Malcolm* and *Codrington*.

He saluted the quarterdeck as he stepped aboard.

'Didn't expect to see you back so soon, sir,' ventured the quartermaster, rather as if Archie had returned early from a game of golf.

Archie concealed his true feelings behind a mask of brisk bonhomie. 'Bad luck! Thought you'd got rid of me, eh? First lieutenant about, is he?'

'In the wardroom, sir.'

He went along the irondeck and looked in as he knocked on the open door to the wardroom. Armitage was breakfasting alone at the head of the table, reading the signal log.

'Morning, Number One. What chance of an invitation to breakfast in the wardroom this morning?'

Armitage sprang to his feet. '*Very* good to see you back, sir! There's a signal here just in from the vice admiral. He wants to see you the moment you return.'

522

'Does he, indeed?'

Armitage showed him the file. The signal was very short: USM IMMEDIATELY ON YOUR RETURN. 'USM' was signalese for 'You see me'. It was the most peremptory way a senior officer could summon a subordinate and, almost invariably, meant that the officer concerned was to be carpeted.

'Best bib and tucker again I suppose,' Archie muttered, and left Armitage to his sausages and tinned tomatoes.

Twenty minutes later, having washed, shaved, changed into his best doeskin and caught a lift in a lorry that happened to be going up to the castle, Archie descended the tunnel into the underground headquarters, and when the Royal Marine sentry at the entrance had examined his identity card he was escorted by the flag lieutenant along the main corridor to the admiral's office.

'Lieutenant Commander Trendle-Home, sir!' announced the flag lieutenant, and a moment later Archie found himself on the admiral's balcony.

Ramsay was sipping a cup of tea. Archie's latest confidential report – the dreaded Form S.206 – was rather obviously open on his lap.

'You sent for me, sir.'

'I did indeed, Trendle-Home. And I think you know why.'

'Yes, sir. I intend to make my reasons for landing clear in my report of proceedings –'

But Ramsay was shaking his head. 'I think they're clear enough already, aren't they? It looks to me like a case of failing to delegate. Short-cut methods. Running a one-man band.' He tapped the confidential report with a silver propelling pencil. 'Which is precisely the criticism Captain D makes of you in your latest two-oh-six.'

Archie had been in the Royal Navy long enough to know that there was never any point in taking issue with a senior officer when you were on the carpet. So he remained standing to attention and said nothing.

Ramsay took another sip of tea, and gazed out over the

harbour. 'Good destroyer captains aren't ten a penny, I'm sure you know that. You took a foolish, ill-considered risk last night. You risked yourself, and you risked your ship.'

'Sir, I apologize if –'

'No. Don't apologize to me. Apologize to my staff who spent valuable time sending signals back and forth across the Channel trying to locate you. And, what's more, apologize to your daughter. You frightened her very badly last night, and I don't like my Wren officers being frightened, not even by their fathers.'

'Sir.'

'Was there any good reason for leaving your ship in that way?'

Archie had no desire to air dirty linen before the admiral. 'Well, sir, it – it seemed a good idea. I felt like stretching my legs.'

'And your first lieutenant at the same time, eh?' Ramsay said quietly, and shot a penetrating glance in Archie's direction. 'All right, Archie, consider yourself privately and unofficially reprimanded.' Ramsay nodded to dismiss him, then, as he turned to go added: 'And Archie –'

'Sir?'

'Next time you have an afternoon free, give me a ring and we'll have a round of golf.'

'I'll do that, thank you, sir.'

He met Christine in the tunnel outside the Dynamo Room. She looked as if she had been crying, but it might have been fatigue.

He said: 'Your boss says I owe you an apology.'

'I'm just so relieved you're safe,' she said. 'I got the news that Nick was back in one piece and then just a few hours after that the signal that you were missing in Dunkirk. I thought . . . I was sure that something had happened to you.'

'Well. It didn't, did it?'

She looked at him and shook her head.

He said, 'If we were anywhere else I'd give you a big hug,

Chrissy. But I don't think that would go down very well here.'

'I don't suppose it would.'

He hesitated. Should he tell her about Griff? She would have to know sooner or later. 'There is some bad news, though. I don't know if I ought to tell you now, but last night I – I found Griff –'

Suddenly, for the first time, he felt the full impact of it.

Christine was staring at him. He knew now that he should not be telling her, but he had already started, and the words, bottled up all night, poured out. 'He . . . was at the shore end of the pier. He had been wounded, and he must have tried very hard to get back, but he didn't make it, poor old chap. I don't expect Simone knows yet. I think it's probably better if she hears through official channels first. I know that you two haven't got on all that well, Chrissy, and I know, well, that you disapproved of – of what was going on, but I wanted to tell you that – that's all over and – and –'

Tears were streaming down her cheeks. 'Oh Daddy!' she whispered. 'Not Griff! Not Captain Griff!'

'I feel like a murderer,' he said softly. 'Griff was closer to me than a brother, and I feel as if I murdered him . . .'

She did not appear to hear him. She glanced at a group of officers who came down the tunnel and went into the admiral's office. He could almost feel her pushing him away to arm's length again. 'I've got to go,' she said. 'I'm sorry.'

'Of course.'

She went back into the Dynamo Room and he was left in the corridor with people coming and going around him. He heard his own footfalls echoing in the tunnel and on the iron steps of the spiral staircase as he went back to the entrance. Outside, the sun was very brilliant and the castle lawn very green. He walked down through the town and back to his ship. When he got into his cabin he sat down and took out the little photograph he had discovered on Griff's body. He was still staring at it when the yeoman brought him another signal from the Vice Admiral Dover.

As the morning went by and the previous night's work was assessed, it quickly became apparent to Ramsay's staff that Operation Dynamo was not yet over: thirty or forty thousand men of the French army were estimated to remain within the Dunkirk perimeter, and it was unthinkable for Britain not to go to their rescue. This was confirmed by Churchill in a telegram to Weygand that morning:

> WE ARE COMING BACK FOR YOUR MEN TONIGHT. PLEASE ENSURE THAT ALL FACILITIES ARE USED PROMPTLY. FOR THREE HOURS LAST NIGHT MANY SHIPS WAITED IDLY AT GREAT RISK AND DANGER.

Ramsay informed the ships that they would be going back in a general signal that morning and, like several other commanding officers, Archie cleared lower deck at midday to break the news to his ship's company in person.

They assembled on the fo'c'sle, a hundred or so officers, senior ratings and men, their faces gaunt from strain and lack of sleep. The coxswain reported them present and correct to the first lieutenant and the first lieutenant reported them to the captain.

Archie was still in his best uniform. He had a white silk handkerchief in his top pocket, his shirt cuffs protruded half an inch from his best doeskin reefer, and his messboots gleamed in the June sunshine. It was all part of the naval tradition: by parading himself in his best finery, all he was doing was repeating the example Nelson had set to his men when the going was roughest. The fact that 'Father' was unusually red-eyed caused no comment, because nearly every single officer and man was similarly red-eyed from lack of sleep.

He walked for'd up the cable deck and stood in the eyes of the ship, facing aft, to address his men.

'Stand at ease, stand easy,' he said, and then told them to break ranks and gather round him so that he did not have to shout over the noise of fans and the repair work going on aboard neighbouring ships.

He paused for a few moments, during which time he sought to look every single man in the eye. And then, just when he was about to start, Knocker White, an irrepressible Geordie stoker who had been in and out of trouble ever since the ship was commissioned but who, during the last week, had worked tirelessly in the impossible conditions of a boiler room full of steam leaks, shouted from the very back rank, 'Get a bit last night, sir?' and the sheer cheek of it broke the tension.

Archie shook with laughter and his ship's company laughed with him. 'No such luck, I'm afraid. There wasn't any skirt worth looking at and I couldn't get a drink for love nor money.'

He looked round again at them. Most were still smiling. Even the first lieutenant looked amused.

'Well,' he said, 'I had a toffee-nosed speech all ready for you, but I think I'll save it for another day. All I need to do is read out the signal we received an hour ago from the vice admiral. It says everything I want to say only better, and it'll help to explain why we were kept waiting by the Frogs last night. So here it is: "From Vice Admiral Dover to Force K. I hoped and believed that last night would see us through, but the French who were covering the retirement of the British rearguard had to repel a strong German attack and so were unable to send their troops to the pier in time. We cannot leave our allies in the lurch, and I call on all officers and men detailed for further evacuation tonight to let the world see that we never let down our ally."'

Archie looked up. 'Just in case you're still in any doubt, *Vagabond* has been detailed for cross-Channel operations tonight. So there you are, lads. We're going back for one more trip, and with a bit of British luck the French'll turn up for the party this time and we'll bring every last one of them back. So – good luck to us all. One more big heave, and the job'll be done.'

iv

While Dover planned, Dunkirk fought. Bit by bit the French defences were chipped away, until the ring had closed to within two miles of the port. By evening, it ran from just outside the burning oil storage tanks on the west of the port, through the outer suburbs of Coudekerque-Branche and St Georges to Rosendael and thence to the dunes on Malo beach.

But in spite of the confident ring of Churchill's telegram to Weygand, and the willingness of the ships' companies and crews that would be going back that night, there was among the staff working an Operation Dynamo an un-stated awareness that complete success that night was probably beyond the capability of the forces detailed for the task.

It was not so much a problem of ships or men now as of time available and the speed of embarkation. Although ships with a lifting capacity of thirty thousand men were available, no one could be sure that the Dunkirk facilities were sufficient to take those ships, or that Admiral Abrial and the French generals were capable of organizing their ships and troops sufficiently to fulfil their share in the operation. So although it was never stated openly by the staff, those of them who knew the arithmetic of men, ships and hours of darkness were aware that it was not so much a question of whether any French troops would be left behind, but how many.

At 1440, Ramsay promulgated the plan for the night:

COMMENCE 2230/3 WITHDRAW 0230/4. FROM EAST PIER EVACUATION BY PERSONNEL VESSELS, DE-STROYERS AND PADDLE MINESWEEPERS. FROM WEST PIER, NEW OUTER PORT, BY OTHER MINE-

SWEEPERS, CORVETTES, SKOOTS, AND FRENCH
VESSELS. DRIFTERS AND SMALLER CRAFT INTO
THE INNER HARBOUR, LOCUST REMAINING OUT-
SIDE ENTRANCE RECEIVING LOADS FERRIED OUT
BY SMALL BOATS. TUGS AVAILABLE OUTSIDE
ENTRANCE TO ASSIST SHIPS IN BERTHING AND
LEAVING.

At Ramsgate, Captain Phillimore's orders to the skippers of
small craft leaving from Ramsgate and Margate came on two
pieces of roneoed foolscap. Each motorboat was to embark
two ten-foot ladders; every available fast motorboat would
be required; boats were to be ready to sail by 1600 and were
under orders to enter Dunkirk at 2230 and leave at 0230.
They were to ferry craft from the Quai Felix Faure out to
the gunboat *Locust*, which would use a box-lamp with a
group of long flashes every two minutes to identify herself.
The five schuits were to sail at 1500 and had orders to go
straight to the western pier in the Nouveau Avant Port,
fill up with troops and return to Ramsgate. Those with
knowledge of French were to be spread throughout the craft
operating. A sketch plan of Dunkirk harbour showing the
Nouveau Avant Port and the Quai Felix Faure was attached,
and the final paragraph, in capital letters, stated: ALL CRAFT
ARE TO LEAVE DUNKIRK HARBOUR AT LATEST BY
0300/4.

v

On arrival at Ramsgate that morning, *Daisy Belle* had been
taken alongside one of the repair berths to have her rudder
post straightened and the damage to her starboard quarter
repaired. While Sid Imrie assisted, Pringle and Odell slept.
Three hours later, when David awoke, the boat had been
moved back to a buoy in the outer harbour and Sid's
oil-smudged face was hanging upside down over the coach
roof and looking in at him.

'Wakey-wakey, rise and shine! You've had your time, laddie but I hav'nae had mine!'

David had slept fully clothed. He yawned, sat up and rubbed the sleep out of his eyes.

'Got any plans for the night?'

'Excuse me?'

'I said have you got any plans for the night? 'Cos if ye hav'nae, the navy's got plans for you.'

David pulled on his boots and went up into the blinding sunlight, where Sid handed him Captain Phillimore's order. 'Take a wee peep at that.'

David glanced at it and felt his heart sink. 'What about the rudder?'

'Fixed. And the sprung plank down aft. They did a fine job, no error.' Sidney glanced at him sidelong. 'Not feeling so keen, eh? Well, you've no reason, have you? I mean, being a Yank . . .'

Pringle had emerged from the forecabin where he had taken a wash and shave. 'Ah – good man, you're up. Seen the orders? We'll be taking on fuel and water at midday. They offered to put a new crew in, but as I didn't relish the thought of *Daisy* being knocked about by some throttle-happy sub lieutenant, I said we'd keep the same crew and do another trip. Happy?'

David yawned another gigantic yawn. 'Ecstatic,' he said.

vi

HMS *Malcolm*'s wardroom had planned a mess dinner on board that evening to celebrate the end of the operation. The dinner had been cancelled, but the officers insisted on sailing in their evening 'mess undress' and the ship went out of harbour to the sound of bagpipes played on the forecastle.

On the way over, fog came down, and there were many close shaves as the faster ships overtook slower ships or encountered vessels that had broken down and were return-ing. One of the closest of these involved *Vagabond*: while the ship was steaming at twenty-five knots in visibility of a hundred yards or less, the for'd lookout suddenly bawled, 'Ship dead ahead, sir!' and a paddle minesweeper appeared out of the gloom, broadside on.

There was no time to make a major alteration: a large wheel order would have thrown *Vagabond*'s stern in the wrong direction. Very calmly, Archie ordered. 'Starboard ten: midships; port ten; midships,' in little more than the time it took to give the orders and have them repeated back by the coxswain in the wheelhouse. The result was a small 'jink' to starboard, and the two ships missed each other by five yards.

Without turning, or ceasing to stare ahead into the mist, Archie said to Armitage, who was standing at his elbow, 'I suppose you're thinking we ought to reduce speed, Number One?'

'I would probably have recommended it, sir,' Armitage replied, 'before last night.'

Archie had detected a marked improvement in his first lieutenant's general attitude since returning on board that morning. Giving a man command of a ship – even for only a few hours – changed his entire perspective. He remembered something Griff had once said about getting the best out of one's men. It was always more effective, he had said, to reward a man for doing something well than to criticize him when he did badly. 'Give a man credit every time he does well,' he had said, 'and you give him something to live up to and improve on; pick on his faults all the time – or worse, bully him – and you turn him into someone who resents your leadership and will seek to undermine it, whether consciously or unconsciously.'

Perhaps, he mused, he had been making that mistake with Armitage.

'By the way,' he said, still peering for'd through the fog. 'I meant to tell you. I watched you take the ship out last night. I thought you handled her very well. And you were right to sail when you did, too. I saw that shell land in our

531

berth. You probably saved the ship for me, and I give you full credit for it.'

There was a pause, as if Armitage could hardly believe his ears. Then he said quietly: 'Thank you, sir. Thank you very much indeed.'

Archie continued to stare ahead. Don't thank me, he thought to himself. Thank my good friend Griff Wilmot.

vii

When *Vagabond* arrived at Dunkirk, the harbour was swarming with French fishing boats and small craft of every sort, and boats were crowding alongside the east mole, which was already thick with French troops. But there was no sign of a French naval berthing party: although Dunkirk was one of the principal French naval ports, there were no French ratings able or willing to assist the destroyers by taking their lines, and everyone seemed to be yelling advice to everyone else.

HMS *Whitshed*, which had brought a naval shore party over in advance of the main fleet, was still trying to get alongside against the effects of the easterly wind and a strong west-going tide. *Kingfisher, Sabre* and Admiral Wake-Walker's MTB were having similar difficulty, and at the same time a continual stream of small craft was going back and forth through the harbour entrance.

There was a wrecked trawler off the end of the pier and another wreck alongside the pier itself; a blockship sunk the previous night had reduced the usable channel between the two breakwaters; it was pitch dark, magnetic mines were known to have been laid in the harbour by the enemy, and debris, much of it half-submerged, was everywhere. On top of it all, six enemy MTBs had been reported heading west from Ostend. Fortunately, they never materialized.

The destroyer *Kingfisher* was rammed by a French trawler,

and as her degaussing equipment – which provided protection against magnetic mines – had been put out of action, she was sent back empty to Dover. With hundreds of French troops on board, the transport *Kellet* went aground on a falling tide off the western breakwater and by the time the troops had been transferred to other ships and she was floated off it was too late to embark more men and she too was sent back empty. Because of the huge crowds still on the west quay of the Nouveau Avant Port, Admiral Wake-Walker guided two large transports alongside, the *Royal Sovereign* staying until the very last minute in order to load to capacity.

viii

Sub Lieutenant Beale made the crossing in the cabin cruiser *Mermaiden*. He had an elderly gentleman called Mr Macpherson as his second in command and a stoker and an air gunner on leave as crew. For part of the way Commodore Taylor, who had organized the fleet of little ships for Admiral Ramsay, took passage on board, transferring to the faster War Department boat *Marlborough* just after passing W Buoy.

After avoiding some floating mines in the approaches, the little ships reached Dunkirk without mishap and Beale took *Mermaiden* straight in to the Quai Felix Faure, just west of the east mole. The *Marlborough* was the only one alongside when they arrived, so there was no difficulty in filling up: men poured in over the bow and stern until there was not an inch of space unfilled.

With two hundred troops on board, the for'd deck was so crowded that the helmsman could not see at all, and Beale had to manoeuvre *Mermaiden* by shouting wheel orders above the incessant French chatter. They made a safe passage out of the harbour, but could not find *Locust* as she did not appear to be flashing the prearranged signal. To make matters worse, the swell outside the breakwater and the wakes of passing ships were making the boat roll heavily.

Having transferred the troops to a sloop, *Mermaiden* went back into the harbour but found the Quai Felix Faure deserted. Beale nipped ashore to make quite sure Commodore Taylor had not been left behind, then took his boat back down the harbour.

Ordered to assist a French fishing boat which had engine trouble, *Mermaiden* was just turning to obey when she was hit by a small French tramp steamer, which ran into her bows. Little damage had been done, but in the darkness and confusion, Beale and his crew were not to know that.

They went alongside the French trawler but when Beale enquired civilly of the coxswain if he would like a tow, he was told in no uncertain terms to 'hop it', the message being rammed home with the butt of an oar wielded by one of the French crew. In the conversation that ensued Beale discovered that the French were convinced he had come to stop them leaving. Nothing could change their minds and they were adamant that they did not want a tow, insisting that they would save themselves '*comme tous les autres.*' Beale left them to get on with it.

Further down the harbour he was hailed by a motor-boat which had gone aground off one of the inner piers. She had a rope round her screws and had fouled a large piece of timber. The crew was taken aboard and it turned out that the boat was Vice Admiral Ramsay's ceremonial barge. The rescue was somewhat delayed by the barge coxswain, a Scot, who insisted on returning aboard to collect his boots.

A hundred yards further on they came on yet another broken-down boat with a few men aboard. They towed it out to the harbour entrance, where the tow parted, took it in tow again, found the tugs, transferred the two crews and set the boat adrift. After that they were ordered to remain outside with the tugs, and because the engine was giving trouble accepted a tow back to Ramsgate.

Daisy Belle carried four boatloads from the Quai Felix Faure that night, lifting twenty men on each trip. After transferring the fourth load to the *Locust*, Pringle was ordered to make the next trip his last, but soon after they passed between the breakwaters, while sitting on the foredeck keeping a lookout, David felt a sudden pain in his upper arm.

'You all right?' Pringle enquired.

David nursed his arm. 'I guess I just stopped a bullet.'

'You *what*?'

'I just got myself a slug in the arm.'

'Can you get yourself back aft?'

David explored with his hand and felt a warm sogginess of blood just below his left shoulder. In a strange way he was quite relieved and pleased with himself. It was hurting like hell, but he knew he'd live, and having stopped one bullet gave him confidence that he wouldn't stop another. It was also good to be able to play at being a hero. 'It's okay! I'm okay to stay up here for a bit. Can you see this garbage on the port bow?'

'I'm turning round.'

'Why for God's sake?'

'We're going home.'

'It's only a scratch! Not that bad!'

'Bad enough,' Pringle said and spun the wheel to take the boat out between the breakwaters.

By the time they got clear of the harbour the tugs were rounding up the smaller boats and taking them in tow for the journey back, and Pringle decided it would be more risky to go in among them and transfer his casualty than to keep clear of the mêlée.

Once reasonably clear of other shipping, he stopped the boat and helped David down to the forecabin; then, with *Daisy Belle* rolling heavily in the confused water of Dunkirk Roads, he cut the left sleeves off David's jersey and shirt and applied a padded field dressing, tying the tapes with a reef knot in accordance with the instructions on the wrapper.

'How are you feeling?'

David grinned. 'Fine. It was only a nick, wasn't it?'

Sid had come up from the sternsheets. 'What d'you say, skipper? Think this might be an excuse for a wee dram?'

'Alcohol's not good for shock,' Pringle said.

'Very good for morale though,' David said, and Sid added, 'Aye, ye cannae beat Scotch whisky.'

'A small one then,' Pringle agreed.

'I'll go an' get it right away,' Sid said; and as the flotilla of small craft headed back from Dunkirk the crew of the *Daisy Belle* had a good-sized tot each, washed down with hot, sweet coffee from a flask.

x

The plan for the evacuation of the last of the rearguard French troops had been General Barthelemy's. His intention for the 68th Division had been that all troops disengage rapidly as soon as it was dark and move inwards to the east mole in the hour before midnight. Most of the battalions achieved this, though one or two units holding bridges had difficulty in getting clear.

Marching back, the rearguard troops had been told that there would be ships waiting to take them off, and were cheerfully confident; but General Barthelemy had not bargained for the fact that many thousands of men who should have departed the night before, while the ships lay alongside empty, were still in the city, and were emerging once more from the dunes and cellars and descending upon the port to claim first place in the queues to embark.

So, as the 68th Division approached in an orderly column along the Malo promenade, General Barthelemy was horrified to see, from the roof of Bastion 32, a huge disorganized mass of men already swarming out along the mole ahead of them.

The 68th Division marked time, then halted. The long

wait began, and as the minutes turned into hours and the new day approached, a sombre realization began to dawn with it.

xi

On the east mole, after a two-hour wait for other ships to load and get clear, HMS *Vagabond* finally secured alongside and embarked 800 troops. It was not as many as the ship had taken on previous trips because, in spite of all the pleas to the French to leave their equipment behind, every *poilu* still carried an enormous pack on his back, and the ship seemed fuller than when it had carried over a thousand British troops.

Just after *Vagabond* had sailed and when *Malcolm* was alongside loading, the gunboat *Locust* – which had been lying off the harbour entrance – signalled that she had completed loading from small boats and had room for another hundred; accordingly she came alongside the mole ahead of *Malcolm* and filled up, although this meant staying on after the last time ordered for departure of ships. At about the same time, Rear Admiral Wake-Walker hailed *Malcolm* on loudspeaker from his MTB and gave orders that the last two ships should use their discretion about remaining later than 0230. *Malcolm* signalled *Express* to wait no longer than 0300, but she waited until 0318 before shoving off, loaded to capacity and with the last of the British naval shore party embarked.

HMS *Shikari*, the oldest destroyer still operational and the one which, of all the destroyers, had perhaps made the biggest single contribution to the success of Operation Dynamo, had been detailed to escort Captain Dangerfield's block ships, and had anchored off Dunkirk to await the completion of the operation. At 0230 she weighed anchor, but as she did so a mine detonated close off her port bow. Minutes later, as she led the way into the harbour with the three blockships following close in her wake, the first in the line detonated another mine and sank rapidly.

While Wake-Walker's MTB picked up survivors and the remaining two ships carried on and were scuttled in the harbour entrance, *Shikari* went alongside the east mole and took 400 troops on board, including General Barthelemy, who told the captain, Lieutenant Commander Richarson, that there were twelve thousand troops still ashore.

But *Shikari* had already stayed far beyond the latest time ordered, and at 0340 Captain Dangerfield ordered her by signal to withdraw. She was the last destroyer to leave.

xii

As dawn approached, the final efforts to lift troops from the quays turned into a frantic last-minute rush, with boats coming and going in the darkness, bumping into one another, taking each other in tow, hailing each other, cursing, rescuing, encouraging and blaming one another. And as the first light came up, machine guns and artillery started firing on the jetties and approaches to the harbour.

Fallen in on the Quai Felix Faure with the light of flames glinting on their helmets, over a thousand men of General Lucas's French 32nd Division were still waiting patiently for embarkation. They had been promised that the Royal Navy would come to collect them, and had clung to that promise for four long hours while thousands of others were lifted off before them. But now the shuttle service of boats had stopped and only a small War Department boat, *Pigeon*, lay alongside.

She was commanded by Sub Lieutenant Gabbett-Mulhalleu. It was his fourth night of operations, and he knew Dunkirk harbour and its many wrecks and navigational hazards as well as anyone, having been in and out about forty times in the past three nights. He was now waiting alongside for Commander Troup, who had been taking charge of embarkation on the quay all night. It was already well after three, and Gabbett-Mulhalleu was beginning to think it was time to get going.

At last, Commander Troup arrived with a French general and his staff.

'How many can you take, Sub?'

'Twenty-five, sir.'

Troup turned back to confer with the French officers. It would clearly be invidious to select any small section of men for embarkation, and the decision was taken by the French battalion commander that the formation should remain behind as one, and that only the general and his staff should go in the boat.

It was one of those occasions when honour seemed to be at stake, and the French troops rose magnificently to the occasion. Silhouetted against the flames of a burning warehouse, with dawn coming up and machine-gun fire echoing in the streets behind them, the whole battalion stood rigidly to attention as General Lucas and his staff prepared to embark. No one spoke; no one broke ranks; no one so much as muttered a complaint.

One by one, the staff officers descended the ladder into the boat, and to Gabbett-Mulhalleu and his crew the time they took seemed interminable. Finally it was General Lucas's turn, and before he went he turned smartly about to face the troops fallen in on the quay and saluted them; then, when he was safely in the boat, Commander Troup came aboard, *Pigeon*'s engines rose to a roar, and she moved away into the darkness.

xiii

It was over. As dawn came up, white towels and sheets were hung out of a scattering of windows in the buildings that were still standing. Advancing cautiously, covering each other with sub-machine guns, shooting up buildings where allied troops might be making a last stand, the advance German troops arrived.

From the west, from the south and from the east they came, and gradually, as confidence increased that Dunkirk would offer no further resistance, the shelling stopped and the machine-gun fire dropped away until there came a great and terrible silence over the city.

Much of it had been reduced to smoking heaps of brick and stone. Here and there faces peeped out of boarded windows at the victors. Dogs, cowering with their tails between their legs, followed their new masters in hope of food. In the city slums some children remained: they came out into the misty morning to gaze wide-eyed at these booted supermen who tramped in.

On the beaches east of the port, the advancing army found an extraordinary litter of debris. Lines of lorries ran down into the sea. A spiked heavy anti-aircraft gun pointed its split barrel to the sky like a half-opened banana. A French Chasseur lay beached, a Thames barge was high and dry, its tattered mainsail still hoisted and flapping gently in the morning breeze. On the sands, haversacks, canvas webbing, greatcoats, corpses, rubber tyres, timber, wrecked lifeboats, private cars, bicycles – even armchairs, dining room tables and mattresses – lay strewn everywhere. But though there were thousands upon thousands of ammunition boxes, hardly a round of live ammunition was to be found.

The prisoners of war – twelve thousand of them, and all French – were gathered into a few large groups on the quays, the moles and the beach. Dog-tired, dishevelled, hungry, dispirited, they sat in silence on the Quai Felix Faure looking across the dock into the muzzles of heavy machine guns and light anti-aircraft guns which the Germans had brought up to cover them.

In the cathedral, two German infantrymen were experimenting with the organ, and out of the silence there suddenly sprang a devilish diapason as an Aryan thumbnail ran downwards over the yellowing keys.

'Ah, that's good! It works!' muttered one, and sitting

down with grenades still hanging from his belt, he began playing Luther's *Nunc Dimittis*, singing in a fine baritone:

> *Mit Fried und Freud ich fahr dahin*
> *In Gottes Wille . . .*
>
> In peace and joy I now depart,
> As God would have me.
> At rest and still are mind and heart,
> He doth save me.
> As my God hath promised me,
> Death is become my slumber . . .

The Germans arrived at Chapeau Rouge soon after dawn, and surprised the British medical team there by appearing to be normal human beings. They asked for marmalade and swapped cigarettes and used their immortal cliché to tell the wounded that, for them, the war was over. Later, the administrative units came in, but they were not so friendly.

There were camera-carrying propaganda troops as well, and they roamed the streets and the beaches in the hope of getting some photographs of British prisoners. But they were to be disappointed: apart from the thirty-three medical staff who had remained behind at Chapeau Rouge, the only British soldiers still at Dunkirk were stretcher cases.

They reached Bastion 32 and entered, grenades and machine guns at the ready. But Admiral Abrial and his generals had gone during the night: only a few junior clerks remained in the guttering candlelight to greet them, and all the codes, maps, records and plans had been destroyed.

Soon after nine o'clock, General Beaufrère received General Cranz, the commander of the German 18th Division, in the Hôtel de Ville, and the city was formally surrendered. But it was the east mole that was the very last part of the port to fall into German hands. French troops, mostly of the 68th Division, were still packed in a solid mass along its length when they arrived, and the last thirty men to escape from it did so by a ship's lifeboat at ten o'clock.

Twenty minutes after that, while the last hundreds of dejected *poilus* were still filing back to assemble on Malo Beach, half a dozen German infantrymen gave a cheer as the Swastika was hoisted at the end of the mole.

PART FOUR

FORTY

Griff came back to England – Simone was convinced of it – just before dawn. They had broken the news to her the previous afternoon, when most of the returning French soldiers had already been processed and her work as an interpreter was all but over. She had been called away from the reception tables on the quay at Ramsgate and, while the WVS women laughed and joked among themselves as they packed up the tea urns and washed up the last of the mugs and cups, a lieutenant colonel in the Sappers – she didn't catch his name – told her quite simply that her husband had been killed.

'I am so very sorry, Mrs Wilmot,' he had said. 'Although I only knew your husband slightly, it has been reported to me that he led his section with courage and distinction.'

She thanked him: it seemed the thing to do at the time, but later she reflected that it was a little odd to thank someone for informing you that your husband was dead. And at first the news didn't seem to make any sense. It didn't seem to have anything to do with her. She didn't shed a tear. Griff was gone, that was all. She was almost relieved: hadn't she expected him to be killed? Well, now he had been. She wouldn't have to wait any longer.

She had wanted to go on and finish the day's work, but Major Pearce had insisted she return home. It was no good arguing. He could not understand that the last place she wanted to be was alone in the house she had shared with Griff for nearly twenty years. But the army decided she must go home, so home she went.

She wandered from room to room for an hour or so, and in the evening went across to the school and collected

Blashford from the guardroom where he had been the guest of the military police at the gate. She took him for a short walk behind the school grounds, but didn't go to the cliffs. She came back into the house and began wandering from room to room again. She had only had a sandwich and a cup of tea since breakfast, but could not be bothered to cook herself a meal. She wanted to think about Griff, but something in her mind stopped her. She felt as if there was a mental path which was somehow barred to her, blocked off. She knew where that path led: it wound back over the years through all the glades of happiness, the winters of regret, the stormy nights of bitterness and argument. It went back, back almost out of sight to the green hills of her youth, to the dizzy heights of happiness and the caves of despair. Yes, she knew where that path led, but she could not follow it. All she could do was stare bleakly out of the sitting room windows at the riot of Griff's flowers that for some reason had chosen to bloom in the last few days.

The minutes passed like hours and, later, the hours seemed to have gone by like minutes. She went upstairs to her bedroom, came downstairs again to the hall. Once, standing in the kitchen, she was so sure that he was near that she said his name aloud. The silence that followed was so oppressive that she had to run from the room.

She found herself standing in her bedroom in the dark. She hadn't noticed the light go, only that it was now quite dark. She didn't put the light on. She didn't want to see. She sat down on her bed. For quite a long time she heard her own voice speaking, but was not sure what it said.

The dog came upstairs and slumped at her feet. She lay back on the bed, but did not sleep. From time to time the dog whined softly. And then she must have slept, because she was suddenly jerked awake by the knowledge that Griff was in the room with her.

'Griff?' she said. 'Griff?'

She did not see him with her eyes, but he was there nevertheless. Straightbacked, military, the old Griff.

He was so real that it seemed quite natural to talk to him. 'What is it?' she asked. 'What do you want?'

She did not hear him with her ears, but he spoke quite clearly all the same. 'Your forgiveness,' he said. That was all. 'Your forgiveness.'

'I need yours, Griff,' she whispered.

'I forgave you long ago,' he said. 'Now you must forgive me.'

'I do forgive you,' she managed; and felt a torrent of love and sadness gathering inside her and beginning to break. 'Oh Griff . . .' she whispered, and the tears were coming now. 'Oh Griff darling, why couldn't we have said this before?'

But Griff was gone; dawn was in at the window, and the first blackbird of the morning was bursting into song.

ii

As soon as *Daisy Belle* arrived at Ramsgate, David was seen by a naval sickberth attendant who cleaned and dressed the wound – which was only a superficial one – and put his arm in a sling. Afterwards, he went back on board to say goodbye to Pringle but found him asleep in the forecabin and he decided to take a nap himself. Eighteen hours later he woke with a start as the Stuart-Turners throbbed into life.

'Thought that'd stir you!' Pringle remarked when he appeared on deck. 'How's the arm?'

David touched it cautiously. 'Stiff.' He looked round the harbour. A couple of tugs were taking a string of little cabin cruisers in tow and preparing to move. 'What's going on?'

'They're taking the Thames craft up-river. I'm going with them, so if you want to hop off, you've got about five minutes left to do so.'

The bustle of boats in the harbour, the brilliant summer sunshine – even *Daisy Belle* herself – were oddly reassuring

547

and he felt loth to leave them. There were some big decisions he would have to take soon, but he didn't want to take them just yet.

'How far up-river will you be going?'

'She'll have to go back to Teddington for repairs, but I've a mind to berth her at Kew for the time being. I can step ashore and go right into my back garden from the landing stage there.'

'I won't be much use to you.'

'You can take some of the steering.'

David nodded. 'Okay, I'll string along if you don't mind.'

Pringle smiled. 'Pleasure,' he said.

So they took their place in the convoy and went off through the narrow harbour entrance for the last time; and as they passed the breakwater a small crowd of people cheered and waved, and a naval officer with a megaphone shouted, 'Well done, *Daisy Belle*!'

Then they were outside the harbour and rounding the North Foreland; Margate drew quickly abeam, and then Herne Bay, and as they approached Sheerness another two tows of small craft joined them, the tall-funnelled tugs at their head looking like the teachers at the head of a school crocodile. The enlarged convoy puttered past the Isle of Grain, Canvey Island and up the Lower Hope reach to Gravesend and the docks at Tilbury. Here and there, as they passed, a few people waved from the shore or a tug tooted its siren.

'I wouldn't have missed this!' David remarked.

They came to Greenwich. 'Built as a thank offering for one of our naval victories, I believe.' Pringle said. 'It was a palace, then a hospital. Now it's the naval college.'

'Worth fighting for, eh?'

Pringle nodded and looked away.

The convoy rounded the long ox-turn enclosing the Isle of Dogs, and a few minutes later the distinctive parapets of the Tower of London came into view.

'London Bridge!' David exclaimed.

'No, Tower Bridge. The next one's London Bridge.'

'You know the river pretty well, I guess.'

'Well, it's where I live, you know. See that square rigger? That's the *Discovery*.' Pringle raised his binoculars. Lining the bulwarks were several hundred sea scouts, and as the convoy approached they began cheering and waving.

The skippers of the little ships waved back, and the tugs tooted their sirens. And then, from up ahead, came the sound of more cheering, and as they approached London Bridge they saw it was crowded with people waving Union Jacks and shouting their heads off.

They were singing 'There'll Always Be an England' at Waterloo, and 'Land of Hope and Glory' at Westminster. Taxis and motor cars were sounding their horns; and when David glanced at Pringle he saw that his mouth was clamped very tightly shut, and that there was a crumply smile on his face and tears in his eyes.

As the convoy continued on its way past Fulham, Mortlake and Barnes, some of the craft were dropped off at the landing stages; and soon after going under Kew Bridge Pringle slowed to go alongside a pontoon.

There was a narrowboat moored nearby and the owner's wife, a cockney lady in an old pink dressing gown, fluffy bedroom slippers and hair curlers, obliged by taking *Daisy Belle*'s bowrope.

'Ow, Mr Pringle! What 'ave you been up to? I never seen a boat in such a bleedin' 'arvey Nichol!'

'We just took a weekend in France,' David ventured.

'Looks like it was the black 'ole of bleedin' Calcutta, I'd say!'

Pringle coiled up the stern rope and checked that the fenders were properly placed on both sides. 'So what'll you do now?' he asked David.

'Haven't decided. Spend a night in town, I guess. I need to buy some clothes.'

They finished securing the boat. Pringle put a padlock on the cabin door and helped David to step off onto the pontoon. 'Would you like to come into the house? I know my wife would like to meet you.'

'Well, that's very kind of you –'

Pringle led the way ashore and fifty yards along the tow-path put his hand over the back of a garden gate and lifted a latch to open it. David had a glimpse of a long, narrow lawn running up between herbaceous borders to the back of a tall, narrow house. But at the same time he sensed that something was not quite right. Within the space of a few seconds they had become strangers again, just as they had been when he had first accosted Pringle on the quay at Ramsgate.

'Er – look – if you don't mind, I guess I'll take a rain check.'

'A what?'

'I – er – don't think I'll come in after all.'

Pringle didn't look very surprised or disappointed. 'Oh! Are you sure?'

'Yes – thanks all the same.'

'Well, in that case, many thanks for your help.'

'That's okay,' David said, and they shook hands. 'Goodbye then.'

'Goodbye,' said Pringle, and a moment later the wooden gate clicked shut behind him.

David turned and made his way along the towpath towards the main road. Walking over Kew Bridge, he stopped for a minute to look down at the pontoon landing stage where *Daisy Belle* was berthed.

Suddenly he felt a terrible sense of anticlimax. The only time he had felt happy since arriving in England had been that evening he spent with Gwynneth. But he had lost touch with her, and the chances of ever finding her again seemed remote.

So where does that leave me? he wondered, gazing down at the water as it slipped along below him. Right back where I started, I guess . . .

But he knew that that was not the case. Something important had happened to him over at Dunkirk with the shrapnel falling all around and the men cursing and struggling in the water. He had been changed in some way, but he was only just beginning to understand how radical a change that was.

iii

Along with the rest of Ramsay's fleet, HMS *Vagabond* had been ordered back to her home port, and on her arrival at Chatham the officers and men were given forty-eight hours' leave in two watches.

Archie telephoned Christine from his cabin as soon as the shore telephone was connected. He tried to get her at the Dover Headquarters first and was told she was at the Lord Warden Hotel, but when he tried there they said she had gone back to her lodgings at St Margaret's-at-Cliffe. So, with a slight qualm of apprehension, he rang Simone's number.

Simone's voice, flat and emotionless, came on the line. 'Oh, hello, Archie. I was wondering if you would ring. Do you know about Griff?'

He had already decided to say nothing of that last encounter he had had with Griff by the east mole. In a strange way he needed to keep it to himself. It was like a secret that Griff had made him promise not to share with anyone else. 'Yes,' he said. 'I did hear. I am so sorry, my dear.'

There was a slight pause. When she spoke she sounded frighteningly calm. It would have been easier for him had she broken down and wept. 'I'm sorry too. I mean – for you. For all of us. Christine's terribly upset.'

'Is she with you?'

'Yes. She's sleeping at the moment.'

'Well don't wake her now. I'll ring again.'

'Did you know the wedding's going ahead on Saturday?'

'I wasn't sure.'

'It's at eleven o'clock. They're having the reception here

afterwards. Nick's getting forty-eight hours' leave. Will you be here for it?'

'If I possibly can.'

'I'll tell Christine you called,' she said. 'Can she ring you?'

'Better not. I'll try again this evening.'

'Fine.'

They said an awkward goodbye and he rang off. He sat at the desk in his cabin with his head in his hands. He felt like an accomplice to crime, as if he and Simone had deliberately engineered Griff's death. Did Simone's chillingly calm manner disguise similar feelings? Perhaps not: women were strange creatures. It was impossible to know exactly how they felt. All he could be certain of was that he would not shake off this burden of guilt he felt until he and Simone could meet and talk frankly about it all, face to face.

iv

The marriage of Flight Lieutenant Nick Massingbohm and Third Officer Christine Trendle-Home was announced in *The Times* and took place on the Saturday after the evacuation.

The service was conducted by a Royal Naval chaplain. Christine could have worn her mother's wedding dress, but with invasion imminent it seemed out of keeping to wear anything but her uniform. Nick invited his squadron friends from Manston, and several of the naval staff at Dover came along, as well as some old family friends. Beeby Perowne turned up in uniform – she was now a first officer – having snatched a morning off from her post at the Whitehall Signals Centre.

David, who had returned to Prowse after spending two nights at a guest house in Hampstead, was the only male guest not in uniform.

Archie was unable to attend: *Vagabond* had sailed earlier that morning to resume North Sea patrols, so while the organist played Purcell and Nick and Chrissy stood in the church porch for the photographer, Archie was doing captain's rounds – which are customary on a Saturday forenoon in the Royal Navy – somewhere off the Dogger Bank.

A joint naval and air force guard of honour drew swords and formed an arch for the newly-weds and then the whole wedding party walked back together along Reach Road to Prowse Lodge for a reception on the lawn.

David was last in the queue to meet the bride and groom. The evening before, over supper, Christine had asked him about his days aboard the *Daisy Belle*, but he had been reluctant to talk about it. The result was that Christine now held him in rather higher regard than previously.

'I guess even Yankees get to kiss the bride, isn't that right?'

Christine laughed and offered her peach-soft cheek for him to kiss. He turned to Massingbohm and shook him warmly by the hand. 'You've got to be the luckiest guy in England right now, Flight Lieutenant!'

Massingbohm was unable to keep his eyes off his new bride. 'No doubt of it!' he boomed.

Later, after the speeches, David returned to have a more serious word with him. 'Something I want to ask you. Did I ever tell you I hold a private flying licence?'

Massingbohm looked surprised. 'Really? No, I don't think you did.'

'Well I do, and I've been doing some hard thinking these last few days. I figure you British are going to need every pilot you can lay hands on in the next few months, right?'

Since returning to his squadron Massingbohm had flown several operational sorties over France, and it was now apparent to every pilot at Manston that the Luftwaffe was preparing to launch a massive attack aimed at overwhelming the RAF prior to launching an invasion across the Channel.

'Yes, I think you're right there.'

'So what are my chances of getting myself trained up as a fighter pilot? You reckon that'd be possible?'

Christine had been engaged in conversation by Beeby, but she now turned back to hear the rest of the conversation.

'I really don't know,' Massingbohm was saying. 'But no reason why you shouldn't try.'

'There was a Yankee squadron last time round,' David said. 'I checked it out. Seventy-one Squadron – Camels and Snipes. They got themselves disbanded at the beginning of '19. You reckon they'd start up the same outfit again?'

'Are you really serious about this?'

'Sure I'm serious! I got over fifty hours single engine!'

'Well . . . I suppose there's no reason why you shouldn't try. As you say, we'll probably need every pilot we can lay hands on before the year's out.'

'That's the way I figured it. So what do I do to get a piece of the action?'

'I know what I'd do. I'd go straight to the squadrons.'

'Which squadrons?'

'Six-oh-nine. Sixty-four. Six-oh-five. You could try any of those.'

Christine took Nick's arm and leant against him. 'What on earth are you two cooking up?'

'David wants to be a fighter pilot.'

'Honestly! Is there anything you *don't* want to be, David?'

'Oh sure! A newspaper reporter for one, and a grunt for another!'

'What's a "grunt" for goodness sake?'

'It's what we call a GI in the States.'

'They're known as the PBI over here,' Nick said. 'Poor Bloody Infantry.'

'Captain Griff always used to call them that.'

'Oh, is that right?' David shook his head, frowning. 'You know, I was really sorry to hear about Captain Wilmot. I mean, I never met him, but I read some of those books in that library of his and, well, I guess I kind of got to know him through them.'

'Griff was a good man,' Christine said quietly. 'There aren't many like Captain Griff.' She looked up at Nick. 'Only a very, very few.'

Standing a little way off, Simone watched David talking

to Nick and Christine and remembered her own wedding. She had never clung to Griff's arm as Christine clung to Nick's. Her married life had been prefaced by the hurt of losing David, and she had laid all the blame for that on Griff. She had seen Griff as a lord and master, that was the trouble, and when he had turned out to be a mere mortal, the disappointment had been huge. Poor Griff! It hadn't been all his fault. Hadn't she already suspected she was pregnant before he took pity on her that spring day in 1918? They had failed to talk, that had been the trouble. They had both professed their love, but had held something back. How many opportunities for happiness they had missed! How many chances for happiness and reconciliation had been idly thrown away . . .

In one of their more bitter arguments, Griff had once accused her of being unable to love a man until he had been killed on the battlefield. It now seemed that he had proved his case: if she loved or was loyal to anyone or anything now it was the memory of Griff. But Griff was dead, and Archie had gone off without so much as a word of comfort or affection. She felt suddenly cheated by them both. They had let her down, abandoned her at the very moment when she needed them most. Their triangle of interdependence was finally broken and scattered. The centre to her life had gone.

There was no reason to stay on at Prowse any more. David had been talking about returning to the States and Christine had moved out. Everyone around her – the whole country – seemed to be bracing themselves for what was to come. And here she was, alone, useless. What was it Mr Churchill had said to the nation only a few days before? 'We shall not flag or fail . . .'

She must do something!

But what? She had enjoyed working as an interpreter, had felt needed and useful. But she was sure she was capable of far more effective work than that, and an idea was beginning to form in her mind that had to be approached obliquely. The news from France was getting worse every day: Paris was all but surrounded. It was only a matter of days before the capital fell.

Paris. Since hearing of Griff's death she had felt a new urge – almost a compulsion – to return. Her old phobia was gone. She had met and mingled with her fellow countrymen during the past few days, and had felt totally at ease with them. So if she was no longer afraid of returning to France, what was there to keep her in England?

The newly-weds were about to leave, and as the wedding guests moved round the house to the drive to wave the couple goodbye, Christine came out of the house and took Simone by the arm.

'Simone, before we go – I just wanted to thank you for everything. You've been such a brick!' She smiled awkwardly and then blurted out: 'I know there have been times when – when we haven't exactly hit it off, and I'm sorry about that and hope you'll forgive me.'

'My dear, if anyone needs forgiveness it's me. But that's all behind us now. Yes – completely behind us.' She held Christine's hands tightly. 'Now Chrissy, you mustn't cry on your wedding day!'

Christine dabbed her eyes with a folded handkerchief. 'I do wish Mummy could have been here . . .'

Simone gave her a hug, and then Nick appeared.

'Take care of each other,' Simone said. 'And come and see me sometimes, won't you?'

'Of course we shall,' Christine said, and taking Nick's arm went with him round the side of the house to the drive.

A cloud of confetti billowed in the sunshine; the guests waved and cheered; the exhaust of Nick's wire-wheeled MG roared – and even before the car had gone past the rhododendron bushes and out of sight, Simone knew with complete certainty what she was going to do.

v

She went to see Major Pearce that evening, and as a result of their meeting an interview was arranged for her at a

London address the following week. Dressed in a plain grey suit and low brimmed hat, she took a taxi across London and entered a Georgian building by an inconspicuous door. A wheezing pensioner escorted her up two flights of linoleum-covered stairs and along a corridor to a cluttered office where a dark-eyed, rosy-cheeked young woman sat at a typewriter.

Simone gave her an envelope which contained a card with a note of authentication from Major Pearce. She glanced at it and picked up one of two telephones on her desk. 'Mrs Wilmot is here,' she said simply and, having replaced the receiver, turned to Simone and said, 'They'll see you in a few minutes.'

They saw her after quarter of an hour. She was shown into an adjoining room that was more of a large study than an office. Behind a desk with brass-handled drawers on its front sat an elderly, military man in a light-weight suit smoking a pipe. Sitting on the arm of a leather upholstered chair to his right was a younger man, immaculately turned out, in his thirties.

There were no introductions. When the door had clicked shut and Simone had taken the upright chair facing the desk, the military man launched straight into the interview, which was conducted entirely in French.

Nearly two hours later, when she stepped back into the office where the dark-haired girl was typing, Simone felt as if her whole life had been unravelled like a piece of knitting.

'You'll be contacted in due course,' said the young woman. 'I believe you're on the telephone, aren't you? Can I make a note of the number?'

A few minutes after Mrs Wilmot had gone, the major called the receptionist into his office. 'Details for your card index,' he said, and handed her a sheet of paper with some notes on it.

'Shall I start a file for her, sir?'

'Yes, please.'

'Very good, sir.'

She went back into her office and began to read the major's notes before typing them on a card. She hadn't got very far when a few lines leapt off the page:

Son (illegitimate) David Odell. Adopted 1919.
Adoptive father Irish, adoptive mother German Jewess.
Resided New York. Entered UK as journalist Nov '39.
Reunited with subj. Jan '40. Entered France May '40.
Evacuated Boulogne. Volunteer crew during Op
    DYNAMO.
At present resident with subj. Seeking entry to RAF.

She bit her lip and gazed at the words for a full minute. Then she got up from her desk and knocked on the major's half-open door.

He looked up. 'Yes?'

'Sir, I think I ought to tell you something. I know Mrs Wilmot's son personally.'

'Oh?'

'Yes, sir. I met him last Christmas. When I was training. I thought I'd better mention it, because he was the young man that – that caused me the spot of trouble I was in, sir, if you remember.'

The major looked vaguely amused. 'Yes, I do remember. But there's no reason why you should come into contact with this chap again, is there? Unless . . . unless you want to, of course.'

She blushed.

'Do you want to?'

'Well, sir –'

'Ah. So you do!'

'Only with your permission, sir.'

'Well, provided you don't reveal the nature of your work, I have no objection at all. It might even be of some use to us.' He smiled and added, 'You can use the phone if you want. But only this once, understood?'

'Thank you, sir.'

She went back into the adjoining office and sat down at her typewriter. She was so happy that she was smiling and crying at the same time. After a while she lifted the telephone and asked for a trunk call to Dover. A minute later his voice came on the line.

'Hullo, David,' she said. 'It's me. Gwynneth.'

vi

Simone was in Griff's study packing his books into tea chests when the front doorbell rang. Since receiving confirmation a few weeks before that the War Department could use her services, she had acted on the major's instructions and had gone ahead with the business of getting rid of Griff's and her own personal belongings. Griff's clothes and most of her own wardrobe had gone to the Salvation Army. All the furniture and household things were to stay with the house. The books were going as a gift to the Prowse school library. Her Wren lodgers had moved out and, at her own request, the telephone had been disconnected. David – who had somehow regained contact with his long-lost girlfriend – had moved to lodgings in Croydon and was awaiting a reply to his application to join the RAF. In three days' time, Simone would close the front door behind her, deposit the keys with Major Pearce and leave Prowse for ever.

She was to be sent to 'a secret location', as the major had put it, for specialist training. She had been warned that the training would be very tough and that if she failed to make the grade she would have to be interned for the duration of the war. If she passed . . .

They had not said a great deal about what work she would be required to do, but having volunteered on the understanding that she would be sent into France she knew that she would almost certainly have to place herself in situations of personal danger. She would not have wished it otherwise.

She came into the hall with her head in a scarf and her

hands covered in dust. She wasn't expecting visitors. She presumed it was Major Pearce or the parcel post.

But it was neither. When she opened the door, Archie stood in the porch in his best uniform with his hat cocked at a Beatty angle over one eye. His face broke into the old grin.

'The cat came back,' he said. 'How's tricks?'

vii

He came into the hall and saw the tea chests.

'What's this? Are you moving?'

'Yes.'

'Where?'

She shrugged. 'Away.'

He put his hands on her shoulders. 'Where, Simone?'

She turned away from him and made for the kitchen. He followed her. She washed her hands at the sink. 'Somewhere the Germans won't be dropping bombs. I'm running away, you see. Would you like a coffee or something? Oh – no, it'll have to be tea. By the way, I hope you don't mind, but I've given your dog to the MPs on the gate. They're training him up as a guard dog.' She turned, and smiled quickly. 'Oh! I should have noticed. You've been promoted, haven't you? Congratulations.'

He watched her drying her hands on a roller towel.

'We need to talk, Simone.'

'Isn't that what we're doing?'

'You know what I mean.'

She moved away. 'I don't think I want to talk, Archie.'

'Why? Because it hurts too much?'

She shook her head. 'Perhaps.'

There was a long silence.

'Why don't we go for a walk?' he said eventually. 'We don't have to talk if you don't want to. I promise not to embarrass you. I just – I just want to be with you for a bit. Is that too much to ask?'

'Look,' she said. 'I've bitten off a nail.' She turned to him, her head back in the way she had. 'I'm a mess, Archie. I've made a complete mess of my life. I've wasted twenty years.'

'That's just not true.'

'Yes it is. I was no good as a wife to Griff and I took you away from Olivia. And now they're both dead and I'm to blame. So. I think that says all that needs to be said, don't you?'

But then her control broke without warning and she began sobbing quietly, her hands at her side, her face turned away.

He reached out to her and she looked up at him – with her face tear-blotched. When he folded her in his arms it was not out of sympathy or kindness to her but because he needed her; and they stood there like that in the middle of the kitchen for a long time.

She looked up and managed a watery smile. 'Perhaps we should go for that walk on the cliffs after all.'

He nodded. 'I could collect the dog if you like.'

'Yes. Let's take him. Like old times.'

While he was gone she went up to the bathroom. She washed her hands again and held a hot flannel against her face: it was supposed to be terrible for the skin, she knew that, but it was soothing, and she didn't care about her skin any more.

'All set?' Archie called from the hall. She came downstairs. The dog wagged and barked.

They went down the garden to the gate at the end and along the narrow path to the limit of the school grounds. Archie let the dog off the lead and he bounded joyfully ahead, burying his head into rabbit holes and digging furiously.

'It's the first good walk he's had for weeks,' Simone said.

They went down into the little valley of grass and scrub and up again onto the cliff path. It was a clear day, and the hump of the French coast at Calais was plainly visible. The fires of Dunkirk had been extinguished: the cloud of smoke was gone.

For a while they walked in silence. They had turned left

along the cliffs, away from Dover. 'Would you like an arm?' Archie offered.

'All right.'

'You don't have to, Simone.'

'I know. It's just . . .' She sighed. 'Practically everything I do, everything I see or hear is a reminder of Griff. Even when I wash my hands it's as though I'm trying to wash the guilt away.'

'If it helps at all, I feel every bit as guilty, you know. I know exactly how you feel.'

She accepted his arm. 'Do you? I wonder.'

'Like . . . a murderer.'

'Yes,' she said. 'That's right. That is exactly right.'

'But I'm not a murderer. And nor are you. It just turned out that Griff was the one to get killed and we were the ones to survive.' He laughed. 'And we may not survive, Simone. This war's going to last a long time.'

'Maybe it will. That doesn't change the way I feel.'

'You're not the only one. Most of our generation have the same sense of guilt. Griff felt it too, did you know that? Guilty because he was alive. I'm sure that was why he joined up again. He felt – we all felt – that we had left a job unfinished.'

They walked on a little way in silence.

'You know when he decided, don't you?' Simone said. 'To join up, I mean. It was on our way back from Eggardon last August. Something happened that morning. Something I've never mentioned to either of you. You know how we fell asleep on the sofa that night? Well I *didn't* sleep. I was wide awake the whole time. And – and Griff came downstairs and found us. He came to the door and saw us. And for some reason –'

'For some reason, he backed away, didn't he? He backed away and tiptoed upstairs. I was awake, too, my dear. I didn't sleep either.'

She stared at him. 'Why didn't you say anything?'

'Why didn't you? Why didn't Griff?'

They stopped. The cliff edge was only a matter of yards away. Simone faced out across the Channel, the wind fluttering her headscarf. 'I didn't say anything because Griff didn't, and you kept silent because I did.'

'I wonder what went on in Griff's mind . . .'

'Shall I tell you something that always annoyed me about him? He seemed incapable of fighting for *himself*. It infuriated me, you know that? He always had to be fighting someone else's battles for them, but never his own. If he'd had just a bit more push . . .' Simone laughed sadly. 'But it's all very well for me to say that. If he'd had more push he wouldn't have married me. If he'd had more push he would have stayed in the army where he belonged. If he'd had a bit more push he'd have been a general by now.'

'And if he'd had a bit more push,' Archie added, 'he'd have read the riot act to us that morning. But Griff had love and gentleness instead of push, didn't he, and he didn't want to hurt either of us. Poor old Griff. We had a housemaster when we were here at Prowse – old Mr Colson. He was known as Coal-Hole. He used to call us the Two Impostors. Triumph and Disaster – from Kipling, of course. Old Coal-Hole used to say he could never make up his mind which of us was which. I was always getting into trouble and losing things and coming bottom of everything, but Griff was a bit of a duffer on the playing fields. I used to get quite het up about it, do you know that? And even now, well, I feel that Griff has somehow scored another triumph. Who was it that said you should die at the right time? Well, that's what I think Griff's done. Not in a revengeful way. More a case of tidying up a piece of unfinished business, something he felt he should have done in '18. And he didn't waste those twenty years, did he? He did a good job of work as a schoolmaster, he kept true to himself, and when the time came to fight for what he believed in all over again he did so without making a song and dance about it.'

Simone smiled. 'He'd get so angry if he could hear you talking like that, Archie. He really hated any sort of hero-worship, you know. He would never *ever* talk to me about what he did or saw when he was in the army.'

'No, he wouldn't.'

They began walking again. 'But you two probably discussed it, didn't you?'

'Sometimes.'

'What did he say?'

'Oh . . . various things.'

'You see? You're the same.'

'Possibly.'

'Tell me something of what he said, Archie. Please.'

Archie looked out across the Channel to the coast of France and remembered the talks he and Griff had had, usually over a pint of beer at the local, or sitting in the garden after lunch at Prowse. 'He once told me that it was the injured and dying horses that hurt him most of all. He said that there was something about horses that set them above humans, and that using them to wage war aggravated the crime of it tenfold. He said it was one thing for soldiers to kill each other, but a quite different thing for them to force animals to take part in the killing as well.'

Somewhere to their left, Blashford was yelping excitedly, in hot pursuit of a rabbit.

'But you've been through it as well, Archie.'

He shook his head and said nothing.

She removed her arm from his and took his hand instead. 'Tell me,' she said simply. 'Don't make the mistake Griff made. Don't bottle it up. Share it. Please.'

They had stopped again. She felt his hand tighten on hers and when she looked up he was frowning into the path of sunlight that was reflected on the sea.

'Fighting on land,' he began – and Simone felt that he was thinking aloud as much as speaking to her – 'is a much more horrific affair than fighting at sea. The sea always looks the same, however many lives it claims. At sea you can bury your dead over the side and you can hose the ship down and give her a lick of paint and polish up the brasswork and –

and *forget*. But on land the blood soaks into the earth and carcasses leave their bones in the mud and the fields and woods are left scarred and wounded and burnt. The sea forgets, but the land remembers – for generations afterwards.'

'How long do you think it will take?' she asked, and it was a question that had been asked so many times and by so many people in the past few weeks that he knew immediately what she meant.

'Years, probably. Years of bloody fighting.'

A little while later, when they had reached the path that descended towards St Margaret's Bay, Simone said: 'I don't expect I shall ever come on this walk again, you know. And I don't expect we shall see each other again, Archie.'

He turned and faced her and she held both his hands. Somewhere in the distance, a formation of aircraft was approaching. The drone of their engines was growing slowly louder. 'You know I loved you, don't you, Archie? Don't ever forget that I loved you.'

He whispered, 'My dear,' and took her in his arms.

'I loved you both,' she said. 'And I think Griff loved us both, too, didn't he?'

'Is there no possibility –' he began, but she put a finger to his lips to stop him going on.

They stood on the cliff for a little while longer. While they did so, the throbbing of aircraft engines rose in slow crescendo until it could no longer be ignored. They looked up: several formations of German aircraft were approaching from the south, appearing and disappearing behind clumps of brilliant white cumulus.

Simone said, 'We'd better go back,' and moments later, as they retraced their steps along the cliff path, six Spitfires thundered overhead, joining up in formation, climbing away and leaving a trail of exhaust smoke behind them.

Within minutes the sky was full of the zoom of engines and the rattle of gunfire. A little way inland, a black pall of smoke was billowing up from a crashed aircraft.

'This is it,' muttered Archie. 'It's begun.'

ACKNOWLEDGMENTS

I am grateful to the library of the Institution of Royal Engineers at Chatham, where I obtained a copy of Ralph Lionel Clarke's unpublished memoir 'Three weeks to La Panne', from which I have quoted several excerpts, and M. J. Lee's article 'Boulogne – 23rd May 1940', also quoted. At the Imperial War Museum, I consulted a number of diaries and accounts and used material from Gregory Blaxland's unpublished memoir and Major Archdale's unpublished account of his activities as liaison officer on General Billotte's staff. The Public Record Office at Kew provided me with a huge store of reports, signals and accounts all of which served to bring immediacy and authenticity to the text. Quotations from radio news bulletins are by kind permission of the BBC. From the Bundesarchiv in Freiburg I obtained a copy of the anonymous war chronicle of an infantryman in the Grossdeutschland Regiment. It was ably translated in part by my sister, Janice Gidley Wheeler, and in part by Thames Translations of Winchester. The delightful poem 'To the House' is by Susannah Wadeson, and was found on the kitchen wall of Eggardon Farm House.

I wish to thank the archivists, librarians and staff of the Public Record Office, the Imperial War Museum, the BBC department of written archives, the School of Military Engineering, the Dover Museum, the Public Libraries at Maidstone, Dover and Winchester, and the Records Office at Boulogne, all of whom were most helpful in providing me with research material.

Individual thanks go to Terry Sutton, editor of the *Dover Express*, who spared time to talk to me of his early memories of Dover; Bernard Tanter, of Winchester College, who lent me his notes on the fall of France, and Lieutenant Colonel Cetre, who served with Captain Ervine-Andrews at the time the latter won his Victoria Cross on the Dunkirk perimeter, and who provided me with useful atmospheric material.

CHARLES GIDLEY WHEELER

The Far Side of the World
Patrick O'Brian

'All true lovers of the sea will find this a most enjoyable book.' *Nautical Magazine*

It is still the War of 1812. Patrick O'Brian takes his hero Jack Aubrey and his tetchy, sardonic friend Stephen Maturin on a voyage as fascinating as anything he has ever written. They set course across the South Atlantic to intercept a powerful American frigate outward bound to play havoc with the British whaling trade.

If they do not come up with her before she rounds the Horn they must follow her into the Great South Sea and as far across the Pacific as she may lead them. It is a commission after Jack's own heart. Maturin has fish of his own to fry in the world of secret intelligence.

Aubrey has to cope with a succession of disasters – men overboard, castaways, encounters with savages, storms, typhoons, groundings, shipwrecks, to say nothing of murder and incipient mutiny. That the enemy is in fact faithfully dealt with no-one who has the honour of Captain's Aubrey's acquaintance can take leave to doubt.

'Aubrey has rarely undertaken a more hazardous mission or one more packed with exciting incident.' *Gloucester Citizen*

FONTANA PAPERBACKS

After the War
Frederic Raphael

An epic novel of great scope and vision
from the author of *The Glittering Prizes*

When Michael introduces Joe to his sister, he warns
her: 'Careful of this character - he's motorized
mayhem.'

Michael Jordan, playwright, screen writer and
director, grew up in the long shadow of the Second
World War. Separated from his beautiful sister Rachel
by wartime evacuation, they were like two only
children. At prep school Michael meets Joe Hirsch, a
refugee. Both Jewish – Joe, brash and uninhibited;
Michael deferent to the England in which he grew up
– their long, angry friendship and Rachel's life and
loves form the kernel of this sweeping portrait of the
postwar years.

From the seclusion of wartime Devon, to occupied
Germany, and Paris, the action moves from showbiz
London to Greece and Africa: but Israel provides a
constant backdrop. When the threatened attack by the
Arabs on Israel brings Michael, estranged from his
wife, to his own year of decision, the irony of the
masterly novel is manifest: since 1945 new wars have
rendered that wonderful era 'after the war'
systematically unattainable.

FONTANA PAPERBACKS

The Andros Passage
John Hallows

The day lone yachtsman and journalist Harry Lancaster came across an abandoned white boat foundering in the storm-swept Aegean, it was the thought of salvage money that led him to risk his life boarding the unanchored *caique* in the middle of a raging sea. The boat had been abandoned only recently, for the blood that stained the deck was still fresh.

Then when he discovered a beautiful girl, stripped, bound and left for dead below deck, he realised that the apparently worthless cargo of fake antiquities must conceal something much more valuable. So valuable, in fact, that he and Nina Millen, his newly found companion, were soon to be plunged into an international smuggling conspiracy and forced to embark on a terrifying voyage for survival, pursued by the Turkish police, the Greek police . . . and some ruthless and determined people who wanted their property back.

FONTANA PAPERBACKS

Shining Through
Susan Isaacs

'In 1940 when I was thirty-one and an old maid, while the whole world waited for war, I fell in love with John Berringer.'

Linda was a legal secretary; John Berringer was her indecently handsome, brilliant, unattainable boss, the man of her dreams. Four years later, Linda Voss Berringer emerged from the ruins of Berlin a self-determined woman of shining courage and a war hero.

Shining Through is the compulsive, engaging, heart-stopping saga of an American working girl and her transformation. Her story involves passion – a blazing affair with John Berringer; betrayal – when John's faithlessness rips their marriage apart; and intrigue – ultimately of a lethal kind when Linda joins the war as an OSS spy. Her story soars to its breathtaking conclusion in a blazing explosion of danger, death and unexpected love.

'Three cheers for Susan Isaacs, *Shining Through* keeps you turning the pages because you care what happens to the characters . . . her most ambitious novel to date.' *Daily Express*

'Give me the unashamed blockbuster any day, especially of the Susan Isaacs' tear-jerking, breath-catching variety . . . marvellously engaging.'
Financial Times

'Truly compulsive . . . has all the hallmarks of a runaway bestseller.' *Publishers Weekly*

FONTANA PAPERBACKS

Hold My Hand
I'm Dying
John Gordon Davis

'This is the best novel coming out of Africa that I have read for a number of years. *It is Africa today*. It has the inevitability of a Greek tragedy . . . both moving emotionally and full of adventure.'
Stuart Cloete

The great heart of old Africa is dying. Joseph Mahoney, the last colonial commissioner in the spectacular Kariba Gorge, is there to witness the death throes. Somehow, he must also ease the birth pangs of the new Africa that will take its place. His companions are Samson, his Matabele servant, and Suzie, the girl he loves.

But Mahoney and Suzie are drifting apart, and now Samson has been accused of murder. And all too quickly, it seems, the country is heading towards a bloodbath of revenge.

Hold My Hand I'm Dying – a compelling story of freedom, friendship and love in the face of hatred, violence and death.

'A great, compassionate and deeply moving book. I did not know how to put it down.'
Marguerite Steen

FONTANA PAPERBACKS

Ramage and the Saracens
Dudley Pope

When Captain Ramage is ordered to Naples, neither he nor the crew of the frigate *Calypso* expect to meet hostile ships in the Mediterranean so soon after the battle of Trafalgar. Yet hardly have they cleared the Straits of Gibraltar than they sight two French battleships of the Line.

Arriving eventually in Naples, Ramage reports to Admiral Rudd, expecting to be given the tedious task of escorting merchantmen. Nothing could be further from the truth. The mission he is given is one far better suited to his reputation: he is to sail to Sicily where the Barbary Coast pirates – the *Saraceni* – have been terrorizing the fishing ports.

'The first and still favourite rival to Hornblower.'
Daily Mirror

FONTANA PAPERBACKS

Fontana Paperbacks: Fiction

Fontana is a leading paperback publisher of fiction. Below are some recent titles.

- ☐ THE SCROLL OF BENEVOLENCE John Trenhaile £3.99
- ☐ A CANDLE FOR JUDAS David Fraser £3.50
- ☐ THE FIREMAN Stephen Leather £2.99
- ☐ BLACKLIST Andrew Taylor £3.50
- ☐ SACRIFICIAL GROUND Thomas H. Cook £3.50
- ☐ THE GREEN REAPERS R. W. Jones £3.99
- ☐ THE BLIND KNIGHT Gail van Asten £2.99
- ☐ GLITTERSPIKE HALL Mike Jefferies £6.99

You can buy Fontana paperbacks at your local bookshop or newsagent. Or you can order them from Fontana Paperbacks, Cash Sales Department, Box 29, Douglas, Isle of Man. Please send a cheque, postal or money order (not currency) worth the purchase price plus 22p per book for postage (maximum postage required is £3.00 for orders within the UK).

NAME (Block letters)_____

ADDRESS_____

_____

While every effort is made to keep prices low, it is sometimes necessary to increase them at short notice. Fontana Paperbacks reserve the right to show new retail prices on covers which may differ from those previously advertised in the text or elsewhere.